"It's our first Christmas together."

"Our first Christmas," Elise repeated as they touched their glasses together. They sat for a while, just enjoying the moment and this quiet time together, but Elise had to tell Jake how she felt or she thought she'd burst.

"I saw the cradle," she said quietly. "It's beautiful. I can't believe you ordered it."

He swirled the wine in his glass and leaned back on his elbow. "I didn't."

"Sure you did. I saw it."

"I made the cradle."

"What?"

"I made the cradle," he repeated.

"Oh, Jake, why?"

"Because I wanted a baby, too."

Silence followed his words and Elise knew he wasn't telling her his true feelings. "There's another reason, isn't there?"

The words were in his throat, but he couldn't force them out. He'd waited for this moment forever, but fear kept him silent, kept him prisoner, kept him chained to the past. He found it hard to express something he felt so intensely, especially since *his* ghost was always there.

Elise took a breath. "Say it, Jake."

Dear Reader,

A *Baby by Christmas* is the story of a couple, Jake and Elise McCain, who get married for the wrong reason—to have a baby. Their plans begin to unravel when they discover Jake already has a child by another woman. The book is about how two people struggle with this situation, how they learn to cope and, most important, how they find love. It's also about a special little boy named Ben who changes their lives.

This book is a little different than my others, but I hope you will enjoy it no less. May the Christmas season embrace you and your families as you journey with Jake and Elise to find the true meaning of love.

Happy holidays,

Linda Warren

You can reach me at LW1508@aol.com, superauthors.com, or visit my Web site www.lindawarren.net, or you can write me at P.O. Box 5182, Bryan, TX 77805. Your letter will always be answered.

A Baby by Christmas

Linda Warren

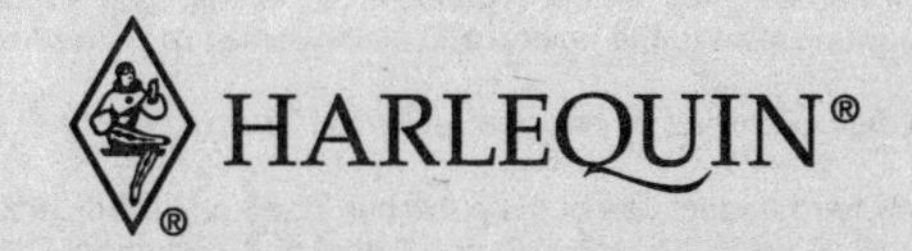

TORONTO • NEW YORK • LONDON
AMSTERDAM • PARIS • SYDNEY • HAMBURG
STOCKHOLM • ATHENS • TOKYO • MILAN • MADRID
PRAGUE • WARSAW • BUDAPEST • AUCKLAND

ISBN 0-373-71167-0

A BABY BY CHRISTMAS

This edition published by arrangement with Harlequin Books S.A.

Visit us at www.eHarlequin.com

Printed in U.S.A.

DEDICATION

This book is about a special little boy, so I dedicate it to the special little boys (the great ones) in my life:

John Fuller, Matt Fuller, Jake Fuller, Josh Rychlik, Tyler Phillips, Layne Tharp, Scott Patranella and Taylor Siegert.

And to Ty Siegert, a special nephew, who never fails to ask about my books.

Books by Linda Warren

HARLEQUIN SUPERROMANCE

893—THE TRUTH ABOUT JANE DOE
935—DEEP IN THE HEART OF TEXAS
991—STRAIGHT FROM THE HEART
1016—EMILY'S DAUGHTER
1049—ON THE TEXAS BORDER
1075—COWBOY AT THE CROSSROADS
1125—THE WRONG WOMAN

CHAPTER ONE

A BABY. A BABY. A BABY.

The words resounded in Jake McCain's head as he entered the house. He stopped and took a deep breath. Damn, he hated this. It ruined his whole workday. *Then why was he here? Because he* didn't *hate it.* It was just so...hell, he couldn't explain it to himself. Elise had called and he'd come running. Ever since he'd met her he seemed to be jumping through hoops. At times it irked him, like today; at others he found it quite enjoyable. That was the problem with their relationship, their marriage—he never knew what the hell was going to happen next. But he'd signed on for better or worse...and a baby.

"Jake, is that you?"

"Yes," he shouted from the kitchen.

"I'm in the bedroom."

Where else would she be? he thought with resignation. He made his way to the living room and paused for a moment. The room was completely white with touches of silver and mauve. There wasn't a comfortable chair anywhere, and after a long day he needed a place to relax other than the bedroom. Everything in there was white, too, but he had ways of blocking it out. Why he'd let Elise convince him to live here he had no idea. She could make him do the impossible, though, even live in the city among these houses all crowded together. He was beginning to think she had him under a spell, because he wasn't acting like himself.

He needed to tell her how he felt.

ELISE WEBER MCCAIN SLIPPED out of her suit and underclothes and reached for a silk robe. She didn't bother with a gown. She didn't need one—all she needed was Jake and his sperm. They'd been married for six months and they were trying for a baby. That was the reason they'd gotten married; they were two people who wanted the same thing—a child.

At thirty-five, Elise had been certain she'd never fall in love again. Ten years ago, after a year of marriage, she'd lost the love of her life, Derek Weber, in a plane crash. Heartbroken, she sank into depression, then eventually picked herself up and went back to school and got her Ph.D. Now she was a professor of American literature and had the respect of her peers. In her professional life everything was perfect, but her personal life had been nonexistent—until she met Jake.

It had happened unexpectedly. She was traveling home to Waco, Texas, from a lecture at Rice University when she got a flat tire between Marlin and Waco. It was almost dark and she was in the middle of nowhere. She'd taken out her cell phone to call for assistance when a truck pulled up. She was nervous about a stranger stopping to help her, but as soon as the man, who was tall with strong, chiseled features, introduced himself, her fears vanished. She was acquainted with Jake's mother and his brothers and stepfather. They belonged to the same country club as Elise and her family, and Elise had heard of Jake's estrangement from his mother. Althea had left her husband for another man; her ten-year-old son, Jake, wouldn't go with her, so he'd stayed with his father. After that, Althea had had little contact with Jake and Elise knew that troubled her a great deal. She'd heard Althea talk about him for years and it was an odd twist of fate that he'd stopped to help her…or maybe it was meant to be.

Elise didn't find Jake's brothers as interesting as Jake. He was kind, honest, forthright. Not that his brothers weren't, but with Jake it was different. She couldn't explain it. She was only aware that she felt drawn to him in a way she hadn't experienced in a long time.

When she'd tried to pay him for fixing her flat, he'd refused. The next week she'd phoned and invited him to dinner as a thank you. Why she'd done that, she had no idea. Asking a man out was so unlike her, but she'd wanted him to know how much she'd appreciated his kindness. To her delight, he accepted.

Her mother and sister were appalled at her actions. They'd told her Jake McCain wasn't their kind and that Althea's other sons were more suitable. She'd ignored them. Her mother and sister were snobs and she'd struggled with their attitudes all her life.

Elise had enjoyed that first date. They'd discussed all kinds of things and Elise learned a lot about Jake McCain. He ran the McCain farm, which extended along the Brazos River Bottom from parts of Highbank and Marlin to Waco, and raised cotton and corn like his father, who expected Jake to follow in his footsteps. He'd added that he'd farmed all his life.

When she'd told him she knew his brothers, Beau and Caleb, he wasn't surprised, but he was quick to remind her that Caleb was his half brother and he'd never met him. That made her so sad, and even sadder when he wouldn't talk about his mother. The subject was clearly off limits.

That was one small thing that bothered her about Jake. Everything else she liked. He was easy to be with and he listened with such compassion. He made her feel as if her problems were important, and she'd found herself telling him about her marriage, how much she'd loved her husband and how her whole world had come apart the day he died. She also told him she wanted a baby—she couldn't believe she'd brought that up. She and Derek had planned a family, but after his death she'd pushed that idea to the back of her mind. As she grew older, though, she found herself thinking once again about having a baby.

Jake surprised her by saying he'd love a child, too. After

a few dates and several conversations on the subject, she was asking him to marry her. Just like that, out of the blue, no second thoughts. He was shocked, understandably so. But they both wanted the same thing very badly. Even though they weren't in love, the arrangement seemed perfect.

When he agreed, she was thrilled. Her mother and sister told her she was losing her mind and obsessed with having a baby. They begged her to take some time, but as usual she'd ignored them and married Jake, anyway. They were married by a justice of the peace and spent their honeymoon at her house—in her bed. Jake was everything she wanted in a lover, in a husband.

She glanced at the full bed with its lacy white comforter and bed skirt. Their first night she'd been so nervous, but she and Jake were very compatible in that area and she'd responded to him in ways that surprised her. She wasn't sure what she'd been expecting, but it certainly wasn't warm, tantalizing kisses that drove her to a frenzied state. Jake's touch brought out her sensual, passionate nature, and sometimes it made her angry, because she always believed that part of her belonged to Derek. But she had to admit when she was with Jake, she never thought of Derek. Jake became her main focus…and she was uncertain how she felt about that.

JAKE MOVED TOWARD THE BEDROOM. He had to see her, then he'd forget about his negative feelings. That was the way it was with him: one look at her and nothing else mattered. She folded the comforter, looked up and smiled. She was beautiful with her slim, curved body and patrician features, but it was those soft, inviting blue eyes that always pulled him in. The natural blond hair didn't hurt, either. His bad mood evaporated.

"Hi." She continued to smile.

He clenched his jaw and pushed attraction for her aside.

He had to talk to her, make her understand that he wasn't a puppet on a string.

"I'm in the middle of harvesting a cotton crop and that makes it rather difficult to drop everything and hurry over here," he said in a rush.

She placed the comforter on a chair and tucked her hair back behind her ears. It was medium-length and hung like a bell around her face. "You should've said you were busy."

"Yes, I...should...have." His words got slower and slower as he glimpsed her body through the opening of her robe. He wanted her. It was that simple, that basic. It had been like that since he'd met her. Regardless of how irritated and frustrated he felt, it still didn't change the effect she had on him.

She stood in front of him and began to unbutton his shirt. "I'm sorry I interrupted you, but according to my calculations this is the perfect time, and I thought we could spend the afternoon making our dream a reality. Pregnant by Christmas, isn't that our goal?"

"Elise..." he began, then forgot what he was going to say as she ran her hands across his chest, lightly, provocatively, then tasted the warmth of his skin with her lips. Desire ripped through him and his breathing became labored. She unbuckled his belt, stepped backward and guided him toward the bed. All the words he'd planned to say went right out of his head. Elise, her allure, encompassed every part of him.

He quickly slipped out of his clothes. He'd left his boots in the garage by the door—afraid of getting something dirty. Another thing he was tired of doing—but he never grew tired of this. His arms circled her small waist and he drew her against him, skin against skin, his lips taking hers in an urgent, hungry kiss.

Her soft curves melted into him as he placed her on the bed. His lips and hands found those curves with eagerness and he soared with all the emotions she brought to life in him.

"This is the right day," she breathed against his lips. "We've been trying for six months, but this has to be our time."

"Shh," he said in a ragged tone, his lips trailing to her neck. She liked to talk about getting pregnant when they were making love. He didn't.

"I should've been pregnant by now, Jake. I want to be pregnant."

"Shh," he said again, kissing her mouth. That was the only way to keep her from talking and he needed to taste, to feel every nuance of her. His body moved to cover hers and nothing else was said for some time.

Afterward Jake tried to move away, but Elise held him tight. "No, don't," she said, her legs and arms like a vise around him. "I read that if a man stays inside longer the sperm has more of a chance."

Jake groaned and buried his face in her damp neck. That was all she thought about—having a baby—and there was a stack of books on conception by the bed. She was obsessed with the idea, and he couldn't make her see that they had to let it happen naturally.

After a moment Jake rolled to the side and Elise turned around and placed her legs on the headboard and shoved a pillow beneath her hips.

"What are you doing?" he asked out of curiosity, but he should have known better.

"I also read that if a woman holds her legs in an upward position, it gives the sperm a much better chance of reaching the egg."

He shook his head and got up, then found his scattered clothes on the floor and began to put them on.

"Jake, please don't dress. We need to have sex again in a little while. We have to make sure."

He stopped in the process of buttoning his shirt. Sex. That was what they were having. Love had nothing to do with it. Was that what bothered him? He caught sight of the picture on the nightstand—Derek Weber, Elise's dead husband. That bothered him even more. Elise didn't need Jake McCain; any man would have done. He'd just been crazy enough to go along with her wishes. That was the crux of his irritation. He didn't like being used, but that was the way he'd begun to feel.

"I'm not a machine," he muttered.

She turned so she could see him. "Is something wrong?"

"Yes."

"If you have to get back to the farm, we can try tonight."

God, the woman had a one-track mind, and he wondered if she even saw him as a person. Was he nothing more than a sperm bank?

"Elise..." The doorbell interrupted him. He looked at her. "Are you expecting anyone?"

"No, I...oh, I forgot. A woman phoned earlier. A Ms. Woods. She said she had to speak with you and that she'd be by later."

"I don't know any Ms. Woods. Did she say what she wanted?" He couldn't imagine why anyone would try to reach him at Elise's. Everyone called him at the farm. He only slept here—and had sex.

"She said that your aunt had given her this number and it was important."

That explained it. It was probably some minor farm business Aunt Vin didn't know how to handle. The doorbell rang again as he stuffed his shirt into his jeans. His boots were in the garage so he'd have to answer the door barefoot. He hurried to the foyer.

A woman with short brown hair and light green eyes stood on the doorstep. She held a briefcase in one hand. She was pretty and somewhere in her thirties and Jake didn't recognize her.

"Jake McCain?" she asked politely.

"Yes," he answered.

"I'm Carmen Woods." She held out her hand and he shook it. A salesperson, he guessed. He had to get rid of her so he could talk to Elise.

"May I come in?"

"I'm kind of busy. Could we do this another time?"

"It's very important."

"Ms. Woods, I..."

"I'm from the Harris County Children's Protective Services, Mr. McCain, and it can't wait."

Children's Protective Services. What the hell did they want with him? They had to have the wrong person. He could clear this up easily, he was sure.

He stepped aside and she entered the living area. Elise came out of the bedroom in a white robe and Jake introduced them.

"I'm sorry if I'm interrupting," Ms. Woods apologized as she took in Elise's attire.

"That's okay," Jake said. "But I believe you have me confused with someone else."

"I don't think so, Mr. McCain. Just let me explain."

"Okay." Jake still felt she had the wrong man, but he was willing to listen. "Have a seat."

Elise and Jake sat on the sofa and Ms. Woods took the Queen Anne chair. "I'm glad you're here, Mrs. McCain. This concerns you, too." She opened her briefcase and took out some papers.

"Oh" was all Elise said.

"Mr. McCain, do you know a Sherry Carr?"

Jake frowned. "Sherry? Yeah, I met her about, gosh, maybe four years ago. I went to Texas A&M for a program on increasing cotton production and she worked at the hotel where I stayed. We dated, but it didn't work out. I haven't seen her since."

"Then you knew her...very well."

His frown deepened. "What are you getting at, Ms. Woods?"

"Are you aware that Sherry has a son?"

Jake shook his head. "No, she never mentioned a son."

She pulled a paper from the ones in her hand. "I'm not sure how to tell you this, but I've learned that it's best just to come out with it. Your name is on his birth certificate."

"What!" Jake and Elise said simultaneously.

Ms. Woods leaned over and handed him the paper. It was a copy of a birth certificate and there, in black and white, he was listed as the father. Elise moaned softly. Jake wanted to reassure her, but he kept staring at his name, trying to make sense of what he was reading.

"This can't be true," he said in a low voice. "I was only with her for a week and we always used protection. And she said she was on the pill. Why she put my name on the birth certificate is beyond me unless..." His eyes narrowed. "Is she trying to extort child support from me?"

"It's nothing like that, Mr. McCain," Ms. Woods said firmly.

"Then what is it like, Ms. Wood, because you'd better tell me and fast."

"Ben's grandmother passed away two weeks ago. By the way, his name is Benjamin, but everyone calls him Ben. He just turned three."

Jake had noticed that on the document. Benjamin Jake. Sherry had even named the boy after him. Why would she do that? They had not parted on amicable terms.

"As I was saying, Ben lived with his grandmother. Sherry left him with her mother and she called a couple of times, but no one's heard from her in years. The authorities have searched, and they can't find a trace of her. Mrs. Carr was worried because Sherry's boyfriend was involved with drugs."

"That's why I stopped seeing her," Jake said quietly. "I caught her doing cocaine in the bathroom and that was it for me."

There was silence for a moment, then Ms. Woods spoke, "Mr. McCain, this little boy is all alone and we're trying to find his father."

Jake met her gaze. ''I'm not him.''

''Are you positive of that?''

He stared at the brocade drapes and wished he could say with certainty that the boy wasn't his, but he couldn't. They'd used protection. Maybe it didn't work. If it didn't, then…

''No,'' he admitted reluctantly.

Elise moaned again and Jake wanted to tell her it wasn't true, but he really didn't know.

''There's an easy way to find out,'' Ms. Woods said.

Through his confusion, Jake breathed one word, ''How?''

''A DNA test. It's a simple blood test and it'll tell us if you're Ben's biological father or not.''

Jake didn't say anything. This was so unreal, but he felt that if he had a son, surely he'd have some inkling, something…

''Is there a possibility that someone else is the father?'' Elise asked into the silence.

''Yes,'' Ms. Woods replied. ''We know there were two other men she was seeing at the time.''

''Have they taken a DNA test?''

''No, we're starting with Mr. McCain, but I have appointments set up with the other men as well.''

''I see.''

Ms. Woods's gaze centered on Jake. ''Are you willing to take the test?''

He rubbed his hands together. ''Yes,'' he replied, knowing this was hurting Elise, but he had to do it to ease his mind.

Ms. Woods reached over and handed him a card. ''That's the name and address of a lab here in Waco. You can have it done first thing in the morning and—'' she reached into her purse ''—I'll leave my card in case you have any questions.'' She laid it on the table. ''I work out of the Houston office, but I'll be here until tomorrow to finalize the paperwork.''

He fingered the card in his hand. "How long will it take before we have the results?"

"A week or two, maybe more. Depends how busy they are."

"I see," he said, studying the card. "I'd like it done as soon as possible."

Ms. Woods rose to her feet. "I'll put a rush on it. Maybe that will help. If you're not the father, I have to keep searching."

"What…what does *he* look like?" Jake asked, suddenly needing to know. He felt Elise stiffen beside him.

"Actually, a lot like you. He has brown eyes and hair, and a smile that'll steal your heart. He's a well-mannered, adorable little boy. His grandmother raised him well."

Elise jumped up and ran to the bedroom.

"I'm sorry if I've upset her," Ms. Woods said.

Jake got to his feet. *Upset* was a mild word for what they were about to go through. He'd never expected this and he damn well didn't plan it. They had to face it, though. He was hoping they'd face it together, but he wasn't sure.

"I'll call when I get the lab results," Ms. Woods added, and Jake showed her to the door. Earlier he'd been feeling irritated. Now he was stunned and wondering how to explain this to Elise. He'd had sex with another woman, but that was years before he'd met her. If the boy was his, though, it wasn't going to make a difference. Their marriage, such as it was, would be over. He knew that for a fact.

ELISE PACED BACK AND FORTH in the bedroom, her movements agitated. *A child.* Jake could have a child—with another woman. No, *she* was going to have Jake's baby. She ran her hand over her flat stomach. It could be conceived already—growing inside her. Jake couldn't possibly have a child. It would ruin everything they'd planned. She'd waited and waited and…

Jake stepped into the room and she swung around to

confront him. ''He can't be yours. He can't,'' she cried desperately, not even recognizing her own voice.

He shrugged. ''I'm not sure.''

A sob left her throat.

''It wasn't intentional. I met Sherry years ago.''

''She was a drug addict.'' Her words sounded more accusing than she'd intended.

His jaw tightened and he picked up his socks from the floor. ''I'm going to the farm. I'll give you some time to cool off.''

She bit her lip. ''You can't leave. We haven't talked.''

''Maybe tomorrow.''

''You're not coming back tonight?''

''No, I need time to think.''

She waved a hand. ''So you're just...leaving?''

''Yes,'' he replied woodenly.

''That won't help.''

He watched her for a second. ''As I said, we both need some time right now. You're upset and I'm in a state of shock. I don't want to say anything I'll regret later.''

''Fine,'' she snapped, astounded by how much his words hurt her.

He nodded and walked out.

''Jake...Jake...don't go.'' But no one heard her plea. Painful silence echoed through her and she started to cry. The future was so bright and now... She caught sight of Derek's picture. *Derek wouldn't hurt me like this...never.* With Derek's picture in her hand, she curled up on the bed. More tears followed.

After a while, she wiped her eyes and sat up. What was wrong with her? She was overreacting—dramatically. The boy probably wasn't even Jake's and she'd spoken impulsively and selfishly. Now she'd have to spend the night alone. She stared at the photo in her arms. A picture wasn't much company in the middle of the night and she'd gotten used to having Jake in her bed.

Please don't let the boy be Jake's, she prayed.

JAKE SLEPT IN HIS OWN BED for the first time in months, but it wasn't the same. He kept reaching for Elise. She had a habit of snuggling into him, and then he'd wrap his arms around her. He could almost smell her perfume, her feminine scent. He got out of bed and went to the kitchen for a glass of milk and a banana. He sat at the table in his underwear and took a look around the room. Everything was new and shiny. Mistakenly thinking Elise would want to live here, he'd had the farmhouse completely redone. The house had belonged to his grandfather and had a wraparound porch and lots of mullioned windows for air circulation. But Jake had installed central air and heat years ago. Still, the house retained the ambience of older days. He'd painted it inside and out, put on a new roof and given it a makeover that included new appliances, enlarging the master bedroom and adding its own private bath. There'd been only one bathroom in the house and Jake had also installed a bath in the utility room. He put as much white as he could in the house because Elise liked it, but there was a lot of natural wood, which he kept. The result was very rustic with a modern touch. He'd done everything for Elise.

He ran both hands over his face. They'd gotten married in such a hurry and it had seemed logical to live in Elise's house because it was close to the university, as Elise had pointed out. Her days were full with teaching, and her summer schedule had already been planned with graduate students—he saw very little of her except at night. Of course, he was occupied harvesting a corn crop and watching over his planted cotton, too. Both their lives were so busy and they'd never talked about where they would eventually live. Was he crazy to think she'd ever come here?

He'd certainly hoped that she would, because all he could see in his future was Elise and he knew he'd fallen... His whole body jerked as the thought ran through him like an electrical shock. *In love with her.* Love? What the hell did he know about love? *Not a thing,* he answered himself.

He knew that it hurt and he was feeling a lot of that, plus a few other emotions that left a hollow ache in his belly, not to mention his heart. Was this love? How did it happen? And when?

Maybe it was that first time he looked into her blue eyes or when he'd kissed her or made love to her. Made love? Oh, God, he was making love and she was having sex. He recognized the difference. Painfully.

Somehow his feelings had deepened between that first look and the many heated encounters. Now what? He wasn't familiar with this type of love, but it was a powerful feeling. That was what all the irritation was about. Elise didn't love him. If she did, she would've tried to be supportive about the possibility of his having a son. Instead she was blaming him for an indiscretion he wasn't even aware he'd committed. A son? He could have a son. The realization threatened to overwhelm him, but he couldn't dwell on it or the what-ifs. First, he had to have the truth.

He heard a noise and saw Wags, his dog, coming through the doggy door. Wags rested his head on Jake's thigh and Jake rubbed his ears. Wags was a medium-size, yellowish-brown Labrador retriever mix. Mike, his foreman, had gotten him as a puppy and given him to Jake. Wags wagged his tail constantly, as he was doing now, hence his name.

"Where you been, boy?" Jake asked, continuing to stroke him. "Out chasing rabbits?"

Wags growled.

"What are you gonna do if you ever catch one?" Jake laughed.

Wags barked.

He got up and opened a can of dog food and spooned it into his dish. Wags gobbled up the food, his tail working overtime. "Life is pretty simple for you, isn't it, boy? No responsibility, no worries, or guilty conscience. Just basic primal needs."

Jake returned to the table; Wags followed and curled up beside his chair. His thoughts turned to Sherry. She'd been friendly, helpful and outgoing, and he was attracted to her energetic personality. His room at the hotel had a water leak in the bathroom and she'd quickly arranged a move to a suite, even though the hotel was crowded. To make up for his inconvenience, she offered to buy his dinner. He assumed she'd meant the hotel would pay for his dinner, but when he went down, she was sitting at his table. He didn't mind. She was pretty and good company. Being away from home, he found it pleasant to have someone to talk to.

When they returned to his room, she began to rip off his clothes and he knew she wasn't the woman he'd thought she was. But he didn't do much resisting. Later in the week, he found her in the bathroom doing cocaine. He didn't want anything else to do with her and told her so. She called him a few names and that was the last he'd seen of her. Could she have already been pregnant? They'd used a condom and she'd said she was on the pill, so there was no way she could have gotten pregnant. No way. *The little boy had brown eyes and hair and Jake's name was on his birth certificate.* Those facts kept torturing him.

He sighed tiredly. No, he wouldn't do this to himself. Tomorrow he'd take the blood test and wait. The results would determine the rest of his life—a life with or without Elise.

CHAPTER TWO

THE NEXT MORNING JAKE WOKE up to the smell of bacon frying and knew he was home. Wags was asleep on his mat in Jake's room. When Jake rolled out of bed, Wags trotted into the kitchen, enticed by the smell of food. Jake hurriedly dressed, trying not to think about Elise and how it felt to wake up with his arms around her.

Aunt Lavina stood at the stove—a short, thin woman with permed gray hair and blue eyes. She was his father's sister and Jake had always called her Aunt Vin; everyone did. She'd never married or had children and when Althea left, she came to help raise Jake and she'd been at the farm ever since. She'd worked as a secretary for years, but now she was retired.

"Morning, Aunt Vin." Jake kissed her cheek.

She raised an eyebrow at him. "The honeymoon over?"

He was well aware she was referring to the fact that he'd slept in his own bed last night and he avoided the question. "Mmm, that smells good."

Aunt Vin gave Wags a piece of bacon, then set a plate of eggs, bacon and homemade biscuits in front of Jake. "I knew this was going to happen. Any woman who isn't interested enough to even come here and see the beautiful work you've done to this house is not good enough for you. I'm glad you've finally realized that. The only interest you had in her was making the bedsprings sag."

Sex *had* been a big part of their relationship. Hell, it was the only relationship they had. They hadn't built any type of foundation to sustain the news they'd received yesterday.

Ignoring her words, Jake bit into a biscuit. At Elise's, they usually had muffins and fruit in the mornings, and now the big breakfast seemed too much.

"I've got bingo tonight, so you'll have to fix your own supper. I'm not missing bingo." She put the frying pan in the sink. "Some woman's been calling. Did she get you?"

Jake put down his fork. "Yeah, I talked to her."

"I just hope Mattie isn't there tonight. She always manages to win. I believe she's cheating and I wish I could catch her."

Aunt Vin was on another channel as usual—at times it was hard to keep up with her.

"So what did the woman want?" she asked abruptly.

Jake wondered how much to tell her, but then made the decision. Aunt Vin was like a mother to him and he had to share this with someone. He told her about Ms. Woods and Ben. Aunt Vin just stared at him.

"A son? You could have a son?"

"Yes. I have to take a DNA test and then we'll know."

She clapped her hands. "Oh my, there hasn't been a child in this house for years." She looked down at Wags, who was begging for more bacon. "Isn't that great, Wags?"

Wags growled.

"Aunt Vin, you're not listening to me. I said *might.* I have to take a test, so don't start planning anything."

"Okay, okay, don't get riled up," she said, giving Wags another piece of bacon.

"I just want you to be aware of what's going on."

Aunt Vin smiled. "Oh, now I see. That's why the fancy lady kicked you out. She's not happy with this development."

"Please don't call her that," Jake said, hating that Aunt Vin didn't like Elise. But Elise hadn't made any effort to get to know her, either. Still, Jake found himself defending his wife. "And no, she's not happy. No woman would be."

"Well, well, well," Aunt Vin murmured, pouring him

more coffee. "This should be interesting, but you can count on me. I raised you and I can raise another boy."

Jake stood and hugged her. "I know, and thanks, but like I said, please don't start making plans. We have to wait before we do anything. Now I have to find Mike and then go to the lab."

"Will you be sleeping here tonight?"

He turned at the door. "I'm not sure."

"You'll be sleeping here," she muttered under her breath as he walked out the door, Wags right behind him.

Wags missed him at nights, but there was no way he could take a dog to Elise's. Elise didn't even know he had a dog. So whenever he was at home Wags followed him everywhere he went.

JAKE TALKED TO HIS FOREMAN, Mike, to go over which cotton fields were scheduled to be harvested today. It was late September, one of the busiest times of the year, and he needed to be here, but he had no choice—he had to go. He had good people working for him so he left things in their capable hands.

The lab work was easy and simple, as Ms. Woods had said, a few minutes out of his day that could change the rest of his life. Driving home, he started toward Elise's, then realized she'd already have left for the university. He should've called her this morning, but he wasn't sure what to say. Maybe by tonight she would've cooled off and they could talk without tempers flaring.

When he got back to the farm, he picked up Wags and drove to the fields. Wags loved to ride in the truck with his head stuck out the window. The machines were already picking cotton, which would be stored in a module to be taken to the gin a little later. Right now the goal was to get the cotton out of the field. The corn had been harvested in July and so far he was having a good season. The weather was always a deciding factor in his business. It could make or break him.

His office was attached to a big barn that housed most of his farm equipment. After he checked with Mike and found they were on schedule, he headed there. Wags curled up at his feet as Jake tried to focus on paperwork that had piled up on his desk, but he couldn't concentrate. He kept thinking about Elise. He wished he'd called her, then he'd know what kind of mood she was in and maybe, just maybe, he'd be able to get some work done.

At noon, his brother Beau stopped by. Beau was a lawyer, single with dark good looks that made him popular with women. They'd had very little contact when they were growing up. Beau was eight when Althea left and the battle lines had been drawn—Beau and their mother against Jake and their father. Joe McCain had refused to let Jake have anything to do with them and that was the way it stayed for years. When Jake was twenty-five, Joe passed away and Beau came to the funeral. He and Jake started talking, getting reacquainted. Since then, Beau had been on a crusade to bring Althea and Jake back together, but so far Jake had resisted all his efforts. He couldn't forget the hurt she had caused him and his father.

"Hey, Jake," Beau said, throwing himself down in a chair. "How's business?"

Jake lifted an eyebrow. "Busy."

"Yeah, I saw the machines in the field. Looks like you're having a good year."

"Yep, even the shortage of rain didn't hurt. Irrigation took up the slack."

Beau looked around the office. "It's strange coming back here. I feel as if *he'll* walk in at any minute and yell at me to do something. I was always frightened of him."

"We have different memories of our father," Jake replied with a somber face.

Beau eyed him speculatively. "Just like we have different memories of our mother."

Jake leaned back in his chair. He didn't want to discuss

their parents; that was the past. He was more concerned with the present and Elise and the DNA test.

"What are you doing here, Beau?"

"Aunt Vin wanted some advice on her will. She's leaving everything to you, which is no secret, but I think she just wanted to make sure I didn't feel hurt. I told her that by the time she dies, she'll have spent it all on bingo, anyway."

"Yeah, it's an obsession with her." He glanced at Beau. "Are you sure you're okay with her decision? I tried talking to her, but—"

Beau held up a hand. "I'm fine with it, Jake. Besides, I've only gotten reacquainted with Aunt Vin in the past few years."

Silence stretched for a moment, then Beau slipped in, "Aunt Vin said you slept here last night."

Jake's eyes caught Beau's. "Don't pry into matters that don't concern you."

"Ah." Beau crossed his legs. "Something *is* wrong."

It certainly was, Jake thought, but not in the way Beau meant. How much had Aunt Vin told him? Not much, Jake guessed; that was why Beau was fishing for information. Well, if the boy was his, it wouldn't be a secret too long, but still, he wasn't good at confiding and the last person he wanted to know was his mother. And he couldn't trust Beau not to tell her.

"Nothing's wrong," Jake replied in a cool tone.

"Come on, Jake, I'm not stupid," Beau kept on. "Something's wrong or you wouldn't be sleeping at the farm."

"If there is, it's between Elise and me." He'd never told Beau why he and Elise had gotten married so quickly. His relationship with Elise was private.

"Okay, okay, I'll stop prying."

"Don't you have an office you should be in?"

"Sure do." Beau stood. "If you need to talk, you know where to find me."

"I won't."

Beau frowned. "Why do you have to be so hard and unforgiving?"

"That's just me" was the quick answer.

"No, it isn't. It's just a front to hide your emotions." Beau took a breath. "For God's sakes, why can't you talk to her?"

"I don't want to."

"Why not? She's your mother."

"Not anymore."

"Sometimes, Jake, you make me so angry."

"Close the door on your way out," Jake said, then went back to his paperwork.

"One of these days, Jake, you're going to need someone, and I hope to God that person's not as hard as you are."

Jake tried to shut out Beau's words, but he couldn't. All he could remember was a ten-year-old boy who cried himself to sleep wanting his mother—a mother who'd deserted him without a second thought. That might be hard for Beau to understand, but he wasn't the one left behind. Jake refused to see Althea under any condition; that was a vow he'd made to himself when she walked out of his life—the day she abandoned him to start a new life with Andrew Wellman. That kind of betrayal he couldn't forgive and neither could his father. A heartbroken man, Joe McCain died way before his time.

Jake had never met his half brother, Caleb, the child of Althea and Andrew Wellman, nor did he want to. Caleb was now almost twenty-eight, but Jake still had no desire for any type of relationship. He realized that was a flaw in his nature, but he couldn't get around it. The pain from the past was always with him, and even though Caleb had nothing to do with it, he represented part of that betrayal.

Jake reached for his hat. If he had a son, he'd never be able to walk away from him. He'd never do to a child what his mother had done to him—even if it meant losing Elise.

THAT EVENING JAKE DROVE TO Elise's house, unable to stay away any longer. Her car was in the garage, so he knew she was home. At the door he started to pull off his boots, then changed his mind. He wasn't doing that anymore. He wondered if he should knock but decided against that, too. He used his key, as always.

Elise was sitting on the bed staring at Derek's picture but thinking about Jake. She'd thought about calling him all day but wanted him to make the first move. *He* was the one who'd created the turmoil in their lives, so *he* had to make it right. She heard the back door open and jumped to her feet. It had to be Jake. She glanced at herself in the mirror and straightened her blue suit.

"Elise," she heard him call.

She slowly made her way to the living room. Jake was standing in the middle of the room with his hat in his hand. He wore his customary jeans, boots and cotton shirt and he looked so handsome. Just seeing him made her heart beat a little faster. Now he'd tell her that the boy wasn't his and everything would be okay. They'd have their baby as planned.

"Hi," he said softly.

She noticed him looking at her hair, which was pinned up. She wore it like that to work. She thought it gave her an added edge of maturity, but Elise knew Jake liked her hair down—he enjoyed taking it down.

"Hi," she replied, her heart beating so fast now she could barely breathe. They had to resolve this situation; that was all she could think.

"We have to talk," he said.

"Yes." She sat on the sofa and he took a chair.

"I had the test done this morning," he told her, placing his hat on the end table.

"But you still don't have the results?"

"No," he admitted. "But I need to tell you how I feel."

Elise leaned back and grabbed a decorative pillow for support.

"My mother walked away from me when I was ten years old. I would never do that to a child. If the boy is mine, I have to take responsibility."

God, she knew that. She knew Jake. This nightmare was not over.

"What about our plans for a baby?" She had to have an answer to that question. It had been with her day and night.

Jake drew a deep breath. "We have to wait for the test results before we can go any further."

"Our lives have changed," she had to say. "We have this tension that wasn't there before."

"Yes, and I apologize for that, but this has been a big shock."

"I'm having a hard time dealing with it."

"I can see that."

"So where do we go from here?"

Jake swallowed. "If the boy is mine, you'll have to ask yourself a big question. Can you raise another woman's child?"

Another woman's child.

Suddenly she felt a deadweight in her arms and fear clogged her throat, her senses, her thinking. How did she explain to him what she was feeling? She had a hard time understanding it herself.

Jake was taking in the expression on her face, looking like he'd been punched in the chest. He swallowed again. "I suppose the DNA test will decide our future."

She stared at him. "Have you considered that I might be pregnant?"

"Yes," he said, and looked away. "We'll have to wait about that, too. So I'll stay at the farm until this is resolved. It'll give us the time we need."

"Yes," she muttered, squeezing the pillow so tight her fingers were numb.

He walked over and kissed her cheek. She felt cold and didn't respond to his touch. How could she? He straightened and picked up his hat.

"I'll call when I get the results." Then he walked out of the room.

ELISE'S HAND WENT to her cheek. She could still smell his aftershave. She closed her eyes and her body started to tremble. Placing both hands over her stomach, she prayed a baby was growing inside her. If she had Jake's baby, he'd come back. They would be together, but that didn't make the other problem disappear. It only made things worse. God, she was losing her mind, just like her mother and sister, Judith, had said. And she was losing Jake.

She wiped a tear away and tried to understand what she was feeling. A little girl's blue face swam before her eyes and that old fear gripped her, just as if it were yesterday. Then the memories came flooding back.

Her mother was getting ready for a party at the university. She was going with her friends, the Abbotts. Even though Elise's father had passed away, her mother still had close ties to the university.

Mae Abbott called at the last minute in a panic because her baby-sitter had canceled. Elise's mother had volunteered her for the job.

Elise was fifteen and didn't know a thing about babies, but her mother gave her a list of instructions and told her it would be easy. Tammy was eleven months old and adorable and Mrs. Abbott had brought a playpen full of toys to occupy her. Elise fed her, changed her diaper and let her play while Elise lay on the floor reading. Engrossed in her novel she forgot about Tammy, then she heard her gagging. Elise jumped up to see what was wrong.

Tammy's face was red and tears rolled from her eyes as she continued to gag. Elise picked her up and patted her back, but it didn't work. Tammy turned blue and stopped breathing. Elise was horrified and didn't know what to do. She shook the baby, turned her upside down, but nothing worked. Tammy was limp and unresponsive. Clearly there was something obstructing her breathing so Elise had no choice but to stick her finger down Tammy's throat, trying to dislodge whatever it was. At first, she couldn't feel a thing, so she rammed her finger farther into the baby's windpipe and pulled out an object. Tammy coughed and started breathing, then wailing. Elise sat with her in a chair, both of them crying hard. That was the way her mother and the Abbotts had found them.

Mrs. Abbott was very angry and accused Elise of being irresponsible and negligent. Her mother had asked what Tammy had choked on and Elise opened her hand to reveal an eye from one of the large teddy bears in the playpen. The Abbotts whisked Tammy away to the emergency room and Elise's mother told her to go to her room and to forget what had happened. Tammy had almost died because Elise hadn't been watching her—there was no way she'd ever forget that.

Later, Mrs. Abbott had apologized and said she shouldn't have sent the bear because she knew the eye was loose, but the damage had been done. Elise couldn't stop thinking that she'd almost killed a baby. An innocent baby.

After that she avoided babies, her fear of them continuing through her teens, college and adult life. A lot of people gravitated toward babies, but Elise was just the opposite. Derek was the only person she'd ever told about her experience and her fear. For the first time someone made her understand it wasn't her fault, and Derek had her actually planning the birth of their own baby. Then he died.

When she turned thirty-five, she began to have inner stirrings—yearnings—and she found herself looking at babies, wondering what it would be like to be a mother. Derek had told her she would be a good mother and she believed him. She wouldn't be scared of her own child; she would love it, care for it and protect it.

Her biological clock was ticking, the sound a silent alarm that kept reminding her *time was running out.* If she was going to have a baby, she'd have to do it, and soon. Somehow she reasoned that if she gave birth, she could forget that horrible day, finally put it behind her as Derek had told her. She would experience those nurturing, motherly feelings and prove she wasn't a horrible person.

She got up and walked to the bedroom. How could she tell Jake that awful story? How she'd almost killed a child. He'd see her differently and she didn't want to see the loathing in his eyes.

The little boy needed a mother. And he might be Jake's son. Could she care for him? Be his mother? She honestly didn't have an answer. All she could feel was the fear inside her, and before she could find an answer she'd have to tell Jake the truth. Derek had understood, but then Derek had loved her. Jake didn't love her and it made this problem so difficult.

He's just a little boy, though.... She swiftly closed that door. She wouldn't open it. She couldn't. Selfishly, painfully, she pushed those thoughts aside. Tomorrow would be brighter. It had to be.

THE NEXT COUPLE OF WEEKS were difficult. Jake worked himself to exhaustion. He talked to Elise several times to see how she was doing and she was always happy to hear his voice. Still, their conversations were stilted and the waiting was getting to both of them.

Elise went through her regular routine of teaching and attending meetings, but Jake was never far from her mind. She was surprised she missed him so much. She missed his presence at night and she missed his company in the mornings. He always brought her a cup of coffee to wake her up; she enjoyed that and enjoyed what followed even more. She became angry every time she thought of how that had been taken away from her without warning. But she had to learn to cope, to deal with the situation.

She had a dinner engagement with her family at the club and came up with several excuses, but they all seemed lame. Besides, she had to get on with her life.

The club was busy and Elise spotted Althea Wellman

and her family eating at a table. She purposely avoided them because she didn't want to be asked questions about Jake. She hurriedly slid into a seat at her mother's table and forced a smile.

"You're late," Constance Graham said before Elise could speak. Constance's hair was blond, as was Judith's, but now her color came out of a bottle. In her sixties, Constance was regal and proper and expected the very best of her daughters. Being late wasn't tolerated.

"The husband not with you?" Judith asked in her catty way. "I'm not surprised. He's never with you."

Stan, Judith's husband, spoke up. "Leave Elise alone. For God's sake, she just sat down."

"Thanks, Stan," Elise said pointedly. "And it's nice to see everyone, too."

Constance patted her hand. "How are you, darling?"

"Fine," she replied, gritting her teeth. Her family had that effect on her.

"Stan's ordered wine," Constance informed her. "Oh, here it comes now."

The waiter poured wine into a glass and Stan tasted it. "Great, just great," he murmured, and the waiter filled the glasses around the table.

Elise took a sip of wine. She was going to need it to muddle through the evening. Why had she come? She just wanted to be by herself. She didn't like the way she was thinking or feeling these days and she couldn't seem to do anything about it.

"I've had a horrible day," Judith was saying. "I'm not satisfied with Duncan's school and I can't get through to his teachers. It's like talking to robots."

"He's at a very good private school," Elise said. "Their academic record is excellent."

"There's nothing wrong with the school," Stan put in.

Judith turned in her seat to confront her husband. "Our son is not excelling the way he should. He has to be pushed. You're too lenient. Why can't you understand that?"

Stan shoved back his chair. ''I need something stronger.'' He headed for the bar.

''Oh, he makes me so angry,'' Judith said, tipping up her glass. ''He lets Duncan get away with anything. I caught them watching sports the other night instead of doing homework. I won't have it. I won't.''

''Calm down, dear,'' Constance said. ''We're in a public place.''

Judith drank more wine.

''Duncan is eight years old,'' Elise had to say. ''He's bright and energetic. I'm sure he'll excel in anything he chooses.''

''I don't need your advice, Elise.''

Normally Elise wouldn't say anything to her older sister because when Judith was in a bad mood, it was better to leave her alone. But tonight she was out of patience. ''Then stop giving me advice.''

Judith's head jerked up. ''And do you ever take it? No. You just had to marry that McCain man. Lord only knows why. Look at his brothers over there. They're educated and respected in their fields, but you chose the farmer in the family. What were you thinking?''

''It's my business,'' Elise shot back.

''Yes,'' Judith settled back with a smug expression. ''The business of making a baby. But has it happened? No. I think you should cut your losses and get out while you can.''

Anger bolted through Elise at her sister's words. Judith didn't even know Jake, but she'd judged him because of his profession. ''I will thank you to stay out of my life.'' She rose to her feet. ''I'll pass on dinner.''

Constance caught her arm. ''Darling, no. Judith is just upset and not acting rationally, are you?'' She looked at Judith. ''I won't have this kind of behavior at the dinner table.''

Judith waved a hand. ''Okay, I'm just upset with Stan. I promise I won't say another word about the farmer.''

"You just did," Elise said heatedly, and walked away. She didn't even pause when Constance called her name. Before she could escape, Althea stopped her at the door.

Althea was petite with short brown hair now highlighted with shades of gray. Her eyes were brown like her son's.

"I'm sorry to bother you, but I was wondering how Jake is." She asked the same question every time Elise saw her. Tonight she didn't think she could take much more.

"He's fine, Althea. Busy as ever," she managed to say.

"That's good. I just want him to be happy."

"I really have to go," Elise said, and hated that look in Althea's eyes—as if she'd hurt her. "I'll talk to you later."

She quickly made her way to her car, resisting the urge to run. She wanted to go to Jake, to feel his arms around her and…what? She didn't know anymore. All she knew was that she was falling apart and the worst wasn't over.

JAKE WAS FINISHING FOR the day when the phone rang. He'd spent hours in the fields, making sure things were done to his specifications. He was dirty and tired and he longed for a shower and a change of clothes.

"Hello," he said into the receiver.

"Mr. McCain, this is Ms. Woods."

Jake immediately sat down. He had to, because he knew what the call meant.

"Yes."

"I have the DNA results."

"Yes," he said again, and tried to swallow, but his throat seemed to be locked.

"You're the father. The test is 99.9 per cent reliable. You can't be any more positive than that. You're definitely the father."

You're the father. You're the father. You're the father.

The room and Ms. Woods's voice faded away, and he was alone with those words holding him in a mindless void of pleasure and pain. *He was the father.* He had a son. He now knew the truth, and the truth was a bitter sweetness that permeated his whole body.

"Mr. McCain? Mr. McCain?"

Jake finally heard Ms. Woods calling his name. "Yes," he said.

"Are you okay?"

"I'm not sure, but I will take responsibility for my son."

"I'm glad you feel that way. We offer counseling for you and your wife…to help make this transition."

"Right now I just want to see my son."

"First, I'd like to meet with you and discuss Ben."

"Why? What's to discuss?"

"Ben's just lost his grandmother. He's very confused and we have to take things slowly."

"Yes, yes, I understand."

There was a pause, then Ms. Woods asked, "How does Mrs. McCain feel about this? She was pretty upset the other day."

"Does it matter?" he countered, not wanting to discuss Elise with her.

"Yes, it matters a great deal. At the hearing a judge will look favorably upon a couple having custody of Ben."

"Hearing? What hearing?"

"Ben is a ward of the court, Mr. McCain. Sherry's rights as a parent were severed long ago and Mrs. Carr had full custody. A judge will now review Ben's case before awarding custody to anyone else. The court will do what's in Ben's best interests."

"I'm his father. Doesn't that mean anything?" It was the first time he'd said the words and they felt good. He had a son. Ben was his.

"Yes, that will weigh in your favor, but as I said, a judge will make the final decision."

"Are you saying I might not get my son?" He suddenly felt nauseous.

"I'm saying that with your wife beside you, it shouldn't

be a problem. But from this conversation, I'm guessing she's not supporting you in this.''

Jake couldn't lie to her. ''She's having a hard time accepting the news.''

''I see'' came the reply. ''I'll be in Waco at nine in the morning to discuss this. The address is on the card I gave you. We'll talk about Ben and everything else. Maybe by the time the hearing comes around, your wife will feel differently.''

''Maybe,'' he mumbled, but he felt she wouldn't.

As he hung up, he didn't think about Elise or Ben. He thought about Ms. Woods and their conversation. There was a note in her voice that bothered him. A hesitation—as if she was keeping something from him. But what?

LATER THAT EVENING JAKE DROVE to Elise's house. He let himself in and saw her working at her computer in the study. When she saw him, she came into the living room, wearing black slacks and a cream knit top, her expression vulnerable. He wished he wasn't about to shatter her world. He searched for words to tell her, but she took it out of his hands.

''You have the results, don't you?''

''Yes,'' he said quietly as his insides coiled tight.

She bit her lip. ''Well?''

His eyes met hers. ''I'm the father.''

''No, no!'' She shook her head, not wanting to believe it, then saw that look on his face. ''Oh, God.'' She sank onto the sofa and linked her fingers together. ''You're the father.''

''Yes.''

''This changes everything.''

''Yes,'' he said again.

Silence. Loud, heartbreaking silence.

He squeezed a question from his locked throat. ''Can you raise another woman's child?''

She raised her head. ''I...ah...I'm not sure.'' She needed

to tell him now what she'd done. Maybe he would understand. Maybe...

"I want my own baby" came out instead.

"I'm aware of that, but I can't walk away from my son. My mother did that to me and I will not do that to my child."

They stared at each other, and the pain in her eyes tightened his stomach even more. "I'm sorry, Elise. I didn't plan this. I would never intentionally hurt you."

Tears rolled down her face. "But you have, can't you see that? You've ruined our lives."

Something in him snapped. She wasn't even trying to see this from his point of view. She had only one thought in her head—herself and a baby.

"Yes, I've ruined your life, Elise, and I'd find all these tears and emotions easier to understand if you cared one iota for me. But I'm just a sperm donor to you. You've never considered my feelings or much of anything else where I'm concerned."

She blanched. "What are you talking about?"

"Derek's picture. How do you think it makes me feel to make love to you with *his* picture on your nightstand?"

"You never said anything."

"My God." He shoved both hands through his hair. "Why should I have to say anything? You should've had enough consideration for my feelings to remove it."

"You know how I loved him."

"Oh, yeah, and I'm tired of hearing that, too. He's dead and it's time you accepted it."

"Now you're being cruel." She buried her face in her hands, sobbing.

Jake inhaled sharply, but it didn't keep the grief and anger from coming out. "And I don't like living in your house. I'm afraid of getting something dirty or breaking a priceless heirloom. I'm a farmer and I have a house and that's where I should be." She looked up at him with her bottom lip trembling but still he didn't stop. "You've never showed the slightest interest in seeing my home, my farm. That's because you don't care about me. The only thing you care about is having a baby.''

She stared at him through watery eyes. ''That was our agreement—to have a child and raise it together. We never discussed the other things. I didn't think they were important to you.''

''They are and you've stomped on my feelings long enough.''

''Then I think you'd better go.''

Some of his anger evaporated. He didn't want it to end like this. He'd wanted to say so many things to Elise and everything had come out wrong and harsh. ''I...ah...''

She gritted her teeth and took a deep breath, composing herself. ''It's okay, Jake. I'll survive.''

No doubt she would, but he hated hurting her. ''The social worker is setting up a meeting with Ben.'' He didn't know why he said that. It just seemed to slip out. Maybe he was hoping for a break in her demeanor, something to give him a sign that the marriage wasn't over.

''I hope you'll be happy with your little boy.''

Her head was bent and he couldn't see her eyes, but he knew it took every bit of emotional energy she had for her to say that. It also told him that there was no hope for them. Ms. Woods had said his chances for custody would be better with Elise. Now he'd have to take his chances alone.

''If you want to file for divorce, I'll sign the papers.''

Her eyes jerked to his. ''Is that what you want?''

No, I want us to raise my son together. But he said, ''Yes, it's what I want.''

CHAPTER THREE

JAKE HAD TROUBLE SLEEPING. He kept seeing Elise's face, the hurt in her eyes…a hurt he had put there. Not intentionally, but still, he was the cause of her pain. He sat up and slipped on his jeans, grabbed a T-shirt and shoes and headed for the door. Wags followed. Jake went straight to his workshop, which was off the garage. Wags settled in his spot by the door, watching Jake.

The smell of fresh-shaved wood clung to the air. As a hobby, Jake did woodwork and it was something he loved. He flipped on the light and strolled over to a baby's cradle that occupied the middle of the large room. Elise had seen it in a magazine and he was planning to surprise her with it when she became pregnant. He drew in a deep breath and pulled up a chair, staring at the cradle. Wags trotted over and barked.

"I know, boy," Jake said. "We'll go to the house in a minute." He couldn't take his eyes off the cradle.

It consisted of round spindles connected to a half-circular base at each end. The crib swung from a sturdy stand. He had spent many hours doing the intricate pattern of flowers on the circular base and the stand. The spindles were rounded in the middle and smaller on each end. Mrs. Myers, a friend of his who sewed, was making the mattress and lining out of some of the finest cotton ever grown and he'd ordered lace from Italy as a finishing touch. The picture in the magazine was white, but Elise had said if the baby was a boy she wouldn't want white, so Jake was waiting to paint or stain the crib. Now he didn't have to worry. It would never be finished.

He pushed the cradle and it swung gently back and forth as "Rock-a-Bye, Baby" played. He'd had a hell of a time figuring out how to get the tune to play when the cradle rocked, but a visit to the electronics store solved his problem. It worked on the same principle as a music box. Now it was all for nothing.

Wags barked several times at the sound and Jake nodded his head. Glancing up, he saw the new wood stacked against the wall. He was starting on a baby bed next, to match the crib. A tremor of despair ran through him. For the first time he realized how much he wanted a baby...how much he'd planned for it, too. Letting go of that hope wasn't easy for him, either.

But now he had Ben. Tomorrow he'd see his son for the first time and that filled him with new hope. It didn't diminish the feelings he had for his and Elise's baby; it just made the whole situation difficult.

What would he do if Elise *was* pregnant? He ran his hands over his face. He'd deal with that if it happened.

"Jake, what are you doing working so late?"

Jake turned to Aunt Vin standing in the doorway.

"It's almost eleven," she added, walking farther into the room. "I just got in from playing bingo and... Oh, oh, the cradle is beautiful."

"Yes," Jake said in a low voice.

Aunt Vin watched him for a moment. "What's wrong?"

Jake clasped his hands together. "Ms. Woods called. I'm...I'm Ben's father."

"Oh, and from your expression I'm guessing the fancy lady isn't taking this well."

"No," Jake admitted, seeing no reason to lie.

Aunt Vin clicked her tongue. "She wants a baby and God just gave her a ready-made one. What's the difference? They all need love."

Jake pushed to his feet and put his arm around her shoulder. "Yeah, and I'm going to give my son all the love I have."

"So you're raising Ben alone?"

"It looks that way."

"Don't worry, I'll be here."

"Thanks, Aunt Vin."

They slowly made their way to the house, Wags running ahead. "I guess we need to get a room ready," she remarked.

"Let's wait for a few days. I want to meet Ben first."

"Okay." Aunt Vin paused. "*She's* not even going to meet Ben?"

"No."

Aunt Vin shook her head and went to her room.

THE NEXT MORNING JAKE WAS UP early and drove into Waco to meet Ms. Woods. He found the building without any problem. She was in an office that consisted of a small space cluttered with filing cabinets and a desk.

She rose to her feet. "Good morning, Mr. McCain," she said as she shook his hand. "Have a seat."

Jake sat in a straight chair by her desk.

Ms. Woods clasped her hands across a large folder. "Mrs. McCain not with you?"

"No," Jake replied, and to avoid answering uncomfortable questions he asked, "When can I see my son?"

Ms. Woods looked as if she was going to press the issue, but then said, "There are a few things we have to discuss first."

"Like what?"

"Ben. I want you to be fully aware of his situation."

He heard that note in her voice again and Jake knew something was wrong. "What situation?' he asked carefully.

She opened the folder. "Ben has special problems."

Jake's chest tightened. "Problems?"

"As before, the only way I know how to do this is just tell you."

"I wish you would."

"Ben was a twenty-seven-week baby—a preemie—and he wasn't breathing when he was born. The doctors worked with Ben and it took nine minutes before he could breathe on his own. He was then flown to Memorial Hermann hospital in Houston. He was basically in a comatose state and the doctors didn't expect him to live. Sherry was supposed to make the trip to Houston a couple of days later, but she never showed up. That's when the hospital called Children's Protective Services. They had no one to contact if the baby died. We were able to locate Sherry's mother and she immediately came to Houston. She didn't even know Sherry had given birth." She paused. "They fed him from an IV because he had no sucking reflex and he was getting oxygen to help him breathe. When Mrs. Carr arrived she was devastated at the sight of Ben, but she was a very religious person and wouldn't leave Ben or give up on him. On the third day, Ben's sucking reflex began. It was as close to a miracle as I've ever seen, but Ben had a long way to go. The doctors did test after test and ruled out several disorders, including cerebral palsy. Finally Ben's diagnosis was developmental delay and his prognosis wasn't good."

"Developmental delay?"

"Yes. Ben does everything much slower than other children."

The pain in Jake's chest became so tight that it was unbearable.

"Mrs. Carr was Ben's lifeline and she was determined that Ben would be a normal little boy. She lived in Bryan but she relocated to Houston so Ben could be near the hospital and doctors. At first Ben didn't have the muscle tone to accomplish simple tasks. Mrs. Carr, under a developmental pediatrician's guidance, began an exercise program for Ben. She massaged his arms and legs, even the inside of his mouth, to stimulate him. When she took Ben home, she continued the exercises. They took from three to four hours and she did them at least twice a day, but it was worth it. This little boy—who was supposed to be a vegetable if he lived at all—was able to roll over at ten months. At fifteen months he crawled and he took his first steps six months ago. Mrs. Carr was working on his speech and he was starting to say words and whole sentences, then…"

Ms. Wood stopped. "Irene was diagnosed with pancreatic cancer and she died quickly. She was so busy caring for Ben that she didn't take care of herself. She was devoted to Ben, I suspect mainly because she'd had such a disaster with her daughter." She stopped again. "When you met Sherry at that hotel, she was supposed to be clean and working but, as you found, that wasn't true. She also lied to you about birth control. Irene said Sherry was never able to take the pill and Irene worried about pregnancy all the time because Sherry's boyfriend was a drug dealer. He was in prison when you met her. CPS hasn't been involved in Ben's case since Mrs. Carr was granted custody, but we've checked on him from time to time. When Mrs. Carr became ill, she contacted us. That's the reason I'm here today."

Jake listened to all of this in a state of shock, hardly able to believe what he was hearing. His throat burned with an ache he couldn't assuage. His son had needed him and he hadn't been there.

"Mr. McCain, are you okay?" Ms. Woods asked with concern.

"Yes," he answered with difficulty. "Sherry…where is she now?"

"As I told you earlier, we don't know. When Ben was about a month old, her boyfriend, Rusty, was released from prison. Mrs. Carr was in Houston with Ben and Sherry was in their Bryan home. The boyfriend went there and Sherry and Irene argued. Irene didn't want him in her house and she was trying to get Sherry to return to Houston and Ben. Sherry came one more time to see him, then she left with

Rusty. Two months later Irene got a phone call from the police. Rusty shot a woman in El Paso when a drug deal went bad. The Texas Rangers became involved and said they were in Mexico. Irene got several phone calls from various border towns, but they still haven't been located.''

Jake frowned. ''She just left with her boyfriend?''

''Yes.''

''How could she abandon her own son?''

''Mr. McCain, Sherry has had lots of problems since her father was killed in a freak accident when she was sixteen. He was the center of her world and she never recovered from it. She got in with a bad crowd, got into drugs. From what I understand, Mrs. Carr did everything she could to help her daughter, but Sherry was bent on a course of self-destruction.'' She arched an eyebrow. ''I'm sure you noticed some of this when you met her.''

''Yes,'' he murmured. He recognized early that Sherry had problems he didn't want to get involved with. He remembered her talking constantly about her father and how he understood her and her mother didn't. But that didn't explain how she could just leave Ben.

Jake stood on shaky legs. ''I want to see my son.''

She was taken aback. ''I'm not through, Mr. McCain.''

''There's more?'' he asked hoarsely.

''Yes. Ben has regressed since Mrs. Carr's death. He's stopped speaking, he falls often and he rarely smiles. So we have to handle this very carefully.''

''Please, I want to see my son,'' he repeated.

''You will, I promise, but I wish you would listen to everything I have to say.''

''What else could there possibly be?'' He was losing patience and could feel his tension building.

''You haven't asked where Ben is.''

''I assume he's in a foster home somewhere,'' he replied. ''All the more reason for me to take responsibility for him.''

''It's not that simple.''

"Why?"

"Mrs. Carr's sister and her husband moved in when she became so ill. She wanted someone there for Ben."

Thank God. At least Ben was with family. "I'm glad," he said simply.

Ms. Woods picked up a pencil, then glanced directly at him. "Our office got a call this morning from an attorney. The Fosters have decided they want to adopt Ben and they're filing for custody."

"What!" His eyes burned into her.

"They're very fond of Ben."

"He's *my* son," Jake stated as if he needed to remind her of that.

"Yes, but Ben is comfortable with Peggy and Carl. He knows them and they know how to take care of him."

Jake's eyes narrowed. "Are you saying I might not get my son?"

"As I told you, a judge will make that decision, but I want you to be aware of this new development."

He gulped in a breath at the injustice of it all and then anger quickly overtook him. It seemed as if they were conspiring to keep him from Ben, and he wasn't letting that happen. He placed his hands on the desk and leaned in close to Ms. Woods's face. "You came looking for me, lady, and you found me. I'm Ben's father and I want to see him…now."

"I have every intention of taking you to Ben," she said crisply.

Jake straightened. "Good. Let's go."

Ms. Woods let out a long sigh. "I have to make arrangements with the Fosters. We can't barge in on them."

"Okay, make the arrangement." He tried to remain calm.

"Mrs. Carr lived in Houston, as I told you, and that's a four-hour drive. We may not be able to do it until tomorrow."

Jake glanced at his watch. "I'll be back at one. That'll

give you enough time to inform the Fosters that I'm coming." He turned toward the door.

"Mr. McCain, I can't—"

"One o'clock, Ms. Woods," he said, and closed the door.

ELISE WAS HAVING A BAD morning. Her eyes were red and puffy and makeup hadn't helped. She should have been at the university by now, but she couldn't seem to pull herself together. Jake was gone and he wasn't coming back; she couldn't get past that and the hateful things he'd said.

She went into the closet to get her gray suit jacket and saw Jake's clothes...a couple of pairs of jeans and a few shirts. He also had some socks and underwear in a drawer. In six months of marriage, that was all Jake had brought to her house. It was as if he'd been visiting her, and in a way she supposed he was. Now that visit was over. A shiver ran through her as she moved to the bedroom for her briefcase and purse. Picking up her purse she saw the magazines by the nightstand...magazines with articles on conception. She dropped her purse and gathered an armful and headed for the garage. She wouldn't be needing them anymore. Jake was gone and so was her dream of a baby. She made three trips to dump the magazines in the garbage.

With the last few in her hands, she straightened to see Derek's picture on the nightstand. Suddenly Jake's words echoed through her head. *"How do you think it makes me feel to make love to you with* his *picture on your nightstand? You should've had enough consideration for my feelings to remove it. You've never considered my feelings or much of anything else where I'm concerned."*

Oh my God. The magazines dropped to the floor at her feet as a fog lifted from her mind and she could see her insensitive actions clearly. *Oh my God.* Her legs trembled and she sank onto the bed. What had she done? Up until this very moment, she had never seen anything wrong with having Derek's picture in their bedroom. And it *was* very wrong. She could see that now. Why couldn't she before? Maybe she was more like her mother and Judith than she'd ever imagined, because the insensitivity of her own behavior bordered on cruelty. Yet Jake had never said a word until yesterday. Why not? He wanted a child as much as she did; that was the only reason that made sense. And now he had a child—a little boy named Ben. She wondered if Jake had seen his son. What was Ben like?

Tears welled up but she refused to cry. She couldn't. She had a class to teach and she had to get moving, although her body wasn't cooperating. All she could see was Jake's face, and she knew she had to apologize. But how could she explain the mental fog she'd been in? By being honest. Years of grieving had clouded her thinking. Jake's words had brought her to her senses.

She stood and turned Derek's picture facedown. He was dead. She had to accept that, as Jake had said, and she had to get on with her life...a life without Jake...or a baby. She picked up her purse and walked toward the door, trying not to think about Jake. But she knew he'd be in her every thought.

JAKE THOUGHT THE SITUATION OVER. He now knew what Ms. Woods had been hiding—Ben was not a normal little boy. His mind reeled from the revelation and he tried to stay focused on the main objective. The Fosters wanted to adopt his son—a son who had problems, severe problems. As easy as that would make his life, he couldn't even consider the possibility. Ben was his flesh and blood, and even though he'd need special attention, Jake would do everything he could to be the boy's father. Because he was.

He decided he needed a lawyer. If he had to fight for custody of Ben, he'd need a good one. He drove straight to Beau's office. Beau specialized in family law and Jake knew his brother could help him, give him some advice. He'd never been to Beau's office, since Beau always visited him at the farm. They met for dinner every now and then, but other than that, they had very little contact. Jake knew that was his fault. He couldn't face seeing his mother.

He located Beau's office on the fourth floor of a tall glass structure. A young woman at the reception desk smiled at him as he entered.

"I'd like to see Beau McCain, please," he said.

"Do you have an appointment?" she asked politely.

"No."

She flipped through a book. "He has an opening on Friday at two."

Jake frowned. "I need to see him now."

"He's with someone and—"

Her words faded away as Jake headed down the hall to find Beau.

"Come back here." The young woman ran after him, but Jake didn't stop. He heard Beau's voice, tapped on the door and went in.

As he did, his stomach caved in with such force that it cut off his breathing. His mother was there talking to Beau. He hadn't seen her in twenty-eight years—not since the day she'd left the farm and him behind. He'd made a point of not seeing her, of not having anything to do with her, and he'd succeeded until today.

Just like that, his childhood flashed through his mind, his mother reading to him, singing to him, kissing his forehead, patiently helping him with homework, and from out of nowhere the taste of her cinnamon rolls made his mouth water. Then just as quickly those good feelings slammed into a wall of pure pain—the pain of her betrayal—and that was all he felt. All he could remember.

"Mr. McCain, I tried to stop him." Numbly the receptionist's voice penetrated his mind.

"It's okay, Cindy," Beau said as he came around his desk. "I'll take care of this."

Jake wanted to turn and leave, but his feet wouldn't move. When he was younger, he used to dream of things he'd say to his mother if he ever saw her again, but those words were locked away so deep, under layers of heartache and resentment, that he couldn't dredge them up.

Almost in slow motion he watched his mother get up from the chair and walk toward him. The pain in his chest intensified and he was beyond thinking. *Don't speak to me,* screamed through his head.

But her words came as soft and sweet as he remembered. "I was just leaving. It's good to see you, Jake." She stared at him a moment before walking out the door.

She didn't look any older than she had years ago, Jake thought inanely, except for the gray in her hair.

Beau closed the door and glared at Jake. "Would it have killed you to say hello?"

Jake was still having a hard time finding his voice.

"When are you going to let go of the past?" Beau snapped.

Air swished back into Jake's lungs. "Some things can't be forgiven."

"Like what?"

"Like a mother leaving a ten-year-old boy."

Beau shook his head. "You have a convenient memory, Jake. You refused to go with us. Remember?"

He remembered it vividly. His mother begging and pleading with him, but his father had already told him what she'd done. She was leaving him for Andrew Wellman. "I remember a lot of things," he said harshly.

"Do you remember Mom had custody and could have forced you to go, but she didn't? She knew how much you loved the old man and how loyal you were to him. In the end, she couldn't hurt you anymore. She let you stay and I don't think she's ever forgiven herself for that."

Jake had had all he could take. "She *chose* to leave. I remember that. Or is your memory convenient, too?"

Beau threw up his hands. "What do you want, Jake? I'm tired of talking to a stone wall."

Ben—he was here about Ben. For a paralyzing moment he'd forgotten that. Now he wasn't sure if he wanted Beau to help him or not. Too much tension existed between them, and he needed someone willing to fight for him. Was Beau that person?

"Since you've never been to my office before it must be important," Beau said, moving back to his desk.

"Yes, it is," Jake admitted. "But I'm having second thoughts now."

"Why?"

"Because it's awkward."

"I don't feel awkward. Do you?"

Jake didn't answer as he took the seat his mother had vacated. Awkwardness or tension didn't matter. What mattered was his son. He told Beau about Ben.

Beau eyes widened. "You have a son?"

"Yes, and the Fosters, the people caring for him, want to adopt him."

"How bad is Ben's health?"

"I'm hoping to meet him this afternoon and determine that for myself. Ms. Woods is trying to set it up and from what she's said, Ben needs lots of care and attention."

"And you're willing to do that?"

"Of course I am. He's my son."

Silence, then Beau asked, "And Elise?"

Jake swallowed. "She'll be filing for divorce."

"I'm sorry."

"I can't dwell on it. I have to move forward for Ben." That was his one goal. As long as he had that, the pain wasn't so bad.

"I have to be honest," Beau said. "It would go a hell of a lot better if she was with you."

"She won't be."

"Why not?"

"Dammit, Beau, I'll be fighting for my son alone. That is all you need to know." He wasn't discussing his marriage with Beau or anyone else.

"Okay," Beau muttered.

Jake's eyes caught Beau's. "What are my chances?"

''If Ben has severe problems and these people know how to care for him and he's familiar with them, a judge'll think twice before removing him from their home. Being the biological father carries a lot of weight, though. I'll look up some case law and see if we can even the odds.''

''Thanks, but…''

''But what?''

Jake had trouble expressing what he felt. He cleared his throat. ''I want what's best for Ben and I feel that's being with me, but I haven't seen him yet. The Fosters might be able to give him more than I can. If that's the case, I'll have to leave him there.''

A slight grin tugged at Beau's mouth.

Jake frowned. ''Why are you smiling?''

''I was thinking that to do what's best for your son, you might have to relinquish your claim on him—like Mom did with you.''

Jake drew in a long breath. ''I don't want to get into that again.''

''There're two sides to every story, Jake. One of these days, you might want to hear the other side.''

Jake stood. ''I'd better go. I want to be ready when Ms. Woods calls.''

''Call me after you see Ben and let me know your decision.''

''All I can think right now is that I want my son,'' Jake said. ''That won't change unless Ben is in such bad shape that I'm unable to handle him. I don't know anything about kids, but I'm willing to learn. I'm bracing myself for the worst and hoping I can be the father Ben needs. He may need more than me, though. That's what I have to find out.'' He moved toward the door. ''I'll talk to you later.''

''Jake.'' Beau stopped him.

Jake turned back.

''Give me the word and I'll fight for you any way I can.''

They stared at each other, two brothers with different points of view bound together by blood—the most powerful connection in the world.

"Thanks," Jake replied, and walked out.

CHAPTER FOUR

WHEN JAKE WALKED INTO the kitchen, the phone was ringing. He immediately picked it up. Ms. Woods's voice came through, clear and impatient. "Mr. McCain, I've set up a meeting for four o'clock today. Is that fast enough?"

"Yes, thanks." He felt a moment of relief.

"I'll meet you at the office in Houston. The address is on the card I gave you. When you get to Houston, Mrs. Turner, head of our department, will want to explain the situation more fully."

When were they going to stop explaining things to him and just let him see his son? "Fine," he said.

"Try to get there a little after three. I know that's rushing it, but—"

He cut her off. "I'll be there, and thanks again, Ms. Woods."

As he hung up, a sense of excitement ran through him. He was finally meeting Ben—his son—and he didn't have any time to waste. It was already after eleven. He ran into his aunt Vin on the patio.

"Where're you going in such a rush?" she asked.

Jake grinned. "To see my son."

Aunt Vin patted his shoulder. "That's wonderful. When will you bring him home?"

The grin left his face. "It's a long story and I'm in a hurry. We'll talk tonight."

"I'll be at bingo," she shouted after him.

"I'll talk to you in the morning, then."

"Okay. Drive carefully."

Jake made a stop at the barn to talk to Mike, to check if there were any problems he couldn't handle. There weren't. The machines were out of the fields and the cotton was stored in modules waiting to be taken to the gin. Wags jumped into the truck.

"Sorry, boy, you can't go," Jake said, pulling him out by the collar.

Wags whined in protest.

"You can ride with Mike and I'll be home tonight."

With Wags barking loudly, Jake climbed into his truck and within minutes he was on the highway to Houston.

He didn't know what he'd find when he arrived, but as he'd told Beau, he was preparing for the worst. Ms. Woods hadn't said Ben was mentally challenged. He was just slow. Did that mean the same thing? He wasn't sure and it didn't matter. Ben was his son and he'd love him no matter what.

Sherry crossed his mind and Jake wondered again how she could have abandoned her own son. He grunted. What was he thinking? Women abandoned children all the time—children who didn't have anything wrong with them—like his mother had abandoned him. He still felt a queasiness in his belly from just seeing her. Beau had said there were two sides to every story, but he was wrong. His father had been a hardworking man who loved his family, and his mother had had an affair and become pregnant. She had destroyed a home and a family and Jake couldn't see any other side than that.

Gently rolling hills, dense woods, farms and ranches flashed by as he drove through Hearne to College Station to Navasota and hit Highway 290 into Houston. The highway merged with Loop 610 South, and as he negotiated heavy traffic, that sense of excitement returned. He couldn't stop thinking how much more thrilled he'd be if Elise was with him, but she wasn't.

He wondered how she was. He'd purposefully tried not to think about her, which was impossible because she was always there at the back of his mind. Had she seen an attorney yet? Probably, he decided. What they'd shared was something basic to her. To him, it had developed into something much more.

He had been so shocked when she'd called and asked him out. He didn't date women like Elise Weber—beautiful, educated and with an air of being untouchable. He preferred women who were soft and natural. Not that Elise wasn't those things. She just seemed way out of his reach. That was his first impression, but then he got to know her and she was a completely different person. He responded to her warmth and vitality. They seemed to be able to talk forever. He wasn't a guy who liked to talk, but with her it came easy.

He shifted uncomfortably as he realized Elise had been in control from the start. She knew what she wanted and she didn't have any problem getting him. Hell, after that first date, he wanted her like crazy. Elise had been a big surprise in the bedroom. Her cool professorial facade disappeared into a warm, inviting woman, and that sensuality blinded him to the problems in their marriage. Her dead husband's picture on the nightstand was a big example. So many times he'd resisted the urge to knock the damn thing to the floor, but he respected her enough not to do that. He kept waiting for her to remove it. That never happened. And it hurt. His feelings didn't matter to her.

He didn't have to worry about Elise, though. She'd be fine because her emotions weren't involved—not the ones that counted, anyway. It bothered him that he'd hurt her, and it would be a while before he'd lose the feelings he had for her…if ever. She loved someone else and she'd told him that up front. That didn't keep him from falling for her. But it kept him locked in a pain of his own choosing.

IT WAS TEN AFTER THREE by the time Jake found the office. This office was basically the same as the other, only much larger and there were people in the waiting area. He told the woman at the desk who he was and took a seat. In a few minutes Ms. Woods came out and he followed her into an inner office where an older, gray-haired woman sat at a desk. She stood and shook Jake's hand.

"It's nice to meet you, Mr. McCain," she said. "I'm Gail Turner and I worked with Carmen on Ben's case when his mother left him at the hospital."

"Then you know Ben very well?" he asked, taking a chair by the desk.

Mrs. Turner resumed her seat and Jake had a feeling he was in for some cold, hard truths.

"Yes. After Mrs. Carr was granted custody, we checked on Ben for several months and saw that she was very capable of caring for him. We didn't become involved again until Mrs. Carr called us two months ago. She knew she was dying and she asked us to locate Ben's father." She paused. "We weren't aware until this morning that the Fosters want to adopt Ben. They knew we were searching for the father and they never gave us any indication that adoption was a possibility. But in all fairness I have to admit that they know Ben and his routine and they care for him deeply."

Jake frowned. "Are you saying the Fosters would be better for Ben than me?"

"A judge will make that decision," she replied coolly.

Same old line. "On your recommendation."

"Well, yes, our recommendation will weigh heavily in the decision."

Jake chose his words carefully. "So, Mrs. Turner, what you're trying to tell me in not-so-subtle terms is that Ben would be better off living with the Fosters."

Mrs. Turner clasped her hands on the desk. "Dr. Howard Ruskin, Ben's doctor, a developmental pediatrician, feels very strongly that it would be detrimental for Ben to be moved out of his familiar surroundings at this time. After several visits with Ben, I have to agree with him. Ben's taken a step backward because of Mrs. Carr's death. I'm not sure how much he understands. All he knows is that his grandmother's gone and he's retreated into himself. The Fosters are working with him and I'm hoping to see some signs of improvement."

"But you haven't?"

"No. He was walking everywhere. Now he stumbles and falls. Mrs. Carr had him talking, but now he won't say a word."

"What does Dr. Ruskin say about Ben's falling and refusal to talk?"

"That he's grieving and needs some time."

Jake's stomach curled into a knot. "You mentioned you didn't know how much Ben understood. What I'm asking is whether he's mentally challenged."

"At first the doctors thought so, but Mrs. Carr refused to believe that. The doctors also thought Ben would be a vegetable and Mrs. Carr proved them wrong. Ben was working on his ABCs and numbers and he was able to repeat them. Mrs. Carr felt he had the ability to learn. He just has to try harder, and I must admit I agree with her. The bottom line, Mr. McCain, is that we want Ben's progress to continue."

"I do, too."

"That's good."

Something in her voice alerted Jake. His eyes narrowed. "You're not going to try to keep me from seeing Ben, are you?"

"Of course not," she said. "You're his father. You have every right to see him, and our goal, whenever possible, is to unite child and parent. But Ben's case is very different."

That told Jake more than he wanted to hear. They were pressing him to relinquish his claim on Ben. She hadn't come out and said it, but it was there in her voice. He stood. "I understand the situation, Mrs. Turner, and now I'd like to see my son."

"Sure," she nodded. "Carmen will take you to the Fosters'."

"One more thing," he added before leaving. "I want Ben to know that I'm his father."

Mrs. Turner glanced at Ms. Woods. "As I said, we're not sure how much Ben understands."

"I still want him to know—to feel that he's not alone anymore."

She seemed to hesitate, then nodded again. "It's probably best."

"Thank you," he said, and left the room.

In the hall Ms. Woods said, "You can follow me over there if you like. I'll bring my car around."

Jake did as she asked and tailed her white Corolla through the busy Houston traffic. They made several stops for lights and finally turned into a residential area with brick homes and small landscaped yards. How did people live so close together? He'd grown up with lots of fresh air and space and he wanted Ben to grow up the same way, but it might not be a possibility. He had to prepare himself.

Carmen pulled into a driveway and he parked behind her. Jake glanced at the house. Very neat and clean, he thought, then realized she was waiting so he quickly made his way to the front door.

"Mr. McCain," she said before ringing the bell. "I need to tell you that the Fosters are not pleased by this visit."

"I'm not pleased that they have my son, but I'm trying to make the best of a bad situation. I hope they'll do the same."

She seemed to want to say more then changed her mind. She pushed the doorbell.

A slim, gray-haired man opened the door. Jake guessed he was somewhere in his fifties.

"Oh, it's you," he said gruffly.

"Yes, Mr. Foster, we're here to see Ben," Ms. Woods replied.

He opened the door wider and they stepped into the foyer. "This is Jake McCain. Carl Foster." Carmen made the introductions.

"We know who he is, Ms. Woods," a woman said as she joined them. She was also thin with graying blond hair. The expression on her face was unfriendly. Jake received that message loud and clear.

"This is Peggy Foster," Ms. Woods murmured as if nothing had been said, then quickly asked, "Where's Ben?"

"He's in the den, but I won't have him upset," Mrs. Foster answered.

"We're not here to upset Ben," Carmen told her. "We talked about this and I thought you understood."

"I don't understand how he can have any rights where Ben is concerned," Mrs. Foster snapped angrily.

Carl put an arm around his wife and led her to the kitchen. Ms. Woods didn't say anything and Jake followed her into a large den. His eyes froze on a little boy sitting on a sofa with a pile of Lego blocks in his lap and a tattered teddy bear by his side. He held two pieces in his hands and was trying to fit them together. *He looks normal* was Jake's first thought. He wore jeans, a T-shirt and sneakers like other kids. He was small for his age, though. And so thin.

Jake didn't know what he was expecting, but at the sight of his son he felt as if the sun had burst open inside him, filling him with so much warmth that for a moment all he could do was absorb the wonderful feeling.

Ms. Woods sat beside the boy. "Hi, Ben."

Ben didn't answer. He kept fiddling with the plastic pieces.

"I brought someone to see you."

Still no response.

"Ben, do you hear me?"

Nothing.

"I brought your daddy to see you."

Ben slowly raised his head and stared at Jake. Jake's stomach tensed at the sight of that precious face. Ben looked so much like the boy in Jake's baby pictures, with his sandy brown hair and brown eyes. *This was his son.*

The pain in his stomach shot straight to his heart. His son was waiting, but he couldn't seem to move.

Finally, he took several leaden steps to sit by Ben. He tried to ignore the pain in his chest and concentrate on the pleasure.

Ben's eyes followed him.

"Hi, Ben," he said, his voice rusty.

Ben just stared at him.

Jake glanced down at the Lego blocks. "What are you building?"

No answer.

"It's been a while since I played with these. Are you making a house? A car?"

Still nothing, but Ben's eyes never wavered from Jake's face.

"How about a tractor? I know a lot about tractors. I have several on my farm. Would you like to build a tractor?"

Ben held out a green Lego.

At the unexpected gesture, Jake felt exquisite joy. Ben was responding to him. He took the block, so desperately wanting to touch his son, to hold him. Instead he picked up several more and started working on a tractor. Ben continued to hand him pieces and Jake thought maybe Ben should help. "Okay." He smiled. "Your turn."

Ben tried to snap two green ones together, but couldn't because he didn't have them lined up correctly. Jake resisted the urge to help. In deep concentration, Ben worked until finally he'd figured out how to join the pieces.

"That's great!" Jake gushed, feeling as if Ben had split the atom or something equally important.

After that, they continued fitting pieces together until they had a strange-looking tractor. "I don't know, son, but I think I've forgotten the finer points of building a tractor."

Ben held the model against his chest, his eyes huge.

"Next time I come to see you, I'll bring you a toy tractor. Would you like that?"

Ben nodded.

Jake's pulse accelerated. Ben understood what he was saying.

"Mr. McCain, it's time to go," Ms. Woods spoke up.

No. He couldn't leave his son, but he knew he had no choice. He wanted to take Ben in his arms and hold him, but he was afraid it might frighten the child. It took all the strength he had to resist.

Jake got to his feet. "I'll be back, Ben," he said, and he noticed the look on Ms. Woods's face. Surely she wouldn't try to keep him away from Ben.

The Fosters came into the room and Jake and Ms. Woods left. Outside, Ms. Woods said, "I wish you hadn't told Ben you were coming back."

"Why?"

"Because it's a very sticky situation."

"And it will get stickier if you deny me access to my son."

"I'm not doing that," she insisted.

Jake raked a hand through his hair. "I'm sorry. I'm a bit overwhelmed at the moment, but I want to spend as much time as I can with my son. I realize, though, that I have to clear that with you."

Carmen relaxed. "Yes, and I appreciate your cooperation."

He drew a hard breath, trying to be patient, accommodating, anything to gain time with Ben. "I don't understand what the Fosters have against me. Why wouldn't they encourage a connection to Ben's father?"

"They're still dealing with Mrs. Carr's death, so please try to be understanding and respect their privacy."

Jake tilted his head up toward the smoky blue sky. It was the middle of October and fall was in the air with a robust feeling of cooler temperatures. They wanted him to understand. Did they realize what it was like for him? To have his whole world torn apart? Then be expected to let strangers raise his boy—his own flesh and blood. "When's the hearing?"

"A date hasn't been set, but since you've been located, we're expecting it to be soon."

"Then CPS will tell a judge who should raise Ben?"

"Yes."

"How can you do that when you're hesitating to give me time with Ben?" He held his hand up when she started to speak. "You don't know if I can take care of my son or love him or nurture him. You can't write an honest report unless you give me a chance."

"This would be so much easier if you and your wife weren't separated."

Jake was taken aback. "Are you saying I can't take care of my son because I'm a man?"

"I'm saying Ben needs a loving, stable environment and I'm not sure you can provide that."

"I see," he said slowly. "Then there's only one recourse left."

"What's that?"

"To show you that I can provide that." He moved toward his truck. "I'll be back tomorrow. Set it up. Same as today."

"Mr. McCain, that's very arrogant and I—"

"Do it," he interrupted. "I'll wait for your call."

Jake drove away feeling as if he'd won this battle, but the war was far from over. There was no doubt that he wanted his son. All those fears inside him had dissipated when he saw the face of his child. Now he'd fight for him, because Jake knew in his heart what was best for Ben—to be raised by his father.

He had to learn about Ben's medical problems, how to care for him. That would take time, but he could do it. He felt confident about that now.

THE DRIVE HOME WAS LONG but he hardly noticed. He thought about Ben...and Elise. She kept intruding even though he tried not to think about her. He wanted to tell her about Ben, to share this with her, but that wasn't going to happen, so he'd better get accustomed to the idea of being a single father.

As he neared Marlin, his cell phone rang. He picked it up and heard the voice that had been humming through his head.

"Jake, it's Elise," she said. "You left some things and I have them ready for you to pick up."

Getting rid of all the evidence that he'd ever lived in her house, he thought, but he replied, "I'm not far from your place. I can stop by now and get them." He was such a glutton for punishment. He was closer to the farm than he was to her place. Why didn't he tell her to throw the things out? He didn't need them. Still, he didn't like the way they'd parted and he hoped they could end the marriage amicably. Maybe this was his chance to do that.

"Oh, that's fine," she was saying. "I'll see you, then."

As he clicked off, he wondered if she'd done anything about a divorce. He couldn't help thinking, though, that a divorce was the last thing he wanted. Not today—not ever.

SHE'D DONE IT, ELISE TOLD herself. The clothes were just an excuse to see him, to talk to him. She wasn't uncaring and insensitive to his needs and she had to tell him that. Most importantly, she had to apologize about the photo.

She ran into the closet and gathered his clothes. A fragrance tempted her nostrils and she paused for a moment. Aramis. One day when she was shopping she'd bought the cologne for him, not sure if he'd like it or not, but he had and she now associated that scent with him.

Shaking her head, she put everything in a bag, even his items from the bathroom. When Jake took those, his presence would be gone from the house. She sank onto the bed. *No, it wouldn't,* she had to admit to herself. So many feelings were struggling to surface, but she couldn't let them. The past and the emotions connected to her fears and anxieties kept her bound. But through the mental block one thing rang true: she had to see Jake.

The doorbell buzzed and she jumped. Jake was here.

CHAPTER FIVE

WHEN JAKE STEPPED INTO the foyer, Elise felt almost out of breath. The foyer wasn't small, but suddenly the confines of the entry overwhelmed her...or was it Jake?

"Hi," he said, and her stomach trembled at the warmth in his voice.

Her eyes met his. "Hi."

"How are you?"

She tucked her hair behind her ears and walked toward the living room—to put some distance between them and to sort through her emotions. "Fine," she lied. "Your things are in here." She picked up the bag and handed it to him.

He took it and asked, "Could we talk for a minute?"

"Sure," she replied, sitting on the Queen Anne chair and slipping her bare feet beneath her. She was glad he'd asked to talk. It made what she had to say easier.

He sat on the sofa. "Have you seen a divorce lawyer yet?" he asked.

She shook her head. "No, I haven't gotten around to it." She wondered if he could hear the hesitation in her voice.

"Let me know when you do."

I don't want a divorce. I don't want a divorce. I want a baby...and I want you. The words ran through her head but she couldn't say them. Something inside her wouldn't allow her to do that, and she knew what it was—fear. Despite this, she had to find a way to tell him.

She smoothed the front of her pants. "I have to apologize."

He raised an eyebrow. "Oh?"

"You were right. It was insensitive of me to leave Derek's picture on the nightstand. I shouldn't have done that and I'm sorry."

Jake was dumbstruck. He'd never expected her to admit that. She kept the man on a pedestal, and she wanted the world, including Jake, to do the same. He cleared his throat. "Thanks, and it was insensitive of me to bring it up when I did."

"You were angry and you had a right to be."

He didn't know where this was coming from and he didn't want to say anything that would hurt her more. "Maybe," he admitted grudgingly.

She raised her eyes to his. "I do care about you. You were wrong when you said I didn't. I wouldn't have asked you to marry me otherwise."

"From the start I knew you could never love me. You were still in love with your dead husband, but I wasn't asking for your love—just your consideration."

She bit her lip, his confession obviously cutting deep. "I guess my mother and Judith were right, which I never like to acknowledge, but I've been obsessed with having a baby. I couldn't think about anything else. It took over my life, my thinking, my reasoning…and my treatment of you."

"Elise—"

She broke in. "I took all the magazines on conception and childbirth and threw them in the trash." She blinked back a tear. "It's so hard to let go of that dream, but I realize now that I'm not ready for a child. I just got carried away with the thought."

"How do you know you're not ready for a child?" he asked, puzzled.

"If I were, I'd be able to accept your little boy, to love him, to be his mother—but…"

Jake's heart stumbled, and he realized he'd been hoping she'd change her mind. That hope was now gone.

"Please don't think I'm heartless," she begged. "I wish I could explain to you how I feel, how..."

What was she trying to tell him?

"It's okay," he assured her. "It's a tough situation."

They were quiet for a moment. Jake wasn't sure what to say to her and the words slipped out before he could stop them. "I saw Ben today."

"I'm glad." She had to squeeze the words past her lips.

Jake wanted to tell her everything, but he could see she was uncomfortable talking about Ben. So he had to let it go...and he had to let Elise go.

He stood. "Thanks for the apology. It means a lot. Now I'd better leave because I have to be up early to make the drive to see Ben again." He moved toward the door, then turned back. "If you'd like to meet Ben, just call me. It might change the way you feel." Why had he said that? He had to make her aware that option was still open to her—to be a part of his life...and Ben's.

"It won't," she said quietly.

Jake walked out the door, feeling as if he'd just been sucker punched.

ELISE BLINKED BACK TEARS, refusing to cry. She couldn't do that anymore. Getting to her feet, she noticed the bag on the floor. Jake had forgotten his things. She grabbed them and ran for the front door in time to see Jake's taillights disappearing out of the driveway. She carried the bag to the closet. She'd call him tomorrow. No, she wouldn't. She couldn't see Jake again, it was too painful. She'd give the things to Beau and he could take them to Jake.

Jake's cologne wrapped around her and a whimper left her throat. Why was this so hard? Why couldn't she just tell him the truth? She'd planned to, but looking into his warm eyes she couldn't tell him that she'd almost killed a child with her negligence. She was so afraid of taking responsibility for a child that wasn't her own, so afraid of hurting his little boy. She shook her head and made her way to the bedroom.

She saw Derek's picture turned down on the nightstand and picked it up. Derek was the only one she could talk to. He understood her and loved her unconditionally. Staring down at his loving face, she knew why she kept his picture on display. She never wanted to forget Derek, and if she saw him every day, she wouldn't. She closed her eyes as reality spun its truth. Despite having just looked at the picture, she didn't see Derek's face anymore. Jake was all she could see. She wasn't sure how that had happened. But it had.

Derek and Jake were so different. She'd met Derek in college. They'd been friends first and then study partners because they both loved American literature. One evening as they were studying for an exam, Derek had said, "If I asked you for a date, would you go?" She didn't have to think twice. She answered "Yes" immediately. A few dates later he'd asked, "Do you mind if I kiss you?" Derek was kind, considerate and gentle. His lovemaking was the same, and she'd never wanted any other man in her life.

Until she met Jake.

He was so completely different…or maybe it was the different effect Jake had on her emotions. From the first moment she saw him, she thought he was handsome and sexy and she harbored risqué fantasies about him, which shocked her, then excited her and made her feel alive and feminine again. She'd never realized how much she needed that. She found herself acting on unusual impulses…like dreaming of babies and marriage. Their sex life was unlike anything she'd ever imagined. It was so much more. Derek had been gentle and affectionate, but Jake was passionate and fiery, and when they got into bed she wasn't just lying there being made love to—she was a partner giving and taking until she heard herself moaning with pleasure. She wasn't shy with Jake. She was actually bold and daring and she enjoyed discovering that part of her nature.

She felt as if she'd betrayed Derek because Jake touched a part of her that her first husband hadn't. She and Jake had connected in a special way—the way a husband and wife should. And now it was over. All because of her.

She stood, opened a drawer and placed Derek's picture inside. That part of her life was over, too. The years stretched lonely and empty before her, unless she could talk about it. Share it. No, she couldn't do that. She couldn't tell Jake she'd almost killed a child. He'd think she was a terrible person.

But then she *was* a terrible person. She was letting her teenage phobia control her, allowing her to reject a three-year-old boy who needed a mother. That made her the worst kind of woman—a woman without maternal instincts. A woman who was only capable of caring for a child if he was her own flesh and blood. The pain ripped through her and she let it. She didn't try to rationalize it or to disguise it. She deserved it.

JAKE REACHED THE FARM, feeling numb inside and trying to come to terms with the ending of his marriage. He hadn't eaten but he wasn't hungry.

He walked into the kitchen and stopped short. Beau was sitting at the table feeding Wags some doggy treats.

"What are you doing here, Beau?" he asked as he pulled up a chair.

"Feeding that hungry dog of yours. You should feed him more often."

"Wags is always hungry," Jake commented. "He spends a lot of his time chasing rabbits out of the cotton fields and he burns up a lot of energy trying to catch one."

Wags rested his face on Jake's thigh while Jake stroked him. "Wags is a good dog."

Beau appeared thoughtful. "There's a woman who lives in the condo next to mine and she adopts every stray she finds. She found a cat and was nursing it back to health. I agreed to keep it at my condo while she was out of town.

I'm not too fond of cats, but I enjoyed this one and all her antics."

"Animals are good company and friends." Jake continued to rub Wags and the dog's tail beat a steady tattoo on the floor.

"Actually I prefer the human female variety for company."

Jake did, too. He preferred Elise and…

The silence stretched, then Beau asked, "How did it go with Ben?"

Jake ran both hands over his face and knew he had to talk to someone or he'd explode. "I saw him, Beau, and he was the most beautiful sight."

"Then he's not hooked up to machines or anything?"

"No, he seems like a normal three-year-old except he's small and thin." Jake glanced off to the blue ceramic cookie jar of his mother's. She'd left it behind just like she'd left him. As a kid, he remembered dragging a chair up to the counter and stealing a cookie. Would Ben ever be able to do that? He cleared his head of such thoughts. "He was sitting on a sofa playing with Lego blocks," he continued. "He had a difficult time making the pieces fit but he tried and tried, and his eyes lit up when he did. Even though he didn't speak, he kept watching me. They don't know how much he understands. I think he understood that I'm his father, though."

"Did you tell him you were?"

"Ms. Woods did," Jake explained. "I asked that he be told."

"Good for you." Beau paused. "Can Ben walk?"

"They said he can, but he stumbles and falls, especially since Mrs. Carr's death."

Beau leaned forward. "Why did CPS contact you now?"

"Mrs. Carr was dying and asked them to find Ben's father. I told you that."

"Yes, I know, but why didn't they contact you when

Sherry basically abandoned Ben? Your name was on his birth certificate. Isn't that what you said?''

Jake got to his feet and paced back and forth. ''Yes...yes it was. God, I've been so consumed with the fact that I have a son that I never thought of that. Why did they wait so long to find me?''

''That's a good question and one that bears answering.''

''I will definitely talk to Mrs. Turner tomorrow.'' Jake went on to tell Beau how he felt that the caseworkers wanted the Fosters to have Ben. ''Mrs. Turner said it would be detrimental to Ben's health to uproot him.''

''How do you feel about that?''

''I feel like they're not giving me a chance,'' he answered. ''Ben and I need to spend time together—to form a bond. I was adamant about seeing him again tomorrow and they're supposed to let me know.'' He looked at Beau. ''Can they keep me from him?''

''No,'' Beau replied. ''I'll give Mrs. Turner a call tomorrow and make her aware of a few facts.''

Jake held up a hand. ''No, don't do that just yet. Let's see if they try to keep me away from Ben. A judge will make a decision on who gets custody of him, and right now it's looking like it'll be the Fosters. I have time to convince them otherwise.''

''And Elise?''

Jake's head jerked up. ''What about Elise?''

''She still filing for divorce?''

Jake stiffened. ''Yes.''

''Damn,'' Beau said. ''This would be a lot simpler if you were together.''

''Well, we're not,'' Jake said shortly. ''And I don't understand why everyone thinks that because I'm a man I can't properly care for my own son.''

''Because women give birth and they're the nurturers,'' Beau informed him. ''Every judge, whether male or female, recognizes that.''

''I can take care of him. I know I can.'' Tears stung his

eyes. He hadn't cried in so long, he thought he'd almost forgotten how. But he wouldn't cry for Ben. He'd fight for his son…without Elise.

Beau moved restlessly at Jake's disquiet, then asked, "How did you and Elise get together? It was a known fact around the club that no one was to come on to her because she was still in love with Derek Weber. The few men who tried still have frostbite. Then I hear my brother's actually married her. What was it? Opposites attracting?"

"Sex, Beau, that's what it was," Jake replied before he could help himself. "I enjoy it and so does she."

Beau frowned. "You're being crude."

"And you're being intrusive and nosing into matters that don't concern you," Jake shot back.

Beau held up both hands. "Okay, I get the message."

"I'm sorry," Jake apologized, realizing he was being curt for no reason. "I'm not discussing my marriage. That's between Elise and me."

Beau watched him for a second. "Is there any chance she'll come around?"

"No." That one word sent a chill to his heart.

After a pause, Beau said, "This is a bit ironic and the similarity might escape you, but your attitude toward Caleb is about the same as Elise's to Ben."

Jake's eyed narrowed. "What the hell are you talking about?"

Beau leaned back. "You refuse to have anything to do with Caleb and she's refusing to have anything to do with Ben. Both of you are acting out of some sense of misguided betrayal."

Jake didn't quite see the similarity to Caleb. Elise was hurt, understandably so, that their plans had been shattered. She'd been fixated on her own child and she couldn't get beyond that. He wouldn't explain any of this to Beau. It was none of his business. And it was nothing like his feelings toward Caleb.

"I'm not getting into this with you." His tone was hard and Beau switched to the matter at hand.

"Okay, then, the next step is to find out exactly what kind of care Ben needs. I'm ready to go on this thing. Just give me the word."

"I'll call you after I talk with Mrs. Turner." Jake was glad to change the subject.

"Fine." Beau stood and glanced around. "I like the remodeling job. It's nice."

"Thanks."

"I have so many memories of this place and most of them are bad."

"Not all of them were bad," Jake said in a wooden voice.

"Tell me some that weren't?" Beau asked. "I remember a lot of yelling, arguing and hiding from him because he was so damn drunk Mom was afraid he'd hurt us."

Jake gritted his teeth in denial.

Beau gestured outside. "How many nights did you, Mom and me spend hiding in the barn waiting for him to fall asleep so we could sneak back into the house?"

Jake clamped his teeth together so hard his jaw hurt.

"He drank and he was mean when he was drunk," Beau went on. "Hell, he wasn't all that much fun to be around when he was sober. And his insane jealousy was hard to take. Mom couldn't even speak to a man or he'd accuse her of sleeping with him."

"Maybe she was." Jake found his vocal cords.

Beau drew back as if Jake had hit him. "Come on, Jake, even you don't believe that."

"She left Dad and me for Andrew Wellman. I know that."

"She didn't leave because of Andrew," Beau denied. "The people at the church helped her get out of a bad marriage. Andrew was just one of those people."

"She married him," Jake shouted. "She had his child

six months later, so stop trying to make her a saint. That proves my point.''

''That proves nothing.''

Jake shook his head. ''The other side again?''

''Yeah,'' Beau said. ''If you'd just ask her, she'd tell you her side. But you don't even care enough to do that.''

''No, Beau, I don't, so let's drop it before we both say something we'll regret.''

''Just answer me one question.''

''What?''

''Why did you stay with him? For God's sake, you were ten years old.''

Jake had had all he could take for one night and he wasn't in a mood to mince words. ''Everyone hated him, that's why. After what *she* did to him, I was all he had left.''

Beau's eyes narrowed. ''When you were ten, how did you know what Mom had done?''

''Dad told me.''

''He *told* you?'' Beau asked in disbelief. ''He told you Mom was pregnant with Andrew's child?''

''Yeah, he told me everything.''

''God, Jake, you have to talk to Mom. She's not aware he did that.''

Jake gestured in frustration. ''What the hell does it matter what she knew or didn't? It happened more than twenty-eight years ago and I'm tired of rehashing it. Now, I'd appreciate it if you'd leave.'' Jake walked toward his bedroom.

''Jake…''

''Good night, Beau.''

Jake dropped onto the bed and lay back staring up at the ceiling fan. What an awful day! The only bright spot was Ben. He could still see that precious face, those big brown eyes. At least he had that, but for how long? The caseworkers weren't on his side and at that moment he felt all alone and defeated.

Wags put his paws on the bed and whined as if he sensed Jake's pain. Jake patted Wags and he whined louder. "I'm okay, boy," Jake soothed. "Just a little tired." He was used to taking knocks, but lately there had been too many of them. He questioned his judgment once again in asking for Beau's help. The past was always between them—or at least Beau's attempts to resurrect it were. Jake had closed that door long ago and he didn't appreciate Beau's constant endeavors to open it, to generate a relationship between Jake, his mother and his half brother.

As he continued to stroke Wags, he acknowledged to himself that his father was a hard person. Joe McCain believed in control and discipline and went to extreme measures to achieve both. Exemplary behavior was expected of his sons and he'd dominated his wife's every move. He wouldn't allow her to go anywhere without him. The only place she went alone was to church, and she went with a neighbor his father trusted. That had been the beginning of the end.

He put a forearm over his eyes and acknowledged another truth. His father drank to excess, so much that even Jake became afraid of him. That last year, there wasn't a day he was sober and he talked about Althea constantly. Every time he did Jake's heart broke a little more. As a boy he'd learned to hate his mother. As a man he'd learned that hate and love are closely entwined, and as much as he wanted to find a measure of forgiveness, he couldn't. The past was a shadow on his soul—darkened by the harshness of his father and the weakness of his mother.

Oh, God. He sat up. He had to stop this. It was tearing him up inside. His thoughts turned to Elise and a new pain began. Beau couldn't understand what had brought them together since they were so completely different. When he'd told Beau they enjoyed sex, he hadn't lied. They were sexually attracted to each other and shared a basic need, a need for family. When she'd called with a dinner invitation, he'd wondered what they'd talk about. Farming wasn't on her list of knowledgeable subjects as American literature wasn't on his.

But their careers were the last thing they discussed. The future and family were their chosen topics. They shared dreams and hopes and he opened up and confided more about himself than he ever had. When he was with her, time seemed to fly and he couldn't wait to see her again. She seemed to feel the same way. Their arrangement, their marriage, had only become irritating in the last month and he now knew why. He wanted a lot more from Elise than sex—a whole lot more.

He pushed to his feet and removed his shirt, wondering what she'd meant when she said she wasn't ready to be a mother. For months they'd been working overtime to become parents and all of a sudden she'd decided differently. Where was that coming from? He remembered her excitement over names and discussing things to buy for the baby. She had the nursery all planned; that was why he'd made the cradle. Had he somehow destroyed all her hopes? Was she feeling betrayed, like Beau had said? He should have pressed her more to find out what she'd meant.

When she'd apologized he sensed a weakening in her and something else, but he couldn't define what that something was. Maybe that was why he'd been so bold as to suggest it might help her to meet Ben. She'd quickly shattered that notion. Their marriage was over and he had to move on. But he couldn't, not until... What? Until she met Ben. It was so simple. That's what he needed. For her to look at Ben and say she couldn't be his mother. Then he could move on.

CHAPTER SIX

THE NEXT MORNING JAKE GAVE Aunt Vin a quick rundown on everything that had happened, then he was off to see Mike before heading back to Houston. He wanted to get there early; he and Mrs. Turner had a lot to talk about. A dense fog blanketed Waco but by the time he reached Hearne it had completely cleared and the sun was shining. Traffic was good until he reached the outskirts of Houston. After that it was a slow bottleneck pace. He didn't walk into Mrs. Turner's office until eleven.

"Mr. McCain, did we have an appointment this morning?" She was obviously surprised to see him.

"No," he said, "but I have a lot of questions and I'd like some answers."

"I see." She removed her glasses, that cool facade in place. "Please have a seat."

"Mrs. Turner, I'm going to be completely honest," he said as he sat down. "I feel as if you and Ms. Woods are trying to keep me from my son."

"Mr. McCain, that's not the case at all. Carmen's set up a visit for you this afternoon. She's been trying to reach you."

He was relieved, but he had to add, "Ms. Woods seemed perturbed that I asked to spend time with Ben."

"You're imagining things. After all, this is a delicate situation and we do everything we can to unite children with their parents."

He'd heard those words before. "Then why do you and

Ms. Woods feel the Fosters would be better for Ben than me?''

"Well, Mr. McCain, now I have to be completely honest,'' she said tightly. "Ben is in our custody. He's our main concern and we have to do what's best for him. It would be different if Ben was a normal little boy, but he isn't. He requires lots of attention and a loving, nurturing environment. I'm not convinced you can give him that. You're separated from your wife, which in itself can be the cause of a lot of tension for Ben. He doesn't need that. His whole world has come apart and we'll fight to keep him as comfortable and happy as possible.''

Jake made to speak but she held up a hand. "I realize you have all these new feelings for Ben because you've just discovered he's your son. But it's a whole different ball game when you have to care for a special child on a daily basis. It can be taxing and draining, and I don't think you've even considered what it would be like to have Ben twenty-four seven.''

"Then *tell* me what it would be like.'' He was trying very hard not to get angry.

"As I said, Ben requires constant attention. He needs someone to force him to walk to continue to use his muscles. He's now starting to eat solid foods, but he has to be watched in case he chokes. He has to be on a breathing machine twice a day so his lungs can grow stronger. And most of all, he needs someone patient and loving so he'll start talking again. The Fosters are working on his speech. They're very good with him and they've been caring for him since before Mrs. Carr died.''

"But he's not talking,'' Jake reminded her.

"It's just a matter of time.''

Jake clenched his hands. "Let me ask you a question, Mrs. Turner. Why did your office come looking for me?''

She seemed taken aback. "Because you're his father.''

"Yes, my name is on his birth certificate, but you didn't come looking for me when Ben was born. Why is that?''

Mrs. Turner moved uneasily. ‘‘Sherry had listed Mrs. Carr as next of kin and we located her. She took full responsibility for Ben, and when Sherry finally showed up she said she’d slept with several guys and wasn’t sure who the father was. She’d just put a name on the certificate. We don’t have the resources to go chasing after men who may or may not be the father. Ben wasn’t expected to live and we did the best we could at the time.’’

‘‘And you wouldn’t have come looking for me now if the Fosters had realized sooner that they wanted to adopt Ben. Isn’t that right, Mrs. Turner?’’

‘‘Mr. McCain—’’

‘‘No,’’ he interrupted her. ‘‘As I told Ms. Woods, you came looking for me and now you have to deal with me. I am Ben’s father—his blood father—and that gives me certain rights.’’ He rose to his feet. ‘‘Until the custody hearing is set—’’

She broke in. ‘‘I heard this morning. It’s in six weeks. The Monday after Thanksgiving.’’

Jake took a moment, relieved in a way that the custody issue was moving forward, but he was still apprehensive. He had to make sure she understood how he felt. ‘‘Until the hearing, I’d like to see Ben every day, and I’d appreciate it if you could arrange for me to speak with Ben’s doctor, so I can read over his medical reports and learn exactly how to care for him. If you have a problem with any of that, you can contact my attorney.’’

Her eyes opened wide. ‘‘You’ve hired an attorney?’’

Jake reached into his wallet and pulled out Beau’s card. ‘‘I have a brother who’s a family lawyer. All I have to do is call him.’’ He laid the card in front of her.

Before Mrs. Turner could say anything, Ms. Woods walked into the room. ‘‘Oh, Mr. McCain, I’ve been trying to reach you. I’ve set up a meeting for the same time as yesterday.’’

‘‘Thank you. I’d like to see him every day at whatever time is convenient for the Fosters.’’

Carmen glanced at Mrs. Turner. ''Make the arrangements,'' Mrs. Turner said.

''And please call Ben's doctor so I can see him today.''

''This can't be done at a moment's notice.'' Mrs. Turner spoke sharply.

''Unless you can postpone the hearing, I suggest you do it now.'' Jake spoke just as sharply.

Mrs. Turner nodded to Ms. Woods and she left the room.

''I'm not trying to be difficult, Mrs. Turner,'' he had to say, ''but a moment ago you said you were willing to fight for whatever was in Ben's best interest. Well, so am I. We may have different opinions on what that is, but a judge will have the final say. And before you start writing a bad report on me, please at least give me a chance. I will not do anything to harm Ben.''

Mrs. Turner stared straight at him. ''I have to believe that, and at the first sign that your visits are causing Ben any distress, they will be terminated—lawyer or no lawyer. I hope you understand that.''

''Yes, you've made that very clear.''

JAKE SPENT THE NEXT THREE hours at the medical center, going through Ben's records. Dr. Howard Ruskin, the specialist, had arranged for Jake to read through Ben's medical file before he spoke with him. There were hundreds of pages to examine. Everything was documented from the moment Ben was born. Numerous pictures accompanied the charts. He saw Ben in an incubator attached to many tubes and machines. Ben weighed barely three pounds when he was born. Then he saw a woman holding Ben. He knew it was Mrs. Carr. She didn't look anything like Sherry; she had a soft expression, especially when gazing at the baby in her arms. Many other pictures followed—Ben in a crib, on a blanket, crawling, standing holding on to Mrs. Carr. Each picture buffeted his heart and tears stung his eyes. This was his son and he should have been there for him.

He had to stop himself from looking at the pictures and read through the medical history. Most of it Ms. Woods had already told him, and the more he read the more he understood how dire his son's health was. Ben didn't make a sound until he was two months old. His muscles weren't receiving the appropriate signals from the brain to function. The report said Ben could feel very little and he had a blank expression on his face.

With his heart in his throat he read how a pediatric neurologist had diagnosed Ben's case as hopeless. If he lived, which the neurologist said was unlikely, he would be a vegetable. Then Mrs. Carr asked Dr. Ruskin, a specialist in child development, to look at Ben. Dr. Ruskin felt he could help Ben, and the pages and pages of results proved that he could. They began an extensive exercise program of simple techniques to provide deep stimulation for the legs and arms, which consisted of tickling, gentle slapping and massaging. His mouth was vibrated with an electric toothbrush. A flashlight and flash cards were used for eye exercises. Music stimulated his ears. Ben breathed into a mask several times a day to increase his lung capacity and the supply of oxygen to his muscles and to his brain.

The results were astounding; Ben's muscle tone improved and his whole physique changed. He had a more normal expression on his face and was able to control his tongue. He started to make sounds, his drooling stopped and he became aware of his environment. His program was modified according to his progress. New exercises enhanced his balance, leg muscles, motor ability, comprehension, visual memory and auditory memory. Every day was a new beginning for Ben, and Jake marveled at Mrs. Carr's dedication and love for him. She'd given Ben a life with her selfless commitment to his health.

Jake was so engrossed in what he was reading that he didn't even notice when Dr. Ruskin entered the room. "Mr. McCain," Dr. Ruskin prompted.

Jake stood and shook the doctor's hand.

"It's nice to meet Ben's father," the doctor said. "He's an amazing little boy."

"Yes," Jake replied, glancing down at the medical records. "I've just been reading how amazing."

Dr. Ruskin sat across from Jake. "I wanted you to be aware of Ben's medical history before we talked."

"Thank you," Jake said. "And thank you for seeing me on such short notice."

"Ben has been a priority of mine for a long time," Dr. Ruskin told him. "His story is nothing short of miraculous. Mrs. Carr and I were working on a book to chronicle Ben's progress before she became ill, and I still intend to finish it. I have also written several articles concerning Ben for medical journals."

Jake touched the records. "It's quite a story."

Dr. Ruskin folded his hands on the desk. "So what can I tell you about Ben?"

"How can I care for him now?"

"How much time are you willing to devote to him?" the doctor countered.

Jake frowned. "I'm not sure I understand the question."

"Ben requires constant attention. Are you willing to devote twenty-four hours a day to Ben?"

Jake wasn't certain what he was getting at, but he had to be honest. "I'm sure no one can do that."

"Irene did," he informed Jake. "The first weeks of Ben's life she slept very little. She only slept when Ben slept. Of course Ben doesn't need that kind of attention now. He's much stronger, but you must realize that Ben has a long way to go. Irene's death has been a tremendous blow for him. His refusal to speak bothers me, as does his falling. The Fosters are working diligently and I'm hoping for improvement soon."

Jake had a feeling he was about to have the same conversation he'd had with Mrs. Turner. He took a deep breath. "How do I care for my son now?" he asked again. "What special needs does he have?"

Dr. Ruskin picked up a pencil and studied it, then he raised his head. "You're not going to like what I have to say, Mr. McCain, but the best thing you can do for Ben is to leave him where he is."

"Excuse me?"

"Irene took Ben to that house when he left the hospital. It's the only home he's ever known. The house, the yard, his room are his haven. It would be detrimental to his progress to take him out of that environment."

Jake didn't understand why he was shocked, because he knew this was coming. Mrs. Turner had gotten her information from Dr. Ruskin. They wanted him to acquiesce to their wishes. He couldn't do that. Not now. Not ever.

Jake stared at the doctor. "What special needs does Ben have?" He repeated the question with steel in his voice.

"Mr. McCain..."

"No," Jake cut in. "I'm not giving up my son. I am his father and I will have a part in his life."

"Mr. McCain, I didn't mean that. I'm sure you'll be allowed visitation rights. I'm only saying that for Ben's well-being he needs to stay in familiar surroundings and he needs to continue his medical treatments here in Houston. I'm sure you desire what's best for him."

"Yes, I want what's best for him, but I'm not sure what that is at the moment."

"In my professional medical opinion, I—"

Jake cut in again. "I know what your opinion is, Dr. Ruskin, but until I spend time with my son I'm not budging on *my* opinion."

"I appreciate how you feel, Mr. McCain, but please look at this from Ben's point of view."

"There is no other view for me, Dr. Ruskin."

"Good, then we're in agreement." They stared at each other an extra second, then Dr. Ruskin added, "The Fosters can go over Ben's routine. They're very familiar with it and can tell you anything you require."

Jake nodded and left, feeling again as if everyone was

conspiring to keep him away from his son. In the end, he might have to defer to their wishes, but not until he knew beyond a shadow of a doubt that Ben was better off without him.

IN THE TRUCK HE CALLED BEAU and told him what had happened. Beau was ready to come to Houston, but Jake hesitated. He had to have more time with Ben to make that decision. Above everything else, he would do what was best for Ben…even if it broke his heart.

On the way to the Fosters', he stopped at a toy store and bought a green tractor. When he drove into the driveway, he noticed that Ms. Woods was waiting for him. He let out a long sigh. It seemed they didn't want him to be alone with Ben.

He picked up the tractor in its bag and got out. "I didn't realize you'd be here."

"I'm sorry. I thought you understood that all visits have to be supervised…for now."

"No, but that's fine. I just want to see my son and learn how to care for him."

"I know," she surprised him by saying. "Dr. Ruskin has already informed us of your intentions and, of course, you'd mentioned it earlier."

He shook his head. "Why is it so hard for you, Mrs. Turner and Dr. Ruskin to believe that I love my son?"

"We don't doubt that you love him," she said frankly. "We doubt that you fully grasp the state of Ben's health and the constant care he needs. Ben has endured the rough part and now we're determined to see him develop into a normal little boy."

"I am, too, so let's go see my son."

Carl let them in without a word and disappeared into the kitchen. In the living room, Jake paused for a moment and watched Ben play. He was on the floor on his knees, the tattered bear by his leg as he arranged big colorful blocks with numbers and letters on different sides. Peggy sat on the floor with him. When she saw Jake, she got up and left the room. The Fosters made it very plain that Jake wasn't welcome here.

Jake eased down, sitting cross-legged. "Hi, Ben," he said.

Ben turned his head to look at him. Jake thought again how tiny he was...and how precious. "Remember me? I was here yesterday. I'm your daddy."

Ben reached to pick up something, but he had a block in his hand and couldn't grab the item. He fumbled around until he finally realized he had to put the block down before he could do anything. Jake now understood, from what he'd read, that Ben's brain wasn't receiving the appropriate signals. But Jake could deal with this.

Ben held out the item—it was the mass of Lego pieces they'd put together yesterday. Ben had kept it. Jake smiled as he took the makeshift tractor. "Yes," he said. "We made this yesterday and it's a poor excuse for a tractor, but I brought you a better one today." He pulled the shiny tractor out of the bag. "See." He set it in front of Ben. "It's like the ones on my farm. It even has a closed-in cab like the real thing and good sturdy tires." Jake pushed it along the carpet. "And it rolls."

Ben placed his hand over Jake's, and Jake's heart stopped beating. His son's touch was soft and gentle, yet Jake felt immeasurable power...the power to soar, to climb great heights and to experience unknown pleasure. Jake felt all that in the sensation of Ben's fingers against his. It was a moment he would not forget for the rest of his life.

They played for thirty minutes and Jake was totally absorbed. Then Ben grew sleepy, his eyes closing, the tractor in his hand.

"He's getting tired. We'd better go," Ms. Woods said.

Jake wanted to protest, but he had to be cooperative. "I've got to go, Ben," he said softly. "But I'll be back tomorrow. Do you understand?"

Ben's eyes opened wide as he stared at him, and Jake

yearned to gather Ben in his arms, to hold his son, to let him know he loved him. As before, he was afraid of frightening him so he made himself get to his feet. He took a couple of steps, then something caught him around the leg and he stopped in his tracks. He glanced down to see Ben holding on to him, little arms locked around Jake's calf. Jake immediately scooped Ben into his arms. Ben laid his head on Jake's shoulder and Jake's arms tightened. He could feel Ben's heart beating like a tiny bird's against his chest. Everything in Jake melted into a wonderful glorious feeling…the feeling of being a father and holding his child for the first time. So many new emotions surged forth, powerful and strong, protective and shielding. In that instant, he knew that he'd never be able to leave Ben in the Fosters' care.

Jake patted Ben's back. "It's all right, son."

"Come to Peggy, Ben." Jake hadn't even realized Peggy had entered the room until he heard her voice. "I've made your favorite chocolate pudding. Let's go get some." She held her hands out to Ben.

Ben raised his head and looked at Peggy.

"Come on," she coaxed.

When Ben went to her, Jake felt a pain he couldn't describe. He choked back emotions that were threatening to overtake him. The only thing that saved him was the fact that Ben kept staring at him.

As Ben and Peggy passed Ms. Woods, Peggy said, "I told you this was going to upset him."

Jake bit his tongue to keep words from tumbling out. He strolled to the front door, Ms. Woods a step behind him. Once they were in the yard, he turned to her. "He wasn't upset." He had to make that very clear.

"I know that, Mr. McCain."

He let out a long breath. He was so afraid his visits might be stopped and he couldn't handle that…not now. "Why did she have to say that?"

"Please understand that the Fosters are very protective of Ben."

The adrenaline slowed. "I do understand that, but what I don't understand is why they seem to hate me."

"They don't hate you," she said.

"If the temperature dropped any more in there, we'd all be frozen."

"This is—"

"A difficult situation," he finished for her. He noticed the way she nervously fiddled with her purse strap and a suspicion formed in his mind. "Is there something you're not telling me?"

"Of course not."

She answered that a little too fast, and Jake's suspicions grew, but he couldn't dwell on it. He had other things on his mind. "I need to spend more time with Ben. Thirty minutes is too short to learn his routine."

"Mr. McCain..."

"Do it, Ms. Woods, or you'll be hearing from my attorney. I'll call first thing in the morning." He didn't want to be difficult but felt he had no choice. Time was running out. As he walked to his truck he couldn't still a sense of exhilaration. He had made a connection with his son—Ben now knew who he was. Things could only get better.

HE DIDN'T REMEMBER MUCH of the drive home. Ben occupied his mind completely, but as he neared the farm his thoughts turned to Elise and he wanted to tell her about his day. He couldn't, though. He couldn't force a child on her that she didn't want.

He glanced at his watch and saw it was after nine. Was Beau still at his office? Sometimes he worked late. He decided to check and drove into the city. He had to let his brother know what was happening.

Beau's Explorer was in the parking area. Jake parked beside the vehicle and went into the lobby, pushed the elevator button and waited. The joy of Ben was still strong and he couldn't be still. He paced back and forth. When the elevator appeared Jake turned to enter, then stopped dead. Beau and Caleb were inside, and as he stared at his younger brother, a spasm of pain gripped Jake. Betrayal. Resentment. The past. Everything crowded in on him at once and he couldn't move or speak.

"Jake," Beau said in surprise, walking off the elevator. "I wasn't expecting you."

"I'll talk to you later," Jake replied in a tight voice, and began to move away, but Beau stepped in front of him.

"This is stupid, Jake. Caleb is our brother and I think it's time you met him."

Jake's face remained stone cold and he couldn't seem to bring himself back from the dark past that had plagued him for years.

"You want custody of your son?" Beau asked with cutting sharpness. "How do you think a judge is going to react when he learns that you're estranged from your family? That you won't even speak to your own brother? That's not good for Ben and the sooner you realize it, the better off you'll be."

Ben. The thought of Ben bolstered him, gave him courage. For his son he would do anything, and that meant sinking his pride so Ben wouldn't be caught in his emotions. He wanted a clean slate for Ben, fresh and exciting, with family love around him so he could grow and develop into a healthy little boy.

He turned to Caleb. Jake saw that they looked somewhat alike—same brown hair and eyes, and they were the same height. Jake was broader while Caleb was lanky. Brothers bound by a common thread…their mother.

Caleb held out his hand. "Hi, I'm Caleb."

Jake stared down at his hand and Beau's words came back to him. *Your attitude toward Caleb is similar to Elise's toward Ben.* He saw it now, clearly. He was afraid of the pain, a pain that he associated with loving his mother, which had nothing to do with Caleb. Was Elise also afraid of the pain? Afraid of not loving Ben because he wasn't her own? Something in him gave way. The past, its hold, wasn't there to paralyze or to blind him. He had a brother and for the first time he was able to acknowledge that. He took his hand. "I'm Jake."

"It's nice to finally meet my other brother," Caleb said.

"Half brother," Jake corrected, unable to stop himself.

"Brother," Caleb emphasized in a hard voice.

Awkward silence followed.

Jake wasn't sure why Caleb took offense at the word *half* and he didn't care. If Caleb had a problem with the truth, then that was *his* problem.

"Was there a reason you stopped by?" Beau asked quickly.

Jake wasn't keeping his son a secret, so he didn't mind talking to Beau in front of Caleb. "I've asked CPS for more time with Ben. Can you help me if they refuse?"

"I sure can," Beau replied.

"Why don't you two sort this out?" Caleb put in. "And, Beau, I can catch you another night."

"No, no," Jake said immediately. "I have my answer and that's all I needed."

"Would you like me to take over now?" Beau asked.

"I'll let you know tomorrow, and thanks, Beau. I'll talk to you later." He nodded at Caleb. "Nice to have met you."

Outside he sucked air into lungs that felt raw and bruised. This was too much for one day, he thought. Hell, it was too much for a lifetime.

Driving away, Jake thought his head might detonate with the turmoil inside him. Through it all he saw Elise's face and he let himself relax with her image. He knew exactly what she was doing at this hour. She'd removed her makeup and had a shower and she was in her study reading the material she'd use in her next class. Sometimes he came home this late and she always stopped what she was doing and they'd talk about their day, but the conversation always came around to the baby. She'd seen an article in a magazine he had to read or she'd thought of a new name and wanted his opinion. He missed that closeness, that togetherness.

If he hadn't eaten, she'd make him a sandwich. That was the extent of her culinary skills. Elise didn't cook, but that didn't bother him. He loved her softness, her intelligence, her desire for a family. He wondered how long it took to stop loving someone. Somehow he knew he'd love her until the day he died.

CHAPTER SEVEN

ELISE PULLED INTO HER driveway and saw Jake's truck. Her pulse pounded in her temple. Jake was here, waiting. She wondered why, but she didn't care. She'd have another chance to talk to him. Grabbing her briefcase and several books, she got out. Jake was standing there and her pulse pounded harder.

"Here, let me take those," he offered. As he took the briefcase and books from her, his hand brushed against her breast and the spot he touched felt warm and achy. She missed that, his touch, and her body throbbed with a need she recognized—a need Jake could satisfy. She reached for her purse, trying to get her emotions under control.

She unlocked the door and they went inside. Jake placed his load on the breakfast table. "How are you?" he asked, looking at her with concerned eyes.

"I'm fine," she lied. "I had a meeting at the university."

"I thought so."

They stared at each other, both of them seeming to need that contact. He looks tired, she thought, and wanted to put her arms around him just for a moment. If she did...

"Did you stop by for something?" She ached with hope. Hope that she could tell him her fears. Hope that this nightmare would go away.

"I forgot my things here the other night."

"Oh, yes. I'll get them." She hurried toward the bedroom to get the bag, glad to escape from the sensual tension. Picking it up, she leaned against the wall for support. She was different now that he was here. She was alive again and the loneliness and the emptiness wasn't so bad. But for how long?

She had to talk to him.

When she came back into the room, she held the bag out to him and he took it. He stared into her eyes, no doubt seeing the naked longing there. She wanted to kiss him so badly that it took everything she had not to reach out to him. Her tongue licked her lower lip, and before she knew what was happening, he dropped the bag and framed her face with his hands, taking her mouth. She breathed him in urgently, and he tasted her tongue, her mouth like a starving man in need of sustenance.

The kiss was long, deep and thorough and Elise forgot her fears—forgot everything except her need for Jake. Then suddenly, he broke off the kiss and he pulled away.

"I'm sorry. I shouldn't have done that," Jake said, looking at the floor.

Elise tried to speak, but she couldn't. She didn't have an explanation for her own actions. She wanted him like she'd never wanted anyone in her life. That scared her. She shouldn't want him this much.

He took one last look at her and walked out.

Elise glanced down at the bag at her feet. He'd forgotten it again. Her hand went to her lips. He'd never kissed her quite that way before...as if he was saying goodbye. A sob left her throat.

JAKE STOPPED AT THE intersection and took a long breath, cursing himself. What had he done? He'd just made a bad situation worse. Earlier he had every intention of going home, but before he knew it, he was parked in front of Elise's house.

He licked his lips and could still taste her hunger, her desire, and he shifted uncomfortably. All he wanted was to make love to her, to shut out the world and everything in it. It would have been so simple, yet so complicated. He couldn't do that to her. That was why he'd stopped. He couldn't hurt her any more than he already had. He had to stay away from her and resolved to do just that in the days ahead.

ELISE'S NIGHT WENT FROM BAD to intolerable following a phone call from her mother. Constance insisted she join them for dinner the next evening, and that was the last thing Elise needed. Constance wasn't pleased when she declined, saying she was busy. She should tell her mother that she and Jake had separated, but she couldn't bring herself to do that. Just like she couldn't contact an attorney. She felt as if someone had thrown her emotions into a cauldron and all her bad traits had risen to the top for the world to see—for Jake to see.

Getting ready for bed, she took one of Jake's shirts out of the bag and breathed in its scent, remembering his kiss. She had invited it, wanted it, and she wasn't certain where she'd hoped it would lead. Not a final goodbye—of that she was positive.

That night she slept in Jake's shirt and knew she was close to the edge. This wasn't the Elise Weber who'd survived the biggest trauma of her life. This Elise was weak and… Her thoughts stopped as she realized something. She wasn't Elise Weber anymore. She was Elise McCain. That was her married name now, but she was still going by Derek's. She hadn't even changed her name on her driver's license or her social security or done anything to acknowledge her marriage to Jake, except sleep with him. What kind of woman was she that she could treat Jake that way? A man who'd been nothing but loving to her. She had to try to maintain a balance between the present and the past. The past became even murkier, but the present was clear. She could see Jake's face plainly and she knew what she had to do.

Talk to him. Talk to him. Talk to him.

She chanted the words in her head as she drifted into a restless sleep.

JAKE HAD NEVER BEEN AWAY from the farm at harvest time. He had always been at the center of the operations, but to spend time with his son he had to delegate some of his responsibilities. The custom harvesters were through picking, now Mike and the farm workers would pick the remaining fields with Jake's own equipment. Jake worked on a schedule and he didn't like falling behind. The sooner the gin picked up the modules of cotton, the sooner it was baled and graded by the Unites States Department of Agriculture. The better the grade, the better the price. That part of the business was important so Jake was the only one who dealt with the cotton buyers. He went over the schedule with Mike in the mornings and at night, returning calls, solving problems that needed his attention. But the strain was getting to him.

His days fell into a routine. CPS gave him the time he'd requested; two hours in the morning and two hours in the afternoon with Ben. The Fosters had to be present and they didn't like it. He went to Dr. Ruskin's office to learn CPR and the Heimlich maneuver in case Ben choked or stopped breathing. He was there when Ben took a bath, when he ate, when he exercised, when he used the breathing machine. Ben was still in a diaper and Jake learned to change them with relative ease. Ben's problem was his coordination and the fact that his brain was slow in getting signals to his body. The stronger he became, the easier life would be for him. Dr. Ruskin said Ben's brain would also catch up, as long as he continued the exercises.

Jake soon found out what the brightly colored blocks were for. They'd sit on the floor and Ben would separate the colors—red, blue, green and yellow. He did the same with the numbers and letters. He did everything very slowly and deliberately. Jake could almost see his little brain working to achieve the simplest task. The longer they worked, the better Ben got; he also got faster, so Jake knew the exercises were working. Jake kept at it meticulously, but it was taxing, just as he'd been told. He didn't mind, though.

He felt Ben was on the verge of blossoming into a healthy child and he intended to do everything he could to make that happen.

Some days, Ben was almost lethargic and would fall asleep on the floor. On those occasions Jake just held him and Peggy complained to CPS, saying that wasn't good for Ben. But CPS let the complaints go, maybe because Peggy complained about almost everything. Jake tried to make some connection with the Fosters so life would be easier for Ben, but they weren't inclined to be too obliging. At times he sensed that Peggy was glad he was there. The stress was obvious on her face; she was in her late fifties and taking care of a three-year-old took all her stamina. Peggy rested whenever Jake and Ben were together. After a few days, Jake had Ben's routine memorized and Peggy didn't need to watch him so closely. Jake was grateful for the time alone with his son.

One day Ben fell and hit his head on the coffee table. Jake quickly picked him up, but Ben didn't make a sound. He only frowned as he rubbed the knot on his forehead. That alarmed Jake. Ben should be crying.

Peggy immediately called Dr. Ruskin, who came to the house to check Ben. Jake thought that was odd. He could have easily taken Ben to the office, but he was told Ben didn't go out much. It was too dangerous. He would be exposed to all sorts of germs and viruses. That meant Ben was virtually a prisoner in the house and that was the way Dr. Ruskin wanted to keep him. Jake later learned that it was the only way Dr. Ruskin could document everything accurately. He didn't understand why this had to continue because Ben was improving each day, except for his speech. He deferred to Dr. Ruskin's wishes—for now.

He found tapes in Ben's room—speech tapes that Mrs. Carr had played for Ben. He learned that Ben had trouble hearing the first syllable of a word. A woman, whom he took to be Mrs. Carr, sounded out a word slowly so Ben could clearly hear it. He then repeated the word, which meant he could talk, and that small voice uplifted Jake's spirits. Jake began to perform these exercises with his son, hoping Ben would speak, but he never did. Jake didn't give up, though. He was determined that Ben would talk, and soon.

Through all this, Jake made a concentrated effort not to think about Elise. After that kiss in her kitchen, it was hard, but his involvement with Ben helped. Forgetting Elise was going to be tougher than he'd ever imagined. At night, as tired as he was, he could feel her lips on his.

And then there was the farm. At least he had good men working for him. When this harvest season was over, they'd start repairing equipment, getting everything in tip-top shape for a new season. At least Jake didn't need to be there for that; Mike was the best mechanic around. That gave him peace of mind, at least, about the farm.

TWO WEEKS BEFORE THE HEARING, Jake had a meeting with the judge. The days had passed quickly, and Jake wasn't sure he'd convinced CPS or Dr. Ruskin that he could care for Ben. He was nervous about the report they'd give the judge. The tension, as well as the long drive, was getting to him, but when he opened the Fosters' door and saw Ben's face it made it all seem worthwhile. Ben was always waiting for him, the tattered teddy under one arm and the makeshift tractor in his hand. Those two things stayed with him at all times. Jake knew they'd connected as father and son and no one was going to convince him otherwise.

On Wednesday, he left for home early because Ben had a checkup with Dr. Ruskin in his office. Jake had wanted to go but was told by Mrs. Turner that his presence wasn't required. Ben would be undergoing routine tests and he'd be informed of the results. Jake didn't argue the point, trying to show CPS and Dr. Ruskin that he was willing to bend on some matters. But not the most important—Ben's future.

He drove into Waco to talk to Beau, who insisted on

being with him for the hearing. Jake didn't object. He would need all the help he could get that day.

For the first time in weeks, Jake sat in his den and relaxed. Wags curled up at his feet after a bout of rubbing and hugging. Wags missed him, but right now Ben was his top priority. Aunt Vin and Mike helped. Still, he didn't like neglecting his faithful friend.

He leaned his head back and closed his eyes. The judge's decision would change his whole life and he had to be prepared, but he didn't know how to prepare for losing his son. He wouldn't think that way. They had to recognize how much Ben meant to him.

As much as he'd tried, a day hadn't gone by that he hadn't wished for Elise's presence, wished she could see Ben, hold him and glimpse his special personality. After the hearing, he might lose everything, and he didn't know if he could survive that without her.

ELISE FINALLY RELENTED and had dinner with her family at the club. She still hadn't mentioned that she and Jake were separated and she knew that rumors would soon start to circulate. She needed to tell them, but she kept putting it off.

The conversation wasn't strained because Judith was in a better mood. Stan was quiet while Judith did all the talking about a private tutor she'd hired for Duncan. Judith's voice droned on, and Elise knew she had to get away. This wasn't where she wanted to be. She wanted to be home with Jake. The thought startled her. Her hand went to her lips and she remembered his kiss that night in her kitchen and she had to admit she wasn't happy without him. She was miserable.

Every day she wanted to call him, but she didn't. She kept telling herself he needed time to bond with his son. She wondered about his little boy and what he was like. Ms. Woods said he had brown eyes, probably the same as Jake's. She also wondered how Jake was coping being a new father. He'd be great, she thought. He was kindhearted and patient and… Suddenly she had to see Jake, to talk to him about Ben and to tell him about her past. She couldn't wait any longer. She had to do this for her own sanity, to resolve some of the tension between them. After she told him what she'd done, he might not want her around his son. But she had to take that chance.

Elise pushed back her chair. "I have to go."

"That's nonsense," Constance said. "You haven't even finished your dinner."

"I'm not very hungry." Elise placed her napkin on the table.

"Elise, you will not leave the table in the middle of dinner. It's not proper."

"For heaven's sake." Judith took a sip of wine. "Let her go. If I were her, I'd be dancing on the tabletops."

"Judith," Constance reprimanded sharply.

"What's the big deal?" Judith shrugged. "Couples separate all the time and I don't understand why it has to be a secret."

Elise clenched her hands in her lap. *They knew. How?*

"Besides, Elise needs our support," Judith kept on.

"You've had too much wine," Constance snapped.

"I have not," Judith insisted, and raised her glass to Elise. "Here's to Elise for having the guts to kick him out. Expecting you to accept another woman's child—it's absurd."

Elise bit her lip to keep the anger from exploding inside her, then asked in a calm tone, "How did you find out?"

"My hairdresser plays bingo with his aunt, and she overheard her talking to a friend about your callous behavior. The nerve! What woman would stay in that kind of relationship?"

Elise got slowly to her feet. "I would."

Judith's eyes widened. "What?"

"I was taking some time to get my thoughts straight.

That's why I haven't said anything.'' It wasn't exactly the truth, but it felt good to see that look on Judith's face.

''You can't be serious!'' Judith said.

''I am. I'm on my way to see Jake now to discuss our marriage.''

Judith took a big gulp of wine.

''Elise, think about this,'' her mother begged. ''He has a son...by another woman.''

If Elise had any doubts, they vanished with her mother's words. She could hear herself saying almost those same words to Jake and in that same demeaning tone. How it must have hurt him. Like it was hurting her now. Maybe there *was* hope for her. Maybe there was hope for them.

''I've done nothing but think about this.'' She picked up her purse. ''I've decided I want Jake in my life. I hope you'll support my decision in some small way, but you really don't have to. After all, it's my life and my decision.''

''Stan, aren't you going to say something?'' Judith prodded her husband.

''Yes.'' Stan raised his head. ''A child is a precious gift and should be raised in a loving environment. I hope you and Jake can works things out to make that happen.''

''Thank you, Stan,'' Elise said warmly. ''I appreciate that.'' She wanted to hug Stan, but she knew public displays of emotion were not acceptable to her mother. A lot of things weren't acceptable to Constance, and Elise had lived according to her mother's guidelines for way too long.

At thirty-five she should be past her mother's influence. Finally, though, she could feel herself emerging into a woman who could think and feel on her own without the worry that she was going to disappoint her mother. When Derek died, her mother had told her how she should act and what was expected of her as a widow. Grieving became part of her daily life...but not anymore.

She looked at Constance. ''I'm sorry if you're displeased, Mother, but I don't really care what people think.''

"Elise," Constance whispered in a hushed voice as she glanced around to make sure no one had heard her.

Elise slipped her purse over her shoulder. "If you can't accept Jake and his son, then you can't accept me. Goodbye." She turned and walked toward the door, feeling good about herself for the first time in ages.

BEFORE SHE COULD REACH the door, someone called her name. She turned to see Beau coming after her.

"Can I speak with you for a moment?" he asked.

"I'm in a hurry. Could we do this another time?" She had to find Jake and didn't want to stop for anything.

Beau shook his head. "No, I have to talk to you tonight."

There was a note in his voice that alarmed her. Her stomach coiled tight. "Is something wrong with Jake?" she asked guardedly.

"Yes," Beau answered bluntly. "Come on, let's go into the bar and I'll tell you."

She followed him willingly. They took a seat and Beau ordered wine. Elise was hardly aware of anything but the pain in her abdomen.

"Have you talked to Jake lately?" Beau asked.

Elise shook her head.

"You're aware that he's been seeing his son?"

"Yes."

"Do you know he might not get custody of him?"

Her eyes shot to his. "What? Why?"

Beau told her a story that coiled her stomach tighter until she couldn't breathe without difficulty. "His little boy has problems?" she managed to ask.

"Yes, they were severe, but Ben is better and hopefully that will continue."

"And the Children's Protective Services think that the Fosters are better qualified to care for Ben?"

"Yes, and do you know why?"

Elise could only shake her head again.

"Because Jake is separated and in the process of getting a divorce. To a judge, that can only add to Ben's problems, and Ben needs a stable, loving environment."

"I see," she murmured numbly.

Jake could lose his son because of her.

"I know nothing about your marriage to my brother and I apologize for intruding," Beau was saying. "But if there's the slightest chance you can work things out, I—"

The waiter brought the wine, cutting Beau off. Elise's hand gripped her glass.

"Elise, are you okay?" Beau asked as he noticed her pale face.

"Where's Jake?" She avoided his question because this wasn't about her anymore.

"He's at the farm, but not for long. He leaves before daylight and comes back late."

She stood and had to grab the table for support.

Beau quickly rose to help her, but she didn't need his help. "I'm fine," she told him. "I just have to see Jake right now."

Beau looked concerned. She was trembling visibly. "Sit for a bit first," he suggested.

"No, thanks," she said, and moved away.

"Elise…"

Elise wasn't listening and she wondered if she'd ever listened to anything Jake had said to her. She didn't know, but she was listening now. All the emotions she'd been fighting suddenly dissipated with five little words. *Jake could lose his son.* She was the only one who could stop that. The fear inside her told her to let it be, but her heart wouldn't allow her to do that.

Ben had problems. The thought almost had her changing her mind. Almost—until she heard those words again. *Jake could lose his son.*

ALTHEA WELLMAN SAW ELISE leave the club and went to look for Beau in the bar. ''What's wrong with Elise? She seemed upset.''

Beau laid some bills on the table. ''Let it go, Mom.''

''No, I won't,'' she said stubbornly. ''It's about Jake, isn't it? Something's wrong.''

''I'm not sure I should tell you.''

Althea's face crumpled.

''Mom, don't look like that,'' Beau pleaded.

''Then tell me.''

Beau pulled out a chair for Althea, then he sat close to her and told her the same story he'd told Elise.

''Jake has a son?'' Althea said quietly. ''I have a grandson.''

''Yes.''

''And he has problems? You said developmental delay.''

''Yes, he's slow in doing things.''

''Is Elise having a hard time dealing with this?''

''Elise and Jake have been separated for weeks now, and the judge may not award custody to Jake because he'll be a single parent. The people who want to adopt Ben know how to care for him and Ben's familiar with them.''

''Beau, you're a lawyer. You have to make sure Jake gets his son.''

''I'm doing all I can, but Jake's trying to manage this on his own.''

Tears filled Althea's eyes. ''Jake can't lose someone else he loves.''

Beau glanced away. ''I know, Mom.''

''It's all my fault. I handled the past so badly and it continues to hurt my children.''

''It's not your fault,'' Beau was quick to tell her. ''If Jake wasn't so damn stubborn, then—''

''Don't you dare say anything about Jake.'' The tears became a storm brewing in her eyes.

''Heaven forbid that Jake take the blame for anything in his life,'' Beau replied in an angry tone, but his voice softened as he saw the expression on his mother's face. ''Why can't you tell Jake the truth? He's a grown man and he can take it now. Keeping it a secret isn't helping anybody.''

Althea stood. ''I will not hurt Jake again. He's had too much of that in his life because of me.'' Her eyes darkened. ''You're a good lawyer, so do what you have to. Do you understand?''

Beau nodded and Althea joined her family in the dining room.

ELISE TURNED OFF THE HIGHWAY onto a country road, and after a mile or so, the headlights caught rows and rows of cotton stalks in their beam. Some fields were bare and the rows freshly plowed; other fields were snow-white with bushy plants that looked sheared, as if their yield had been harvested.

Jake had talked about the farm so Elise knew where it was but she'd never had the chance to visit it and Jake had never asked her to come. He'd probably been waiting for a sign of interest from her. A flash of guilt struck her and she was shaken by her own behavior, at her insensitivity to Jake's needs, his life. Now she had to make it right.

When the cotton fields ended, she saw tall oak trees and an enchanting older house with a long veranda and white railing. Because of the floodlight, she could see that the house was also white and had dark green shutters. Parking on the paved drive, she sat for a minute. What did she say to Jake? How did she explain her feelings? Her change of heart?

She got out and walked to the front door. A porch light shone brightly, as did lights inside the house, so she knew someone was here. She pushed the doorbell, noticing that the big door was also dark green.

The door swung open and a gray-haired woman stood there, her mouth open. ''My, my, it's the fancy lady,'' she finally said. ''Found your way here, did you?''

Elise frowned. ''Excuse me?''

''You're Elise, aren't you?''

"Yes."

"Then I don't think I have anything else to say."

The woman, who had to be Jake's aunt, didn't like her; that was obvious. Another stab of guilt.

"Is Jake here?" she asked.

"Yes," his aunt replied, but made no move to let her in the house.

"May I speak with him, please?"

"Why?" she asked point blank. "Haven't you hurt him enough?"

Elise took a breath. "May I come in?" The north wind was blowing and she could feel its chill. Or was it the ice that had been around her heart for so long?

The woman opened the door wider and Elise entered the house.

"If this can wait—"

"No," Elise interrupted. "I have to speak with Jake now."

Jake's aunt eyed her strangely.

"What is it?" Elise asked, because her stare was making Elise edgier than she already was.

"You're not like I imagined. You actually seem…nice."

"Thank you, and I apologize for not meeting you before." Elise held out her hand. "I'm Elise."

"Lavina, but you can call me Aunt Vin," she replied, taking Elise's hand.

"Thank you," Elise said again.

"I'll probably never understand young folk. I'm from an older generation and I think a little differently." She waved a hand. "Jake's in there, and I've gotta get to bingo or I'll be late."

Aunt Vin hurried through a large living room on the right. Elise stood in the oversize foyer, studying the dark hardwood floors beneath her feet. The planks were wide like those in pioneer homes; she remembered that this house had been in Jake's family since the Civil War. It had originally been an overseer's home on a large plantation.

The big mansion had been burned to the ground and all that was left was this house that Jake's ancestors had purchased. It had been in the McCain family ever since. She *had* listened to some of the things he'd told her. Uplifted by that discovery, she slowly stepped toward the doorway.

The room was a large den dominated by a huge stone fireplace with a crackling fire that radiated a calming warmth. But her total attention was riveted on the man sitting in a recliner, feet stretched out in front of him, his back to her. The only light in the room, besides the fire, was a lamp burning by the beige leather sofa.

An enormous dog lay at Jake's feet, his head raised, watching her.

"Who was it, Aunt Vin?" Jake called. He'd heard the doorbell, but he wasn't in a mood to talk to anyone.

"It's me, Jake."

Jake froze. She'd been on his mind so much that now he was hearing her voice. Jake drew a deep breath and pushed to his feet. It was Elise. She was standing there, dressed in her usual business suit and heels, and she looked tired and drained. But he couldn't tear his eyes away. What was she doing here? *The divorce.* That was the only reason she'd make the trip out to the farm. She probably had the divorce papers and wanted him to sign them. Oh, God, not today.

CHAPTER EIGHT

"ELISE," JAKE SAID in a startled tone.

"I...ah...I..." she stammered, unable to articulate a word. She regularly spoke in front of students, faculty and groups, but looking at Jake, she found that her thoughts were jumbled.

The dog trotted over and sniffed her. She stared down at him, a little wary. She'd rarely been around dogs; she wasn't allowed to have one when she was a child so she was naturally spooked by them. The dog barked and she jumped backward.

"Wags," Jake scolded, and walked to Elise. "His bark is worse than his bite. The only thing he attacks is a T-bone." He patted the dog's head. "Be nice. This is Elise."

Wags rubbed his head against her stocking leg and she stopped breathing.

Jake caught the expression in her eyes. "Are you afraid of dogs?"

She nodded as Wags took an interest in her shoe and licked it eagerly.

Jake took her arm and pulled her down to the floor so they could be on Wags's level. When Jake scratched Wags behind his ear, the dog rolled onto his back and Jake rubbed his stomach. "See, he's just a lazy old dog who needs attention. Go ahead and touch him. He won't hurt you. I promise."

"Jake, I..."

"Touch him, Elise. That's the way to conquer any kind of fear—to face it."

When she still hesitated, he took her hand and placed it on Wags's stomach. She felt the warm fur and the rapid thumping of the dog's heart. Her fingers slowly moved and the dog made a humming sound, then flipped over and licked her hand. She jerked out of reflex. She wasn't afraid, though, and a warm feeling suffused her. The dog was friendly and she liked touching him.

The dog continued to lick her, and Jake ordered him away. "Sorry, he gets a little too enthusiastic sometimes," he said, helping her to her feet.

His hand was strong and steady, and words again eluded her as she stared into his eyes. How did she tell him what she had to? She cleared her throat. "Could we talk?"

"Sure," he replied. "Have a seat."

She sat on the sofa and he resumed his place in the chair. Wags curled up beside him.

"I've been meaning to call you," he said before he could change his mind.

"Oh."

"I wanted to apologize for kissing you when I stopped by to pick up my things."

Her stomach trembled at the memory. "Should I apologize for kissing you back?"

Their eyes clung together as Jake struggled for an answer. "Since we're getting a divorce…I assume you're here about the divorce."

"No, no, that's not why I'm here. I talked to Beau, and he told me about Ben."

His eyes narrowed. "What did Beau tell you?"

"That Ben has health problems and you might not gain custody."

"He didn't have any right to do that."

"He just opened my eyes a little. It seems I've had them closed for a long time."

Jake frowned and she rushed on, needing now to tell Jake

everything. ‘‘I don’t know where to start, so I’ll start at the beginning. When you asked me if I could raise another woman’s baby, my immediate reaction was no. I couldn’t take responsibility for someone else’s child. That sounds a little crazy, but...’’ The words locked in her throat. She smoothed the fabric of her skirt, gaining strength, gaining courage. ‘‘Once...I...I...almost killed a child.’’

She waited, but Jake didn’t say a word and she couldn’t make herself look at him. That expression in his eyes would be too much for her.

‘‘Elise, what are you talking about?’’ His voice was a mixture of confusion and annoyance.

She clasped her hands tightly and told him about Tammy and how she’d swallowed the teddy bear’s eye and stopped breathing. The whole story came pouring out.

Jake scooted to the edge of his seat. ‘‘Let me get this straight. The mother knew the eye was loose and she continued to let her child play with the bear?’’

‘‘She said she was in a hurry and forgot. I don’t think she’d have admitted that except her husband made her. She later apologized for calling me careless and irresponsible and a lot of other things, but I couldn’t get her words out of my head.’’

‘‘It was an accident, Elise. It wasn’t your fault.’’ She hadn’t even realized that Jake had moved to sit by her until she felt the sofa move.

‘‘Yes, it was. I was reading and I should have been watching her, but once I get involved in a book I block out everything else.’’

‘‘You saved her life,’’ he reminded her.

‘‘Thank God,’’ she mumbled, gripping her hands so tight they were bloodless. ‘‘After that, I stayed away from babies. My fear of them intensified as I got older. I planned to never have children because I was afraid I’d hurt them. I felt I didn’t have motherly instincts.’’ She paused. ‘‘Derek is the only other person I’ve told this to and he was shocked that I had harbored these inner fears about children. He said we had to have our own child, then I'd see what a wonderful mother I'd be. He had me convinced and I agreed to have a baby. We were so excited and the fear wasn't so strong anymore. Then Derek died and my life fell apart. I forgot about babies and lived in my own private hell.''

She took a breath. ''When my nephew, Duncan, was born, I didn't hold him until he was two months old. I was scared to death to touch him. He didn't cry, but I was very uncomfortable since his head seemed to wobble and I was afraid I'd do something I shouldn't. I realized then I wasn't ready for a child and I didn't know if I'd ever be.''

She unlinked her fingers. ''Then I met you and I'm not sure what happened. My biological clock must have shorted out part of my brain, because I reasoned I could still have my own child—a child I wouldn't be frightened of—a child I could love and who'd love me.'' She raised her head and looked at him. ''When you said you didn't know a lot about love because of your mother, but you wanted a child, too, it all seemed to fall into place for me. I'd never fall in love again and you didn't want that from me. It was a perfect arrangement, and I was so looking forward to having a baby, to put to rest all those bad feelings inside me. I desperately needed to know I wasn't some sort of monster.'' She stopped. ''Then we found out about Ben and those irrational fears returned. I could actually feel Tammy's deadweight in my arms, see her blue face and the hysteria took over. I was afraid I'd hurt Ben and...''

Jake looked completely dumbstruck. Had she shocked him? He reached for her hand.

She clutched his hand tightly. ''You must think I'm a terrible person.''

''I don't,'' he told her. ''I just wish you would've confided in me.''

''I couldn't. Derek was so understanding and I wasn't sure how you'd react if you knew I'd almost killed a precious baby.''

''Stop being so hard on yourself.'' His thumb moved

against her skin and a familiar warmth skimmed through her. "Can I ask you a question?"

She wiped away a tear. "Yes."

"Your desire for a baby, did that have something to do with Derek?"

She bit her lip, needing to be honest but also not wanting to hurt him. "It started with Derek." She paused, wanting the words to come out right. "He was the one who made me want a baby of my own."

He pulled his hand away. "When we made love, did you pretend I was him?"

"No, of course not," she assured him, her eyes meeting his. "In the beginning, I'm not sure what I was expecting, but..." She swallowed, needing to gather her wits. "I thought I wouldn't respond to you and that we'd just have sex to create a child. But I was...unprepared for my own reaction and at times it delighted me, other times it made me feel guilty."

"Why?"

"Because when I'm with you, I have a hard time remembering Derek's face. I guess that's why I had to keep his picture."

He looked down and released a deep sigh.

"I put Derek's picture away," she said abruptly.

His body jerked in surprise, giving her the courage to continue.

"You have to be the most patient man in the whole world to have tolerated my late husband's picture on the nightstand."

Jake stood. "I think we got in so deep, so fast, that we skipped the getting-to-know-each-other part."

"Yes," she agreed. "If we'd taken it slower, it would probably have occurred to me how callous that was." Her eyes held his. "I'm sorry, Jake. I'm the reason you might lose your son."

"There's so much involved that it's hard to explain, but if I don't gain custody of Ben, it won't be your fault."

This was the Jake she'd come to care for—the kind and giving man. The man who'd taught her how to feel. She'd never felt so intensely attracted to anyone—not even with Derek.

He shoved a hand through his hair. "Why are you telling me this now?"

Because I'm miserable without you. I want to be your wife...again.

What came out of her mouth was "I don't want you to lose your son and I'd...I'd...like to help...raise him...if you can trust me."

He drew in a sharp breath as if he couldn't quite believe her words. "You want to be Ben's mother?" he asked tentatively.

"Yes, but..." Her voice trailed off and she could feel the panic rising in her.

"Let me ask you another question," he said. "If you had been driving down a street and a child darted out chasing a ball, and you swerved and missed him, would you stop driving because you'd almost hit him and killed him?"

She stared at him, imagining the situation. "No, I...don't think so. I mean, if I wasn't driving recklessly or anything and I had no control over—"

"Exactly," he smiled slightly. "Just like you had no control over Tammy choking. It was her mother's fault, and because of that you've suppressed a vital part of yourself, the nurturing maternal side. You say you feel you don't have motherly instincts, but I've seen you look at baby magazines with that infatuated expression on your face, so don't let yourself believe that." He stopped. "And I'd trust you with Ben, anywhere, anytime."

"You would?"

"In a heartbeat."

Jake didn't hate her. She could see it in his eyes and the adrenaline began to pump through her veins. He trusted her with his child. She wasn't a terrible person. For so long she'd thought otherwise.

Elise slid back on the sofa. "Please, tell me about Ben." She hoped her question wasn't coming too late.

He sat beside her again. "Ben's a special little boy. He has big brown eyes and a smile that's joyous to watch. He's three years old, but he looks much younger. He's tiny and thin."

From the love in Jake's voice she could almost see those eyes, that smile, and she yearned to know more.

"Beau mentioned he has problems."

"Its called developmental delay. He was very premature and at birth he didn't have the vital survival reflexes, like sucking. They didn't expect him to live, but Mrs. Carr brought in a specialist, Dr. Ruskin. They worked diligently with massage and exercises, and their efforts began to pay off. Ben got a lot better. He's slow in doing things, but to me he's a normal little boy who needs lots of love and attention."

At the ache in his voice, she swallowed. "That's why CPS thinks the Fosters are better qualified to handle Ben?"

"Yeah, they keep saying it would be detrimental for Ben to move him to another residence. He's been in that house since Mrs. Carr brought him home. He goes outside to play in the backyard, but that's about it. They don't take him out much because Dr. Ruskin's afraid Ben'll catch a cold or the flu and that would weaken his already weak lungs. It seems so drastic. I mean, Ben's never played with other children. That house and Mrs. Carr have been his whole life." He paused. "Sometimes when we're playing, he'll walk across to Mrs. Carr's room and look around and I know he's searching for her. When he does that, it breaks my heart." He took a breath. "I love him, but I don't think they're going to let me have him. I…I…I can't live with that decision."

He loved his son—she was sure of that—and inwardly she screamed against the forces that had brought them to this point. Mostly her inability to accept Ben when they'd first heard of his existence. Now it was up to her to try to rectify the damage.

"Wouldn't it help if we reconciled?"

Jake shrugged. "It may be too late."

She chewed on her lip. "I'll try to be Ben's mother."

"Elise," he groaned. "You can't *try.*"

At her expression, he quickly added, "It has to be all or nothing. There's no trial run. Ben can't endure that and frankly I can't, either."

She fought the panic rising in her again.

"You have to do this from your heart…your whole heart," he said quietly.

"I can," she told him earnestly. "I'm afraid, I'll admit that. But as long as you're there I'll be fine." At his silence she added, "I have to do this for you, for Ben and myself."

It shocked her that she wanted this so badly. Before the prospect had terrified her. But now Ben and his future were foremost in her mind. One question kept torturing her, though—could she love Ben the way Jake did? The way he needed to be loved by a mother?

Jake took her hand and led her down the hall. He flipped on a light in a child's room—a boy's room. The walls were painted a pale green and the wide border halfway down was decorated with John Deere tractors, as was the skirt on the twin bed.

"I've started on his room," Jake said. "What do you think? And keep in mind that Ben loves tractors."

"It's warm and lovely."

He touched the wooden headboard. "This used to be mine and I got it out of the attic. It has a side rail, but I haven't had time to put it on. I'm not sure this will work, since Ben still sleeps in a baby bed. Hell—" he sank onto the mattress "—I'm not even sure they'll let me bring him here. I have this fear that the judge and everyone else will want to keep Ben in that house with the Fosters."

She sat close to him. "When do you see the judge?"

"Friday. He'll give his decision the Monday after Thanksgiving."

"I'll go with you and show the judge that we're willing to make a home for Ben."

He sighed heavily. "We have to talk about a lot of things first."

"What?" she asked, surprising herself with the knowledge that she was willing to compromise.

"Like where we'll live."

"Oh." She hadn't even thought of that.

"I want my son to be raised here on the farm."

"That's not a problem."

He glanced at her. "Are you sure?"

"Yes, it would be good for Ben to be here."

"What about your house? Your job?"

"I can sell my house," she said immediately. "But my job could be a problem. I've worked a lot of years to get where I am."

"I don't want you to give up your job."

"I can work something out with the dean of my department. I was planning to take a leave of absence when I had a baby."

"I thought that might be what you'd come to tell me tonight—that you were pregnant."

"I'm not pregnant," she said.

"I would've been happy," he had to say.

"We grabbed at that too quickly."

He nodded, admitting, "Sex clouded our minds to a lot of issues."

"Yes," she agreed as they went back into the den. Sex had been the sole basis of their relationship, and now they had to learn to be husband and wife. Sex would be a result of that bond. A much-needed result.

Jake turned to look at her. "I appreciate your coming out here and telling me this, but you have to be absolutely certain. No doubts, no fears. I don't think you're at that point yet. Until you are, I can't see us moving forward. You need more time.''

Her heart fluttered and stalled, and she experienced a pain so great that she wanted to cry out. But Jake was right. She had to be positive—absolutely positive—that she could be a mother to Ben.

Jake waited for Elise to speak—staring at her hard as if he could will the words out of her. *Say you love me.* If she said that, time wouldn't make a difference. Only love would.

But she kept silent. She walked to the door and Jake resisted the urge to run after her. Instead, he just said, ''I'll call you tomorrow.''

So many emotions collided inside him, and he struggled to contain his own fears, his own hopes. Through the turbulence, one fact rang true: Elise had come to his home. She was making an effort, something he'd thought she would never do. She had to take the next step herself.

''Jake, where are you?'' he heard Beau calling, and Jake went to meet him in the kitchen. ''I saw Elise leaving. How'd it go?''

Jake didn't answer. He walked back to the den and stood staring at the dying embers in the fireplace. The temperature was in the forties, and since the central heat was on, a fire wasn't necessary. But he'd made it because it was comforting. He wasn't feeling any comfort now.

''Jake?''

He turned to his brother, his body rigid. ''Why did you tell her?''

Beau shrugged. ''She needed to know.''

''That wasn't your decision.''

''Maybe,'' Beau conceded. ''But *she's* the person who can help you get your son.''

Jake sank down on the brick hearth. ''I can't force Ben on her,'' he mumbled.

Beau watched him for a moment. ''What did she say?''

''She said she didn't want me to lose my son.''

"That's great." Beau smiled. "That's what you wanted, isn't it?"

"More than anything, but Elise has to do it for the right reason—not because she feels guilty."

Beau shook his head. "What does that mean? You didn't send her away, did you?"

Jake studied his hands. "She needs time."

"Her idea or yours?"

"Mine."

"Dammit, Jake, what's it going to take to get through to you?"

Jake didn't answer.

"Let me say this again," Beau said impatiently. "Without Elise your chances of getting Ben are next to nothing."

"I...I..." Jake stammered, the words tangled among emotions he couldn't express. Elise had loved Derek Weber; she still did. Jake couldn't tell Beau how much that hurt, how it tore him up inside.

Beau clicked his tongue, reading the emotion on Jake's face. "It isn't how Elise feels about Ben. It's how she feels about *you.*"

"Beau." A warning darkened Jake's eyes.

"You love her," Beau stated. "It's written all over your face, but you're not sure how she feels. That's it, isn't it?"

"You can't make someone love you," Jake murmured in an aching voice.

Beau dropped down beside Jake. "I'm sorry," he offered.

"Don't be," Jake told him. "I wasn't expecting her to love me. I just wanted a life with her, but that life got derailed and I'm not certain we can get it back."

Beau stood. "Elise was very upset when I told her about Ben. Not about the fact that he had problems, but that you might lose him. She didn't seem like a woman who didn't care. As a matter of fact, she seemed like someone who cared very deeply."

"Still..."

"Don't expect too much at this point," Beau said. "Just take what she's willing to give. Your future with Ben depends on it."

Jake was having difficulty accepting that reality. He wanted it all.

"I'd better go," Beau said. "You have an early morning. On Friday when you see the judge, do you need me there?"

"No, I can manage that."

"Jake..."

"I'll be all right."

"Call Elise and work this out."

Jake sighed, rose to his feet and put his arm around Beau. "I'll talk to you tomorrow."

After Beau left, Jake took a shower and crawled into bed, but he couldn't sleep. His mind was like a grasshopper on speed, jumping from Elise to Ben to the judge to the Fosters to Dr. Ruskin. In the early hours of the morning he came to the conclusion that his pride and his feelings didn't matter. Only Ben mattered. And that meant he had only one option.

ELISE DROVE AROUND, UNABLE to go home to an empty house and Jake's memory. Tears burned her eyes, but she couldn't allow herself to sink into self-pity and despair. Jake said she had to face her fears. How did she do that? She answered her own question: by being around children. Where would she find children at this hour of night? Well, *she* might not be able to find any children, but she knew someone who could. She picked up her cell phone and called Stan. He was a pediatric cardiologist and would be making his rounds at the hospital now.

"Stan, it's Elise," she said when he came on.

"Elise?" he asked, surprised.

"Could I talk to you, please?"

"Sure, I'm at the hospital."

"I can meet you there."

"Fine, I'll wait in the lobby."

A few minutes later she was sitting in the hospital lobby with Stan. It was after ten and the place was quiet except for the occasional person coming in and going to the elevators. Now that she was here, she had trouble explaining what she wanted. Instead she burst into tears. Stan waited patiently.

She wiped her tears away with the back of her hand. "I'm sorry. I'm an emotional mess."

"I can see."

"Mother would have a fit if she could see me," she hiccuped. "A lady's not supposed to reveal her emotions, and crying in public is a definite no-no."

"Your mother's opinion has always been important to you," Stan commented.

"Yes, those ingrained habits are hard to break."

"I'd say you broke them when you married Jake after dating him for only a few weeks. You did that even though Constance disapproved."

She took a deep breath and the words tumbled out about her fears and how desperately she wanted to be there for Jake and Ben.

Stan gaped at her in complete shock. "Elise, my God, how long have you felt this way about children?"

"Since I was fifteen."

"You're an educated woman. Surely you understand that what happened was an accident due to the mother's negligence."

"Yes, but I've never really convinced myself of that."

"For heaven's sake, Elise. You did nothing wrong. You saved that child's life."

"That's what Jake said."

"Jake's right. I've lost count of the number of times we've left Duncan with you, and not once have I worried about him and neither has Judith. He loves you and he enjoys every minute he spends in your company. You have him reading Mark Twain and he won't turn in a paper unless you read it, which really gets to Judith."

"That's now. When he was a baby, I was scared to death of him."

Stan stood. "Come with me."

Elise followed. "Where are we going?"

He pushed an elevator button. "I have one more patient to see and I want you to meet him. He's three years old and I repaired a valve to his heart. He's still awake because he's excited about going home tomorrow."

To face her fears she had to do this now—tonight. That was why she was here. They walked down a corridor and Stan paused outside a door.

"Just be yourself," he advised.

She smiled slightly as they entered the room. It consisted of a large baby bed and a cot. On the cot was a woman holding a little blond-haired boy.

"Dr. Harper," the woman said nervously when she saw them.

"It's late and I was told Jamie's still awake."

"Yes, he won't sleep in his crib. He wants to go home."

"Home," Jamie mumbled into his mother's neck.

"In the morning, Jamie," Stan told the child. "I promise."

Jamie grinned, his blue eyes sparkling.

"Mrs. Denton, would you like to stretch your legs while I examine Jamie?"

"Oh, thank you," Mrs. Denton replied as she scrambled to her feet with Jamie in her arms. She handed Jamie to Stan and slipped out. Stan eased down on the cot with Jamie, patting the spot beside him. Elise's knees wobbled and she quickly did as Stan instructed.

"Jamie, this is Elise," Stan said. "Do you mind if she holds you while I listen to your heart?"

Jamie shook his head and Stan placed him on her lap. He stared up at her, his eyes curious, his little body soft and warm. Elise tried hard to battle the fear welling up inside of her. Then Jamie grinned and her heart leapt with hope. She could do this. She could.

Stan took out his stethoscope and placed it on Jamie's chest. Tentatively Elise pushed the hair away from Jamie's forehead in a gentle caress. When Jamie rested his head on her breast, so many emotions burst forth and she knew beyond a shadow of a doubt that she could be a mother to Ben. She *wanted* to be his mother. But she was also aware that she had a long way to go.

Later, in the hall, Stan said, ''Come with me. There's a place I want you to see.''

That place was the nursery. The curtains had been closed for the night, but Stan asked the nurse to open them. The nurse pulled the curtain back partially so Elise could see the newborns. Her heart beat erratically as she stared at the five infants—four girls and one boy, the boy in blue and the girls in pink. Three little girls were crying at the top of their lungs while the other babies slept peacefully.

''They're upset because they haven't been to their mothers yet,'' Stan said. ''They're hungry.''

Elise was mesmerized by the babies, so tiny, so precious and so full of hope and promise—everything that life encompassed. Everything she wanted with Jake.

Out of the corner of her eye she noticed a nurse bringing an incubator forward. Elise's breath caught in her throat at what she saw. A little boy was inside, hooked to numerous tubes. His naked body trembled severely and his movements were agitated, as were his cries.

''What wrong with that baby?'' she asked.

''He's a crack baby,'' Stan told her. ''I didn't mean for you to see that.''

''A crack baby? You mean his mother was on drugs?''

''Yes. She's sixteen and doesn't know who the father is. Children's Protective Services has been notified, and as soon as he's ready to leave the hospital, he'll be placed with a foster family until someone adopts him.''

''Then he'll be okay?'' Her voice was barely a whisper.

''Eventually, but the first days of his life are traumatic. He's suffering through withdrawal.''

"How can a woman do that to her own child?"

"It's a sad statistic. Broken homes, shattered children, trying to self-destruct. We have kids out there having kids and they haven't got a clue what they're doing to themselves and others."

Elise's hand touched the glass partition as she kept watching the torment the little body was enduring. In that instant, something happened inside her; she felt herself opening up, reaching out, longing to hold and touch the baby. Yesterday she would have turned away, uncomfortable witnessing such a situation. But today, because of Jake and Ben, she wanted to let that baby know there were people who would love him, care for him in ways his mother never could.

Ben's mother had been selfish, inconsiderate and uncaring. *Much as Elise had been when she'd learned about Ben.* She'd let fear control her reaction. But not anymore. That baby had no one and she ached to hold him, to let him know the world wasn't all bad. And she'd love Ben even more because he was Jake's. She wasn't a bad person. She saw that now. She would never hurt a child.

Then why had she believed those terrible things about herself? In a moment of clarity she knew. Her mother. Constance's opinion was important to Elise, as Stan had pointed out, and her mother had perpetrated the fear by not telling Elise it wasn't her fault and that she hadn't done anything wrong. Jake had said it was an accident—and it was. *It was an accident.* She had to talk to Constance. She turned and headed for the elevator.

Stan caught her before she poked the button. "Elise, I'm so sorry you had to see that."

She brushed away tears through her smile. "It's all right, Stan, I did have to see that. I'm going to be fine—really fine now."

He seemed perplexed and she gave him a quick hug. "Thank you so much." He wasn't aware of the revelation inside her that she was finding herself again—the real Elise who cared for people from the heart.

"You're very welcome," he replied.

"Please don't mention this to Judith." She couldn't deal with her sister at this point.

"Judith and I share very little these days." A hard expression came over his features and Elise hoped he wouldn't confide the problems in his marriage. Even though she and Judith were at loggerheads, she was still loyal to her sister. As if sensing her discomfort, he added, "Don't worry. I won't mention it."

She hugged him again, then left realizing she'd always be grateful for Stan's compassion. How she wished Judith could see that side of him.

THE FIRST THING SHE DID when she reached home was call her mother. It was late, but Constance didn't go to bed early and Elise was hoping this night wouldn't be any different.

It wasn't long before Constance was on the line.

"Mother, I need to ask you something."

"Elise, is that you?"

"Yes, and I'm sorry it's so late but this is important."

"What is it, darling?"

"All those years ago when I looked after Tammy Abbott and she choked you told me I wouldn't be baby-sitting anymore. What did you mean by that?"

"Elise, why are you bringing this up now?"

"Because I have to know. The Abbotts stopped coming to our house and you looked at me differently. Did you blame me for what happened?"

"Of course not," Constance said sharply. "The Abbotts stopped coming to our home because I didn't want them there. After the things she said to you, I didn't want anything else to do with her."

Relief trembled through her and she kept on. She had to know everything. "Then why did you say I couldn't baby-sit again?"

"You've always been my sensitive child who felt things deeply and I could see the pain you were going through. I wanted to ease your pain and make you understand that you'd never have to do that again."

"I thought you didn't trust me." Her voice wobbled. "I thought…it was my fault…and I believed that until tonight, but it wasn't. I did nothing to harm Tammy."

"Of course not, darling."

"Then why didn't you try to make me believe that?"

Silence.

"Do you know that I shut myself off from children? That I'd decided never to have a baby because I was terrified I might hurt it? Do you even understand the turmoil I've endured?"

"Oh, darling. I'm so sorry. I just wanted you to forget what happened. I never blamed you, Elise."

Elise closed her eyes briefly and drew a deep breath. "Thank you, Mother."

"Elise, are you okay?"

"I'm fine." She meant it.

"I'm glad you called. I've been worried about you. Are you still separated from Jake?"

"I'm going to try to make my marriage work." She meant that, too.

"Elise…"

"Just be happy for me."

"Elise, I wish I could, but—"

"Good night, Mother."

She hung up the phone and a smile spread across her face. She was free—free from a past that couldn't hurt her anymore. The thought was euphoric. She wanted to tell Jake but decided to wait until morning. She was well aware the days ahead wouldn't be easy, but she'd faced that crippling fear inside her and she was now ready to be a mother to Jake's son.

She removed her makeup, took a quick shower and slipped on Jake's shirt. His scent wrapped around her and she looked forward to tomorrow—and their future. She just hoped Jake believed her. He had to.

Their plans hadn't turned out the way they'd envisioned, but Ben would now be *their* baby and she was fine with it. She thought of the baby in the incubator and prayed he'd find a mother who'd love him, too.

Lying in bed, she touched the pillow next to her…Jake's pillow. She pulled it to her and held it tightly. Soon they'd be together again.

CHAPTER NINE

AT 5:00 A.M. JAKE WAS PARKED in front of Elise's house. Last night he'd realized that he had only one choice. He and Elise had to fight for Ben as a couple. His feelings had to be put aside and he had to concentrate on the big picture—a future for all of them. Elise had come around, the way he wanted her to, and now getting custody of Ben would be their focus.

It was still dark and he wasn't sure how to let her know he was there. He could use his key, but that might frighten her. So would the doorbell. He turned on the light in the cab of his truck and reached for his cell phone. The ringing of the phone would be less alarming, he decided.

The persistent ringing awakened Elise. She sat up and flipped on the bedside lamp, then picked up the phone, wondering who was calling this early in the morning.

"Elise, it's Jake. I'm outside. Would you let me in, please?" His voice came through loud and strong.

She swung her feet to the floor, her heart hammering loudly in her ears. "Yes, yes." Slamming down the phone, she ran for the front door, turning on a light as she went.

She turned the dead bolt and felt the gust of cold air that ushered Jake in. He wore dark slacks, a sports shirt and a black leather dress jacket. A whiff of aftershave greeted her nostrils and she felt a familiar stirring.

"I'm sorry to wake you," he said, and quickly closed the door. "But I need to talk."

"It's okay. You know I get up at six, anyway." She shivered at the outdoor chill and hurried into the living area.

She curled up in a wing chair, her feet beneath her, while Jake sat on the sofa. Looking at him in her house, she recognized how uncomfortable he was in her very feminine home. His house was homey and comfortable—a place for a family. Funny she could see that now. Why had he tolerated her insensitivity for so long?

"I'm on my way to see Ben," Jake said.

"I figured that."

He leaned back and crossed one ankle over his knee. "I didn't sleep much last night. I kept thinking about what you'd told me and the difficult dilemma we find ourselves in." He swallowed. "Marriage to me is a commitment for life."

"I feel the same way." She held her breath.

"I don't want to force Ben on you—"

"Jake," she interrupted him. "I know you have doubts about my true feelings for Ben, and I did, too, until last night."

"What happened last night?"

She told him about her visit to Stan at the hospital. "As I looked at that tiny baby in such pain because of his mother's selfish actions, I could see myself and my recent behavior so clearly. I'm really not that person. I would never hurt a child. You said what happened to me was an accident and now I can believe that."

He just stared at her in awe.

"I finally realized my inner fear had to do with my mother and the fact that she never told me it was an accident. I naturally thought she blamed me and I blamed myself."

"So you talked to Constance?"

"Yes. And I'm so sorry for my recent behavior. Why did you put up with my mental block?"

Because I love you. But the words never left his mouth.

He shrugged instead. "I was too busy enjoying what we shared."

A smile threatened her lips. "Yes, we are good together,'' she admitted, smoothing the cotton shirt against her thighs. ''But there's a lot more to marriage than sex.''

He scooted forward, watching the slight tinge of color in her cheeks. She seemed shy, but she wasn't shy in bed. They hadn't talked about their personal relationship, but they would—later. Right now he had to concentrate on what was important. ''Yes, there is,'' he agreed, plunging in. ''I see the judge on Friday.'' He looked into her eyes. ''I trust you with Ben completely. Do you believe me?''

''Yes, now I can,'' she answered with certainty.

Jake continued to stare at her, searching for doubts and fears. He didn't see any. Her eyes actually sparkled with anticipation. He drew a ragged breath and carried out the decision he'd made last night.

''Then we'll forget about the divorce and raise Ben together.''

''Yes.''

''Would you like to meet Ben...today?''

The anticipation in her eyes intensified. ''Oh, yes, yes.'' She jumped to her feet. ''I can be ready in ten minutes. I'll call the dean on the way. I haven't taken a sick day in years and it won't be a problem.''

He grinned.

''What's so funny?''

''I've never seen you get dressed in ten minutes.''

''I'll show you, Jake McCain,'' she teased. ''This Elise Web—'' The mirth in her voice died as she caught her error. ''My name is Elise McCain,'' she stated emphatically.

''Yes, it is,'' he said, loving the changes on her face.

''And this Elise McCain is a new woman who has to get dressed—now.'' She rushed toward the bedroom.

''I rather liked the old one,'' he shouted after her.

Jake rested his arms along the back of the sofa and sighed heavily. He'd done the right thing in coming here. Maybe soon the knot in his stomach would ease. Maybe soon he'd have custody of his son. Maybe soon Elise would learn to love him. Maybe soon…

ELISE QUICKLY WASHED HER FACE and brushed her teeth, then slipped on a plum-colored pantsuit. She applied a little makeup and pinned her hair at the back of her head. That was all she had time for. She shoved her feet into a pair of black flats and grabbed her purse and coat. In nine minutes, she was in the living room again.

"Wow," Jake said as he rose to his feet. "You actually did it."

"Yes." She took a much-needed breath. "I'm ready." And she was. She was ready to face whatever lay ahead for them.

SOON HE AND ELISE WERE on the road to Houston. Jake explained that Mrs. Turner would have to approve her visit. He'd call Beau if there was a problem and as soon as Mrs. Turner's office opened, he'd inform her of the new development.

Elise was full of questions about Ben and he was glad to answer everything. But Ben's medical records would tell her more than he ever could.

They talked easily, with their former rapport, and Elise was just happy to be with Jake again. He had come to mean a lot to her, more than she'd ever imagined, and it wasn't just the sensual magnetism. It was a lot more. But right now her thoughts were on Ben and on Jake's voice as he talked so lovingly about his son.

"There's a lot that bothers me—Ben never leaving the house, Ben not having any interactions with other children. But what bothers me most is the fact that he won't speak. I've tried everything and still he won't utter a sound."

"He doesn't even cry?" That was so hard to believe.

"No, and I've seen him fall and bump his head hard and he never made a sound."

"But he can talk?"

"Yes. Mrs. Carr has tapes of him talking and I've played them for him, but he doesn't respond."

"What did the doctor say?"

"That he's grieving and in time he'll talk again."

"That's so sad," she murmured, and that sadness gripped her heart. It also made her think about herself and her ability to help Ben. She had to be honest. "Don't take this the wrong way, but I'm nervous. I feel so…inadequate."

He glanced at her, a grin on his face.

"What?"

"I had those same doubts," he told her. "As much as I wanted my son, I thought if the Fosters could help him more, then I'd have to let them."

"What changed your mind?"

"Meeting Ben" was his simple reply. "In my head I had pictured him needing all this medical attention with machines and medications, but what Ben needs is someone who's patient and loving while his motor skills improve and his brain starts to react more quickly. I can do that and I know Ben understands I'm his father. So I'm trying to do what I can with him until a judge tells me otherwise."

"Do the doctors know Ben's mental capacity?"

"They've run several developmental screening tests and numerous other kinds of tests. Dr. Ruskin said he's not mentally challenged, but very slow. I can see that, but I also see how eager he is to learn."

When she'd thought of having a child with Jake, it was nothing like this. It surprised her that she wasn't panicking at the monumental task facing them. There was no doubt in her mind, though, that she could do it. That surprised her even more.

"Thank you," Jake said softly.

She didn't have to ask for what. She knew and she hated herself for having caused him more pain, more distress over his son. Now they would help Ben together—the way they should have from the start.

She smiled and that was all Jake seemed to need.

"When I described my doubts to Beau, he thought it was ironic," Jake went on.

"Why?"

"Beau said that now I knew how my mother felt when she had to leave me with my father."

Jake never talked about his mother, and for a moment Elise was nonplussed. But she quickly recovered and she had to ask, had wanted to ask for months, "Why *did* she leave you?"

"I refused to go with her."

"Weren't you ten?"

"Yes, and I stood my ground because Dad told me what she'd done and that she was pregnant by another man."

"Your father told you that?" she asked, unable to disguise her shock.

Jake recognized the tone of her voice—it held the same shock he'd heard in Beau's voice. "Yes," he replied hesitantly.

"You were *ten.* That doesn't say much for your father."

For the first time Jake saw his father through someone else's eyes and he didn't like what he was seeing. Why would his father tell him that? He'd never tell Ben bad things about his mother, especially the fact that Sherry had abandoned him. Years of loneliness and resentment ballooned inside him and recurring questions began to nag. Questions he'd ignored before. Why had his father forbidden any relationship with his mother? Why had he encouraged the hate?

"I'm sorry," Elise apologized when Jake became quiet. "I shouldn't have said that."

"No, it's all right," he assured her. "I'm trying to understand why he did it. I guess he was afraid of losing everything, including me."

"I've known Althea for years and I can't imagine her leaving you without a fight."

"She called repeatedly until Dad had the number changed to an unlisted one. She wrote letters, but he burned them. When the sheriff came, he hid me in the barn. I hid every time until the sheriff stopped coming."

Elise bit her tongue, then clamped her lips tight. Still she said, "I wish you'd talk to your mother."

Jake heard her words, but he was locked somewhere between that boy who'd loved his mother and the man who still held loyalties to his father. To block out destructive emotions, he grabbed his cell phone.

"It's after eight, so I'd better try to reach Mrs. Turner."

She wasn't in yet so Elise called Ron Smythe, dean of her department, and explained the situation as best as she could. He was very understanding. She had an unblemished record and that worked in her favor.

Jake soon had Mrs. Turner on the line. Elise gazed out the window as he talked. Stands of thick oak, serene farmland and peaceful country communities slipped by. They had a direct route into Houston and were making good time. But the scenery couldn't hold back her awareness of Jake's past. She felt so much pain for that lonely boy who was torn between his parents. That must be why she was so drawn to him. The ache in her was assuaged by the ache in him. Her childhood hadn't been idyllic, either, and her whole life had changed after the incident with Tammy.

Constance was a controlling, domineering mother who set goals for her daughters and expected them to be achieved. Failure was not an option. Maybe that was why she'd kept waiting for Constance to tell her she hadn't failed.

Her father had died when she was twelve, but he'd had very little involvement in their upbringing. He was a history professor, more interested in the past than the present, but she'd inherited her love of books from him. As long as she could escape into a book, she could deal with her mother. The older she got, though, the harder that was to do.

She didn't call to tell her mother where she was going. She was cutting the cord, so to speak, and it was way past due. A well-respected professional in her field, she needed to become a woman in her own right—a woman who knew what she wanted. She looked at Jake and saw exactly what that was.

Jake put down the phone. ''Ms. Woods is going to meet us at the house. They feel this might be too much for Ben, but I kept insisting, so Mrs. Turner wants Carmen there.''

Those words kept her trapped as Jake maneuvered through the heavy Houston traffic. She was hardly aware when they turned off the freeway. What if meeting another person was too much for Ben? What if her fears controlled her reactions? No, she wouldn't allow that to happen. Jake needed her and she wouldn't let him down.

She'd felt so good, but now anxiety had taken over. ''Jake, I...'' She stopped as they pulled into a driveway and Ms. Woods got out of a car.

Jake looked at her and she gave a tremulous smile. She saw everything she needed in his eyes: strength, faith and trust. Her tension eased...somewhat. It was time to meet Ben.

''Don't be nervous,'' Jake said.

''I'll try.'' But her stomach quivered sporadically.

''He's always at the door waiting for me, so be prepared.''

''Okay,'' she replied as they climbed out.

''Mrs. McCain,'' Ms. Woods said brightly. ''I'm so glad you and Mr. McCain have worked things out.''

''Thank you.''

The woman's expression changed as she glanced at Jake. ''Mrs. Turner is allowing this because the hearing is in two weeks and she feels you and Ben have a good rapport. But at the first sign that Ben's distressed I'll have to ask you to leave.''

"No problem," Jake answered. "I don't want Ben distressed in any way."

"Good."

Ms. Woods rang the bell and they could hear voices and bumping. It became clear that someone was trying to get Ben away from the door in order to open it. Finally the door swung in and Elise saw a woman in the entry. A man stood a few feet away, holding a little boy. Ben wriggled out of the man's arms and tottered straight to Jake, who picked him up. They strolled toward a den.

"Hey, son," Jake cooed. "How are you today?" His voice was so gentle that Elise could practically feel it.

Her focus was riveted on Ben. He favored Jake so much that she couldn't tear her eyes away from that beautiful face. He was small, as Jake had told her, but he'd forgotten to say how precious Ben was. How absolutely precious...and petrifying.

She was vaguely aware of Ms. Woods introducing her to the Fosters. When they left the room, Jake said to Ben, "I brought someone to see you."

Ben held a clump of Lego blocks in his hand and showed it to Jake. "Yes, I see," Jake responded lovingly. "We'll play tractor later, but now I want you to meet Elise." He pointed to her. "That's Elise. Can you say hi?"

Ben looked at her with big brown eyes, but he didn't say a word.

Her breath froze painfully and she fought a sense of suffocation.

"Why don't you show her our tractor?" Jake suggested, standing Ben on his feet.

Ben's eyes grew bigger, then all of a sudden he darted toward her, but tripped and fell flat on his stomach.

In a split second fear gripped her—not for herself, but for Ben. Without thinking, just reacting, she bent down and scooped him up. Staring into his eyes, she felt something unfurl inside her and she knew what it was. Motherly love. She'd had a similar sensation holding Jamie, the young boy at the hospital, but this was stronger, more real, more potent.

She stroked his hair. "Are you okay?" Her voice was soft and tender and for a moment it sounded unfamiliar to her own ears.

Jake watched all this with a knot in his throat. He didn't rush to help Ben because Dr. Ruskin wanted him to get up on his own. He'd forgotten to tell Elise that and now he was glad he hadn't. His father had once told him that the only way to learn to swim was to jump right in and that was exactly what had happened. If she was going to be Ben's mother, she had to start now. And she was.

She moved gingerly to the sofa and eased down with Ben in her lap. Ben pointed to the makeshift tractor he'd dropped on the floor when he'd fallen, and Jake brought it to him.

Ben gave his clump of Lego pieces to Elise. She took it and asked, "What is this, Ben?"

Ben just stared at her.

"Is it a tractor?"

He nodded.

He understands, she thought. He clearly understood what she was saying. It was an exhilarating moment.

"Where did you get the tractor?" She knew, but she wanted to get Ben's reaction.

Ben pointed to Jake.

"Oh, you and Daddy made it?" She knew that, too, because Jake had told her.

Ben nodded.

"Let's see, what kind of noise do tractors make?" She appeared thoughtful. "They don't sound like a car or a train. Do they go putt-putt?"

Nothing but big eyes.

She ran the tractor over his jeans, murmuring, "Putt, putt, putt, putt."

When she reached his stomach, Ben smiled the most gorgeous smile she'd ever seen. Her heart melted from the sheer impact and she wondered how she could've possibly thought she might harm him in any way. He already held her heart in his tiny hand and she'd move heaven and earth for him…if he'd only ask.

Unable to stay away any longer, Jake sat beside them. Ben immediately crawled into his lap and Elise could see how much Ben loved Jake—it was there in his shining eyes. Why couldn't Ms. Woods and Mrs. Turner see that? She searched for Ms. Woods and saw she was in the kitchen talking to the Fosters.

For the next hour, they played, sitting on the floor with the blocks, and it was obvious how hard Ben had to concentrate to match colors, shapes and numbers. He was slow but determined, and he seemed to know when the colors or shapes were wrong. When they were, he became frustrated and stopped or threw them. Jake always told him it was okay, and coaxed him to relax and start again. She'd believed that Jake would be a great father, and his patience and gentleness with Ben proved her right.

Jake gave Ben a breathing treatment, placing an oxygen mask over his face. It was clear that Ben knew exactly what to do, how to breathe. He eventually fell asleep and they sat just holding him. When Ben awoke, they went outside so Ben could exercise his arms and legs on the swing set and other equipment in the backyard. Ben ran, fell and played with a smile on his face. He was so adorable that Elise's heart was in her throat.

They were so wrapped up in Ben they hadn't even noticed the time until Mrs. Foster opened the patio doors. "I have Ben's lunch ready."

"Ready to eat, Ben?" Jake asked.

Ben nodded and took Jake's hand. They headed for the kitchen with Elise tagging along. "I'll feed him, Peggy," Jake said.

"You always do," Peggy retorted. "Why would today be any different?"

"Thanks," Jake replied, not reacting to the barb.

He settled Ben in his high chair, and Peggy put a plate in front of him and a plastic cup that had a lid and a spout. Jake pulled up a chair.

"Can I feed him, please?" Elise asked Jake, surprised by her request. The fear had disappeared and all she wanted was to help Ben, to do everything she could for him.

Jake didn't hesitate for second. "Sure, but he eats slowly and has difficulty swallowing sometimes."

She was uplifted by the trust and confidence she saw in his eyes.

Jake snapped a bib around the child's neck and Elise sat and began to feed him. As Jake had said, he ate slowly and swallowed even slower, and her eyes filled with tears at the effort it was for him. But he continued to eat the potatoes and chicken that had been mashed in a blender. He spit out the green peas, though, so Elise mixed them in with the applesauce and he ate them.

"Would you like to feed yourself?"

Jake was instantly alert. Ben wasn't allowed to feed himself. He didn't have the coordination. Another thing he'd forgotten to tell Elise. He started to stop her when Ben nodded.

"Dr. Ruskin said he's not ready to do that." Peggy could be heard as she spoke to Ms. Woods. But Ms. Woods did nothing. Nor did Jake.

Elise handed the spoon to Ben and he stared at it, then at her. She realized he didn't know how to put his fingers around it.

"Open your hand," she said, then stretched out her fingers so Ben would understand what she meant.

Ben looked at his clenched fist, then at Elise's hand, but he couldn't seem to do it. Elise tugged gently on the little fingers and Ben opened his hand. She placed the spoon in his palm and his fingers made the simple action of gripping. Elise guided his hand to the mashed potatoes, scooped some up and moved the spoon to his mouth. She did that several times. When she let go of his hand, the potatoes landed on his cheek, but she just pushed the spoon over until he found his mouth. After many attempts, Ben made the movement all by himself.

Elise clapped her hands. "Yes, yes. You did it."

Ben beat the spoon against the high chair in response, and potatoes and peas splattered on the floor.

"He's making a mess," Peggy said.

"I'll be glad to clean it up," Elise said, unable to let the remark slide.

"Don't worry," Jake added. "We'll make sure everything's clean." He was upset that they had to listen to this when it was plain to see that Elise had a way with Ben. He was responding to her and Jake was excited just watching them. He'd known from the start that she'd be like this as a mother: loving and tolerant.

Jake wiped Ben's mouth and held his glass for him to drink from the spout. "Ben's a big boy. He can feed himself."

Ben banged the spoon again.

Say something, Ben. Just say something. But Ben kept banging the spoon.

"We'd better put him down for his nap," Carl said.

Jake glanced at his watch and saw it was almost twelve. He'd lost track of time; he always did when he was here. He never wanted to leave Ben, but he had to abide by the rules.

"I'll get him cleaned up," Jake said as he removed Ben from the chair.

"Don't bother," Peggy replied. "I'll have to give him a bath now."

Jake kissed the boy's cheek before handing him to Peggy. Ben glanced at Elise and she hurried over and kissed him, too. It was so easy. "We'll see you this afternoon," she called as Peggy walked away with him.

Elise began to clean up the mess and Jake helped. They left the kitchen spic and span and went out the door. Ms. Woods followed.

Outside she said, "I have an appointment this afternoon, so I won't be able to be here."

Jake's eyes narrowed. "You're not going to say that we can't see Ben again, are you?"

She sighed. "No, actually, the visit went very well and there's no reason you can't return. Just try to keep things amicable with the Fosters."

"Thank you," Jake and Elise said in unison.

"Don't thank me. My opinion hasn't changed." Saying that, she walked toward her car.

A heavy feeling settled in Jake's stomach. CPS had made up its decision and nothing would change that—not even Jake and Elise's love for Ben.

They got into the truck, then Jake backed out of the drive. He glanced at Elise and saw she was silently crying. He pulled over to the side.

"Don't do this," he begged, tucking a stray tendril behind her ear.

"I have maternal instincts," she hiccuped.

Jake blinked. "What?"

"All these years I've been afraid to even get near a child. I thought something was lacking in me, but it isn't. The moment I held Ben, all these strong emotions came to life inside me and I wanted to soothe and comfort him. And he responded to me. I wasn't nervous or afraid and I ached to hold him forever." As she said the last word, her voice cracked and sobs shook her body.

His stomach tightened. "Elise, don't..."

"And because of me, we're...we're going to lose him."

Jake dragged her into his arms, which wasn't easy since they had a console between them. "It's not your fault," he whispered in her hair as he breathed in her fragrant scent. Holding her trembling body, he felt whole again and his own body reacted instinctively, like it always did when he touched her. He pushed those feelings aside as more important needs took over. "I don't know if our being together would have made a difference," he told her softly.

"If we lose custody, it'll be because a judge thinks we're not qualified to deal with Ben's medical problems."

She drew back and wiped away a tear. "Then let's convince him we can care for Ben." She was almost high from Jake's touch and his compassion. When Derek had died, she'd vowed she would never need anyone that much again, but looking at Jake through her tears, she realized she needed him more than she'd ever planned. And she didn't feel guilty for feeling that way.

CHAPTER TEN

AFTER A QUICK LUNCH, they strolled through Memorial Park to stretch their legs. They decided against visiting the Houston Arboretum & Nature Center located in the park; instead they chose a scenic jogging trail for peace and quiet. Several bikers and joggers spoke to them, but they hardly noticed, both eager to get back to Ben. Promptly at two they were at the Fosters and again, Ben was waiting at the door, refreshed from his nap. They spent the afternoon playing and working with him. It was the most enjoyable experience Elise had ever had. When it was time to go, she felt a moment of sadness and Ben obviously did, too. He clung to Jake and refused to look at Peggy. Elise hoped he'd cry, say something in protest, but he didn't. Eventually he went to Peggy.

Outside in the truck, Elise asked in a forlorn voice, "I wonder if he understands we'll be back?"

"Of course he does," Jake replied, also shaken by the parting. "That's why he's always at the door."

The drive to Waco was made in comfortable silence, both of them preoccupied with thoughts of Ben. Soon Jake turned into Elise's driveway.

"Do you want to come in?" she asked tentatively.

He wanted that more than anything. But he couldn't make love to her again without telling her how he felt. She wasn't ready for that yet. And he found he wasn't, either. He had to be honest, though. If their relationship was going to work, they both had to be honest.

He shifted in his seat. "If I come in, we'll make love."

The darkness hid her expression. "Probably."

"We talked earlier about there being more to marriage."

"Yes."

"First we have to decide what we both want." He felt a tension in his stomach as he waited for her answer.

"I thought we had," she replied. "We both wanted a child and now we have Ben."

"What about our own baby?"

She took a long breath. "Right now, our main concern is Ben."

The tension eased somewhat. She was telling the truth—she wanted Ben as much as he did. So what was still bothering him? *Her feelings for him.* Before it had been so simple—they had sex to create a baby, love wasn't involved. Now that they had Ben the situation had changed drastically. He wanted their lovemaking to be a result of their feelings for each other. He knew how he felt and he was well aware of how she felt. As his wife she was motivated by duty. He didn't want duty sex.

When they made love again, he'd want to say those words—I love you. But he couldn't. He remembered his mother leaving and that pain cut too deep to ever experience again. He couldn't risk losing Elise a second time.

"Jake, is something wrong?" she asked.

He stared into the night, finding it difficult to be honest. "Before we were on a sex marathon to make a baby. That's changed."

"Yes."

When she didn't say anything else, he rushed on, "So maybe now we need to take it slow."

"Why?"

He cleared his throat. "I thought you might want to."

She sighed tiredly. "Jake, what are you getting at? Are you saying you don't want to sleep with me anymore?"

"Of course not, I..."

She cut in. "We have to create a loving family environment for Ben. To do that we have to be husband and wife just as we have been. Is that a problem for you?''

Yes—he wanted more now, but all he could hear was duty and responsibility in her voice.

''Jake, say something,'' she prompted.

He ran his hands along the steering wheel, his chest expanding with clogged emotions he couldn't express. ''I want this marriage to work.'' The words were unexpected, unplanned.

''I do, too.'' She paused then groaned as if she could read his mind. ''Jake, are you afraid that if we lose custody of Ben, you'll also lose me?''

''Something like that.'' It was close to the truth. He and Elise were held together by a responsibility for Ben. If that were taken away, would their marriage survive? Would he survive?

''You must have a very poor opinion of me if you think I'd do that. In this case, I'm going to be generous and forgive you because of my own actions in the past. But Jake, please, don't make that mistake again. You're Ben's father and *he* will be a part of our lives, even if we have to continue fighting for him the rest of ours. And I'll be right there with you. Understand?''

''I'm beginning to,'' he said quietly.

''Good. I'm letting you off the hook tonight because we're exhausted and we have an early day tomorrow and the meeting with the judge.''

''Yes, and if I came in, we wouldn't sleep much.''

''No. We have to have our heads clear for tomorrow.'' She swallowed hard, needing to say more. ''I'm not doing this just for Ben. I care about you, too.''

He stared at her through the dimness, and unable to resist, he cupped her face and kissed her softly, his thumb caressing her cheek. ''Thank you,'' he whispered against her lips.

Her heart hammered wildly from the contact as she breathed in his familiar masculine scent. She returned the kiss for an extra second, then quickly got out of the truck. If she didn't, she knew he wouldn't be leaving. "I'll see you in the morning," she said, closing the door.

He waited until she unlocked her door and went inside. When the lights came on, he started the engine. Driving away, he kept thinking of what she'd said—that she cared about him. *Why couldn't she love him?*

ELISE CALLED THE DEAN and arranged to have more time away from the university. She didn't want to miss any time with Ben; she was committed to being his mother and Jake's wife. Sex had been the basis of their marriage and now they would build on that to form a solid relationship. She'd gone overboard with her obsession for a baby and made him feel insecure, as if sex was all she wanted from him. Now she wanted more, a home and a family. She'd wanted that before, but it was tempered by her irrational fears. The fog had lifted from around her and she could see the future clearly…with Jake, happy and secure. She'd work every day to accomplish that, to prove to Jake that she'd never leave him.

When Jake reached home, Mike was waiting for him. They'd received the card from the USDA for the grade of the cotton. It was good—better than he'd expected, but he knew he averaged about three bales of cotton per acre on his best fields and the quality was superior. Now he'd get the price he wanted. He felt uplifted by that. He wished he felt the same about his personal life.

TIME MOVED SWIFTLY, and soon they were back in Houston. The judge's interview was at one o'clock, so it didn't interrupt their visit with Ben. As Jake rang the doorbell they could hear the bumping at the door again. Jake grinned. "I think someone's waiting for us."

The door opened and Peggy held Ben in her arms; he was still in his pajamas with the clump of Lego pieces in his hand. "I'm sorry," Peggy said. "When Ben woke up, he came straight to the door and I haven't been able to budge him. He won't let me change his diaper or put his clothes on."

Jake gathered Ben out of her arms. "Hi, son," he said, and Ben smiled. "I'll change him, Peggy, if that's okay," Jake added.

"Sure, I could use a cup of coffee," she answered, and joined Carl in the kitchen.

Elise followed Jake down a hall, entering a baby's room that had dark oak furniture, stuffed animals and toys. Jake placed Ben in the crib, then went in search of clothes and a diaper.

Ben was too big to still be in a baby's bed, Elise thought, and the room was for a baby, not a three-year-old boy. That didn't concern her now; Ben's welfare did.

"Hi, Ben," Elise said brightly. "Remember me?"

Ben nodded, then he stuck out the tractor toward her. She could feel her heart thumping rapidly. "Yes, I see, it's very beautiful and so are you."

Jake found jeans and a long sleeved T-shirt. "Boys aren't beautiful. They're handsome, aren't they, Ben?"

Ben's eyes opened wide.

"Can I change him, please?" Elise asked, amazed at this newfound freedom inside her—the freedom to love uninhibitedly.

Jake handed her the clothes and a diaper, then let down the rail of the bed and laid Ben on his back. He removed Ben's pajamas effortlessly, as if he was used to dressing children.

"Your turn," Jake said, and stepped away.

Elise set the clothes on the mattress. The last time she changed a baby's diaper was with Tammy. She waited for the paranoia, but it didn't happen. She wasn't afraid. Maybe it was Ben's trusting eyes or the new joy in her.

She undid the tabs on the diaper and removed it. Jake took the diaper and handed her baby wipes; she cleaned

Ben's bottom then put on a clean diaper. Slipping the shirt over his head, she pulled his arms through. The jeans had an elastic waist and snaps on the insides of the legs. She managed to get them on without a problem. Now for the socks and tennis shoes. She stared at the small white socks and wondered how to get them on Ben's feet.

"Raise your foot," she said, but Ben only gazed at her. She tickled the bottom of his right foot and he squirmed, a big grin on his face. "Lift your foot, Ben," she said again, and this time he did. She slipped the sock on, then she tickled his left foot and Ben lifted it. When both socks were on, she clapped her hands. "We did it. We did it."

Ben tried to clap his hands, but he couldn't make them meet. Elise guided them together and Ben bounced on the bed in excitement.

"Shoes," Jake said, marveling at Elise's naturalness with the child. He worked Ben's feet into the shoes, which had Velcro tabs, then picked him up and stood him on the floor. Ben pointed to the bed. "Sorry, son, I forgot the tractor." Jake grabbed the Lego tractor and Ben cuddled it to him.

Ben gazed up at them and Jake's heart fluttered at the love and trust he saw in those eyes. He'd do whatever it took to keep Ben. He slid an arm around Elise's waist. Whatever it took.

The morning was spent entertaining Ben while incorporating his routine exercises into his play. Ben seemed to know what was expected of him and when he grew tired he just lay on the floor and refused to move. After a few minutes, Ben would crawl into Jake's lap and they'd start over again. As Elise watched, she thought the rigorous, constant routine had to be wearisome for someone so small. But it was normal for Ben because it was all he'd ever done. He should be outside in the fresh air playing with other kids. That would happen, she vowed.

Elise again helped Ben with lunch and let him feed himself, to his great excitement. Of course, there was a mess and Peggy complained. Elise agreed with Jake that the Fosters weren't right for Jake; they were too strict and rigid.

Jake explained to Ben that they'd be late coming back. He wasn't sure Ben understood and it was hard to leave, but they had to. He couldn't be late for the interview.

THEY STOPPED FOR A QUICK BITE and made it to the judge's office at twelve-fifty. Sitting in the waiting room, Elise asked, "Are you nervous?"

"A little," he replied, his gut churning. "Hell, I'm a lot nervous. What we say in there will determine the rest of Ben's life...and ours." He glanced at her. "And you?"

"I'm past nervous, but I..."

"You can control it," he finished for her.

"Yes." She smiled slightly, pleased that he was beginning to know her so well. "Speaking in front of people, I learned to focus on my subject and not my nerves. Right now Ben is my only focus."

"Come this way," the judge's secretary said, and led them into a large room dominated by a mahogany desk. "Have a seat. The judge will be with you shortly."

Jake and Elise sat in the dark leather chairs across from the desk. Jake noticed a family portrait on the wall—a husband, wife and three teenage children. The judge was a family man; that was good. He'd understand that kids should be with their parents.

An inner door opened and a man in a suit walked in. He was of medium height, balding, and a little older than the man in the portrait. Jake and Elise shook his hand.

"I'm Judge Alfred Reynolds," he introduced himself. "It's nice to meet you, Mr. and Mrs. McCain."

"Thank you, Judge," Jake replied as they took their seats.

The judge clasped his hands over the folder on his desk. "This is a very difficult case, as I'm sure you're both aware. Your son has very special problems and my decision will be based on what's best for Ben and his future." The judge looked directly at Jake. "What do you see in Ben's future, Mr. McCain?"

Jake swallowed, unprepared for the question, but he answered from his heart. "I see Ben living on our farm near Waco and I see a lot of work, love and attention given to Ben by Elise and me. And because of that I see Ben growing into a healthy, happy boy."

The judge's gaze swung to Elise. "And your answer would be the same as your husband's, am I correct?"

"Yes."

"It's my understanding that you were upset when you learned of Ben's paternity."

Elise bit her lip, wanting to be honest, but also not wanting to say the wrong thing. "Yes, I was," she admitted. "We'd been married for six months and we were trying to have a baby. Suddenly discovering that Jake already had a son was more than I could take. To be honest, I was uneasy about raising another woman's child." She wouldn't tell him about her past. It wasn't relevant now.

"What made you change your mind?"

"Realizing that this was an innocent three-year-old boy who needed someone and that the boy was Jake's. Everything fell into place for me after that, and yesterday, when I held Ben, I knew without a doubt that I could be his mother."

"Even though he's going to demand constant attention for a while."

"Yes," she replied promptly.

"How will you handle your career?"

"Ben will be my top priority. I plan to take a leave of absence."

"You mentioned children. Do you still plan to have children?"

They had touched on this last night and she was aware how Jake felt so she answered easily and truthfully. "I don't think we'll have a child until Ben doesn't need us so much."

"Do you agree with that, Mr. McCain?"

Her words played in Jake's head. After being so obsessed with wanting a child, he marveled at her ability to give up something she wanted so desperately because she cared about Ben—and him.

"Mr. McCain?"

Jake gathered himself. "Most definitely," he said. "Ben will require our full attention."

"That's very selfless and I applaud your devotion to your son, but—" he tapped the folder in front of him "—Dr. Ruskin, a developmental pediatrician, and the case workers at CPS all agree that Ben's health depends on his familiar environment. He's taken several steps backward because of his grandmother's death, and that concerns me."

"Me, too," Jake said. "But I don't agree with what Dr. Ruskin and the others are saying. I feel that house is more harmful than good for Ben. It reminds him too much of his grandmother. Her memories are everywhere and sometimes he wanders into her room and I know he's searching for her." Jake had mentioned some of this to Elise, but he realized now how strongly he felt about it. "Dr. Ruskin and the others think Ben doesn't understand a whole lot, but he does understand that I'm his father. I'm not sure what that means to Ben. It means something, though, because he's happy to see me, and with Elise's and my love and support, I feel Ben can make a move without a problem. That's what I feel in my heart as his father."

"Your dedication to Ben is commendable," the judge said. "But I have to look at facts. I make my decisions on facts and the fact is, Mr. McCain, you can't give me any evidence to support your claim."

The judge's words weren't encouraging and Jake felt a moment of hopelessness, but he had to keep trying. "The fact is, Judge, that Ben is falling and hasn't uttered a word since his grandmother's death. He's still in that house and those facts haven't improved. And it might be presumptuous of me, but Ben is happy when I'm there. He's always at the door waiting for me. When I leave, he clings to me. Another fact is that he bonded with Elise immediately and they have a great rapport. She has him learning to feed himself, something Dr. Ruskin said he wasn't ready to do. Those are facts I see every day. Facts that say a lot to me."

The judge opened the folder and studied the papers in front of him as if Jake hadn't even spoken. He raised his head. "Mr. McCain, would you be willing to move to Houston to care for Ben?"

Jake blinked. "Move to Houston?"

"That's the question."

"I'm a farmer," Jake answered in a confused voice. "My father was a farmer, as was my grandfather. I…I…" He stopped and started again, "Frankly, I'm thrown by the question. I have to be able to make a living for Ben and I'm not certain how I'd do that in Houston."

The judge gave him a minute. "So what is your answer?"

Jake drew in deeply. "To get custody of my son, I'd do anything…even sell my farm and move to Houston." Jake meant every word he said. Any sacrifice he made would be minimal compared to the rewards.

"And you, Mrs. McCain, how do you feel about moving to Houston?"

Elise gripped her hands together. "Whatever decision my husband makes, I will support wholeheartedly."

Jake heard her voice, her words, and felt renewed by her faith in him. He'd never realized how much he needed that from her.

The judge closed the folder. "I'll have my decision next Monday at one. Thanks for your time and answering my questions." He stood and left the room.

Jake and Elise rose to their feet and stared at each other. "How do you think it went?" Elise asked.

He was still caught in a maelstrom of emotions. "I'm not sure," he said. "The judge said he'd make his decision based on facts, and that has me worried. He didn't seem concerned with the facts I told him.'' He noticed the clock on the wall. ''We'll talk later. Ben will be waiting.''

On the drive to the Fosters', they didn't talk much, but a question was burning through Elise and she had to have an answer.

''You'd actually sell your farm?''

''Yes,'' he answered swiftly. ''If that's the only way I can get Ben, then I'll do it. I hope it doesn't come to that, but I'm preparing myself.'' He glanced at her. ''I'm sorry that was thrown at you. I don't expect you to give up your career.''

Elise watched the busy traffic. ''Let's see what tomorrow brings, then we'll argue about it.''

''Oh,'' he raised an eyebrow. ''We're going to argue?''

She looked at him. ''Yes, because I meant what I said. Whatever you choose to do, I'll be with you.''

He smiled. ''I don't know how we got to this point, but I like it.'' And he'd like it a whole lot more if it was for another reason...*that she loved him.*

''Me, too.'' She smiled back. ''I've been afraid for so long and now I just want to be a mother. I have these feelings that have been dormant for years and suddenly they're free. The sensation is wonderful. I have a tendency to go overboard so you'll have to tell me when I do.''

They pulled into the Fosters' driveway. ''I will,'' he promised, knowing she'd make a great mother. ''Just take it slow, that's all I ask.''

THE WEEK PASSED QUICKLY with the constant trips to Houston. Elise obtained a leave of absence from the university, though she'd stay in touch via computer with her teaching assistant until the semester was over, then she'd have to make a decision about whether or not to return. Every possible moment was spent with Ben, and Elise still slept at her house and Jake at the farm. She planned to change that when they weren't physically exhausted and mentally drained. All that was on their minds was the hearing on

Monday. They did manage to finish Ben's room and Elise had packed some of her clothes, but there wasn't much time to do anything else.

Thanksgiving was just another day spent with Ben, no fanfare, no big dinner, and they wouldn't have had it any other way. Ben had totally bonded with them and was now becoming agitated when they left. Every time Jake said they had to go, Ben would run to his room and fall on the floor. He never cried; he just had a sad look on his face. Jake and Elise sat with him until Ben accepted that they had to leave. It broke Elise's heart whenever it happened.

Two days before the hearing, Jake received a call from Mrs. Turner, saying that Ben was becoming distressed and Dr. Ruskin felt the McCains' visits were harmful to Ben's progress and had to stop. Jake was livid and told her there was no way they were keeping him away from Ben. She said they'd get a court order. It was best for Ben.

Jake immediately called Beau, who managed to get the visits reinstated with supervision by Ms. Woods until after the hearing. Jake was thankful, but the atmosphere became increasingly tense with the Fosters. It was a stressful situation and would end with the judge's decision.

Sunday before the hearing they decided to spend the night in Houston so they would be refreshed for the court proceedings. After their visit with Ben, they drove to the hotel, but they were both worried. Ben wasn't his usually lively self; he was almost lethargic. He fell asleep in Elise's arms as she was giving him a breathing treatment. He was still asleep when they left.

"I think all of this has taken a toll on Ben, too," Elise said anxiously.

"And it shouldn't be this way." His hand hit the steering wheel. "Something's not right. I feel it in my gut."

Elise felt the same way, but there was nothing they could do.

They sat in silence for a moment.

Suddenly Elise realized she hadn't talked to anyone in her family in weeks.

"What is it?" Jake asked when he noticed her expression.

"I was thinking I haven't told Mother or Judith about the hearing."

"They're not pleased we reconciled, are they?"

"Mother and Judith are never pleased." She made light of it because she wouldn't have Jake feeling it was his fault. "I think it's a family trait, but *I'm* finally happy and they can't ruin that for me."

"Elise..."

"I'm happy, Jake, please believe me."

He did. He could hear it in her voice and see it in her eyes, and that was all he needed to know. They checked in to the hotel and went out for dinner. When they returned to the room, they were both exhausted. It had been a long, tiring day. While Jake called Beau, Elise took a shower.

Elise came out of the bathroom in a beige silk gown with thin straps, rubbing lotion on her long arms. Jake just stared at her. Her skin glistened, waiting to be...

"What did Beau say?" she asked, continuing to rub the lotion in.

He watched every sensuous stroke. "What? Oh... I..." he stammered, completely lost in the allure that was Elise. "He'll be here for the hearing."

"That's good. We're going to need him."

Ben's face loomed strong in his mind and Jake knew he couldn't face any disappointments tonight. They had to discuss their relationship, but he didn't want to hear her say that she cared for him deeply but that she could never love him the way she'd loved Derek. He couldn't take that—not tonight—with tomorrow closing in on him.

He went to take a shower, and when he came out of the bathroom Elise was already in bed. He flipped off the light and crawled in beside her. She curled into his arms so naturally, and he needed just to hold her.

"I'm so tired," she whispered against his chest.

"Me, too," he murmured, unable to believe he could actually be in bed with her, touch her and not have sex. But he needed her in a way he never had before, a way that had nothing to do with sex. It had to do with love and…

Within minutes they were both asleep.

ELISE STIRRED AND REACHED for Jake, but the bed was empty. She sat up, tucked her hair behind her ears and saw him sitting in a chair by the window. Her heart twisted at the turmoil on his face.

"Jake?"

"Hmm?"

"Are you okay?"

"It's raining outside," he said without answering her question. "Kind of fitting for today, don't you think?"

"Jake."

He stood and walked toward the bed. All he had on was his underwear and her senses ignited at the sight of his lean, masculine body. A body she knew intimately… Suddenly heightened needs, too long denied, clamored through her.

Jake dropped to the bed. "Today's the day they could take my son from me and give me visitation rights. I can't be a weekend father. I just can't."

"Oh, Jake." She scrambled to him. "I don't see how they can do that when you're willing to do so much to keep him—even move here."

"But the experts, the people that count, are against us and—"

"Shh." She placed her finger over his lips.

That soft touch from her blocked everything else out. It was what he needed and he was tired of denying himself something he wanted so badly.

"We have to stay positive and…" Her words trailed off as he took her finger in his mouth, and her breathing stopped completely when his lips traveled up her arm to her shoulder. He reached her neck and she turned her head, meeting his lips with mind-throbbing urgency. The aching exploded inside her as his lips and tongue tasted, explored and rekindled the most basic of needs. He pushed her down on the bed, his mouth moving sensuously down the arch of her neck to her breast.

"I know we should take it slow," he said hoarsely, gazing at her through heavy-lidded eyes. "But I don't think I'm equipped with that feature when it comes to you."

"Me, neither." She kissed his broad shoulder, her hands bold as they moved down his chest to the hair tapering into his underwear. His body was hard and she reveled in that masculine reaction.

Jake's thumb found her nipple and his lips followed suit. Thought was impossible as her body welcomed Jake's touch, Jake's possession. But a warning kept niggling at her.

"Jake," she moaned raggedly.

"Hmm?"

His hand slid beneath her gown, stroking, and she forgot what was so important, then it came blaring back, and she couldn't ignore it. "I'm not on anything and...and I don't want to get pregnant."

Jake sagged against her and laughed into her heated neck.

"What's so funny?"

He raised his head to look at her. "I never thought I'd hear you say that."

"I know, but we have Ben to think about now."

"Yeah," he agreed, kissing her briefly. If there were any lingering doubts concerning her love for Ben, they vanished with those words. "But this isn't easy. We could..." The ringing of his cell phone stopped him. "Damn, who could that be?" He jumped up and found his phone.

Elise straightened her gown as she listened to him talk. Judging by the expression on his face, the news wasn't good. He put the phone down and came over to her.

"We can't see Ben this morning," he said.

"Why?"

"That was Mrs. Turner, and she said Judge Reynolds wants to see Ben in his chambers. The Fosters are taking him in."

"I thought Ben wasn't allowed to leave the house except to see Dr. Ruskin."

Jake sank down beside her. "Dr. Ruskin is meeting them there. What could that mean?"

"It could be fine," she told him. "Judge Reynolds might be checking to see how Ben does in another environment."

"Then I need to be with him. He'll be scared and..." His voice clogged with emotion and he couldn't go on.

She wrapped her arms around him. Jake gripped her so tightly she thought her ribs would crack. But she didn't mind. She kissed the side of his face, just needing to comfort him. Their passion was now overshadowed by the reality of this day. She had to do something or they'd get bogged down in crippling emotions. "Let's dress and have breakfast, then we'll decide what to do."

Elise dressed in record time, but before they could reach the door, the phone rang again. It was Beau, already in Houston, and they arranged to meet him after breakfast. Jake was quiet and ate very little. Afterward they went for a walk. The rain had stopped, but the pavement was still wet as they strolled past the hotel to a small secluded park. They found a bench and watched a mother push two babies in a stroller. Another child was playing on the swings. There was a subdivision behind a wooden fence and later the park would probably be filled with children. But Jake didn't seem to see anything. His thoughts were all directed inward.

He leaned forward, his hands clasped between his legs. "I don't understand why the judge had to see Ben again. He's visited him twice that I'm aware of. With this rain, I'm surprised Dr. Ruskin allowed it."

"Dr. Ruskin has a lot of power where Ben is concerned," Elise remarked.

"Yes, that was a little hard for me to understand at first, but he's really the reason Ben's still alive." Jake jerked to his feet. "Come on, let's go over to the medical center so you can go through Ben's history and understand what condition he was in when he was born and how much he's progressed."

"Okay," she responded, eager to learn about Ben. And it would give them something to do besides sit and worry.

On the drive over, Jake called Beau and suggested he meet them at Dr. Ruskin's office. Once there, however, the nurse wouldn't allow them to see the records without Dr. Ruskin's permission. They waited while she contacted him. Finally Elise was ushered into a small room with the records and Jake left her to go meet Beau in the lobby.

As Jake got off the elevator, he heard "Hey, Jake," and turned to see Beau coming through the double glass doors.

"Why are you here, anyway?" Beau asked.

On the ride up in the elevator, Jake told him everything that had happened. They found seats in a waiting area. "Why do you think the judge asked to see Ben again?"

"He has a tough decision to make and he's not going to make it lightly. In the end, he'll do what's best for Ben."

"I keep hearing that, but I'm not convinced anyone's thinking of Ben."

"What makes you say that?"

"Just this feeling I have. A father's intuition I think it's called." Jake paused in thought before asking Beau a question. "Why did you come to Houston so early? The hearing isn't until one."

Beau cleared his throat. "Actually I've been here since Friday. Mom insisted. She's worried about you."

Jake clenched his jaw. "Don't start."

"You asked."

Jake got up. "I'd better check on Elise."

"I'm glad you're back together."

"Thanks."

Beau shifted uneasily. "I've been checking out Dr. Ruskin. I hope you don't mind."

"That's why you came early?"

"Yeah."

Jake rubbed the back of his neck, which was painfully tight. He should be angry Beau had taken matters into his own hands. He wasn't. As Elise had said, they needed help. "No, but why?"

"I have the same feeling you do. Something's not adding up, and I'm not going into that courtroom unprepared. I'll meet you at one." Beau swung around and headed for the elevator.

Jake shook his head, unclear as to what Beau meant, but he didn't have time to ponder the remark. He found Elise crying, holding a picture of Ben in an incubator.

He knelt beside her. "Elise, don't."

"I never realized Ben was in such bad shape." She brushed away tears with a shaky hand. "He was so tiny and they didn't expect him to live."

"Dr. Ruskin and Mrs. Carr saved him."

Elise looked down at the picture in her hand. "He's come so far."

"But he has a long way to go."

"We can help him. We can." Her voice held a note of urgency.

Jake wiped away a few more tears. "Let's hope the judge sees it that way."

CHAPTER ELEVEN

THEY ARRIVED IN THE designated courtroom at twelve-thirty. The room was empty and they took a seat on the left side and waited. Jake needed this moment of quiet with Elise before the proceedings began. They sat close together, not speaking, drawing strength from each other for the ordeal ahead.

A bailiff and a court stenographer came in. Jake wondered where Beau was, but his attention was diverted as Dr. Ruskin and another man found seats on the right. What was he doing here? Was he going to testify? Jake didn't have time to contemplate that as Mrs. Turner and Ms. Woods walked in and also sat on the right. It seemed as if they were lining up against him. His thoughts were only reinforced when the Fosters, followed by their attorney, arrived with Peggy carrying Ben. He hadn't known Ben was going to be here. He didn't want him exposed to all this. He failed to understand why they'd brought him.

Again Jake wondered where Beau was. He should be here by now, and Jake had a bad feeling he was going to need him. The judge entered then, and Jake focused his full attention on him.

Court convened, and the judge started to speak. "I want to thank everyone for coming today to settle Benjamin McCain's future. I've already spoken with all the parties involved, and if anyone has anything to add, I'd like to hear it now."

Where the hell was Beau? Jake fumed as the judge continued. "I've gone over this case very carefully because I fervently believe that a parent should have every opportunity to raise his or her child. But this case is very different. Ben has special needs and I can't ignore that." The judge glanced at Jake and Elise. "Mr. and Mrs. McCain, there is no doubt in my mind that you have bonded with Ben and that you care for him deeply. That's why I asked to see Ben again to try to elicit some reaction from him indicating that he understood or was even aware of what's going on, but he was unresponsive. He has regressed in his behavior and Dr. Ruskin fears this could be permanent if Ben is moved. That's a fact I can't ignore. Ben's mental and physical health is my top priority and I see no recourse but to—"

Oh God, no, no, no! screamed through Jake's head, and he shut out the judge's words. He couldn't listen anymore. They were taking his son, and there was nothing he could do.

Jake reached for Elise's hand and gripped it tightly. Her arm went around his shoulders, but even this attempt to comfort him wasn't enough.

"Look at Ben," Elise whispered.

Through a haze of misery, Jake heard Elise's voice and glanced toward Ben. He was leaning forward, straining away from Peggy, who was trying to make him sit still. Was Ben trying to get his attention? Suddenly Ben broke free from her and darted toward Jake. In his haste he tripped and Jake swiftly caught him as he fell, swinging him into his arms. For a moment he'd been suspended in hell, but now he could breathe again. The judge had stopped speaking and Jake sat quickly, holding Ben in his lap.

"'A-dy," Ben said, gazing up at Jake.

The room became very quiet. No one moved, spoke or took a breath.

Jake looked into the bright eyes of his son and could feel his heart hammering against his ribs. Had Ben spoken? "Ben," he said tentatively.

"'A-dy," Ben answered loudly, and there was no mistaking that word.

Tears rolled down Jake's cheeks and he held Ben close, kissing his face. Elise put her arm around Jake again, her heart so full she couldn't speak.

Jake was so absorbed in Ben, he didn't notice that the judge had left the bench and come to stand in front of them. He knelt down to Ben's level.

"Ben," the judge said. "Can you tell me who this man is?" He pointed to Jake.

Ben looked at Jake, then back at the judge. Jake held his breath, praying, *Please, Ben. Say it again. Please.*

"Who is this man?" the judge repeated.

Ben stared wide-eyed.

"Who is this man?" the judge repeated again, patting Jake's knee.

"'A-dy," Ben said.

Elise bit her trembling lip and Jake released a taut breath.

"Is he my daddy?" the judge kept on.

Ben shook his head strongly.

"Is he Mrs. Foster's daddy?"

Ben shook his head again.

"Whose daddy is he?"

Ben thought for a minute, his brow furrowed in deep concentration, then he poked a finger into his own chest.

"I see," the judge replied. "Jake is your daddy?"

Ben nodded and pointed to the Lego tractor he'd dropped when running to Jake. The judge picked it up. "What's this?"

Ben looked at Jake again.

"Tell the judge it's a tractor. A tractor like Daddy has on his farm. Can you say *tractor?*"

Ben continued to stare at Jake.

Jake took the tractor from the judge and held it in his hand. "Tell Daddy what this is. Is it a tractor?" *Please, Ben, please. Keep talking. Our future depends on it.*

"'Ac-tor, 'A-dy." Those words were the most beautiful

sound Jake had ever heard in his life. Ben was talking again. Thank God, Ben was talking.

But the judge wasn't through.

He pointed to Elise. "Who is this lady?" he asked Ben.

Ben looked at Elise, deep in thought.

Elise smiled, waiting with her heart in her throat.

Ben smiled back.

"If this is Daddy—" the judge pointed to Jake "—who is this?" He looked at Elise.

Jake couldn't stand it. He whispered in Ben's ear, "Tell the judge who she is. You know her name. Say it for Daddy."

"E," Ben shouted, crawling into Elise's lap. "E," he said again, and Elise kissed his face over and over, oblivious to the fact that the judge and everyone else was watching. Jake would never forget this moment.

The judge stood. "Mrs. Turner, Dr. Ruskin, I want to see you in my office."

"Your Honor," Beau said, finally arriving. "I'm Beau McCain, Jake's brother and attorney, and I'd like to be present at this meeting."

"So would I," the Fosters' attorney spoke up.

"Fine, then," the judge replied. "We'll do it here." He marched to his bench. "I've been led to believe that Ben understands very little. As a matter of fact, he's been subdued and unresponsive whenever I've seen him, as he was in my office this morning, making me believe that assertion was correct. But it's very plain to see that Ben knows Jake is his father and he knows Elise McCain, too."

"'A-dy," Ben said, staring at the judge.

"Thank you, young Ben." Judge Reynolds smiled.

Jake whispered to Elise. "Take Ben in the hall. I don't want him to hear this."

Elise nodded and said to Ben, "Let's go play tractor."

She carried him toward the big doors. "How does a tractor go? Putt-putt-putt?"

"'Utt-'utt," Ben answered as the doors closed.

"I'm wondering a lot of things right now," the judge said. "My main concern is why Ben was different this afternoon than he was on my last visits. This morning he seemed almost—" He turned to Peggy. "Mrs. Foster, did you give Ben any medication before bringing him to my office?"

Peggy twisted her hands. "Just the medication Dr. Ruskin prescribed. Since Ben was going out in the weather, Dr. Ruskin didn't want him to catch a cold."

"Did you give Ben something the days I came to the house?"

"Yes, the same medication."

"Your Honor." Dr. Ruskin got to his feet. "It's just Tylenol. Ben is very susceptible to disease. His lung power isn't what it should be and we have to be careful."

"Why would he need the Tylenol when I came to the house?"

"Because Tylenol also helps to calm Ben when he becomes agitated, and you were a stranger so I wanted to insure that you had a good visit with him."

The judge focused his attention on the CPS caseworkers. "Mrs. Turner and Ms. Woods, every report I've received from you has indicated that a move or a change would be detrimental to Ben's health. Yet here's Ben in my courtroom and he's talking, and right now he's in the hall playing tractor with Mrs. McCain. Tell me why that doesn't add up."

Mrs. Turner stood. "Your Honor, Dr. Ruskin has been very particular about Ben's progress and we had no reason to doubt him."

"Didn't you visit with Ben yourself?"

"Of course, and we saw nothing to indicate otherwise."

"Then you're a poor social worker, Mrs. Turner."

Mrs. Turner paled. "Your Honor—"

"I've always been impressed with the work done by your office under extreme pressures, but you have grossly mishandled this case."

"Yes, Your Honor," Ms. Turner answered, and resumed her seat.

"I have a document that might shed some light on this." The judge reached for a folder on his desk. "I also have to appoint a guardian for Ben's estate."

Ben's estate. What the hell was he talking about? Until that moment, Jake had been listening in a state of shock. They had basically been drugging Ben. He couldn't get that out of his head. He remembered all the days Ben had been listless; now he knew why. A burning rage filled him. He tried to get to his feet, but Beau gripped his arm.

"Just listen," Beau said.

Jake frowned as he sank back. Evidently Beau knew what was going on.

"Before I can do that," the judge was saying, "I have to address a petition that's been filed against that estate. The petition allows that Mrs. Carr planned to allocate money in Ben's name for further research on developmental delay." The judge glanced up. "Is Mrs. Carr's attorney here?"

A man Jake hadn't even noticed stood up. "Yes, Your Honor, I'm Ted Garver and I've worked for Mrs. Carr since the inception of the trust."

Jake didn't understand any of this.

"Did Mrs. Carr plan to donate money to Dr. Ruskin's clinic?" Judge Reynolds asked.

"She was very dedicated to research for developmental delay, but she never asked me to stipulate such a bequest on paper."

"Did she ever confide her wish to fund research?"

The lawyer glanced at Dr. Ruskin for a brief second. "No."

Dr. Ruskin jumped to his feet. "You know she did!"

"I don't know any such thing," the lawyer responded. "Mrs. Carr's life was Ben and his welfare. That's all she ever talked about."

"She gave me power of attorney," Dr. Ruskin stated

fiercely. "She did that for a reason—to ensure Ben received the medical treatment he needed. She wanted the same for other children."

"Dr. Ruskin." The judge's voice rang out. "In light of this evidence, it is my belief that you have tried to perpetrate a fraud on this court."

"Your Honor, no, that was never my intent." Dr. Ruskin spoke in his own defense. "My life is treating children other doctors have given up on. Ben has been a shining example, and my only desire was for Ben to continue progressing. Irene Carr and I were writing a book to inform parents that there's hope for children who are diagnosed with developmental delay."

Jake couldn't stay quiet any longer. "Excuse me, Your Honor," he said politely, struggling to keep his anger at bay. "I don't mean to interrupt, but this is the first I've heard of an estate."

The judge glared at Mrs. Turner. "Mr. McCain was not informed of Ben's financial situation?"

"Your Honor, I was uncertain of what to divulge to Mr. McCain. I didn't want the money to be a deciding factor in his decision to see Ben. I had to be positive his motives were sincere."

"Mrs. Turner, the first time I spoke with Mr. McCain, I could see his only motive was his love for Ben. Money wouldn't have made a difference. As a social worker, you should have seen that. I will be drafting a censure to your superiors."

"Yes, Your Honor."

Jake stared at the judge. "How much money are we discussing?"

The judge glanced down. "It started at 2.4 million, but it's unclear what the figure is now."

Beau stood. "Your Honor, I think I can help clarify the situation."

"By all means, Mr. McCain."

Beau placed a folder in front of the judge; he looked through the contents.

"When my brother first told me about Ben's circumstances, it struck me as odd that a woman so devoted to Ben wouldn't leave a will stipulating who should have custody of him. She knew she was dying, yet she did nothing. I kept asking myself why, and finally I did some checking. What I found is in the folder."

The judge raised his head. "Go ahead, Mr. McCain."

"My brother and mother came with me to Houston to be here for Jake and Elise."

Jake stiffened when he heard Beau say his mother and Caleb were here. Beau had failed to mention that earlier, but he couldn't dredge up much anger. Too much was at stake.

"My brother Caleb is a police officer, which helped in my quest for answers tremendously, and my mother talked to Mrs. Carr's neighbor and her dearest friend, Gladys Simpson, and Gladys's husband. The Simpsons met Mrs. Carr three years ago when she moved next door. She was struggling to make ends meets and caring for a grandson who had to have constant attention. The Simpsons helped her when she needed someone. They sat with Ben so she could get some rest. Then a miracle happened. A lawsuit, which had been ongoing for ten years, was suddenly settled. Mrs. Carr's husband was a truck driver and he had been killed in a freak accident caused by faulty brakes. The trucking company finally honored Mrs. Carr's claim and she was awarded 2.4 million dollars after the lawyers' share. At the time, Ben was four months old and not doing well. Dr. Ruskin's fee was expensive and Mrs. Carr was saving money so Dr. Ruskin would treat Ben on a daily basis. When Mrs. Carr received the money, Dr. Ruskin gladly began to treat Ben regularly. He had phenomenal results, mainly because Mrs. Carr worked tirelessly for Ben's improvement."

Beau placed another piece of paper in front of the judge.

"The more money Mrs. Carr gave Dr. Ruskin, the more he demanded. He traveled all over the world in the name of research for developmental delay. Here's a list of his trips, which I obtained easily from his travel agency. I'm not sure how much research was done in the Cayman Islands or the other exotic locations." Beau paused, letting the information sink in. "In the folder is a statement from the Simpsons. If you need them to testify, they're willing. Their statement explains that when Mrs. Carr became ill, Dr. Ruskin insisted she give him power of attorney. When she hesitated, he said he'd stop treating Ben if she didn't."

"That's a lie!" Dr. Ruskin said heatedly.

Instead of answering, Beau placed another piece of paper in front of the judge. "That's a statement from Ella Timms, who's a hospice volunteer and was at Mrs. Carr's house the day she signed the power of attorney. She told Mrs. Timms she didn't want to sign it, but felt she had no choice."

"Anything to say, Dr. Ruskin?" Judge Reynolds asked.

"They're lying. I didn't force Irene to sign the paper."

Judge Reynolds picked up a form. "I'm looking at a list of withdrawals from Benjamin McCain's account, withdrawals made since Mrs. Carr's death. Are these lies, too?"

"No one had access to that account but Irene and me, and I authorized nothing."

"You're wrong, Dr. Ruskin," Beau said. "Two weeks before she died, Irene Carr gave Gladys Simpson access to the account. According to Mrs. Simpson, Mrs. Carr wanted her to keep an eye on the money for Ben's sake. That's how I was able to get the records."

Dr. Ruskin grew quiet.

"Why hasn't Mrs. Simpson come forward before now?" the judge inquired.

"A week after Mrs. Carr passed away, Mrs. Simpson's daughter and grandchild were in a bad car accident. The daughter lives in Bay City, and the older couple is taking care of them there. We only caught the Simpsons because they were in Houston to check on their house. Mrs. Simpson had called Mrs. Foster several times and was told that the situation was under control and that they'd be adopting Ben. The Simpsons weren't even aware that Ben's father had been found.''

''I see,'' the judge said, and frowned. ''Is this the remaining balance?''

''Yes, Your Honor,'' Beau said. ''As of today there's one hundred and ten thousand left in the trust.''

''Can you explain any of this, Dr. Ruskin?'' the judge demanded.

Before Dr. Ruskin could respond, Beau cut in. ''Your Honor, could I add one more thing?''

''Yes, Mr. McCain.'' The judge sighed.

''The Fosters' daughter, Nancy Bailey, also stated that Dr. Ruskin promised her parents Irene Carr's house if they'd offer to adopt Ben and said he'd hire someone to help them with Ben.''

The judge shook his head. ''This gets murkier and murkier. Dr. Ruskin, is this true?''

''I've done nothing wrong,'' Dr. Ruskin mumbled.

Judge Reynolds waited a second, then spoke to Beau. ''Mr. McCain, you haven't answered your original question. Why didn't Mrs. Carr secure Ben's future in writing? I'm sure you have an answer for me.''

''Yes, Your Honor,'' Beau replied. ''According to Mrs. Simpson, Irene wanted Ben's father located. Her daughter wasn't positive who the father was, but Jake McCain's name was on Ben's birth certificate. Mrs. Carr had to have proof that Jake was the father. She asked CPS to find him and also asked her attorney to hire a P.I. Between the two, Mrs. Carr was certain he'd be found and a DNA test could be done. She wanted Ben with his father. She just ran out of time. I'm not sure why Jake wasn't found before her death. It's not like he was in hiding.''

''Mr. Garver,'' the judge said.

Ted Garver rose in a nervous movement.

Judge Reynolds lifted an eyebrow. ''Did Dr. Ruskin ask you not to find Mr. McCain?''

''Yes, Your Honor,'' Ted replied. ''I...I...''

''Sit down, Mr. Garver.''

''Could I please add another note?'' Beau broke in.

''I don't think I can stop you, Mr. McCain.''

''Irene Carr wasn't sure Jake McCain was Ben's father. That was the only reason she didn't put anything in writing. She misjudged how much time she had left to secure the boy's future, but she'd set the wheels in motion and that's why we're here today—to decide Ben's future. CPS finally did something right.''

The more Jake heard the angrier he became. He stood and faced Dr. Ruskin. ''This hasn't been about Ben at all. It's been about money—the money you used for personal reasons in the name of developmental delay research. As long as you had control and kept Ben in that house, no one would discover that the money was almost gone. You were willing to sacrifice Ben's happiness, his future, to maintain that control—that secret. You even went so far as to overmedicate him so others couldn't see the real Ben, a little boy who should be out and playing with kids his age. The terrible part is that you tried to keep me away from my son. And the Fosters helped you. Even CPS helped you. They trusted you because you're supposed to have a doctor's ethics, but you're a greedy, conniving, selfish bastard.'' As he said the last word, he moved toward Dr. Ruskin, feeling anger boiling through him like he never felt before.

Beau jumped in front of him. ''Calm down, Jake. Hurting him is not going to help.''

''Mr. McCain, I—'' Dr. Ruskin began.

''Shut up,'' Jake yelled, trying to reach Dr. Ruskin, but Beau held him back. ''I don't want to hear a word you have to say.'' Jake didn't even realize he was yelling until he heard his voice reverberate around the room. He had to take several deep breaths to still the rage in him.

"Have a seat, Mr. McCain," the judge ordered. "Now."

"Dr. Ruskin, I will be notifying the AMA and the police department, ordering a full investigation into your medical practice and the handling of Ben's estate. Do not leave town. This is far from over." He motioned to the bailiff. "Bring Mrs. McCain and Ben in. I'm ready to rule."

ELISE SAT ON THE FLOOR, her legs stretched out, her back to a wall. Ben played beside her, running the tractor over her legs, murmuring, "'Utt-'utt-'utt."

People strolled by and stared. Ben didn't notice; Elise didn't care. She had to keep Ben occupied, but her ears were attuned to the room behind the double doors. She couldn't hear a sound. What was going on?

The door finally opened and the bailiff said, "The judge wants you in the courtroom."

Elise quickly pushed to her feet and straightened her suit. She drew a steadying breath, took Ben's hand and they returned to the proceedings. Ben ran to Jake, and Elise sat beside them.

"'Ac-tor, 'A-dy," Ben said, showing Jake the tractor.

"Yes," Jake murmured, loving the sound of that tiny voice. He wanted to leave this room with his son and Elise and never look back. But he had to wait for the judge's decision.

"Mr. McCain, I told you I always make a decision based on facts," the judge said. "Today I'm not doing that, because the facts have been distorted, manipulated and just plain fabricated. I've worked in family court for a lot of years and I've found that I can learn more from listening to the children. That's why I wanted to see Ben one more time, why I brought him into my court, something I don't normally do. Ben proved all those facts wrong." He glanced at Jake. "I award full custody of Benjamin McCain to his father, Jake McCain. And from this day forward, Jake McCain has full control of Ben McCain's estate. I trust, Mr. McCain, that you will use what's left of Ben's money for his medical problems and to meet his needs. I have two stipulations. I don't see any reason for Ben not to live with you and your wife on your farm, but I advise you to take it slow, to give Ben time to adjust. The second condition is I want Ben evaluated by another doctor. My office will schedule an appointment and notify you. This has to be done before you leave Houston. In three months, I'm also requesting an evaluation by CPS of Ben and his progress. Other than that, you're free to leave with your son."

"Thank you, Judge Reynolds," Jake said. *Thank God. Thank God.* Enormous relief trembled through him and he reached for Elise while holding Ben. They clung together. It was over. They had their son.

"YOUR HONOR," PEGGY CALLED. "My husband and I have taken care of Ben for weeks, like Irene asked us to. We let our apartment go because Dr. Ruskin promised us the house. I realize now that he was manipulating us, but that doesn't make it right. Could we please stay in the house until we find another place to live?"

"Mrs. Foster, that's Mr. McCain's decision. This hearing is adjourned."

The courtroom quickly emptied, and Peggy and Carl walked over to Jake and Elise. "I guess you want us out of the house," Peggy said.

"Yes," Jake answered, controlling his temper. He and Elise had Ben. That was all that mattered. "I want the house keys and Ben's car seat." He was unaware that his words sounded harsh. All he could feel was that these people had helped Dr. Ruskin to try to take his son from him and he wasn't inclined to be tolerant.

Peggy dug in her purse and found the keys. "Here's mine," she said somberly. "Do you mind if we keep Carl's until we remove our things?"

Jake gritted his teeth. "No, that will be fine."

Peggy nodded. "We'll get the car seat."

Jake turned, and his whole body froze. Three people

stood at the back of the courtroom, Beau, his mother and Caleb. The past and the present collided inside him, triggering so many confused feelings—betrayal, longing, grief and more—and he knew he couldn't face his mother right now. He wanted to be alone with Elise and Ben.

Beau saw the expression on Jake's face and walked over to him. ''Mom and Caleb did a lot of work on your behalf in a matter of hours. The least you can do is be civil.''

The past would not let go and a chill spread through his whole body, leaving him cold and unresponsive. ''I want to be left alone'' was all he could say.

Beau shook his head tiredly and moved away; Althea and Caleb followed him.

Elise quickly took Ben from Jake. ''Go after them,'' she said strongly. ''Say thank you. That's all you have to say.'' Jake stiffened, unsure if he could do what she was asking. ''Jake, for our family, you have to do this. Now.'' As she said the last word, she gave him a nudge.

Jake looked at Elise and Ben and their shining faces warmed his heart, his body and his soul, making him aware of how much he had…of how much he owed everyone, including his mother and Caleb. Before he could stop himself, he moved toward the doors. He reached them at the elevator, but the warmth of the moment became chilled by memories of the past. For the first time in his life, he forced it back. He had to. He didn't like feeling the way he did.

''Thank…you,'' he said tautly. ''I…appreciate what you did today for Ben, Elise and me.''

Caleb stepped forward and shook Jake's hand. ''I'm glad you have your son.''

''Thank you,'' Jake said again, unable to keep the stiffness out of his voice. He looked from Caleb to his mother, then wished he hadn't. He saw the sadness and pain in her eyes and this time he wasn't able to ignore it. She was hurting. That made him feel rotten, but words still wouldn't come.

At that moment, Elise walked from the courtroom holding Ben's hand. Ben ran to Jake and wrapped his arms around his father's leg. Jake gathered him close.

''He favors you so much when you were that age,'' Althea said, her eyes on Ben's face.

The elevator doors opened. ''We'd better go,'' Beau said suddenly. ''I'll talk to you in Waco.''

''Thanks,'' Jake called as the doors closed. The stiffness was gone and he felt a sense of exhilaration. There was hope—hope the past would not plague him forever.

''That wasn't so bad, was it?'' Elise asked.

Jake smiled. ''No.''

Before he could say anything else, the Fosters got off the elevator, carrying the car seat. ''Thank you,'' Jake said, letting go of his resentment toward the Fosters. They'd been there for Ben when he'd needed someone. Even after what they'd done, he couldn't dismiss that. ''You can stay in the house until you find another place to live. I appreciate that you cared for Ben until I could be located.''

Peggy's eyes widened. ''Oh, thank you, Jake.'' It was the first time he'd seen anything akin to a smile on her face.

''But Elise and I will be staying there until we move Ben to the farm.''

''Yes, yes, we understand, and we won't be a bother,'' Peggy added as they quickly left.

''That was very nice of you,'' Elise said.

''The judge said to take it slow and that's what I'm doing.'' He brushed back Ben's hair. ''Are you ready, son?''

Ben nodded.

Jake stared into Elise's shining eyes. ''Then let's go home.''

CHAPTER TWELVE

THINGS WERE HECTIC WHEN they returned to the house. Ben was running everywhere and jabbering nonstop, which was so good to hear. They couldn't understand him most of the time, but at least he was being vocal. Jake called Aunt Vin and gave her the good news. Peggy and Carl came in and the atmosphere became chilly.

"I'm not pleased that you worked with Dr. Ruskin to take Ben from me," Jake told them.

"We're so sorry," Peggy said nervously. "It wasn't just about getting the house. We do love Ben and we wanted to adopt him, to give him the life Irene had worked so hard for."

Jake believed her; if they hadn't felt that way, they wouldn't have taken such good care of him, and he had to admit they had. He'd thought they were too strict and too stern, but he'd also witnessed their love. He would always be grateful Ben had the Fosters. Jake now understood their attitude toward him a little better, too. It had been instigated by Dr. Ruskin. "As I said, I appreciate what you've done for Ben, but I just wish you'd given me a chance."

"Dr. Ruskin told us so many lies," Carl said.

"Yes," Jake admitted. "We were all taken in by Dr. Ruskin."

"Thank you for letting us stay here until we can find a place," Carl added.

"Let's just try to get along," Jake replied.

After that, the mood in the house improved. Peggy fixed

dinner and Elise watched as she prepared Ben's food. She intended to learn all she could about how to care for him.

Later, the Fosters went to their room, and Jake and Elise gave Ben a bath and dressed him for bed. The house was a split-level, with a bedroom and bath on one side and two bedrooms and a bath on the other. Mrs. Carr and Ben had occupied those two bedrooms, and Jake and Elsie moved their things into her room. Ben fell asleep in Elise's arms as she was reading him a story. She tucked him gently into his crib, hardly able to believe how much she already loved this child. It was an all-consuming emotion she'd thought she would never experience.

A few years ago, she would have laughed if someone had told her she'd ever want to be a mother. Some women needed motherhood, but not her; she'd convinced herself of that. She had her career, and she emphasized strong, independent women in her teaching of American literature of the late nineteenth century. Most of her students knew about the nineteenth-century male authors like Mark Twain, but fewer were aware of the women. Louisa May Alcott was Elise's favorite, and she'd published several articles on the influence of Alcott's writing.

Her life was busy and full—or so she'd believed until she met Jake McCain. When she met him, she started dreaming of babies, rekindling the idea Derek had instilled in her, and thinking about other things besides literature, which shocked her since she'd spent so many years absorbed in it. Now she had something equally fulfilling—Ben. And she loved him with all her heart.

She looked up at Jake and wondered how he felt about her, then dismissed the question. They cared for each other and they would raise Ben in a loving environment. Something in her wanted more, but for now she couldn't concentrate on what that was. Ben required her full attention.

Afterward, they sat on the bed in Mrs. Carr's room and talked until midnight. Jake told her what had happened in the courtroom and how enraged he'd become at Dr. Ruskin.

He also told her about Althea and Caleb and admitted that he couldn't keep holding on to the hatreds of the past. He fell asleep in her arms, much the same as Ben had, and the question resurfaced. How did Jake really feel? Would he ever be able to love after what his mother had done to him? She wished she had an answer.

JAKE AWOKE TO MOVEMENT. Elise was curled into his side—so why was the bed moving? He raised his head and saw Ben on his knees bouncing up and down on their bed. Alarmed, Jake quickly sat up. Ben couldn't climb out of his crib. So how did he get into their room?

"Ben, how did you get here?" he asked softly.

Ben stopped bouncing and smiled at him.

"Did you climb out of your bed?"

"'A-dy E," Ben answered.

Elise stirred. "Ben," she said, surprised, then she glanced at Jake. "Did you wake Ben?" she asked.

"No, I think Ben climbed out of his crib all by himself. Didn't you, Ben?"

Ben nodded and wedged himself between Jake and Elise. Elise gathered him in her arms.

Jake stared at the two of them and the beautiful picture they made. Elise was born to be a mother with her tenderness and compassion. It was a shame she'd thought otherwise for so many years. Slipping from the bed, he said, "I'll go make coffee."

On the way to the kitchen he was smiling. Ben had climbed out of his crib. For a normal child that wouldn't be a good thing, but for Ben it was a milestone because he'd done it by himself. Of course, now they'd have to be careful and make sure he understood that he had to stay in his bed. He'd definitely have to buy a book on parenting because he didn't have a clue about discipline and he was sure Elise didn't, either.

Elise sang nursery rhymes until Ben got bored. He wriggled off the bed and stood transfixed, staring at something.

Elise turned her head to see what it was. A picture of Mrs. Carr and Ben stood on the nightstand. Ben pointed at the photo.

"'Anny." Elise assumed that's what he called his grandmother. "'Anny...go." As he spoke, tears rolled down his cheeks and he started to cry. Elise scrambled off the bed and held him. His body trembled and loud sobs racked his body. "'Anny, 'Anny, 'Anny," he sobbed.

When Jake heard the cries, he ran for the bedroom. Elise was on the floor holding Ben and his face was buried in her shoulder as he cried. Jake sank down and wrapped his arms around them. "It's all right, Ben. Daddy's here," he said hoarsely, the tortured sobs tearing his heart out.

Ben continued to sob.

"Shh, shh," Elise cooed, stroking his back.

"What happened?" Jake asked Elise.

"He saw the picture and I think he's finally admitting that she's gone." She held Ben close, the sobs almost more than she could bear, but something in her knew Ben had to do this. His not speaking had been in defiance of Mrs. Carr's death and now that he was speaking again, the truth had surfaced.

They sat on the floor until the sobs ebbed. The Fosters appeared in the doorway in their nightclothes and Jake told them everything was fine, but he wasn't sure.

"I'll fix breakfast," Peggy said as they left.

Jake caressed Ben's wet cheek. "Daddy loves you."

"'Anny go," Ben hiccuped.

Jake had to swallow before he could speak. "She loved you, too." He wanted Ben always to know that. He was uncertain how to explain death to a child and he was glad when Elise stepped in.

She kissed his face. "E loves you."

Ben rubbed his face against her and rested his head on her chest in total contentment. This was what Ben needed—a woman's touch.

The rest of the day went smoothly and the trauma of the

The Harlequin Reader Service® — Here's how it works:

Accepting your 2 free books and mystery gift places you under no obligation to buy anything. You may keep the books and gift and return the shipping statement marked "cancel." If you do not cancel, about a month later we'll send you 6 additional books and bill you just $4.47 each in the U.S., or $4.99 each in Canada, plus 25¢ shipping & handling per book and applicable taxes if any.* That's the complete price and — compared to cover prices of $5.25 each in the U.S. and $6.25 each in Canada — it's quite a bargain! You may cancel at any time, but if you choose to continue, every month we'll send you 6 more books, which you may either purchase at the discount price or return to us and cancel your subscription.

*Terms and prices subject to change without notice. Sales tax applicable in N.Y. Canadian residents will be charged applicable provincial taxes and GST. Credit or debit balances in a customer's account(s) may be offset by any other outstanding balance owed by or to the customer.

If offer card is missing write to: Harlequin Reader Service, 3010 Walden Ave., P.O. Box 1867, Buffalo NY 14240-1867

BUSINESS REPLY MAIL

FIRST-CLASS MAIL PERMIT NO. 717-003 BUFFALO, NY

POSTAGE WILL BE PAID BY ADDRESSEE

HARLEQUIN READER SERVICE
3010 WALDEN AVE
PO BOX 1867
BUFFALO NY 14240-9952

morning was soon put aside, except for the knot in Jake's stomach. He was glad when Judge Reynolds's office called and said that Ben had an appointment with a Dr. Henry Giles at ten on Wednesday. Jake was relieved it was soon, because he wanted Ben out of this house and away from these memories as soon as possible.

Jake called Mike to get an update on the farm operations. The cotton was now stored in the warehouse and waiting to be sold. The two men went over a few details and agreed that they'd wait until Jake returned to handle the sale. It was hell trying to run the farm from this distance, but he planned to take his family home soon.

That night they put Ben to bed, but he was back in their room in a matter of minutes. He did that four times before they finally had to admit they had a problem.

"What do you think?" Jake asked Elise.

Elise shrugged. "I don't know. After this morning, I'm afraid to force anything."

"Me, too, but something's wrong and we have to figure out what." He raised an eyebrow. "I guess this is our first lesson in parenting."

Before Elise could response, Ben bounced into the room and crawled on their bed, staring at them with big eyes.

"Ben, do you understand that Daddy said you should stay in your bed?"

Ben just stared.

Elise scooted closer. "What's wrong? Don't you like your bed?"

"'A-dy E," Ben replied. That was what he was beginning to call them, as if they were one person.

"Daddy and E sleep in here," Jake said patiently. "Ben sleeps in there." He pointed across the hall.

"'A-dy E," Ben said again.

Jake shook his head, not sure what Ben meant by that. He glanced at Elise as she stroked Ben's hair. "What's wrong, Ben? Are you afraid?"

Ben didn't answer.

She kissed his cheek. "Tell me what's wrong."

"'A-dy E go no," Ben mumbled.

Jake and Elise stared at each other, trying to figure out what Ben was saying. Sometimes Ben got his words wrong or put them in the wrong order. *'A-dy E no go.* The reality of that dawned on both of them at the same time. Ben was used to Jake and Elise leaving—the way they'd done when they visited him. He was afraid they'd go and never come back, maybe as Mrs. Carr had done.

Jake pulled Ben to him with a lump in his throat. "Do you remember yesterday when you told that man I was your daddy?"

Ben nodded.

"That meant that Ben McCain has a daddy and that daddy is never going to leave him." He turned Ben's face up to his. "Do you understand that I will never leave you again?"

Ben nodded.

"Elise and I will be here when you wake up and we'll be here when you go to bed. We'll always be here because you're our little boy. We're your parents and we love you."

"'A-dy E no go," Ben said, but this time it was a statement.

"That's right," Jake answered. "'A-dy E no go." He didn't know exactly how much Ben understood of his reassurances, but he hoped he could understand this. "Now do you think you can sleep in your crib?"

Ben wriggled off the bed and ran to his room.

Jake smiled at Elise. "I guess that's a yes."

She smiled back. "We'd better tuck him in again."

Afterward they went to their room and waited. Sitting against the headboard, they held their breaths and counted. Three minutes...six minutes...ten minutes...Ben was staying in his bed.

Jake gave a sigh of relief. "It's working."

"Yes, I think Ben understands a lot more than Dr. Ruskin or anyone gives him credit for."

"I feel the same way, and I hope we don't have to go through what happened this morning again. I can still hear his pitiful cries."

"Me, too," Elise said quietly. "Ben had to say goodbye in his own way."

Jake turned to her. "I'm so glad you were here. Beau said women are the nurturers and now I understand what he meant."

Her eyes held his. "What did he mean?"

"That women give life, a feat no man will ever equal, and they're equipped to nourish that life. Other than the obvious, they're soft, gentle, warm and..."

When he paused, she asked, "Do you see me like that?"

He stared into her hopeful eyes, wondering how she could've ever doubted it. She was everything a woman should be and he wanted her to know that. "Yes," he replied hoarsely. "I thought I could take care of Ben alone, but I see now that I couldn't. Ben needs a mother. When he was upset, it was your solace, your touch that calmed him."

She expelled a long breath, feeling vindicated, renewed and uplifted by his words. She ran her fingertips along his jaw, then followed it with her lips, feeling her senses spin with need and desire.

"Elise," he groaned, and unable to stop himself, he dipped his head and kissed her tenderly, needing that contact more than he needed anything at the moment. Her lips softened and she returned the kiss with an urgency that had him gasping for air. "I want you like hell," he muttered.

"Me, too."

He drew back and gazed at her wet lips. "We can't take any risks." As much as he wanted her, he was glad to use that excuse. For some reason he could almost feel Derek's ghost in the bed with them. He'd made love to her before knowing how she felt. Why was it so hard now?

"I know," she breathed. "One of us has to buy condoms."

He slipped out of bed and reached for his robe. "I'm putting that at the top of my to-do list." He was tired of fighting his desire for her and soon, ghost or not, he was making love to his wife. "I'm going to fix a snack. You should try to go to sleep." He moved toward the door.

Her body ached for him, but they couldn't take any chances. Somehow that didn't bring her any relief. She pushed up against the headboard and remembered that he did that a lot—made late-night snacks. It was always something like milk and crackers and cheese or fruit. Sometimes she joined him with a bowl of ice cream, not even thinking about the calories. She just enjoyed being with him.

"Jake."

"Hmm." He stopped in the doorway.

She realized what she was about to say and the words burned like acid in her throat, searing until they slowly emerged. *I love you.* Oh God, no, she didn't love Jake. She loved Derek. She would always love Derek. The pain in her throat eased with the admission, but it only created more pain in her heart.

"Elise?" Jake prompted when she remained silent.

She swallowed. "Nothing," she said weakly. "We'll talk later."

"Okay." He watched the paleness of her face for a second, then walked out.

She sank back against the pillows. When had these strong feelings for Jake begun? She *more* than cared deeply for Jake—a lot more. That was why she'd been in such turmoil over his losing Ben.

She remembered that very first day when he'd stepped out of his truck and said, "Can I help you, ma'am?" Her body had connected with him before her heart and her mind did, but her loyalty to Derek wouldn't allow her to admit what she was really feeling. And she couldn't do it now, either.

Now what did she do? She should march into the kitchen and talk to Jake, but what would that accomplish? They had so much on their minds—like seeing a new doctor, the move to the farm and getting Ben settled there—before they could think about themselves. And she wasn't sure how Jake felt. He desired her. She was very much aware of that, but after what he'd endured as a small boy, she wondered if he still believed in love.

Love. She stopped for a moment as she let herself think about what she was feeling. Did she want Jake's love? *Oh, Derek. I'm sorry.* She wanted that more than anything. But Jake could never replace Derek in her heart.

He already has, a voice whispered inside her head.

ELISE PUSHED THE CONFLICTING emotions aside, but at the oddest times she'd found herself watching Jake; changing Ben's diaper, talking with the Fosters. His gentleness, his kindness, was in everything he did. After last night, she seemed more attuned to his every move, but the past still had a strong hold on her.

They spent Wednesday at the doctor's office as Ben underwent test after test. He was a real trooper and it was clear that he was used to being in a medical office. By the end of the afternoon Ben grew tired and fell asleep as they talked to Dr. Giles. The doctor was astounded at Ben's progress, but he emphasized that the therapy, speech and hand-and-eye coordination, had to continue, and Jake assured him they planned to do nothing less. He gave them the name of a doctor and therapist in Waco and set up appointments. He asked to see Ben in six months and Jake agreed.

They had prepared Ben by telling him over and over that they were moving to Daddy's farm and he grew excited about the event. But Jake and Elise worried how Ben would actually feel when they left the house—the house that was so familiar to him.

That evening a detective came by to talk to Jake about Dr. Ruskin. Jake answered all his questions honestly and gave him his address and phone number in Waco. Jake decided to leave Dr. Ruskin and his affairs in the capable detective's hands. He just wanted to take his son home.

Ben eagerly helped to pack his things. He pulled clothes out of his closet and threw them on the floor. Elise stopped him and showed him how to fold the clothes neatly. Ben then wadded a shirt into a ball and dropped it in the suitcase. Clearly Ben did not grasp the folding technique, but Elise had fun just watching him.

They only took the items Ben would need for a few days; the moving van was coming tomorrow to bring the rest. Peggy offered to supervise the movers and Jake thanked her for her kindness. They were getting along in a way they hadn't when Jake had first come here. The Fosters apologized for their involvement with Dr. Ruskin again and again, and Jake knew they were sincere. Greed had blinded them and they admitted that.

Jake and Elise planned to leave in the morning. Elise and Peggy fixed breakfast and everyone was quiet except Ben, who chatted on.

"Go me 'A-dy 'arm," Ben said.

While she was packing Mrs. Carr's tapes on lessons for speech therapy with Ben, Elise listened to a few and she learned that Mrs. Carr used a turnaround signal with her two forefingers to let Ben know when the words were in the wrong order. Elise made the signal.

"Me go 'A-dy 'arm," Ben said correctly.

Elise kissed the top of his head. "Yes, sweetie. We're going to Daddy's farm."

Carl helped Jake put everything in the truck and goodbyes were said. Ben hugged the Fosters tightly, then went to Jake, who buckled him in his car seat. Ben had the tractor and teddy bear in his arms. He was not forgetting those two treasured possessions.

Jake and Elise stood by the truck and stared at each other, and it seemed they were both thinking the same thing. "We don't have any need for this house, do we?" he asked.

"Do what you feel is right," was her answer.

Jake went to the door, knowing he was learning to forgive, learning to accept that people had faults and sometimes made bad decisions.

"Did you forget something?" Peggy asked anxiously.

"Yes," Jake replied. "I don't think I made it clear how much I appreciate you caring for Ben until I was found."

"Yes, you have," Peggy assured him, "and even though our motives weren't the best, we took good care of Ben."

"And for that I'm going to give you the house."

"What!" Peggy held a hand to her chest.

"I have no use for the house."

"But you can sell it," Carl told him.

"Yes, but this isn't about money. It's about my gratitude."

Peggy wiped away a tear and seemed at a loss for words.

"As I said before, I wished you'd given me a chance when I first met you."

"We do, too," Peggy sniffed, then she hugged Jake. "Thank you."

"You're welcome, and my lawyer will be in touch with the details." He walked away, feeling good about himself.

AS THEY DROVE AWAY Elise noticed Christmas decorations in people's yards. It was almost Christmastime. She'd forgotten that. Their first Christmas together as husband and wife—and as a family.

The truck was a four-door cab and she sat in the back with Ben so he wouldn't feel alone. She pointed out the decorations to Ben and he watched avidly, but he became more interested in the cars and trucks on the freeway.

"'Utt-'utt," he said, pointing to the cars.

"Cars go vroom-vroom," Elise told him. "They go fast."

"'Room-'room," Ben repeated. "'A-dy, 'room, 'room."

"Yes, Ben, I see." Jake smiled in his rearview mirror, relieved that he didn't seem upset leaving the house.

At a roadside park outside College Station, they stopped so Ben could stretch his legs and have a snack. Ben could hardly eat his chocolate pudding for staring at the cows across the highway. Ben seemed to love animals and Jake looked forward to introducing Wags to him.

It was almost noon when they reached the farm. A tractor was plowing in the field and Ben immediately saw it.

"'Ac-tor, 'A-dy E, 'ac-tor" he cried excitedly.

"Yes, we see it," Elise said.

"'Utt-'utt-'utt-'utt," Ben chanted as they drove to the barn. A big John Deere tractor was parked outside; Jake had phoned ahead and told Mike to have one ready. Ben was about to take his first ride on a tractor.

Ben could hardly stay still as Elise unbuckled him, and he clambered out into Jake's arms. "'Ac-tor, 'A-dy, 'ac-tor."

"Want to ride in the tractor?" Jake asked.

Ben nodded.

Jake touched his finger to Ben's lips, another technique they'd learned from the tapes.

"Yes," Ben said.

Jake took a couple of steps and Ben started to shout, "E, E, E, E," looking back at the truck. Elise hurriedly got out and went to him.

"He wants you to go, too," Jake said, smiling into her eyes. "Fancy a tractor ride?"

"Sure," she answered as her heart skipped a beat.

A man in his thirties walked up to them. "Mike, this is my wife, Elise." Jake made the introductions.

Mike tipped his hat. "Nice to meet you, ma'am."

"Likewise," Elise smiled.

"And this is Ben."

"Hi there, Ben," Mike said.

Ben raised a hand and Jake touched his lips. "'I," Ben said, burying his face in Jake's shoulder.

Ben's shyness was understandable. "We're going for a tractor ride," Jake said to Mike.

"Okay." Mike grinned. "I'll be in the barn if you need me."

"Thanks, Mike," Jake called.

Jake looked at Elise. "Ready?"

She'd never been on a tractor in her life, but she would do whatever Ben asked her to, even climb the monster machine, which had tires bigger than anything she'd seen in her life. Once inside the glassed-in cab she found it had air-conditioning and heating. The computer astonished her. Modern farming wasn't anything like she'd imagined. Jake told her the computer was programmed to take the guesswork out of planting and fertilizing, and it saved a lot of time.

With the turn of a key, the tractor roared to life. Ben sat in Jake's lap and his mouth formed a permanent O as Jake drove the tractor around the barn and into the field. Elise enjoyed seeing the farm from this height. Cotton fields stretched into the distance, and several tractors were at work plowing and shredding. She suddenly understood that Jake operated a large farm that took a lot of knowledge and effort, and she wished she'd listened to him more in the past. Now she would.

Finally they made their way to the house. Jake had been on the phone several times with Aunt Vin and Beau, preparing the house for Ben's homecoming. They walked into a quiet kitchen.

"Aunt Vin," Jake called.

Wags bounded through the door and jumped up on Jake, trying to reach Ben. "Down, boy," Jake ordered, placing Ben on the floor in front of Wags. "Ben, this is Wags."

"'Og-y," Ben said, wrapping his arms around Wag's neck. Wags moved his head and Ben tumbled on top of him.

Elise immediately bent to help Ben, but Jake held her back. Wags licked Ben's face and Ben started to giggle.

Wags's tail pounded out a rhythm on the kitchen floor as the two became fast friends.

Aunt Vin appeared in the doorway. "Wags, get off him," she shouted.

"It's okay, they're just playing," Jake told her.

At the loud voice, Ben scurried to Jake. "This is Aunt Vin, Ben."

Ben raised a hand and Jake touched his lips. "'I."

"Oh, my." Tears gathered in Aunt Vin's eyes. "He's so darling." She took Ben out of Jake's arms and Ben didn't protest. "Did you have a good trip?"

Ben nodded and jabbered away. Aunt Vin obviously didn't have a clue as to what he was saying and neither did Jake or Elise. But that was okay. They would learn, and more importantly, Ben had made the move without a problem. Still, they worried about the night.

Ben loved his new room and the tractors and he became excited when he saw his big bed. "'Ig-'ig," he kept repeating.

That evening they tucked him in and waited. Wags lay at the foot of his bed as if he needed to be on guard, but Ben made no attempt to get out. He slept soundly, his tractor and teddy clutched in his arms. Ben was finally home.

And Elise felt she was, too.

CHAPTER THIRTEEN

THEY SPENT THE NEXT WEEK getting acquainted with Ben's new doctor, Richard Markham, and therapist, Sue Collins. The two professionals were very encouraging and Ben seemed to like them both. Ben had morning appointments with the therapist and he saw the doctor once a week. They were on a schedule, and Jake and Elise worked diligently, determined that Ben reach his goal of starting school with kids his own age. They had very little time for each other and when they did they were exhausted.

Jake had condoms in his pocket, in their nightstand and in his truck. He wasn't quite sure why he put them there, but he was prepared, waiting for the right moment. He'd made up his mind, and if it didn't happen soon, he was going to die from frustration.

They still hadn't gotten to the point where they could leave Ben. Wherever he was, they had to stay with him. But the speech therapist insisted her sessions be private. Even though they knew it was for the best, Jake and Elise found it hard to leave him. They waited in another room.

Part of Ben's therapy was with a little girl who stuttered. Sue Collins wanted to see how Ben reacted to other children. Ben and Valerie were both very shy and the therapist thought they'd do well together, and Ben needed to interact with children.

One morning when they took Ben into the therapy room, Valerie was already there, drawing pictures at a small table. The blue-eyed girl had blond hair and it was always in a ponytail. Ben ran to the table and sat down. He hardly ever fell these days unless he was in a hurry.

"Ben me." He said this every day.

Elise made the turnaround sign and Ben said again, "Me Ben."

"Me me me." Sue held up her hand and Valerie whispered, "Me Valerie."

Soon after, Sue motioned for Jake and Elise to leave. They kissed Ben and Valerie's mother came rushing through the door, a worn doll in her hand. She gave the doll to Valerie.

"Sorry, baby," she said. "Mommy forgot."

"Bye, Mommy," Valerie said, engrossed in a picture she was drawing.

Valerie's mother left, but Elise stopped as she noticed the look on Ben's face. He stared into space as if in a trance.

"Something's wrong," she said urgently, and moved toward Ben.

Jake caught her. "No, let Sue work with him."

"But..."

"Let the professionals do their job." He led her from the room.

"But what if he needs us?"

"We'll be right here and Sue will come and get us."

"I suppose," she muttered as she sat down, then stood up again. "Maybe I should check on him."

He pulled her back down. "No, sit with me."

She inhaled deeply, realizing he was trying to distract her. "I worry about him."

"I know." He threw an arm around her shoulder, then quickly withdrew it. That action didn't escape Elise. Recently, it seemed as if he tried to avoid touching her.

"Jake."

"Hmm?"

"Why'd you do that?"

"What?"

She arched an eyebrow.

He sighed at the knowing look in her eyes. "Okay." He had to tell her. "I can't keep touching you and not...it's driving me crazy."

"Then why haven't you done something about it?"

He leaned forward with his elbows resting on his knees, hands clasped, and stared down at the floor. How did he tell her? *Because Derek Weber's always between us.* How would she react if he told her that—if he told her he was so jealous of the man that he was beginning to really dislike him and he couldn't make love to her again unless... It hurt that Elise didn't love him.

He'd told Beau that he didn't expect her to love him. He'd lied. He wanted her love, he wanted everything. He already had a life with her; the rest he'd have to live with—like Derek's ghost. He'd already made that decision, that's why he'd bought the condoms. He just wished he could get the man out of his head. More importantly, he wished he could vanquish him from Elise's heart.

He had to get past that, though. Love was just his dream. They had Ben and that should be enough. But it wasn't.

Elise watched the struggle on his face and she was reminded of the conversation they'd had that night in his truck after her first visit with Ben. Something had been bothering him then and it still was. But she knew he wasn't going to tell her what that was until he was ready. He wasn't shutting her out, though.

"We're not teenagers, Jake, and there's no reason for us not to be man and wife in every sense." She kissed the side of his face softly.

"We've been busy." He tilted his head toward her, loving the feel of her breath on his skin.

"Tonight," she whispered. "After we put Ben down, you won't go to the barn to talk to Mike about some equipment that needs repairing or seed that's being ordered, and I won't be on the computer or talking to my teaching assistant. We'll spend some time alone and do what we do very well. Is it a date?"

"Yeah." He grinned. He couldn't keep wishing for the impossible and he couldn't keep depriving himself of something he wanted so badly.

They sat in silence, the tension easing—for now.

"We need to put up a tree and decorate," Elise said as she noticed a poinsettia on a table.

"When I was a kid and Beau and Mom were still living with us, we used to cut a tree from the woods and bring it home and decorate it. It was a big event."

Jake hadn't mentioned his mother since the hearing. Beau had been out to the house to see Ben, but nothing was said about Althea. Elise knew Althea wanted to see her grandson, but she wasn't calling, she wasn't intruding. She was giving them their privacy. Soon, though, they had to discuss Althea and the past, because Jake was starting to relent. The next step was for him to visit his mother and Elise would encourage that in very subtle ways.

Elise hadn't heard from her own mother, not since she'd talked to her about the Abbotts. She couldn't let the rift grow larger. She would make an attempt to reconcile, but in the end it would be Constance's choice. If she didn't accept Jake and Ben, then… In that instant Elise decided to make Christmas a big event for both families and maybe forgiveness would triumph.

"Let's do that," she said excitedly.

He drew back. "Cut down a tree?"

"Yes, Ben would love it."

"Okay," he agreed, joining in her enthusiasm. "We've got some nice big cedars in the pasture not far from the house and there are decorations in the attic and lights that go on the roof, too. We can decorate the whole house."

They talked more about Christmas and the tension completely disappeared, then Ben's session was over and he ran out to them. He seemed fine and Elise realized she'd overreacted. Ben was getting better every day; he was vibrant, more energetic, and he now had a friend, Valerie, whom he called Ree.

That night, Jake made his mind up. He was making love to his wife. If he didn't, sexual frustration was going to claim him. He felt excited and couldn't wait to put Ben to bed. They kissed and hugged him and tucked him in, a ritual they performed every night. Wags slept at the foot of the bed; he'd done this since Ben had come to the farm.

"'Night, Ben," Elise called as she and Jake left the room.

"'Ight, 'A-dy Mom-E."

Elise stopped in her tracks and whirled around. "What did he say?" she asked Jake in a trembling voice. He led her to the master bedroom and closed the door. "He called me Mommy," she said.

"Yeah. Now we know what today was about."

Elise frowned. "What do you mean?"

"He heard Valerie call her mother Mommy. He's finally connected that word to you. You're his mommy."

Elise started to cry as unbelievable joy filled her. She was a mommy. Ben's mommy. It was the greatest feeling in the world.

Jake pulled her to him. "Don't cry."

"I can't help it," she sniffled into his shoulder. "I'm so happy."

Jake gently kissed the tears from her face and she let her arms creep around his neck, giving herself up to this man who'd touched her in ways no man ever had—even Derek. He brought joy to her life and aroused her body to heights of pleasure until she was wanton, wild and brazen, so unlike the stoic, reserved woman she was known to be. She ran her hands up through his hair and pressed her body into his.

When she did that, Jake lost all conscious thought and he just wanted her. His hands cupped her buttocks and held her against the surging part of him. As he deepened the kiss, he heard a tapping sound.

It took a moment for Jake to realize it was a person at the door. He thought it was the sound of his heart beating. Slowly, he drew his lips away and rested his forehead on hers. ''Dammit. Not tonight.''

The tap came again.

''You'd better see who it is,'' she whispered, her voice husky.

He took a deep breath. ''Yeah.'' He walked to the door and yanked it open. Beau stood there.

''Sorry to interrupt,'' Beau said, ''but the lights are on and the doors aren't locked. I knocked and called, but no one answered and I was getting worried. Is everything okay?''

''Elise and I were...talking,'' Jake said. ''Ben's asleep and Aunt Vin's at bingo.''

''Oh, I dropped by for a visit. Guess I missed Ben.''

''He just went down.''

''Do you have a minute for a chat?'' Beau asked.

No. No. He'd waited forever, it seemed, and now... He glanced at Elise and she replied, ''Go ahead. I'll take a shower.''

''Are you sure?''

''Yes.'' She attempted a smile. ''Have a nice visit.''

Jake followed Beau to the kitchen and poured them a cup of coffee. ''Your timing's lousy.''

''Sorry. You should've said something.''

Jake sat at the table. ''Doesn't matter.'' The ache inside him told him differently and in his mind's eye he could see the warm water rushing over Elise's smooth, soft body.

''How are things going?'' Beau asked, sipping coffee.

Jake blinked. ''What?''

''How are things going?'' Beau repeated, giving him a strange look.

''Great. Better than I ever dreamed.''

''That's wonderful,'' Beau said. ''Mom will be glad to hear that.''

Anger didn't sweep through him the way it usually did

when Beau mentioned their mother. He rubbed his thumb over the warmth of the cup as a question nagged at him. To get his mind off Elise, he decided to ask Beau about something that had been bothering him. "Remember that night I met Caleb at your office building?"

"Sure."

"He took offense at me calling him my half brother. Why?"

Beau leaned back in his chair. "Think about it, Jake."

Jake was, finally, thinking about it a lot. "He acted as though we were full brothers."

"Haven't you ever wondered why he goes by the name McCain?"

"No. I try not to think about it at all, but now that I have Elise and Ben, I'm wondering."

"And what did you come up with?"

"Mom had Caleb before she married Wellman and I suppose she put Dad's name on the birth certificate at the time."

"C'mon, Jake, you're well aware that you can put anyone's name on a birth certificate. You don't have to be married."

Silence.

"So?" Jake finally asked.

"So what?"

"So what the hell is the truth?"

Beau rested his forearms on the table. "Okay, you want the truth. I'll tell you the truth. I'm damned tired of secrets." He looked Jake in the eyes. "Caleb is our full brother."

Jake paled under the impact of those words. "No," he uttered in denial. "Dad said she was pregnant with Wellman's child when she left."

"Dad told you a lot of garbage," Beau said. "Mom was pregnant, but with Joe McCain's son. She and Andrew hadn't even slept together."

"No, no, that can't be." Jake was still in denial. "Dad

said…" Suddenly the things he'd been told as a kid began to crumble before him, and he had trouble breathing. Lies. Were they all lies? He turned to Beau. "How?"

"You'll have to talk to Mom," Beau said. "The past is hers to tell."

"I don't understand why Mom didn't want Dad to know he had another son," Jake mumbled. "He thought Caleb was Wellman's."

Beau stood. "As I said, you'll have to talk to Mom. I've told you more than I should."

Jake's eyes burned with renewed anger. "Why the hell are there all these secrets? Secrets kept from me."

Beau shrugged. "You have to…"

"Talk to Mom," Jake finished. "You've been spouting that to me for so long, and I'm tired of it." He ran his hands over his face. "I'm tired of the whole damn thing."

"Then do something about it."

Silence fell again and Beau quietly left.

In a daze, Jake walked to the den and sank into his chair. Caleb was his brother—his full brother—and Caleb knew it. The vortex of pain from the past grabbed him and he could feel himself sinking fast, plummeting into all that misery. He could even hear his father's voice. *Your mother betrayed me, son. She's pregnant with another man's child. She's hurt me and I don't know if I can forgive her deceit.* When Jake had heard that, he'd made a decision. He would never leave his father. His mother had begged and pleaded, but all Jake could hear were those words. *And they were lies…all lies.* Why had no one told him differently? The pain absorbed him until Elise slipped onto his lap. He gripped her body fiercely.

"What's wrong?" she asked worriedly.

He told her about Caleb and he saw that knowing look in her eyes. "You knew, didn't you?"

She brushed his hair back. "I think everyone knows."

"Everyone but me."

"Because you didn't want to," she reminded him. "You

have a blind spot about the past and you refused to hear any version except the one your father told you.''

If anyone else had said that to him, he would've been furious. But from her, he was glad to hear the truth. ''I just don't understand.''

''You know what you have to do to ease your mind.''

''Yeah.'' He gazed into her eyes. ''But I have other plans for tonight.'' He kissed the hollow of her neck.

His lips created chaos within her. She didn't want to let him go, but he had to resolve things with his mother. That was more important now. ''I'll be here when you get back,'' she said with every ounce of strength she had.

''It's late.'' His lips trailed to her ear.

She caught her breath. ''Althea won't mind.''

''I can't leave Ben.''

''Ben sleeps all night.''

''I don't like leaving you alone.'' His tongue found a sensitive spot, and she stopped resisting, just wanting to go with the moment. But she couldn't…

''Jake,'' she murmured, ''that's an excuse. Take your cell phone and you can stay in contact with me. If there's a problem here, I'll call you.'' She moved off his lap. ''Now go.''

''She might not be home.''

Elise handed him the phone and a phone book.

He heaved a sigh, accepting the inevitable, and phoned his mother. Within minutes he was on the road to talk to Althea—something he'd thought he would never do in his lifetime, but he had to find out the truth. Even if it hurt.

Althea lived in an affluent neighborhood in Waco; the houses were big with manicured lawns. He pulled into the driveway of the address in his hand and stared at the white colonial with large columns. What caught his attention were the Christmas lights and decorations. There was a Santa with sleigh and reindeer on the roof and lights trimmed the whole front of the house. In the yard he saw twinkling elves and a snowman. Everywhere he looked were more lights and all he could think was that Ben should see this. He'd be so excited. He remembered now how his mother loved to decorate at Christmas. The farmhouse used to look very similar to this when she'd lived there. After she'd gone, there was very little in the way of Christmas spirit. He suddenly missed that and he wanted Ben to have Christmases to remember. He slowly got out, making his way to the front door. The cold north wind nipped at him and he pulled his sheepskin coat tighter around him.

He stood at the door and stared at the beautiful wreath and the four-foot Christmas trees that adorned either side of the entry. But he wasn't seeing any of those things. He was seeing a sad little boy who'd forgotten how to enjoy Christmas. He wanted answers. But most of all, he wanted the truth.

He punched the bell and his mother quickly opened the door. "Come in, Jake," she said. "It's cold out." She wore a long pale-blue cotton robe and slippers. Her salt-and-pepper hair was in its usual short, neat style. And he thought again that she appeared much the same as she had when he was a boy. "Let's go into the den. There's a fire there."

He followed her, wondering where Andrew Wellman was, but he didn't ask. They walked from the oversize foyer through a formal living area to a huge den. A brick fireplace covered one wall and a ten-foot-tall Christmas tree stood in one corner. It was decorated in white and gold, as was the wreath on the fireplace and the other decorations in the room.

"Have a seat," she invited.

Jake removed his coat and eased onto one of the sofas that were grouped around the roaring fire. He was hardly even aware when Althea sat down at the other end. His eyes were on the carved wood mantel and the Christmas stockings hanging from it. There were six stockings and he read the names in total shock—Andrew, Althea, Jake, Beau, Caleb and Ben.

He swallowed the constriction in his throat. ''Why do you have Ben's and my names on those stockings?''

''Because you're my son and Ben's my grandson. I'm working on Elise's and I should have it finished by the end of the week. I'm putting an angel on hers and it's taking longer to embroider than I thought.''

Jake had forgotten that his mother did beautiful embroidery. There was a tractor on his and Ben's stocking, Beau's had the scales of justice with a gavel, Caleb's had a badge. Andrew's had books and pens, and Althea's had white poinsettias. Jake shook his head as he realized he was getting sidetracked, but he couldn't let it go because there were packages in all the stockings, even his.

''Is this the first year you've put up my stocking?''

''Oh, no, your stocking's been there every year.''

''But why? I don't even come here for Christmas.''

''You may have not been in my life, but you've always been in my heart.''

Jake had nothing to say for a second, then he had to ask, ''What do you put in it?'' For it was very obvious there was something.

''A letter.''

''A letter?'' he echoed in complete bewilderment.

''Yes, every year I write you a letter and put it in the stocking. There are twenty-eight letters inside now. If anything happens to me, Beau has instructions to give them to you.'' She paused. ''Would you like them now?''

''No,'' Jake answered swiftly. He couldn't read the letters, not when his gut was churning as though he had a stomach virus. He didn't think he'd ever be able to read them. ''Beau told me about Caleb,'' he said quickly. ''I want to know what happened back then. Why did you leave?''

''I've waited twenty-eight years for you to ask me that question and now that you have I'm not sure where to start.''

''Just tell me the truth.''

"As you know, my father died when I was small and my mother died when I was nine. An aunt took me in and raised me with her six kids. I never felt I belonged and I wanted my own home, my own family. I met Joe when I was eighteen. He was eight years older, but he made me feel safe and secure and I fell instantly in love. We got married and I soon discovered that Joe was insanely jealous. I'd never had the opportunity to learn to drive and Joe said he'd take me anywhere I needed to go. And he did. Mainly to watch me, I found. If a man spoke to me, he accused me of flirting, so I didn't respond to other men, but that didn't help. The jealousy continued. Joe wouldn't let me wear makeup and I could only wear loose-fitting clothes."

These weren't the answers he was looking for.

"I started going to church because I had to get away from him, to have time on my own. Mrs. Bagley lived not far away and she offered to pick me up and bring me home. She was in her seventies and very religious, so Joe agreed to let me go. I joined the choir and I started to enjoy myself. Then one evening Mrs. Bagley became ill at choir practice and went home early. I wasn't aware she'd left until Andrew told me. He was in the choir, too. I called Joe, but there was no answer. I'm sure you remember all this, Jake, because you and Beau were with me."

He remembered. He remembered the screaming and yelling when his father saw them get out of Andrew Wellman's car. The screaming continued in their bedroom and Jake and Beau had covered their heads with pillows, not wanting to hear any more. The next morning his mother had a black eye and they never went to church again.

"Do you remember?" she asked quietly.

He cleared his throat. "Yes."

"That night Joe hit me."

"I know," he murmured, finally remembering all the things he'd obviously suppressed for years.

"That was the beginning of the end. I couldn't live with

him after that. I just didn't know how to take my boys and get out.'' She paused. ''Your father made that happen because he wouldn't let up on Andrew. He even went to his house and threatened him. That's when the people at the church became involved and hired a lawyer for me. I still didn't know if I had the strength to leave, but then I discovered I was pregnant. I thought that would make things better. It only got worse. Joe said the baby was Andrew's and insisted I have an abortion. He said he would not raise Andrew Wellman's bastard. I tried to talk to him, telling him over and over that the baby was his, but he hit me several times. I lost consciousness and when I came to I immediately phoned the attorney and he set everything in motion. I had to leave.''

The silence grew heavy with shadows from the past.

''I still didn't know if I had the strength to go until a woman came to the house to see me. I'd never seen her before, but she told me things I couldn't believe. She said she'd been having an affair with Joe for over eleven years and she had a son who was almost a year older than you...and Joe was the father. She begged me to divorce Joe so he could marry her and give her son a name. I was completely devastated and I'm not sure what I said to her. I remember asking her to leave my house.

''When I confronted Joe, he became enraged and called the woman names, but he didn't deny the affair. For years he'd accused me of so many infidelities and all along he was the one being unfaithful.''

''Dad was seeing someone else and he had another son?'' He had to be clear on that. It sounded so bizarre, almost made up.

''Yes,'' Althea said.

''What's her name?''

''Vera something. She called her son Eli, but his name's Elijah.''

Jake's breath solidified into pure pain. He knew Vera. She was a waitress at the beer joint his dad had frequented.

He also knew her son. They'd been in the same class at school, but they hadn't been close. Elijah was always in trouble and Jake had thought he'd probably end up in prison...*and they were brothers.* Could that be true?

At the expression on Jake's face, Althea asked, "Do you know her?"

"Yes, she worked at the Tavern and her son was in my class."

"Oh, my God."

"Elijah got expelled from school when he was thirteen and they moved away. Dad stayed drunk a lot after that. Many nights Aunt Vin and I had to go to the Tavern to get him. I blamed you, and yet, there were other things going on that I wasn't aware of." He paused. "It's hard for me to take all this in."

Althea waited.

He had another brother. Elijah Coltrane, the boy who feared nothing. That was what the kids had called him in school. They also called him a bastard because he didn't have a father—but his father was Joe McCain. Lies from the past tangled in his head. He had to hear the rest of the story.

"What happened next?"

"I told Joe I was leaving and taking my boys. He said the boys would never leave the farm. I didn't think there was anything he could do, but I was wrong. I never dreamed he'd tell you those lies about Caleb. I didn't know until Beau told me." She paused. "The sheriff and his deputies came and I was ready to go, but you refused to leave. I was in shock and I couldn't believe your reaction. I pleaded and pleaded, but you had a fierce loyalty to your father. Like I said, I didn't know Joe had put those lies in your head. The sheriff said to let it be and he'd come back for you the next day, but I couldn't leave without you. I just couldn't. Then Joe started shouting obscenities about the bastard I was carrying and I knew that if I stayed, he'd hurt me and the baby. I was torn between my unborn child and the son who was defying me so blatantly. In the end, I left because I didn't have the strength to do anything else.''

Jake remembered that day well. It was etched into his brain. His father had taken him out to the barn and told him filthy lies. As a child, he didn't know what to believe. Mr. Wellman was very friendly and his mother smiled a lot when she was around him. And the fact that she was leaving seemed to suggest that what his father was saying had to be true. But it wasn't. As an adult, he knew that beyond a shadow of a doubt.

''Why did the sheriff stop coming to the farm?''

''Joe was waiting for me one day after work. He said that you were his and if I didn't call off the sheriff, he'd kill the bastard I was carrying. He'd been drinking but I knew he meant what he said. I finally had to admit that Joe had won. He once told me I'd never leave the farm alive and he was right. Part of me died the day I gave up my fight for you. It's something I'll always regret. Looking back, I handled it so badly. I should have told you what I was planning, but I wanted to spare you. Joe had no such qualms.''

Jake felt he'd been cheated in so many ways by two adults who were supposed to love him—and he still felt cheated. ''Why was I never told about Caleb?''

''Would you have believed it?''

He wouldn't have, he had to admit. His father had done a good job of poisoning his mind. He was filled with anger toward the man who didn't know how to love, how to care for his sons, even the ones he chose to acknowledge. Then he felt pity because Joe McCain had been a bitter, unhappy man.

''There was never anything between Andrew and me until after Caleb was born. The church rented me an apartment and Andrew found me a job. He was just a nice man. He'd lost his wife, whom he loved very deeply, and he needed someone to talk to. He checked on us regularly because he was afraid Joe might try to hurt me. When Caleb was born, he showed up more and more. He and his wife had never had children and he doted on Caleb. We grew closer and closer, and when he asked me to marry him, I did. He gave Beau, Caleb and me a home and I've been very happy—except for the missing piece of my heart.''

''It didn't hurt that he had money, did it?'' The words were out before he could stop them. ''I'm sorry,'' he immediately apologized. ''Old habits are hard to break.''

''It's okay,'' she said. ''You have a right to be angry and resentful. You're the victim in all this.''

''And Caleb,'' he said quietly. ''And Elijah Coltrane, wherever he is.''

''I don't know anything about Elijah Coltrane, but Caleb can't complain. He's had a very good life and Andrew spoiled him terribly.''

His eyes caught Althea's. ''But he knows he's a McCain and I've seen the anger in him. Anger that Joe McCain denied who he was.''

''Don't worry about Caleb. He's fine. He might have a temper, but he's very softhearted.''

His questions had been answered and he didn't know where to go from here—other than home to Elise and Ben. That was where his heart was. He now understood his inability to tell Elise that he loved her. The only love he'd ever known was painful, and instinctively he'd been protecting himself. And his jealousy of Derek was clearer now, too. He'd inherited that from his father and he'd definitely curb that. He had too much to do otherwise. Elise had touched a place in him that his mother had left empty, and Ben had filled the rest. Forgiveness was within his grasp and he could feel it edging through him, but the words wouldn't come. The chasm of the past wasn't as wide now, but as much as he wanted to he couldn't make the leap into the present. It would take time. Time to adjust to everything he'd learned tonight.

He stood. "Thank you for telling me. I wish you'd made the effort years ago after Dad died."

"If you remember, I did, and you told me never to call you again and to leave you alone. You were an adult and I had to respect your wishes. I kept praying that eventually you'd want to hear my side."

He remembered. Oh, God, he remembered. He was his own worst enemy, keeping doors closed when people tried repeatedly to open them. "I'd better go," he said awkwardly. "I don't want to leave Elise and Ben too long."

Althea got to her feet and Jake ached to hug her or touch her in some way, but he couldn't make his arms perform the simple task. He didn't seem to be able to force himself to leave, either.

"Mom," a voice called, breaking the silence.

"I'm in the den, Caleb," Althea said.

Caleb rushed in wearing plainclothes, but he wore his gun and badge. He glanced from Jake to his mother. "Are you all right?" he asked Althea. "I saw *his* truck in the driveway."

She patted his cheek. "Yes, son, I'm fine. Jake came by for a visit."

Caleb frowned and Jake again saw the resemblance between them. And if he recalled correctly, Elijah's hair was dark, his eyes blue. *Like Joe McCain's. There are none as blind as those who will not see.* He'd heard that before and it was very true.

"Did you come by to get in a few more barbs, Jake?" Caleb asked sarcastically, and Jake could feel the anger bubbling up in Caleb—the same anger he'd carried for so long.

"No, actually I came to listen."

Caleb glanced at Althea and she patted his cheek again. "Be nice," she smiled. "I'll go to bed so you two can talk." Before they could stop her, she left the room.

Jake and Caleb stared at each other, then Jake held his arms wide. "Take your best shot. I deserve it."

"With my gun or my fist?" Caleb asked, deadpan. They both broke into smiles and sank onto the sofa.

"I found out tonight that you're my full brother," Jake told him.

"The best-kept secret, huh? I'm the unwanted son."

"No, I think there's another son who holds that title."

"Yeah, Mom told me about him a few years ago. I think she said his name is Eli."

"Elijah Coltrane, to be exact," Jake said. "We were in the same grade at school and never realized we were brothers."

"Good God, I wonder if there are any more of us out there."

Each was silent for a moment as they dealt with a true fact of life—the unknown.

"It seems I have a lot of apologizing to do," Jake finally said.

"Yeah, there've been plenty of times when I wanted to kick your ass, and if you hurt Mom again, I will—no matter what Beau or Mom say."

"You've got a temper like him."

"Don't say that." Caleb scowled.

"I have the same temper so I can recognize it. Beau is softer, like Mom."

Silence took over again, then Caleb waved a hand at the mantel. "Every year I've had to look at your damn stocking hanging there. Jake, the son who wanted nothing to do with us, yet come hell or high water, that stocking was on the mantel. Every time I saw it I wondered how you could be so heartless."

Jake rose to his feet. "I'm wondering the same thing. And now…now I have to go home. I've been gone too long."

Caleb also stood. "I'm glad about Ben. A son has a right to be with his father." A somber expression settled over Caleb's face and they both knew what he was thinking. "Don't get me wrong," Caleb quickly added. "I couldn't have asked for a better man to raise me than Andrew. He's the only father I've ever known and he was always there for me. I learned to walk holding on to his hand. He attended every Boy Scout meeting and athletic event from Little League to football. He taught me how to throw a curve ball and how the game was about more than winning. He taught me everything I know, but he could never quite make me understand why my own father didn't want me.''

''I don't have any answers for you, other than to accept what you've been graciously given,'' Jake said quietly. ''I was never allowed to be in any athletic event or to socialize after school. There was farm work to do, and Joe McCain didn't believe that boys should be pampered. He believed they should work and that's how I spent my childhood. So you might think twice before you think you've missed out on something.''

Caleb's eyes darkened. ''Then why'd you choose to stay with a man like that?''

Jake didn't waver under the glare. ''I don't have an answer for that, either, except to say that as a ten-year-old boy I was hurt beyond belief by the two people who were supposed to love me the most.''

Caleb shook his head. ''As a police detective, I see so many bad things being done in the name of love—especially to children.''

''Yeah.'' Jake nodded and slipped into his coat. ''I'm glad I know the truth.''

''Me, too, but Mom had this phobia about never hurting you, so the truth had to be hidden until you were ready to hear it.'' Caleb sighed. ''At times, that wasn't easy for me to understand.''

Jake was sure it wasn't. He'd never realized how much his mother had tried to protect him, but by doing that she'd created other problems for him. But he didn't have time to dwell on it. Jake held out his hand.

Caleb stared at it, then glanced at Jake's face. ''I don't

think so,'' Caleb said. ''Brothers should embrace, don't you think?''

Without a pause, Jake stepped forward and embraced his younger brother.

As Caleb moved back, he said, ''The next time we meet, we're brothers.''

''We've always been brothers,'' Jake replied huskily. ''It's just taken me longer to recognize it.''

Jake walked to the front door, opened it and felt the wind chill everything in him but the warmth of family he'd discovered tonight. His life still wasn't the way it should be, but it was better than the past—much better.

WHEN JAKE REACHED HIS TRUCK, Beau was there. Silently they embraced, holding on, letting go. Neither spoke; there was nothing left to say. Finally Jake got into his truck and drove toward home...and Elise.

CHAPTER FOURTEEN

ON THE DRIVE HOME, the past kept running through Jake's mind and all he could feel was the heartache and pain—but it didn't have to be like that. That was what tortured him most. In time he'd get beyond that, but right now he had so much to think about—especially his feelings toward his father, mother and, most importantly, Elise.

The house was dark and quiet, and Jake stopped for a moment in Ben's room. A night-light burned and Jake could see he was sleeping soundly, Wags beside him. He'd kicked off the covers and Jake tucked them in again, careful not to disturb him. Looking down at Ben, Jake knew that he'd never hurt his own son like Joe McCain had hurt him. That wasn't love. Jake took a deep breath and walked across the hall. He just couldn't think anymore.

The light was on in their room and Elise was sitting up in bed, working on her laptop, probably e-mailing her assistant at the university. He sank down on the edge of the bed and buried his face in his hands.

Elise scrambled to his side. "Jake, how did it go?" she asked worriedly.

He raised his head and she moved into his arms and he held her, needing to hold on to something.

He drank in the comfort of her nearness, felt her softness. She was real. Ben was real. They were his life, everything that kept him focused, and he'd questioned so many times why it was so difficult to tell Elise how he felt. Now he knew. He'd found out tonight. The simple pleasure of saying those three little words had been destroyed by a father and mother that he loved, trusted, and who had betrayed him. If he said the words, he'd lose it all. That was irrational, but it was the way he felt inside. For once he could see that.

"Jake?" She caressed his neck.

Her touch infused warmth into his cold soul. "It was unbelievable, almost unreal, and I'm still having trouble putting all the pieces together."

"What happened?" She settled close to him, her hip and leg touching his. This was what he needed, he thought, her closeness, her compassion, and it would be all he'd ever have of her. In a halting fashion he told her everything he'd learned from his mother.

"Oh, my," Elise breathed, hardly able to believe what she was hearing. Her heart was breaking for the young Jake, who had been used so unscrupulously by his father. "Did you say there's another son?"

"Yes, Elijah Coltrane. My father wouldn't claim him, either, and I'm wondering where Elijah is now."

"Maybe someday you'll meet again," she said, distressed by the anguish in his voice.

"Maybe," he muttered, but he knew that wherever Elijah was, he probably didn't want to be found by a McCain.

"And you and Caleb have a new understanding?"

"It's amazing what the truth can do."

"Now you have to accept it."

A painful sound left his throat. "My father took away my childhood and he took away my mother without any regard for my feelings. I should be angry, but I'm just empty. I've hated my mother for so long and I've been hating the wrong person…that's what I keep thinking. And of course, I keep wondering why no one did anything. Why did they let me go on hating? There's so many whys."

"Oh, Jake." She wrapped an arm around his waist. "When I first met you, you made it very clear that Althea was off limits, and I'm sure you've done that all your life.

You're very formidable when you set your mind to something."

"Yeah, I guess I made it easy for the secrets to continue." He breathed in deeply. "I could never hurt Ben like I was hurt. I don't want him to grow up hating anyone, especially his mother, who abandoned him."

"That's because you're not like Joe McCain and you love much stronger than you hate."

"Thank you," he whispered, needing to hear that. *He was not like his father.*

"I'm sure Aunt Vin instilled different values in you, since she's the one who raised you."

As Elise spoke, they could hear a noise in the kitchen. "That must be her." Jake said, getting to his feet "I need to talk to Aunt Vin."

"Jake?"

He turned around.

"I will never leave you. I hope you understand that." She felt he needed to hear that from her now.

"Thank you" was all he said as he walked out of the room.

She'd never hurt Jake. That was a vow she made to herself.

AUNT VIN WAS SITTING at the kitchen table counting her winnings. She glanced at Jake over the rim of her glasses. "Jake, I thought you were in bed."

"Not yet."

"Is something wrong with Ben?" Her voice grew agitated.

He sat across from her. "No, Ben's fine." He swallowed. "I went to see my mother tonight."

Aunt Vin's eyes opened wide. "You went to see Althea?"

"Yes, and she told me what happened all those years ago. She told me the truth."

Vin removed her glasses and carefully laid them on the table. "And you want me to confirm it?"

"No. I want to know why *you* never tried to tell me?"

Vin frowned. "You remember the way Joe was. He was mean and I was scared to death of him. I only came here because of you and because Althea had asked me."

Jake blinked in confusion. "Althea asked you to take care of me?"

"Yes, living with Joe was not on my list of favorite things to do, but I was in a bad relationship with a man and I finally realized he wasn't going to marry me. He was too attached to his mother. I needed a change of scenery, so after Althea called me, I came here to visit and I tried to talk to Joe about what was best for you. He told me to mind my own damn business and to get out. I couldn't leave you with him, so I stayed the night and cleaned and cooked. Joe didn't mention me leaving again. There were times I wanted to, especially when he'd come home drunk and cursing, but I stayed because of you."

"Then why didn't you tell me the truth? Why did you let me live in that environment?"

Vin ran a hand over her face. "My brother had a violent temper and, as I said, I was afraid of him. He threatened so many times to kill Althea and Andrew Wellman and their bastard son. If I told you the truth and you left, I feared what he might do. He wasn't a rational person. Even though I saw all the pain you were going through, I still couldn't do it. I kept telling myself that at least you were alive."

Jake thought about everything she was saying and memories flowed like vinegar through his system, sharp and distasteful. He remembered so many nights when his dad had come home drunk and cursing, saying he was going to kill Althea and her lover. Aunt Vin would slip quietly into Jake's room and sit there in a chair until his father passed out. She protected him the only way she knew how. She was the reason he'd grown up with morals and values instead of becoming corrupt like Joe McCain. He owed her his life, and for that reason, he couldn't be angry that she'd kept a secret that wasn't hers to share.

After a moment, Jake asked, "Then you know Caleb is my brother—my full brother?"

"Yes, but Joe wouldn't consider it for a moment so I kept my mouth shut."

"Do you also know about Elijah?"

"Who?"

"Mom said Dad had another son by Vera, the waitress at the Tavern."

"Oh, yes." Vin nodded. "I didn't remember his name. Vera said the boy was Joe's, but again, Joe refused to claim him. I stayed out of it because my only concern was you. I don't know if it was true or not."

"It's time we got to know Caleb."

"I've wanted to, but you felt so strongly and I didn't want to upset you."

He inhaled deeply. He'd been wrong about so many things. "I stayed with Joe McCain, took his side against my mother, yet I don't know this man I called my father. He hurt so many people and I don't understand why. I just wish I had some answers."

Aunt Vin leaned forward. "I've never told anyone this, but I think you need to hear it. When we were small, our mother would meet men in motel rooms and lock us in the bathroom while—" she seemed to be searching for the right word "—she visited with them. Joe was older so he knew what was going on. I was just scared. She always lied to our father about where she was and eventually she ran away and left us. Our father's parents took us in and we moved here to the farm, but Joe had been damaged by what he'd witnessed and he never trusted women after that or had any respect for them."

Jake was dumbfounded. He shouldn't be. There had to be a reason his father was the way he had been. That little description explained so much. "Thanks for telling me."

Vin covered one of his hands on the table. "You're a good man, Jake, and don't you ever believe any differently."

"Mainly because of you."

"Well, I don't know about that." Vin picked up her glasses. "Althea had given you a good foundation and I'm so glad you've finally talked to her."

"I'm not sure where to go from here," he admitted.

"To the future—with Elise and Ben."

But she doesn't love me, either.

Vin watched the tortured expression on his face. "I never thought I'd like Elise, but I do. Ben loves her and it's clear to see how much she loves him."

But she doesn't love me.

Jake stood. "I have a lot to be thankful for."

He had to remember that.

"You sure do. Now, skedaddle so I can count my money."

He kissed her cheek, grateful he had Aunt Vin in his life.

JAKE WALKED TO HIS WORKSHOP, sat in his chair and stared at the baby cradle. He hadn't showed it to Elise and he probably never would. He touched it lovingly, remembering all the hours of painstaking work with only one thought in his mind—his and Elise's baby. What was he thinking? Two people could get married, have a child and find happiness? It didn't work that way…*not without love.* A marriage needed love to nourish and sustain it, as did the child. How was he to know? The only love he'd ever known had been taken from him so cruelly.

God, he had to stop this. He slowly made his way back to the house. Elise was in bed and the light was out. He took a quick shower and climbed in beside her. She came to him immediately and he gathered her close. This he understood. She was in his bed, his life, and he had to stop dreaming of being in her heart. He wasn't fooling himself anymore.

His hand ran up her back to her neck and rested there. "We had a date, remember?"

Elise raised her head. "Jake..."

His mouth covered hers urgently, cutting off what she'd wanted to say, then he completely forgot everything as his wife's body responded to his fingers as they caressed and stroked sensitive, needy places. He was home.

A long time later, Jake held her, waiting for his heart rate to return to normal and decided this was better than love. He didn't know a thing about love, other than it hurt like hell, and he didn't want that from her...not anymore.

And soon he'd believe that.

IN THE DAYS THAT FOLLOWED, Jake realized he had a lot of emotions to sort through, but he kept purposely busy with Ben and with the farm and he didn't dwell on it much. Beau was out of town on business so Jake thought he'd wait until Beau returned before seeing Althea again. Why, he wasn't sure, but he needed the time to assimilate all he'd learned. It felt good, though, to admit that he'd be seeing his mother again.

He was now able to leave Ben and work on the farm. He met with his accountant and decided to sell the cotton after the first of the year. It felt good to be back at the helm. Elise had stepped into the role of mother completely and she seemed to thrive on it. They were husband and wife in every way, except one. The love wasn't there—for her. That was okay with him now. He told himself that a hundred times a day.

At times he saw the sadness in her eyes that was always there—for Derek. Other times she seemed like a different person. Aunt Vin was teaching her to cook, and he never knew what to expect when he returned home. Some days she'd be in the kitchen meticulously watching Aunt Vin, usually with flour or chocolate or whatever they were cooking in her hair or on her clothes. Other days, she'd be working with Ben, slowly sounding out words so his brain could recognize the first syllable. One day he came home to the den full of balloons. Wags jumped up and down, biting and popping them as Ben giggled happily and Elise sat in the middle of the floor, a glow on her face, no sadness in sight.

Blowing up balloons was an exercise to increase Ben's lung power. This was the first time Ben had blown up so many and Jake was positive Elise had helped. They worked tirelessly at Ben's program of exercises, but Jake wasn't with him constantly, while Elise hadn't left Ben since they had come home. Ben's speech and coordination were improving and it was all due to her. She needed a break, though, and Jake resolved to provide one, and soon. Convincing Elise to agree to it could be a major undertaking.

When they took Ben to the doctor, they found he'd gained five pounds. He was filling out, and they were excited about the news. But Elise was now worried about Jake. His actions, especially when they made love, seemed forced, almost out of desperation. That was the only way she could explain it to herself. His touch wasn't the same as before. She reacted the same, though, or her body did. It would always be that way for her and she recognized their relationship was changing. She had to find a way to talk to him. But she wanted to give him time to absorb the new revelations in his life.

THEIR ATTENTION WAS NOW on Christmas and making it a big occasion for Ben. It was forty degrees the day they decided to cut down a Christmas tree. Elise bundled Ben up in his big coat with a hood, boots and gloves. All that could be seen was his little face and big smile, especially when he caught sight of the tractor Jake had driven to the garage. A trailer was hooked behind it for the tree, and after they'd climbed into the cab, they set out to find the perfect one. Wags went with them; they couldn't leave him behind. He jumped onto the trailer hitch, then to a wheel and then into the cab. Wags knew his way around a tractor.

Ben sat in Jake's lap while Elise occupied a side bench

with Wags. The cab was very warm and they sang Christmas songs as they rode along. Ben loved "Jingle Bells" and "Frosty the Snowman." Soon they left the farmland and turned into a wooded pasture. All the leaves had fallen from the oak trees so the cedars were easy to see.

"'Utt-'utt 'ong, Mom-E," Ben instructed as Jake drove.

This was Ben's all-time favorite song and he never grew tired of singing it. Elise had used the rhyme and tune of "Baa, Baa, Black Sheep" to create a song about a tractor for Ben.

"Putt—putt tractor, have you any wheels?" she sang.

"'Es-'ir, 'es-'ir," Ben shouted his part.

"Six wheels round." Elise held up six fingers, as did Ben. "One for my Mommy." Ben raised one finger. "Two for my Daddy." Two fingers went up. "And three for the little boy who loves to go..."

Holding three fingers in the air, Ben chimed in, "'Oom-'oom . 'Eels go 'oom-'oom-'oom."

"Yes," Elise answered. "Wheels go vroom-vroom-vroom."

Wags barked, not wanting to be left out.

"'Gin, Mom-E," Ben pleaded, like always.

Jake brought the tractor to a stop. "Okay, Ben, it's time to pick out a tree."

Ben looked blank, his eyes big, so Jake gave him a nudge. "How about that one?" He pointed to a large cedar.

Ben shook his head. They did this several times before Ben nodded his approval.

Jake placed Ben in Elise's lap and he climbed out of the tractor, Wags behind him, and reached for the chainsaw on the trailer. Ben watched avidly out the window as the chainsaw spluttered to life. Within minutes the tree toppled to the ground.

They watched as Jake dragged the tree to the trailer and heaved it aboard. So strong, so capable, she'd always thought that about him. She didn't think there was anything Jake couldn't do. He was unlike any man she'd ever known. She tried to conjure up Derek's face, but she couldn't. It was blurred by memories of Jake. Jake and his loving hands, gentle smile...and tortured soul. All she wanted was to be there for him.

Soon Jake and Wags were back in the tractor.

"Tee, tee, 'A-dy," Ben shouted as if Jake was unaware there was a tree on the trailer.

"I know, son," Jake said patiently. "Now, let's take it home and decorate it."

"'Kay," Ben replied, then switched gears. "'Utt-'utt 'ong, Mom-E."

Jake grinned. "I'm gonna hear that in my sleep tonight."

Elise grinned back, feeling a pull on her heart. She loved his grin. And she... The thought disappeared as she began, "Putt-putt tractor, have you any wheels?"

"'Es-'ir, 'es-'ir," Ben answered. "And t'ee, Mom-E."

"Yes, we have a tree," Elise confirmed as they putt-putted all the way to the house.

THAT NIGHT JAKE GOT ALL the decorations out of the attic and they drank wassail Aunt Vin had made and decorated the tree. Jake and Elise strung the lights while Ben and Wags watched, then Ben helped hang the ornaments. The ornaments were very old and Elise knew they were left from when Althea had lived here. Jake had told her his father refused to have a tree, but Aunt Vin had always put a small one on a table in the den.

It seemed eerie to be hanging decorations from so long ago. She caught Jake a couple of times staring at an ornament in deep thought, and she wanted to say something to ease his turmoil, but the right words eluded her. She hated that lack of confidence in herself.

Soon the tree was complete except for the angel. Jake lifted Ben in the air so he could place the angel on top, then Jake plugged in the tree.

At the glittering sight, Ben's mouth fell open.

"My, my," Aunt Vin said from the doorway. "How

beautiful, and the cedar smell is glorious. Does anyone need more wassail?''

''We're fine, Aunt Vin, thanks.''

''If you don't need anything else, I'm off to bingo.''

''Stay for a while?'' Elise pleaded.

''This is definitely one of those situations when four is a crowd.''

''Aunt Vin, that's not true. You're part of our family,'' Jake told her.

''I know, but I'm still going to bingo. 'Night, all.'' She kissed Ben and left the room.

After turning off the lamps, Jake sank to the floor in front of the fire and pulled Elise down to him. Ben crawled into Elise's arms and Wags stretched out beside them. They sat that way for a long time, just watching the lights on the tree, and then Elise sang several Christmas songs, starting with ''Away in a Manager.'' Jake joined in occasionally and so did Ben. A peacefulness settled over the McCain house that hadn't been there for years, if ever. Finally Ben fell asleep and they still didn't move. This was one of those rare moments and they both wanted to remember...the feeling of Christmas and of being together.

A calmness came over Jake and he kissed the side of Elise's face and breathed in her scent. ''You smell good.''

She rubbed her head against him, feeling more alive than she'd felt in a long time. ''I think it's baby powder,'' she murmured.

''No,'' he whispered into her hair. ''It's you...all you.''

She turned to meet his lips and Ben woke up. She felt bereft, as if she'd been deprived of something special, but now her attention was on Ben. He was full of energy and they had a hard time getting him to bed. He ran through the house singing the putt-putt and t'ee song and Wags ran after him. Discipline was something neither Jake nor Elise was good at. It was after midnight when Ben finally went down, and by then Jake and Elise were drained, and for the first time in days they went to sleep without making love.

Instead they talked about Christmas and what they'd buy for Ben. They also decided to invite both families for Christmas day. It was a start at family unity. Elise wanted that for Jake.

THE NEXT MORNING THE FIRST thing Ben did was run to the tree, Wags at his heels. "Tee, 'Ags, tee," he said, pointing to the Christmas tree. Wags licked his face in response and Ben giggled, "No, no, 'Ags." But Wags continued to lick and Ben wrapped his arms around Wags's neck and they tumbled to the floor amid a sea of giggles.

Elise didn't rush to help Ben because she knew he was fine. She was learning not to be overprotective, and Wags would never hurt Ben. "Breakfast," she called, and Ben hurriedly scrambled to his feet trying to escape Wags.

He hurried to his high chair and crawled in by himself. As Jake pulled it up to the table, Ben grabbed his spoon. He fed himself, and he was getting better and better at it. Soon he'd need no help at all. Elise felt elated by that small miracle.

After breakfast, while Jake dressed Ben, she phoned her mother and invited her for Christmas. Constance replied that she hadn't made her plans yet and she'd let Elise know. That pretty much said it all and Elise felt a moment of sadness that Constance had not accepted her marriage, but she pushed it away. She then called Judith, but there was no answer, which she thought was strange since Judith rarely left the house before lunch. She'd try again later.

She sat beside Jake as he called his mother and then Caleb. They both accepted. Beau was still out of town, but they knew he'd come. Elise watched Jake's face.

"Are you okay?"

He shrugged. "It's just hearing her voice—it does something to me. I feel like that little boy waiting for his mother to kiss him good-night and say she loves him, and then I feel the anger of that ten-year-old and the heartache of my teens and the pain of my adult years. I feel all that and I'm still trying to deal with it.'' He paused. ''The other night when I heard all the bad things she'd gone through, I wanted to hug or hold her in some way—but I couldn't. Somehow, I just couldn't.''

She rubbed his arm, needing to touch him. ''It'll come. Give it time.''

''I suppose,'' he murmured, loving the way she touched him so freely. He looked at her. ''And you, how are you handling your mother's rejection?''

''It's not easy, but it's her decision and...'' Before she could say anything else Ben walked over and crawled between them.

'''Utt-'utt 'ong, Mom-E.''

She pushed his hair back. ''How about another song?''

''No-no-no.'' He shook his head and bounced his legs against the sofa in a temper. '''Utt-'utt 'ong.'' Ben held the makeshift tractor in his hand. He hadn't carried it around in days and Elise knew he was tired.

''Someone's in a grouchy mood,'' Elise cooed.

''Lack of sleep,'' Jake remarked, and lifted Ben into his arms. ''Time for a nap, son.''

''No-no-no,'' Ben screamed, shaking his head vigorously. ''Nap no.''

Jake caught Ben's face with one hand. ''Ben, stop it,'' he said quietly, but his tone was firm.

Ben immediately stopped shaking his head and tears rolled down his cheeks. Elise jumped to her feet, but Jake held up a hand and she understood he didn't want her to interfere. They had to start disciplining Ben, but it was hard, especially with those big tears in his eyes.

''Give Mommy a kiss,'' Jake instructed.

Elise stood on tiptoe to kiss Ben.

'''Utt-'utt 'ong,'' Ben whimpered, and Elise melted. She didn't care about discipline; she just wanted Ben to be happy.

Jake saw that look in her eyes and quickly took Ben to his room. Wags trotted behind them. Jake was back in a few minutes. "He fell asleep almost as soon as I laid him down. We should've made him go to bed last night."

"I know," she admitted. "I don't like this part of being a parent, but as soon as he wakes up I'm singing the putt-putt song."

He smiled. "I can see you're hopeless at discipline."

"Yes, so don't expect me to do a lot of it."

The teasing light in her eyes was as bright as the ones on the tree and for a moment he was caught in its glow, its warmth. And he wished he could be the one to put that light in her eyes. He stopped himself just in time. He'd promised himself he'd never think that again.

He cleared his throat. "I'd better check on Mike. I'll be back later."

The rest of the day Ben was completely off schedule. He was cross and fussy at speech therapy, and Sue finally gave up. Ben fell asleep on the way home and slept until lunch. He'd had two short naps in the span of four hours, which meant he wasn't ready for his usual nap.

THAT AFTERNOON, SINCE CHRISTMAS was a week away, Elise and Aunt Vin made cookies. Ben sat on a stool and watched, totally engrossed in the project. Elise had flour on her face, apron and clothes, but she was having the time of her life.

"Thanks for teaching me all your cooking secrets," she said to Aunt Vin.

"It's been a pleasure, my dear, a real pleasure."

"And I'd like to apologize again for my callous behavior in the beginning."

Aunt Vin looked over the rim of her glasses. "I don't hold grudges and I can see how much you love Ben. So if we got off on the wrong foot, we're on steady ground now."

"Yes, we are," Elise agreed, kissing her cheek.

"Oh." Aunt Vin rushed to the oven. "It's time to check our gingerbread cookies."

The first batch turned out beautifully and she was helping Ben dunk a cookie in milk when the doorbell rang.

"Aunt Vin, would you please watch Ben while I get the door?"

"Sure." Aunt Vin turned from the oven.

"Don't let him put too much in his mouth." Elise kissed Ben. "Mommy will be right back."

"'Kay," Ben said, trying to dunk a cookie in the milk.

Elise hurried to the door and swung it open. She stopped short when she saw Judith standing there.

Judith brushed past her into the living room. Elise closed the door and followed. "You didn't tell me you lived at the back of beyond. I didn't think I'd ever find it."

Elise frowned. "I don't remember telling you where I lived."

"That's rich, isn't it?" Judith snapped. "I had to ask Althea for directions."

Elise stared at her sister and realized something was wrong. She was her usual obnoxious self, but she wore no makeup and her coiffured hair was mussed, her clothes rumpled. She'd never, ever seen her sister like this.

Suddenly Judith dropped onto the sofa and started to cry. Judith never cried in front of people. Elise wasn't sure what to do, then she did what any normal woman would. She sank down beside Judith and hugged her.

"What is it?" she asked soothingly.

Judith wiped at her eyes with the back of her hand. "Stan's left me and he's taken Duncan."

"What!"

"He's filing for custody," Judith hiccuped. "Beau McCain is his attorney. You have to help me. I can't lose my son."

"I'm not sure what I can do."

"Talk to Jake and get him to persuade Beau to drop the case."

"Jake won't do that."

"Elise, please, how will I face people if Stan divorces

me and gains custody of Duncan? What will people say of me as a mother?''

''You're worried about what people will say?'' She couldn't keep the disbelief out of her voice.

Judith put a hand to her temple. ''I can't think straight.''

Elise sighed, knowing it was useless to be angry at Judith. ''Try to work this out with Stan.''

''I tried, but he said he wanted Duncan to be raised in a loving environment without so many restrictions so he can enjoy his youth.''

''I see.'' Elise was remembering her conversation with Stan at the hospital. She'd sensed a restlessness in him then. He had already been thinking of leaving.

''He doesn't understand that Duncan has to be pushed to excel.''

''Why?''

Judith blinked. ''Why what?''

''Why does Duncan have to excel?''

''Are you serious?''

''Yes. I have a little boy who struggles to put food in his mouth. Then it takes all his strength to swallow it. I push him every day to do those simple things, and you have a child who just needs your love. Why isn't that enough?''

''God, you sound like Stan.''

''Maybe Stan's right.''

''Mom-E, Mom-E,'' Ben called a moment before he ran into her arms.

''Are you sleepy?'' She kissed his forehead.

Ben nodded and rested against her chest.

Judith stared at Ben. ''Is this...'' Her voice trailed off and she seemed unable to finish the sentence.

''This is Ben,'' Elise announced, then looked at Ben. ''Can you say hi?''

''Hi, me Ben,'' he said perfectly, and Elise kissed him again.

''Ben, Ben, where's Ben?'' Jake shouted from the

kitchen. It was a game they played when Jake left for any length of time.

Ben was instantly alert and scrambled off Elise's lap. "'A-dy, 'A-dy, Ben me 'ere," he screeched excitedly, and Jake swung him up in his arms as he entered the room.

"Hey, son, how's..." He stopped as he saw Judith. "I'm sorry, I didn't realize you were here." Jake glanced from Elise to Judith. "Something wrong?"

"No, but Ben's ready for a nap." She smiled at Ben. "Want Mommy to sing the putt-putt song?"

Ben nodded.

"Putt-putt tractor, have you any wheels?"

"'Es-'ir, 'es-'ir," Ben shouted.

"Six wheels round," Jake took up, and whispered to Elise, "I'll finish this. Visit with your sister."

"What are they singing?" Judith asked, curious.

"A song I made up to help Ben with numbers and coordination." Elise went through the words. "The more we sing the song, the more he hears the numbers and responds correctly."

"I expected him to be..."

"What?"

"Different. But he seems quite normal."

"He *is* normal," Elise stated emphatically.

"But evidently it's taking a lot of hard work," Judith remarked.

"Yes, but I'm not complaining. I love being a mother."

Judith frowned at Elise's apron and the flour in her hair. "I can see that. You're a regular housewife."

"I wouldn't say that, but I'm learning."

Judith stared at her as if she'd lost her mind. Finally Judith said, "Mother's upset that you haven't been in touch."

Elise gritted her teeth for a second, willing herself not to give in to the subtle blackmail. Constance knew exactly how to provoke her and she was using Judith to apply the guilt, but it wouldn't work the way it had in years past.

Elise didn't need her mother's approval; she just wanted her love. Until that happened they were at an impasse.

"I phoned this morning and invited her for Christmas," she said confidently. "I called you, too, but there was no answer."

"I was watching Stan's new apartment. I know he's seeing someone else. He says he isn't, but he's lying. Another woman has to be involved. That's the only reason he'd leave me."

Elise had to be completely honest. "Think about it. Why would he take Duncan if another woman was involved? Stan wouldn't expose Duncan to that."

Judith put her hand to her temple again. "What am I going to do?"

"Seems to me you have two choices," Elise told her. "You can either accept it or do something about it."

"Like what?"

"Like changing your attitude and being more understanding and willing to listen and compromise."

Judith stood quickly. "I can see you're no help. I shouldn't have come here." She moved toward the door.

"You're welcome here anytime and the invitation to Christmas is still open," Elise managed to say before Judith slammed the door.

Elise sat for a moment trying to absorb this new revelation, and she realized Stan had probably been thinking of leaving for a long time. She remembered what he'd said that night at the club when Elise had discovered that her mother and Judith knew about Ben. He'd said Ben should be raised in a loving environment and he'd meant it...in more ways than one.

She wished that her sister would listen to her, but nothing she said seemed to matter. Judith had always been very headstrong, used to having her own way, and now she'd have to decide if she could bend a little, at least enough to make her marriage work. Elise hoped she made the right decision.

For herself, Elise knew she'd made the right decision in marrying Jake. She wished her mother could accept that, because she was happier than she'd ever been in her life.

Happier than she'd ever been.

No. She'd been happy with Derek, too. Why was that so hard to remember?

CHAPTER FIFTEEN

THE DAYS BEFORE CHRISTMAS were busy with shopping, wrapping, cooking and preparing for the big day. Taking Ben to a toy store was an adventure in itself. His eyes grew bigger and bigger and he wanted everything he saw, but he seemed more enthralled watching the other kids in the store. It was clear he loved children.

They let him buy a gift for Valerie and he chose a Barbie doll. Elise felt it was an excellent choice. Then he picked out gifts for Aunt Vin, Jake and Elise. Of course, they had to pretend to look the other way when their gift was chosen—perfume for Elise and gloves for Jake. When they reached home, Ben had to wrap his gifts by himself. He wadded paper around them with lots of tape and stuck a bow on top and then he and Wags trotted to the tree.

They'd also purchased a new red collar for Wags and a rubber dog bone. Ben insisted on closing the door so Wags couldn't see his gifts while they were being wrapped. Wags barked and howled outside the door until Ben finished his task. Ben soon let the dog in and they rolled on the floor, Ben's giggles filling the room. Jake and Elise just smiled, delighted that Ben was having so much fun.

JAKE RECEIVED A CALL from the Houston police detective, who said that a warrant had been issued for Dr. Ruskin's arrest, but so far they'd been unable to locate him.

Later Jake got a frantic phone call from Dr. Ruskin.

"You have to drop the charges," he insisted. "They're going to arrest me."

"I haven't filed any charges," Jake told him calmly.

"You're lying," Dr. Ruskin shouted. "After all I did for Ben, this is how you repay me. He'd be a vegetable today if it weren't for me."

Jake swallowed hard. "I'm grateful for everything you did for my son, but most of his progress is due to Mrs. Carr's unfailing love and persistence. And you were well compensated for your medical services."

"This is about the money, isn't it?"

"No, Dr. Ruskin, as I've told you, I haven't filed any charges. You'll have to check with the police department for further details."

"You're lying, McCain, and I'll get even. You'll regret this."

Jake hung up on the irate man and immediately phoned the detective to inform him of the call; the detective said he'd take care of it from Houston. Dr. Ruskin's fate was in police hands now, but Jake felt an uneasiness he couldn't explain.

BEAU RETURNED FROM HIS TRIP and he and Jake spent an afternoon reliving the past—the good and the bad. It was Christmastime and everyone wanted peace, and love and goodwill.

Beau finished the papers on the Houston house for the Fosters and Jake mailed them as a Christmas gift. The day the Fosters received it, Jake got a teary call telling him how much they appreciated his generosity. Jake promised he and Elise would stop by when they brought Ben for his checkup.

Christmas spirit filled the McCain house and Elise's happiness escalated when her mother phoned.

"Judith and I have decided to come for Christmas," Constance said.

"Thank you, Mother, I appreciate it."

"We have our differences, but, darling, I do love you."

Elise bit her lip. It had been a long time since her mother

had said that. ''Thank you,'' she said again. ''I love you, too.''

''I tried so hard to do what's best for you and Judith, but my family's falling apart. Stan and Judith's separation is partly my fault. I instilled in Judith that drive for excellence and now it's destroying her marriage. I'm not sure what to do anymore.''

Elise was at a loss for words. Her mother never admitted she was wrong, but it seemed as if they were all taking a deeper look at themselves and not liking what they saw. Elise had already experienced that inner discord and she was hoping for the best for both her mother and Judith.

''Judith says you're flourishing in the role of being a mom,'' Constance added before Elise could find her voice.

''Yes, I'm very happy.''

''I'm so sorry for the anguish you suffered over Tammy Abbott. I should have talked to you, made you understand it wasn't your fault, but I can't go back and—''

''It's okay, Mother,'' Elise said, tears filling her eyes. ''I've gotten through it and as I said, I'm happy.''

''That's all I've ever wanted for you and I'm looking forward to meeting your son.''

Elise held back more tears. This was more than she'd expected from Constance, but it was what she needed from her mother at this time in her life.

''We'll see you and your family on Christmas day,'' Constance said before she hung up.

Elise stared at the phone, then picked it up and dialed Stan. The whole family had to come, she decided.

''Elise, I've been meaning to call you,'' Stan said when he recognized her voice.

''That's great, because I'd like to invite you and Duncan for Christmas.''

''Thanks for the invitation, but I'm not sure. Judith's not taking the separation well and I'm afraid she'll cause a scene.''

''It's Christmas, Stan, and Duncan should be with family. Jake and I will not allow any scenes. We don't want that for Ben, either."

"How's it going?"

"Just wonderful."

"I'm so glad," he said. "I always knew you'd make a great mom."

"Thanks for giving me the confidence I needed that night at the hospital."

A long pause. "I wanted to tell you what I was planning, but I realized that my problems with Judith are mine and I shouldn't involve you."

"Thanks, Stan," she replied. "I just hope you can find a happy solution."

"That's up to Judith."

Another pause, then Elise asked, "Stan, what happened to the crack baby?"

"A couple took him home this week. He'll be fine."

"Thank God." She'd thought about the baby a lot and was glad he had someone to love him. "Stan, please try to come on Christmas."

"I'll be in touch," was all he promised, but Elise had high hopes.

JAKE AND ELISE DECIDED to attend Christmas Eve services to give Ben a sense of the true meaning of Christmas. After therapy, they stopped by Elise's house so she could pack more clothes. She wanted to wear a dress to church, and these days she spent all her time in jeans and slacks. Jake and Ben stayed in the truck because it was drizzling rain and they didn't want Ben out in the weather.

Jake was glad not to have to get out. Derek's memory was in there. Even though he hadn't lived in the house with Elise, his presence seemed to be everywhere. Jake didn't want to be reminded of Elise's love for Derek today. They were both committed to the marriage and Ben; they'd reached a happy medium. Beyond that he couldn't think, wouldn't allow himself to. His insides felt as mangled as the shredded cotton stalks in his fields.

Elise hurried into the house and stopped for a moment. She stared at her perfect white home, everything in order, nothing out of place. This wasn't a home, she thought, it was a place to live. Home was a crackling fire, toys strewn on the floor, dog hairs on the rug and love in every nook and cranny. Home was the farm, and home was Jake and Ben. She wondered how she'd lived in this sterile environment, and then she knew. She'd only been existing, and now she was living.

Rushing to the bedroom, she grabbed a suitcase and began to fill it with clothes. She chose a classic black dress and matching jacket for church and searched for her pearls but couldn't find them. Opening the drawer on the nightstand, she saw Derek's picture. She picked it up and gazed at the face she'd loved for so long. She waited for the pain to engulf her. All she felt was warmth, though—all the other emotions were gone.

She sank to the bed as a truth she'd been suppressing made itself clear. *She loved Jake.* She'd probably loved him from the moment she'd met him.

I love him, Derek, and I'm not sorry for that. She laid the picture in the drawer and closed it. *I'm just sorry it took me so long to admit it.*

In a moment of clarity, she realized what was wrong with her and Jake's lovemaking. That special ingredient, love, the thing that made it right, perfect, was missing. Another truth surfaced. Hers and Derek's love had been young and fresh and never had the chance to develop into a mature, consuming passion, like she had for Jake.

Of course, she didn't know how Jake felt, but she would. She glanced at the drawer, knowing she was truly over Derek. She had finally let him go. As she left the house, she thought she should call a real estate agent and put it on the market, and she would when Christmas was over. The farm was her home now.

She also had to make a decision about her career. She couldn't see herself returning to work, not when Ben still needed her so much. Maybe later. She could finish the book about Alcott that she'd started. Now she just wanted to be with her family.

ELISE WAS IMPATIENT AS she dressed for church. She was dying to talk to Jake, but finally had to acknowledge that wasn't going to happen until later. That was just as well, she told herself. They'd be alone—and they needed that.

Elise wore her black dress and heels and Jake had on a suit. He'd worn a suit the day they'd gotten married, but she hadn't seen him clearly then. Not like she did now.

He was so handsome. She even noticed strands of gray in his hair, which only added to his appeal. He was everything she wanted in a man, a husband and a father. Her impatience grew.

They'd bought Ben a suit, a white shirt and red sweater vest, and he was in the den showing Aunt Vin his new outfit, so Jake and Elise didn't tarry long.

Their main goal was to keep Ben awake during the service, and the little boy sitting in front of them made that quite easy. He and Ben kept smiling and waving at each other and Ben was totally engrossed in the interaction except when the choir sang. Then he whispered to Elise, "'Utt-'utt 'ong Mom-E."

"Later, baby," she whispered back. "Listen." The choir was magnificent. Its rich, melodious sound echoed through the church. At the end, the lights were dimmed and the candles on the altar flickered as everyone sang "Silent Night."

They returned to the house for a late supper. Aunt Vin had prepared a sandwich tray with fruit and cheese before they'd left and she got it out of the refrigerator. Elise set the table and they had a quick festive meal.

"Well, I'm off to a Christmas party at Maggie's," Aunt Vin said. There wasn't any bingo tonight or on Christmas day so the ladies were having a party. "Everything is ready for tomorrow and I'll be up early to put the turkey in."

"I'll be up early, too," Elise promised.

Aunt Vin kissed the top of Ben's head. "'Night, Ben."

"'Ight," Ben repeated. "'Eam, Mom-E."

"First, finish your supper and then we'll have ice cream."

Ben frowned. "No, 'eam 'ow."

"Ben," Jake said in a warning tone that Ben was beginning to recognize.

Ben's frown deepened, but he ate the chicken salad sandwich Elise had cut up on his plate. He chewed, then swallowed the small pieces, and they could tell his throat muscles were stronger because it wasn't much of an effort anymore.

When the food was gone, Elise clapped her hands. "Ben's a good boy."

Ben clapped his hands, too, and they actually synchronized their movements for the first time. Ben was getting so much better.

"'Eam Mom-E."

Jake placed a bowl of chocolate ice cream on the table and tied a small towel around Ben's neck because this was a messy event. They had removed his dress clothes and Ben had on his red Christmas pajamas.

"Daddy loves Ben," Jake said as he handed Ben a spoon. Elise knew how hard it was for him to say no to Ben, but they were learning.

"Me 'ove 'A-dy," Ben mumbled, his mouth full of ice cream, and those little words made everything okay.

As Jake gave Ben a bath, Elise cleaned the kitchen, then went to tie a bow on the tractor they'd bought Ben for Christmas. It had pedals like a bicycle, and they'd thought it would provide good exercise for Ben. Of course, Ben would love it because it was similar to Daddy's big tractors.

She didn't want to have to worry about the bow later, because later she planned to spend with Jake. Her stomach trembled with expectation, as she was unsure of how Jake was going to react when she told him that she loved him.

The tractor and Ben's toys from Santa weren't in the garage, although Elise was sure that was where Jake had put them. A door led off the garage and she opened it and went inside. She found the toys, but her eyes were glued to the object in a corner—a cradle, a baby's cradle. Mystified, she walked over and touched one of the beautifully carved spindles. The cradle rocked to and fro and played "Rock-a-Bye, Baby." For a moment she was caught in a wave of immeasurable joy. She recognized the cradle. She'd shown it to Jake in a magazine months ago and he'd obviously ordered it—for them and their baby. Evidently it was to be a surprise, a gift from him.

Staring at the cradle, she saw everything it personified. It was there in the cradle's beauty, in the tune, Jake's love. He loved her. She held a hand to her chest, overcome by this discovery. He'd never said a word. Why?

Tonight he would.

She tied a big bow on the tractor, but she couldn't take her eyes off the cradle. There would be no baby, and she was fine with that. They had Ben. But how did Jake feel? Did he want more children? Tonight she would find that out, too.

WHEN SHE RETURNED TO the house, Jake was settling Ben in his bed. She walked over and stared down at the boy she loved so much.

"Mom-E," Ben said.

"I love you," she replied.

"I 'ove 'ou, too." Ben held up two fingers, starting another game they played to help him with numbers.

"I love you three." She displayed three fingers.

"I 'ove 'ou 'our," Ben said, and struggled until he had four fingers in the air.

"I love you more."

Ben shook his head. "No, me, 'ore," he insisted, and held out all his fingers.

"No, me more." At this point she usually tickled his rib cage until he dissolved into a fit of giggles, but tonight she just held him. "Night, baby," she whispered, tucking his teddy and tractor beside him.

"'Anta come, Mom-E?" Ben asked. "'O, 'o, 'o."

"Yes, Santa comes tonight. Ho. Ho. Ho."

"'Oys."

"Yes, he'll bring lots of toys for Ben, but Ben has to go to sleep first."

She kissed his cheek and he turned onto his side, the teddy close and the tractor in one hand.

Elise patted Wags on the head as she left the room. Jake watched all this in growing concern. Elise was different and he couldn't put his finger on what was bothering him. She didn't seem upset. She actually seemed happy, but still, there was something…

"Are you okay?" he asked, not quite able to keep the concern out of his voice.

She turned to face him and smiled. "I'm better than I've been in a long time."

He relaxed and slid his fingers through her blond tresses. "Your hair's gotten longer. It's almost to your shoulders."

Her heart skipped a beat. "I haven't had time for a visit to the hairdresser."

"I like it."

She lifted an eyebrow.

He grinned and the skip became a steady rhythm. "Go to the den. I have a surprise for you."

As he disappeared into the kitchen, she headed for the den and clicked off the lamps. Then she kicked off her heels, hiked up her dress and sank to the rug in front of the roaring fire. It was warm and peaceful here, much like she felt inside, and she hoped, prayed, this evening turned out the way she wanted.

Jake came back with a bottle of wine and two glasses

and poured them each a glass and handed her one, the warmth from the fire and Christmas lights creating an inviting glow.

"I like this," she said happily.

He dropped down beside her. "I don't drink, but this is a special occasion. Our first Christmas."

"Our first Christmas," she repeated as they touched their glasses and took a sip. They sat for a while, just enjoying the moment and this quiet time together, but Elise had to tell him how she felt or she thought she'd burst. "I tied a bow on Ben's tractor."

He wondered where she'd gone, and then he knew, and he also knew she'd seen the cradle. He understood the look on her face.

"I saw the cradle," she added quietly, confirming what he'd already guessed. "It's beautiful. I can't believe you ordered it."

He swirled the wine in his glass, leaning back on his elbow. "I didn't."

"Sure you did. I saw it."

"I made the cradle."

"What?"

"I made the cradle," he repeated.

"From wood?"

"Yes."

"It's so professional," she said in awe. "And it even has a song."

"That taxed my intelligence to the limit, but with the help from a man at the electronics store I figured it out."

"I never knew you did woodwork." She was totally enraptured with everything she was learning about Jake. Suddenly she knew why she'd felt his love so strongly—he'd created the cradle with his own hands.

"My dad taught me. He was an expert at making things." He glanced at the fireplace. "He made that mantel. Those designs in the wood are cotton fields."

At least he had some good memories of his father, Elise thought. Jake needed those—and he needed more.

Jake cleared his throat, refusing to let memories sadden him. "I made the headboard on our bed and did all the trim in the new part of the house, too."

"You did?"

"Yes, when we got married I realized the house needed redecorating. Nothing had been done since my mother left. I hired a contractor and we redid the whole house, but I couldn't resist adding my own touches."

The wine burned as it went down her throat. "Because...because you hoped one day I'd want to live here?"

The fire crackled and his eyes met hers in the shimmering glow. "Yeah, I hoped it."

"Oh, Jake, why did tolerate my insensitive behavior?"

"Because I wanted a baby, too."

Silence followed his words and Elise knew he wasn't telling her his true feelings. Feelings that had been there all the time and she'd never noticed. Maybe she hadn't wanted to. She'd had a mental block back then, but now... She had to hear him say the words.

"There's another reason, isn't there?"

"Like what?" The words were in his throat, but he couldn't force them out. He'd waited for this moment—forever—but fear kept him silent, fear kept him prisoner, fear kept him chained to emotions from the past. He found it hard to express something he felt so intensely, especially since *his* ghost was always there.

"Like a deeper emotion," she said. "There's a very good reason you put up with my dead husband's picture in our bedroom and my thoughtlessness about your home, your work." She paused. "Say it, Jake."

He stared down into his glass and said what was in his heart. "Maybe I'm afraid that if I say those words, you'll disappear the way my mother did." There. He'd brought the fear to the surface, the one thing that held him paralyzed, terrified—fear of her leaving him. That was why he couldn't tell her how he really felt. But tonight, for his own peace of mind, he had to acknowledge all the emotions that had brought him to this point.

"Oh, Jake." She took their glasses and set them on the hearth. "I've told you I'm not leaving you—now or ever—and I meant it. And do you know why?"

"Why?" he asked hoarsely, waiting as a knot formed in his stomach, for he knew her words would change his life.

"Because I love you."

The knot dissolved into pure joy. He'd never thought he'd hear those words from her, and for a moment he was caught in a spasm of disbelief and it showed on his face.

"I'm not sure when it started," she went on, "but I know when I first sensed it—the night you were so patient and gentle with Ben for getting out of his bed. I wanted to say I love you and that shocked me because I loved Derek. I felt I would always love him."

"And?" He looked into her eyes, searching for the sadness, searching for a sign that Derek was gone from her heart.

"Today when we stopped by the house, I realized I'd only been existing before I met you, and when I looked at Derek's picture all the pain was gone. I'd finally let him go. I wasn't sad or upset, I was happy. I'd found someone whom I love so deeply I can't remember anyone's touch but his. And I understood why I was so troubled about your losing Ben and why I was willing to do anything to make sure that didn't happen. Tonight when I saw the cradle I knew you loved me, too."

His eyes never left her face. "Probably from the first moment I saw you standing outside your car looking at that flat tire as if it was something from outer space."

"Say it," she said softly.

He had to touch her to get the words out. His hand cupped her face. "I love you," he breathed in a raspy voice, the words coming easily as her eyes shone bright with all the love he'd waited for.

She licked her lips, unable to speak.

"I love you so much that I don't think I can live without you." As he spoke, his lips met hers in a gentle vow of love everlasting, but soon primal needs took over and the kiss deepened. He lowered her to the rug as his lips revisited familiar places along her neck, her ear. "I love you," he murmured again. His hand found her breast through the fabric of her dress. "I'll die if I have to sleep in that bed one more night without your love." His hand slid down the front of her dress. "How the hell do I get you out of this?"

"It has a zipper in the back," she muttered, her body aching, needing his touch, his possession. It wasn't long before she was out of the dress and everything else. The fire glistened on the smoothness of her skin and Jake took in the sensual picture.

"You're so beautiful," he whispered.

"So are you," she answered, undoing the buttons on his shirt and running her hands across his firm chest. Soon his clothes were a heap on the floor as she eagerly helped him.

"Wait," he said before he lost all thought. "I'll get the condoms from the bedroom."

She kissed his cheek, his neck. "You don't have to bother. I've been on the pill for a while."

"How? When?"

"I called my gynecologist and explained the situation, and she ordered a prescription for me and had it delivered to the clinic where Ben goes for his speech therapy. I pretended I had to go to the ladies' room and I went to the office and picked it up."

"Very sneaky." His lips teased her breast.

"This is your Christmas present," she told him. "And mine," she added on a sigh as pleasure ebbed through her from his gentle stroking.

He pulled her to him, their naked bodies caressing, touching and fusing together in a way they never had before. This time every movement was made with love and they both felt it, both rejoiced in the feeling.

Jake rolled her onto her back, his lips kissing every inch of her, her hands equally at work on him. As his mouth touched her intimately, sighs mingled with erotic moans as the world spun away, leaving the two of them alone in a warm oasis of love.

"Jake," she moaned when she couldn't take any more. He parted her legs and thrust deep inside her. She met each thrust, each movement with an urgency of her own, and soon pleasure convulsed through her in a blinding array of fulfillment that was awesome in its power. A moment later Jake reached the same pinnacle and she heard him groan, "I love you."

The sizzling fire warmed their damp, nude bodies and they lay entwined, sharing this moment of discovering sex with love. They were one, completely, forever, and they basked in the joy of that. Neither spoke; words weren't necessary.

Finally Jake kissed the warm hollow of her neck. "It was pretty wonderful before, but this is…" He stopped as words failed him.

"Love," she finished for him. "Real love."

He closed his eyes as he realized he'd found something few men find in a lifetime. The feeling was overpowering, but he accepted it with all his heart. He was no longer afraid of that emotion, although he had been before tonight. That was the main reason he'd accepted Elise's offer of marriage so quickly; it didn't involve love. Now, finally, they had each other and Ben. He didn't think life got much better than this.

"Remember when I was in that insane mood and I said I wanted to be pregnant by Christmas?"

"Yes."

"That didn't happen, but we *do* have a baby by Christmas."

"Yes. We have Ben," he said. "And speaking of him, we'd better put his Santa gifts out and go to bed."

"In a minute," she said, holding tight to his arms so he couldn't move. The fire crackled, and she had to ask, "Do you want more children?"

Jake lay perfectly still. He hadn't expected that question, but he didn't have any secrets from her. "Where is this coming from?"

"I was thinking about the cradle and all the love you put into it."

He stroked her arm. "The cradle was a labor of love, but right now my energy is focused on Ben. I haven't thought much about another baby."

She turned her head to look at him. "Me, neither," she admitted.

"You're amazing, do you know that? For a woman who was tortured by her own fears, you've done a miraculous job with Ben."

"Looking back, I can see I somehow rationalized that if I had my own baby it would heal all the pain in here." She placed her hand on her chest.

"Me, too," he confessed, covering the hand on her breast. "You were clinging to your past and I was trying to escape mine. Not good reasons to conceive a child."

"Maybe not. But it brought us together."

"Yeah," he murmured, cupping her breast. He kissed her softly, lingeringly, and as desire stirred, he rose quickly to his feet and pulled her up. "Mrs. Claus, we've got work to do."

"I love you," she said, gazing into his eyes. "Don't ever doubt that."

He didn't...not anymore. It was there in her eyes, in her voice, and he felt he'd been given the greatest gift on earth. And he had.

Soon all the presents were under the tree and they crawled into bed replete in a most satisfying way.

THEY AWOKE TO Ben jumping on their bed shouting, "'Anta, 'A-dy, Mom-E. 'O, 'o, 'o."

Wags added several loud barks, which was a rousing wake-up call.

"Oh, God, is it morning?" Jake groaned.

"I think so," Elise muttered, and saw it was still dark out. She peered at the clock and saw the time. "It's 5:00 a.m." She made to get up, then realized she didn't have a stitch of clothing on. Jake came to the rescue as he distracted Ben and she slipped out and grabbed her robe. She also threw Jake his.

"Is everyone decent?" Aunt Vin called from the hallway.

Jake tied his robe. "Yes."

Aunt Vin came into the bedroom with a present and handed it to Jake. "This is a gift from me to the both of you. You can use it for the—" she glanced at Ben "—you know."

"Pa-sent, 'A-dy," Ben said.

"Yes, it's a present. Let's see what's in it." Jake quickly unwrapped the box to reveal a video camera. "Oh, my."

"I thought it would be something you could use as Ben grows older."

Jake hugged her. Elise did, too. "Thank you," Jake said.

"It's all set to go and it's so simple to use even I can do it."

"This is incredibly thoughtful." Elise hugged her again.

"Is it time?" Aunt Vin asked. "I didn't want to miss it."

Elise grabbed Ben. "Let me change Ben's diaper, then we'll see if Santa's come."

While Elise was busy, Jake acquainted himself with the camera.

Ben couldn't keep quiet and he jabbered nonstop about Santa.

Elise set him on the floor and he took off down the hall with Wags behind him, and Jake followed with the camera.

Ben came to a complete stop when he saw the presents under the tree. He pointed, eyes wide, then ran to the tractor and climbed on, but he couldn't figure out what the pedals were for.

Jake handed Aunt Vin the camera and he squatted down by Ben. "It's a big tractor like Daddy's. You put your feet here and push to make it go." Ben tried several times, but he didn't understand the action. Jake knew they'd spend hours teaching Ben before he learned it. That was fine because eventually he would.

Ben tore into his other gifts like a hurricane, paper and ribbon flying in every direction. Wags barked excitedly as he tried to catch every piece. The room was full of fun, love and happiness.

Aunt Vin had given Ben a truck that had lights and a horn, and while she was showing Ben how to work it, Jake sank down by Elise on the floor amid all the paper and handed her a small box.

She unwrapped it hastily and gasped when she saw the gold locket with Ben's picture inside. "Oh, thank you, this is perfect. Put it on for me." She turned her back to him.

He slipped it around her neck and clasped it. His hands lingered on her bare skin and she rested her head against him. "You know what I want to do right now?" he whispered.

"Hmm," she answered, an ache in her voice. "The same thing I want to do, but we have to wait until later." Suddenly she was wishing she hadn't invited a house full of people. She just wanted to be alone with Jake and Ben.

She reached under the tree and handed him a carefully wrapped package.

He lifted an eyebrow. "I thought I got my gift last night."

She poked him in the ribs. "You did, but this is something you can show."

"Oh, the other one shows, too. It's written all over my face. I can't seem to stop smiling."

"I know." She had the same goofy expression on her face and it was wonderful.

They stared at each other for endless seconds, both lost in that wonderful feeling, and then Jake opened his gift. Inside was a leather wallet containing pictures of Ben. "I remember you saying that when you met with your accountant, you didn't have any pictures of Ben to show him. I used Aunt Vin's camera and she had them developed for me. I didn't have time for a professional photo. I know we have all those pictures of Mrs. Carr's, but I wanted something recent."

"These are perfect and I especially like this one," he said, holding out the picture of her with Ben. "Thank you." His lips touched hers softly, igniting a familiar flame, and he gathered her close, kissing her thoroughly. He heard a movement and broke the kiss to see Aunt Vin filming them.

"Aunt Vin," he complained. "This is private."

She lowered the camera. "Thought you'd like to remember that, too." Laughter filled her voice.

He didn't need it on film to remember. It was forever in his heart and he would never forget this day and the love Elise had brought into his life.

Love. He finally knew what it was all about.

CHAPTER SIXTEEN

CHRISTMAS DAY WAS EVERYTHING Jake wanted it to be and so much more. Ben was shy at first with everyone, but he soon became the center of attention. Everyone knew he loved tractors and that was the central theme of Ben's gifts. Beau gave him a motorized one that worked from a remote control. Caleb gave him one that had a plow, disk and trailer that could be interchanged. Ben tried hard to make the toys work the way they should, but when he couldn't, he didn't get upset. He just smiled while Beau and Caleb patiently showed him.

Althea had knitted an afghan with a tractor on it and Ben's name. The shocker of the day came when Ben unwrapped Constance and Judith's gift. Ben was sitting in Elise's lap, and when Elise became very still, Jake immediately went to her side to look at the object in her hand. It was a book, and on the cover was a tractor. The title read *Putt-Putt Tractor.* Inside were pictures depicting the little song Elise had created. Jake was at a loss for words and so was Elise.

"Thank you," Elise finally said, fighting tears. "This is so special."

"I remembered your song," Judith said. "And when I told Mom about it, we decided to do this. Mom hasn't drawn in years, but she did a great job, didn't she?"

"Yes. Thank you, Mother. Ben and I will treasure this always." She stood, holding on to Ben, and kissed Constance's cheek.

"You're welcome, darling," Constance responded, her voice unsteady.

Elise then kissed her sister and Ben had to give hugs. "I hope all the words are right," Judith said.

Jake understood now why Elise was so moved. Her mother hadn't bought the book. She had participated in its creation. It was a clear sign that Constance and Judith had accepted their marriage and Ben.

"Let's see," Elise said as she opened the colorful book. "Putt-putt tractor, have you any wheels?" her voice rang out.

"'Es-'ir, 'es-'ir," Ben shouted, and Elise continued the song. Judith hadn't missed a word.

After that, everyone had to sing the putt-putt song and Ben sat on his tractor, joining in. The house was full of laughter and Jake thought it should've been this way years ago, but he was too happy to dwell on sad memories.

When Stan and Duncan arrived, Elise held her breath, hoping Judith wouldn't ruin this day. She remained quiet, though, embracing her son and speaking civilly to Stan. This was a Judith Elise didn't recognize and she kept waiting for the barbs to fly. Again Judith surprised her by being polite and courteous.

Despite their age difference, Ben and Duncan became fast friends. Duncan was eager to help Ben with his toys. After dinner the weather turned nice, and Jake let them go outside to play ball. The men went, too, and the women stayed inside, cleaning the kitchen and visiting.

Elise gathered up the last of the wrapping paper and stood for a moment staring out the French doors, watching the boys playing. Ben and Duncan were throwing a ball to each other, or more accurately, Duncan was throwing it to Ben. Of course, Ben never caught it, but he chased after the ball laughing with Wags right behind him. Ben was having a good time—the way little boys should.

Andrew and Stan sat on the swing, smiling at the antics of Ben, Wags and Duncan. Jake, Beau and Caleb were standing together talking. Three brothers getting to know each other. Jake looked happy, she thought, and felt a sense of pure joy.

Ben grew tired and clung to Jake's legs, and Jake lifted him up. Duncan rested against his father on the swing. Judith came to stand beside Elise, staring out at Stan and Duncan. "He wants another child," she uttered in a voice so low that Elise barely caught the words.

"Who?"

"Stan. It's our biggest argument, other than how to raise Duncan."

Elise didn't know what to say, so she continued to watch the peaceful scene. Ben wriggled out of Jake's arms and ran to Duncan, and they started playing with the ball again. Before Duncan jumped up, he hugged his father, and the expression on Stan's face said more than Elise ever could, but she had to try.

"Would it be that hard to compromise?"

"I miss him terribly," Judith said in a hollow voice.

"Stan or Duncan?"

"Both. That big house is so lonely without them."

Elise put an arm around her. "Like I said before, do something about it."

"I plan to, but I'm not sure if Stan still wants me. Our marriage hasn't been idyllic lately."

"Then do something about that, too."

Judith looked at her. "You're so happy. You're almost glowing."

"Thank you, and thanks for the book. It means so much."

"I do have a heart, Elise," she sniffed. "I haven't acted like it recently, but I do love you...and your family."

That meant more than anything Judith had ever said to her, and they both knew they'd reached a milestone in their relationship—the act of accepting and forgiving as sisters should.

"What's so interesting?" Althea asked as she walked up to them.

Judith couldn't speak, so she turned and moved away.

"Did I say something wrong?" Althea asked with a note of concern.

"No," Elise assured her. "She's just feeling emotional."

"I hope she and Stan can solve their problems."

"Me, too," Elise agreed, and glanced outside. Althea followed her gaze.

"Now I see the attraction," Althea said. "Those McCain boys are sure handsome men," she added, smiling.

"One in particular," Elise replied, her eyes on Jake.

The smile left Althea's face. "Jake and Caleb have suffered a lot…all because of me."

Elise hugged her. "Don't dwell on the past," she said. "It's Christmas, and look at your sons' faces. Can't you see their happiness?"

"Yes, I can," she whispered. "Thank you for inviting us today."

"You're very welcome, and you'll have to give me your recipe for cinnamon rolls and cottage cheese pie. Never heard of cottage cheese pie before."

"My grandmother was Polish, and she used to make it for every holiday. My aunt made it and I learned to make it, too. Jake and Beau wouldn't eat cottage cheese, but they loved it in the custard pie. Caleb was never that crazy about it."

"You made it today for Jake, didn't you? To give him back some of what he missed."

"Yes," she said solemnly. "But nothing will ever make up for all those years." Althea eyes centered on her eldest son. "I want Jake to be happy. That's my fervent wish."

"You don't have to worry about Jake anymore," Elise assured her, and she meant every word. Her goal was to keep Jake happy for the rest of his life.

THE HOUSE WAS VERY QUIET after everyone left. Ben was cranky and fussy; he'd been awake since five and hadn't had a nap and refused to go to bed. Elise couldn't even get him to sing the putt-putt song. Finally, Jake just carried him to his room.

Ben cried, "Mom-E, Mom-E," holding out his arms to her, and it took every ounce of restraint she had not to give in to him. She bit her lip as Jake whisked him away. After a few minutes, the cries stopped and Elise went to take a shower. When she finished, she tiptoed into Ben's room. Jake sat in a rocker, Ben asleep against his shoulder. Jake gingerly rose to his feet when he saw her.

"Mom-E," Ben whimpered.

She scooped Ben out of Jake's arms and placed him in his bed. "Mommy's here," she whispered. "I love you."

"'Ove you, too," he mumbled, but he didn't raise his fingers. Ben was asleep.

Jake led her to their bedroom where she kissed him briefly. "Go take a shower and I'll keep an eye on him to make sure he's sound asleep."

In Ben's room, only the night-light was burning, but she could see clearly. She tucked his covers around him and set his teddy and tractor next to him. She watched him sleep, her heart full of so much love that her chest felt heavy. Taking a sweet breath, she stroked Wags for a moment then left the room.

WHEN JAKE CAME OUT OF the shower, Elise was sitting on the bed staring at the headboard. He eased down beside her. "What are you doing, honey?"

She smiled at him. "That's the first time you've called me that."

He blinked, totally unaware of what he'd said, then he grinned. "You are my honey, aren't you?"

"You bet—always." Their eyes locked for a second, then she touched the intricate carvings in the wood. "I was admiring your beautiful work. It's gorgeous, but I don't understand when you had time to do all this." She looked at the wood trim around the walls.

''A lot of the summer you were busy with graduate students. When you were, I worked on the house. And remember those nights I was late?''

She nodded.

''I was busy on the cradle. You can't do much farm work after dark.''

''If I'd been more astute, I would've realized that,'' she said as she moved toward him. ''We're never getting rid of this headboard.''

''I don't plan to.'' He enclosed her in his embrace.

''Today was wonderful, wasn't it?''

''Yes, but...''

''But what?'' She turned to see his face.

''I still couldn't hug my own mother,'' he admitted. ''I don't understand why that's so hard for me.''

''Give it time.''

''It's like this mask comes over my emotions when I'm around her. I know the truth but something in me won't let it go.''

''Try not to rush it.''

''I've been without my mother for twenty-eight years and I want to be able to love her again.''

She knew that and she didn't know how to make it easy for him. He had to do it by himself, but she'd be with him every step of the way.

''That was a really nice gesture of your mother and Judith.'' He was obviously changing the subject.

''Yes, it was.''

''And you feel good about it?''

''Very,'' she said. ''I'm exhausted, but inside I feel pretty wonderful.''

His hand slid up her thigh under her gown. ''You feel pretty good on the outside, too.''

''Jake.'' She laughed as he slipped the gown from her shoulders and his hands caressed and stroked sensitive places that only he knew about.

She rolled and straddled him, loving the surprise on his face when she took the initiative. Moving her body over his, she felt his arousal and her body grew warm and moist.

He ran his fingers through her hair, holding her head and gazing into her eyes. "I love you," he whispered.

She smiled dreamily. "I know how difficult it is for you to say that and—" Her words were cut off as his lips claimed hers, invoking a burning need that only he could satisfy.

Immeasurable joy trembled through Jake and he knew he held the world in his arms, and the little boy across the hall made it go round. He had everything. His life was perfect.

THE NEXT WEEK PASSED quickly and they soon got back to a normal routine with Ben and his therapy. They paid a visit to Althea's so Ben could see the lights and get the gifts in his stocking. Althea asked Jake if he'd like his and he said no, and Elise knew Jake was still struggling with his feelings about his mother. But they were all trying.

Jake realized that to resolve his feelings he had to read the letters. He called Althea later and returned to her house alone, because this was between him and his mother.

He read every letter with a knot in his gut, but what unfolded was his mother's love—how much she loved him, how proud she was of him and how much she missed him. In every letter she asked for forgiveness. And there were presents she'd kept in the attic. Most of them he'd outgrown, except for a hand-knitted sweater and a watch that had an inscription for his twenty-first birthday.

"Thank you," Jake said in a raspy voice.

"Oh, Jake, don't thank me. I'm your mother and I'm so sorry for the past. I'm so sorry for all the years I wasn't in your life."

Jake fingered the sweater. "I guess we'll never figure out why some things happen…but they usually happen for a reason whether good or bad."

"Yes, I suppose," Althea admitted weakly.

"Thank you for sending Aunt Vin into my life. I really needed her."

"That was the only peace I had. I knew she'd take good care of you."

When he left, there were tears in his eyes and in Althea's and he still couldn't hug his mother. All he could do was say he'd forgiven her. It seemed to be what Althea needed…for now.

BEN HAD A DOCTOR'S appointment in the middle of January for a complete checkup. The day before, they went in for several tests so the doctor could have the results at the time of their visit. Afterward, they took Ben to a restaurant for supper, something they'd never done before, and Ben did fine. He was progressing with each day and they had high hopes for the test results.

The next morning they were at Dr. Markham's office early for the remaining tests, then they went to lunch and arrived at the doctor's office mid-afternoon for the results.

As they expected, Ben's checkup was good.

"Ben's gained seven pounds and he's grown an inch," Dr. Markham said. "I received a glowing report from Ms. Collins. She says Ben is starting to put more and more words together. He's not breaking them up and he's recognizing the first syllables. Also, his coordination has improved tremendously. Keep doing what you're doing, it's working." He closed Ben's file. "I'd like to get an X ray of Ben's lungs. I think we can discontinue the breathing treatments, but I want to see his lungs first."

A young girl knocked on the door. "This is Gloria," Dr. Markham said. "Our X ray technician." He glanced at Ben. "Would you like to go with Gloria so she can do one more test?"

Ben slid from Jake's lap and Elise stood. "I'm sorry, Mrs. McCain, you can't be in the room," Gloria said, reaching for Ben's hand. "Ready, Ben?"

He nodded.

"Are you sure? I mean..."

"Me big, Mom-E," Ben said, sensing her worry. The fact that he put the *b* on *big* made her realize how much he was improving.

"Okay, then. Mommy and Daddy will be waiting," she called as Ben walked away with Gloria.

"He's growing up too fast," she commented sadly, resuming her seat.

"But that's good," the doctor assured her, and she knew that it was. Ben had to learn to go places without them. She didn't like this part of parenting, either.

Jake took her hand and she held it tight. He understood.

They talked with Dr. Markham about Ben's case history, and he said he'd been a colleague of Dr. Ruskin's and that Dr. Ruskin was a brilliant doctor and he wasn't sure what had changed him. He was devoted to researching and treating developmental delay.

"Greed happened," Jake told him. "But I'll always be grateful for what he did for Ben."

Elise grew restless, wondering why the X ray was taking so long. "I think I'll check on Ben," she said, getting to her feet.

"I'm sure he's fine," Dr Markham replied. "But he's down the hall to the right."

"I'll go with you," Jake offered when he realized the time. The film should have been taken by now. "We'll be back in a few minutes."

They walked down a corridor until they came to a door that read X ray Room—Do Not Enter. Jake stopped a nurse. "Our little boy is having X rays and we're trying to find him."

"He's probably in there with Gloria," she answered.

"Would you see, please?"

"Gloria will come out when she's through." The nurse's voice was impatient.

"Would you see, please?" Jake asked again, and when the nurse seemed about to refuse, he added, "If you don't, I'm going in myself." He was beginning to get a bad feeling and he just wanted to see Ben.

"Oh, all right," the nurse sighed, and opened the door. A moment later they heard her scream.

Jake and Elise rushed in and saw Gloria lying on the floor, blood oozing from her head. "Get a doctor," Jake shouted to the nurse, and glanced frantically around, but Ben was nowhere in sight.

"Where's Ben, Jake?' Elise cried desperately. "Oh, God, where's Ben?"

People crowded into the room and a doctor and nurse attended to Gloria. She stirred and blinked her eyes. Dr. Markham came in and knelt beside her.

"What happened?" he asked.

"I don't know," Gloria replied weakly. "I was getting Ben ready to do the X ray and I felt a sharp pain in my head. That's all I remember."

"Where the hell is our son?" Jake demanded.

"Calm down, Mr. McCain," Dr. Markham said sympathetically. "He's in the building somewhere and we'll find him."

That didn't make sense to Jake. Gloria had obviously been hit on the head to knock her out. *And Ben wasn't here.*

He and Elise ran from room to room, calling Ben's name. People rushed into the hall, staring, but no one had seen Ben. After fifteen minutes, Jake experienced fear like he'd never known before and he did the only thing he could; he called Caleb.

Within minutes Caleb came charging in, Beau a few steps behind. Caleb took control and sealed off the clinic until every room was searched. Police officers were everywhere and the Amber Alert for missing children was activated.

''Do you have a picture of Ben?'' Caleb asked.

Jake hurriedly grabbed his wallet and extracted a couple of pictures.

''Good,'' Caleb said. ''We'll have this on every TV station in Texas in a few minutes.''

Half an hour later, Caleb motioned for Jake to come in the hall. ''I have to be blunt,'' he said. ''Ben's not here. That means someone's taken him.''

Jake felt his insides cave in and he fought to breathe. He'd already known this, but hearing it out loud was paralyzing. ''Why?'' was all he could manage to say.

''There are evil people in this world. I see it every day.''

Evil people. Suddenly he thought of Dr. Ruskin and his threat and he told Caleb.

''We'll check him out immediately. A dark gray van with primer stains on one side was spotted leaving the parking lot in a hurry. It scraped a Dumpster and didn't stop. We're searching for the van, too. The best thing you can do now is take Elise home and wait there in case Ruskin or someone phones with a ransom call.''

Ruskin. Ruskin. Ransom call. Ransom call. That was all Jake could hear. Beyond that he couldn't seem to function.

''Jake?'' Caleb said in a loud voice. ''Do you hear me?''

Jake blinked, bringing himself back from a place he didn't want to be. This couldn't be happening.

''You have to be strong,'' Caleb said. ''You have to tell Elise.''

Jake glanced to where Elise was sitting, her arms wrapped around her waist as she rocked back and forth. ''Oh, my God,'' he muttered, and quickly went to her.

''Where's Ben, Jake?'' she cried into his shoulder. ''Where's our baby?''

He inhaled deeply and felt the air rip through his body, but he had to tell her the truth, and it would truly be the hardest thing he'd ever had to do in his life. ''Someone…someone's taken him,'' he finally forced out. ''It might be Dr. Ruskin, and Caleb thinks there might be a ransom call. We have to go home.''

She pushed away, her eyes huge with fright. ''No, I'm not leaving here without Ben.''

''Elise...''

''No, Jake, he's here,'' she insisted, fighting the hysteria rising in her. ''We just have to keep searching.''

''He's not here,'' Jake said in a quiet voice. ''We have to go home.''

Elise looked from Jake to Caleb to Beau. ''No, no, no.'' She shook her head, denying everything she was seeing in their eyes. ''No, no, no.'' Her knees buckled when their expressions didn't change.

She was vaguely aware of Dr. Markham beside her with a needle in his hand. When she realized what he was about to do, she jerked her arm away. ''Don't you dare,'' she spat. ''Don't you give me anything. I have to be awake when Ben returns. He'll want his mommy.'' Plaintive sobs erupted from her, tearing Jake's heart out. He scooped her into his arms and walked from the clinic.

Beau drove and Jake held Elise until her sobs stopped. Then she asked, ''Why, Jake? Why would Dr. Ruskin or anyone take our son?''

He didn't have an answer for her and he was glad when they reached the farm. There were several unfamiliar cars in front of the house. When Jake got out, a man introduced himself as Keith Coleman, an FBI agent. Several more officers were inside setting up a command post, he was told. Aunt Vin met them at the door in a frantic state.

Aunt Vin and Elise hugged tightly. ''It'll be all right,'' Aunt Vin cooed. ''They'll find him.'' She stroked Elise's hair. ''You get some rest and I'll make coffee for these men.''

Jake followed Elise down the hall, but she didn't go to their room. She went to Ben's and picked up his teddy and tractor. Wags rested his head in her lap, whining as if he sensed something was wrong, and she gently rubbed his ears. Jake sat beside her.

"All his things are here," she said. "There's his Christmas toys and his big tractor. He should be on it laughing and playing. He should be here. He—"

Her voice cracked and Jake put his arms around her. "Elise—"

"Don't tell me everything's going to be okay because it isn't. It won't be until he's back."

"We have to be strong."

"I don't want to be strong," she snapped. "I want our son back."

He tried to dredge up words to comfort her, but inside he was slowly bleeding to death and there was nothing he could do to assuage the wound that had burst open the moment he'd realized Ben was gone. But he had to try. He rested his face on hers.

"Hold me, Jake," she cried. "Hold me."

His arms tightened around her and they clung together until Beau came into the room. "Agent Coleman wants to speak with you," he said.

"Let's go to the den," Jake said to Elise.

"No, I need to be here. Wags will keep me company." Wags whimpered in response and she buried her face in his fur.

"What can you tell me about Dr. Ruskin?" Agent Coleman asked when Jake entered the den.

"A warrant had been issued for his arrest. He called at the time and asked me to drop the charges because of everything he'd done for Ben. I tried to tell him I hadn't pressed any charges, but he said I was lying and became angry. He also said he'd get even. I haven't heard from him since, nor have I heard from the Houston police."

An officer motioned to the agent and Keith spoke to him briefly, then he turned back to Jake.

"Dr. Ruskin was released from a Houston jail about fifteen minutes ago. He couldn't have taken your son."

Jake sighed painfully. It seemed obvious that Ruskin would snatch him for revenge, but now it didn't look like it.

"What about Ben's biological mother?" Keith asked.

Jake shrugged. "She abandoned him when he was a baby and I can't see her taking him now."

"Do you have an address for her?"

"No, but you might check with CPS. They've been trying to locate her for years and you can also check with the Fosters. Peggy's her aunt, but if she'd heard from Sherry I'm sure she would have contacted me."

"Do you have her number?"

Jake gave him the Fosters' number and address, then Keith took him through the procedures to follow if the kidnapper called. Jake tried to listen, but all he could think about was Ben. Where was he? Who had him? He'd heard of children being snatched; it was in the papers, on TV, and he always sympathized with the parents, but he'd never even come close to knowing what they were really experiencing. It was indescribable. He just had that death feeling inside, that feeling he couldn't shake.

He raised his head and saw his mother standing in the doorway. In that second, the past came full circle and crashed into the present with symbolic force and he did what he would have done as a kid—went to his mother for comfort, for reassurance. He hugged her tight, something he hadn't been able to do before but now found easy. "Someone took Ben, Mama," he cried.

"I know, son," she said, and guided him to the sofa. "Caleb's a good cop. He'll find him."

"I just keep thinking what he must be going through."

"Don't," she said sharply. "Don't let yourself do that."

"It's awful—losing a child. How does anyone survive this? I can barely breathe or think. I'm lost somewhere and I can't find my way back, and Elise...God, she's close to collapsing and I have to stay strong for her. But someone just took our child from us and I don't know how to deal with the pain. It's eating me alive and..." He stared dazedly at her.

"What?" she asked anxiously.

"Is this how you felt when I took Dad's side and refused to go with you?"

"Jake..."

"It is, isn't it?"

Althea pressed her lips together, but mumbled, "Yes."

The years of anger and resentment ended in that instant as Jake fully understood what his mother had gone through, all the pain, all the suffering she'd endured. Suddenly the past, coupled with Ben's disappearance, hit him like an avalanche, taking him down into a maelstrom of despair, smothering, choking him until the mask that hid his emotions crumbled away. "Mama," he moaned, and reached for Althea. "I'm so sorry. I'm so sorry." He hadn't wept, but now hard sobs shook his body and he couldn't stop. He couldn't stop the pain. He couldn't stop anything.

"Shh, shh, Jake," Althea said in a shaky voice, rubbing his back. "You have nothing to be sorry for."

The heartbreaking sobs echoed through the house, and Beau and Caleb rushed to Jake. Aunt Vin came from the kitchen with tears in her eyes. The FBI agents paused in their tasks. But no one knew what to do.

Elise jumped up when she heard the gut-wrenching sounds and ran to the den. Those sounds drove into her and she dropped to Jake's side, needing to comfort, to hold him, but most of all needing him to know she was here.

"Jake, honey." She smoothed his hair gently. "It's Elise. Please don't. Oh, God, Jake, please don't."

Somewhere in the avalanche of emotion that had just caved in on him, he heard her voice. It was the only thing saving him from the brink of total darkness that threatened to claim him. He wiped his eyes and looked at her.

"I...I..."

"It's okay," Elise said, touching, stroking him. "We're all feeling the same way."

Jake clambered to his feet. As he did, Beau and Caleb embraced him and they stood, three brothers bonded by blood but held together by love. Then he looped his arm around Elise and moved toward Ben's room. He had to get himself under control.

Jake sank onto the bed and buried his face in his hands. "I couldn't take it when I realized the pain I've put my mother through. All those years she begged to see me, to talk to me, and I refused because of the lies I'd been told."

"She understands," Elise assured him.

"I keep wondering how I'd cope if Ben did that to me. If he didn't return because someone had filled his head with lies. It would kill me."

"That's not going to happen." She rested her head on his shoulder. "What are we going to do?"

"Pray and keep praying until we have him home safe and sound."

"I don't understand who would do this."

"It's not Dr. Ruskin. He was in a Houston jail."

"I wanted to believe he had Ben. He knows him and wouldn't be afraid. If a stranger took him, that would mean..." She couldn't finish the sentence. She couldn't say the ugly words. Her hands started to tremble and a chill spread through her body.

Jake gathered her cold hands in his. "Why don't you eat something?" he suggested.

"If I do, I'll throw up." She nestled against him. "Just hold me."

He did, and watched as day faded into evening. One hour passed. There was no word of Ben.

Another hour dragged on. Constance came. Judith and Stan arrived.

Three hours stretched endlessly. People offered help. Others brought food. But there was still no word of Ben. The waiting was killing them both.

Caleb came into the bedroom. "Jake?"

"Hmm?"

"We haven't found the van, but they're questioning Ruskin just to see if he knows something."

Anger jerked through Jake at the helplessness he felt. "Dammit, Caleb, what's taking so long? Why can't you find Ben? It's been hours. They could have him out of the country by now and we're just sitting here waiting. No one's called. Nothing's happening."

"The police department has virtually shut down and every available officer is looking for Ben. Those who were off duty have come in to help. The TV stations are flashing his picture every few minutes and the radio stations are asking for everyone's help. The main thoroughfares are blocked and police are checking every car. Whoever has Ben won't get him out of Waco."

Jake closed his eyes, feeling he should apologize, but he knew Caleb wouldn't expect him to.

"Thanks, Caleb," he offered. "And thank everyone else."

"No problem." Caleb nodded. "The Fosters are here. They asked to speak with you. We haven't told them anything, so go slow in case this visit isn't on the up-and-up."

"You mean..."

"It could be anybody, and I'm just not sure why they're showing up now—at this particular time."

"Maybe they heard about Ben on the news," Elise said.

"They didn't mention it, so let them do the talking."

"Okay," Jake said. "Let's go speak to them."

"I don't think I can," Elise murmured.

He reached for her hand. "I can't do this without you." Together they walked into the den.

Peggy rushed to them. "What's happening? Why are all these policemen here?"

"Haven't you heard?" Jake asked.

Carl frowned. "Heard what?"

Jake glanced at Caleb and he nodded, so he answered, "Someone's kidnapped Ben."

"Oh, no, Carl," Peggy cried. "We should have come last night."

Caleb quickly stepped in. "Do you know something, Mrs. Foster?"

"Sherry came by the house yesterday."

"That's Ben's mother?"

"Yes. Somehow she'd heard about the lawsuit being settled and she wanted to talk to Irene. She wasn't aware her mother had passed away. She said she'd been living in Mexico and she became very angry when she found out Ben wasn't there."

"Did you tell her where Ben was?" Caleb asked.

Peggy twisted her hands nervously. "Yes, I told her Ben's father had been awarded custody."

"Does she know where Jake lives?"

"She didn't ask and I didn't tell her."

"Okay, Mrs. Foster," Caleb said. "Think and try to remember everything that happened."

"After I told her about Irene and Ben, she wanted to know why we were still in the house and I informed her Jake had given it to us. She became even angrier, ordering us out and saying the place was hers and we didn't have a right to it. Carl threatened to call the cops and she left."

"Was she alone?"

"No, her boyfriend was with her."

"What's his name?"

Peggy put a hand to her head. "I don't know. I can't think. Irene refused to allow him in the house because she knew he was supplying Sherry with drugs. She finally ran off with him." She turned to her husband. "What's his name? I've heard Irene say it, but I can't remember."

"Rusty Fobbs," Carl said. "He has red fuzzy hair and a beard and a mean expression on his face."

"Why didn't you phone us immediately?" Jake couldn't keep quiet any longer.

"We did, several times last night and this morning, but there was no answer. Finally I told Carl we had to come in person, but our fuel pump went out near Navasota and we had to have it repaired. That's why we're getting here so late.''

''The kidnapping's been on TV and on the radio. Haven't you heard about it? My God, Ben's been missing for hours.''

''We didn't turn the TV on and our radio has so much static that it gives me a headache.''

There was complete silence as Jake tried to gauge if they were telling the truth.

''Listen, Jake,'' Carl pleaded. ''We wouldn't hurt Ben or you. You've been good to us. I never dreamed Sherry would do something like this. She's never had any interest in Ben.''

''What type of vehicle were they driving?'' Caleb asked.

''A beat-up gray van,'' Carl answered.

''What kind of gray?''

''Dark with some primer stains on one side.''

An agonizing sound left Elise and Jake gulped air into his lungs. They knew who had snatched Ben. *His mother.*

CHAPTER SEVENTEEN

SHERRY HAD BEN. The news gave them hope because they now knew a madman hadn't stolen him. *Just his mother—* and she had taken him for a reason. Sherry wanted something and it had to be money. Jake just didn't understand why she was waiting so long to phone. That bothered him. She should've called by now.

They finally knew the enemy by name and the search intensified. Caleb went directly to Peggy.

"It would help if we had a photo of Sherry. Do you by any chance have one?"

Peggy grabbed her purse. "I don't think so, but I forget what's in here half the time."

"What about that Christmas we spent with Irene when Sherry was home after rehab?" Carl asked excitedly. "Nancy came over and you took a picture of them together. You kept it in your wallet for a long time."

"Yeah, yeah, I remember." Peggy flipped through her wallet. "Nancy hated that picture." She pulled out photo after photo of her daughter and grandkids, but she couldn't find the one of Sherry.

"Keep looking," Caleb insisted. "We need that picture."

"Try under the flap," Carl suggested.

"Oh, my God, here it is," Peggy cried as she found it. "Of course Sherry's much younger and her hair is now bleached blond."

Elise glanced at the photo over Peggy's shoulder. Sherry was pretty with sandy-blond hair. This was Ben's mother, the woman who had given him life. Anger, fierce and hot, ran through Elise. Ben didn't know her and he would be so frightened and lost. What type of mother would put her own child through that kind of misery?

Sherry wasn't Ben's real mother, though. *She* was. Elise knew that with all her heart. She might have had doubts in the beginning about her ability to care for him, but now she loved Ben as if he was her own. And he was.

Caleb grabbed the photo and ran from the room. Elise moved into Jake's arms. "How can she do this? Ben's probably so afraid. They have to find them, and soon."

They sat in the den and waited, Elise holding Jake's hand. She had to hold on to something or she felt she'd come apart at the seams. Silence, loud echoing silence, settled in the room.

Jake got up a couple of times and paced the floor, trying not to look at the clock, trying not to think as time, painful, endless time, slipped away. Just when he thought he couldn't take any more, the phone rang. It sounded like a bomb going off, startling everyone.

Jake ran toward it with Elise behind him, but Agent Coleman stopped them. "If it's her, agree to anything she wants. Don't get angry, just keep asking where Ben is."

"And Jake," Andrew Wellman said from behind him. "Whatever money she wants, I'll give it to you."

Jake stared at Andrew, this man he'd hated for most of his life, and realized the hate had long disappeared. "Thanks," Jake replied, his thoughts shifting to the phone. Was it Sherry? *Please be Sherry.*

"Hello," he said hoarsely, and Elise leaned in close so she could hear.

"Hi there, Jake, remember me?"

It was her. Thank God.

"Yes, Sherry, I remember you."

"I have something you want."

"Where's Ben?"

"He's sleeping. He screamed for a solid hour for

mommy and daddy and 'Ags, whoever the hell that is. I can't understand half of what he says."

Jake closed his eyes in agony and Elise's arm tightened around him. "Wags is his dog," he explained calmly. "Where's Ben?"

"Be patient, Jake."

"He's just a little boy. Please don't hurt him."

"Hurt him? He's my son, and when I told him that he bit the hell out of my arm. You should teach him some manners."

"Bring him back," Elise screamed, unable to listen to any more. Beau led her away so Jake could talk.

"Who's that?"

"Ben's mother."

"Like hell. I'm Ben's mother."

"No, you're not, Sherry, or you wouldn't do this to him. He doesn't know who you are, so please, I'm begging you, bring him back."

There was a slight pause. "I just…just couldn't stand to look at him after he was born. He was so lifeless, and drool was always running out of his mouth. I left him with Irene and I knew she'd smother him with all the love he needed."

"Your mother did a great job with Ben, but you should have called to let me know I had a son. I would've helped with him."

"Hell, Jake, I didn't know who the father was. Rusty was in prison and I was lonely, so how's a girl supposed to know."

"Then why put my name on the certificate?"

She laughed. "You were the only decent man I slept with, and when they wanted a name, I gave them one my mother would be proud of. Odd twist of fate, huh?"

Jake closed his eyes, not wanting to think about what would've happened to Ben if she'd given another name. "Sherry, bring him back."

"He's like a normal little boy and I might just keep him."

His nerves tightened. "You have no rights where Ben's concerned," Jake told her, trying not to lose his temper. It wasn't easy. "Where's Ben?"

"No judge can take away my rights," she spat.

Jake took a controlling breath. "I'm not arguing with you. I just want Ben back."

"I don't really want the kid, anyway. I move around a lot."

"Then why take him?"

Silence again.

Agent Coleman nodded at Jake and Jake remembered he was supposed to keep her talking. "How did you get him out of the clinic without being seen?"

"Well, I knew you lived somewhere outside Waco, and when we stopped for gas in Marlin, I asked about the McCain farm and the man knew exactly where it was. We waited and followed you to the clinic. That was this morning. I checked out the place, but never had a chance to get near Ben. This afternoon, though, I saw a woman walking down the hall with Ben. I knew it would probably be my only chance. I went into the room and hit the woman over the head with some sort of bottle I picked up. I had chloroform ready for Ben. I wrapped him in a blanket and carried him out like a baby. With it being cold, no one noticed. It really was easy."

Jake swallowed. "Bring him back."

"I'll tell you what you have to do before that's gonna happen."

"What?"

"I want every dime my mother got from that settlement and her house. It belongs to me. I'm her daughter."

Jake gripped the receiver. "The money was spent on Ben's health care. There's a hundred thousand in Ben's estate and you're welcome to it."

"Do you think I'm stupid, Jake? I know she received over two million and I want it all—now."

"I don't have two million, Sherry. I told you..." Andrew tapped him on the shoulder, reminding him of his offer. "Okay, I'll get it."

"Now we can do business."

"Where's Ben?"

"You get the money and the deed to my mom's house and I'll call in the morning with details."

"Sherry!" he shouted before she could hang up.

"We have nothing to talk about until you have the money, and Jake, I know you're having this call traced. It's a pay phone and I'll be long gone before the cops get here." The phone went dead.

"Sherry!" he shouted again, but there was only silence.

Elise ran into his arms. "She won't hurt him, will she?"

"No, she just wants money," Jake said in a hollow tone.

"I'll call my banker," Andrew said.

"I don't know how I'll ever repay you. I could mortgage the farm." He'd do whatever it took.

"Don't worry about it." Andrew brushed his concern away. "Just bring Ben home."

Jake's cell phone buzzed and he grabbed it. "We located the van," Caleb said without preamble.

"Thank God." Jake's heart hammered loudly. "Sherry just called here."

"I know," Caleb replied. "I've been in contact with Agent Coleman and we were able to get here as the van was pulling away. It's a pay phone at a convenience store. We followed her to a trailer park around the corner. She drove to one of the trailers and parked inside an attached garage and closed the door. The van's been hidden. That's why no one's seen it and it's probably why she waited until this late at night. They know we're looking for the van."

"Where's Ben?"

"He wasn't with her so we're assuming he's inside the trailer. That's why I called. It would be a good idea for you and Elise to be here before we go in, because Ben's going to need you. Here's the address."

Jake scribbled it on a piece of paper. "We'll be right there, and, Caleb—"

"Just get here."

"Yes, yes." He turned, and Elise already had their coats and Ben's in her hand. Jake hugged his mother, then they ran for Beau's car. Beau drove and they sat in the back huddled together, both hoping that it would soon be over.

As they drove through the night, police cars seemed to be on every corner and Jake realized that what Caleb had said was true. The police department was diligently searching for Ben.

Jake's thoughts stilled as Beau parked behind some police cars in the trailer park. Police had the small trailer surrounded. Jake and Elise walked to where Caleb stood behind a barrier of cruisers.

The wind whipped around them, but Elise didn't feel the cold. All she felt was an ache in her heart. An ache that wouldn't ease until she held Ben in her arms again.

"Is Ben in there?" Jake asked as he stared at the trailer. Two lights shone on each end, illuminating it in the darkness. Policemen were hidden around the perimeter with automatic weapons, ready, just waiting for the nod to go in.

Caleb cleared his throat. "Jake, I'd like you to meet someone."

Jake was so focused on searching for a sign, anything to signal that Ben was inside the trailer, that he didn't notice the other man. He swung around and drew a breath deeply as he stared at the familiar-looking man. A tall man. Jake was tall, but this man was taller, and Jake recognized him immediately. Elijah Coltrane.

"These are Texas Rangers Elijah Coltrane and Jeremiah Tucker," Caleb said, making the introduction. "They've been after Fobbs for some time and know him quite well."

Jake just stared at Elijah, hardly aware of the other Ranger. Gone was the long hair and earring. His hair was short under a Stetson, and he wore dark pants and a jacket with a white shirt. Jake saw the gun and Texas Rangers badge, and thought there was something chilling about this situation. The past had once again erupted into Jake's life, and he had no idea how to respond to Elijah Coltrane.

Jake said the only thing he could. "Do you know who I am?"

Elijah stared straight at Jake, unblinking. "Yes, you're Jake McCain and these are your brothers." He nodded toward Beau and Caleb. "Doesn't mean a helluva lot to me. I'll help the police with Fobbs and try to get your son out unharmed. I won't hold it against him that he's a McCain. I'm a Texas Ranger and that's what I do." He turned and walked away.

Jake sucked cold air into his lungs and started to go after him, but Beau held him back. "Leave him alone. It's clear he doesn't want anything to do with us."

Jake felt sure he was in a nightmare. Elijah Coltrane, a Texas Ranger. There was something wrong with that picture and he couldn't quite make it fit in his head. His half brother would help to bring Ben out. A brother who hated him. That couldn't be true. Maybe he was hallucinating with grief over Ben. He'd been thinking a lot about Elijah and now he'd apparently conjured him up as a Texas Ranger, a member of the most respected law enforcement agency in Texas. But he'd looked into the coldness of his eyes and he knew this was real. Elijah was real.

Elise saw the confusion on Jake's face. "Jake, is that your half brother?"

"Yes, I just can't..." His voice trailed off as lights came on in the trailer.

"Okay, something's happening," Elijah said to Dick Willis, Caleb's captain.

"Everyone stay calm," Captain Willis said to his men, then he spoke to Elijah. Jake couldn't hear his words.

Loud voices erupted and it was clear people were having a disagreement in the trailer. Suddenly a window was broken and a gun poked through.

"He's figured out we're here," Elijah said.

Captain Willis and Elijah conversed again, then Elijah's voice rang out, ''Rusty, send the boy out. You don't want to do this.''

After a moment, a man's voice asked, ''Coltrane, is that you?''

''Yeah.''

''Is Tuck with you?''

''Yeah. He's here.''

''Well I'll be a son of a bitch. You've finally found me. You said you'd have to take me in one day, but it ain't today.''

''Let the kid go and we'll talk.''

''I didn't mean to kill that bitch in El Paso. It was an accident. I swear, Coltrane, but no one would understand that. I knew you and Tuck would come after me, so I stayed hidden deep in Mexico. Sherry wanted to see her mom and kid. That was the only reason I came back.''

''Rusty, send the boy out. His parents are waiting.''

''Wish I could. I really do, but sorry, I can't.''

''Why not?''

''Get me the money and I'll let him go. That's the only way he'll get out of here.''

''C'mon, Rusty. You're not all bad. Don't do something stupid here.''

Rusty laughed. ''You always thought there was some good in me, but there ain't. I'll kill the kid if I don't get what I want.''

Elise gasped and clutched Jake's arm. Jake stood like a statue.

''Rusty…''

Rusty fired several shots at the ground, kicking up dirt. Elise jumped and buried her face against Jake.

''I'm not going back to prison. I can't.''

''Let me come in and we'll talk.''

''It's too late.''

''It's never too late.''

''There's movement at the bathroom window,'' Caleb

intervened in a whisper. All eyes turned in that direction and watched as a window slowly opened. Suddenly a head appeared.

"Oh, my God, it's Ben," Jake cried, and Elise caught her breath.

"Keep him talking," Caleb said to Elijah.

Before Elijah could utter a word, someone pushed Ben out the window and he fell to the ground, unmoving. Without thinking Elise sprinted toward Ben's still body and Jake was a step behind her.

So many things happened at once that Jake wasn't sure of anything until he felt the breath knocked out of him as he hit the ground. Elijah held him and Elise pinned to the ground as gunfire sprayed around them. When Jake tried to move, he realized someone else was holding him. Caleb and the man called Tuck was there, too.

"Goddammit, stay down," Elijah said gruffly. The gunfire stopped and Elijah rolled away to the front of the trailer. As Jake crawled on his hands and knees to Ben, he heard a gunshot in the trailer and saw Elijah ram through the front door, Caleb and Tuck behind him. Another shot echoed chillingly through the night. Jake was aware of the sound, but his concentration was on one thing—getting to Ben.

Elise reached Ben first. He lay in a heap, lifeless, wearing nothing except a diaper. "Oh God, oh God, oh God," Elise cried as she hurriedly gathered Ben's cold body into her arms. He trembled against her and Jake slipped off his jacket and wrapped it around the child.

"He's so still," Elise wailed, cradling him to her and kissing his face over and over.

Jake's hand reached for the pulse in Ben's neck. As Jake touched him, Ben stirred. "Mom-E, 'A-dy," he whimpered, his body trembling severely.

"We're here, son," Jake murmured in a shaky voice, kissing his face, too. An ambulance drove up and Jake took him out of Elise's arms. "We have to get him to a hospital."

Elise tried to rise to her feet but couldn't stand; her body shook violently. With Ben in his arms, Jake helped her up and they climbed into the ambulance. Siren blaring, they were rushed to the hospital.

When they reached the emergency room, reporters and TV crews were waiting. Jake was glad when Caleb arrived and took charge of the scene. Ben screamed when they tried to lay him on the stretcher, so Jake carried him. Inside Ben wouldn't go to anyone except Elise. She held him close, folding a blanket around him. As she did, she noticed his diaper was wet. She managed to place him on the table to change it, but he was immediately clawing to get back in her arms.

"It's all right, baby," she cooed soothingly. "Mommy and Daddy are here."

"No me mom-E, 'ou me mom-E," Ben said.

"Yes, I'm your mommy." She stroked his back, her eyes filled with tears. Her eyes caught Jake's and they both understood Sherry had told Ben she was his mommy. Now they had to undo all that damage.

Dr. Markham came in and tried to check Ben, but he screamed, "No, no, no," and burrowed against Elise.

Finally Jake said, "I'm taking him home. I'm not traumatizing him further."

Dr. Markham examined Ben's shoulder, which was bruised and blue. "I'd like an X ray, but I know that's out of the question right now."

"Yeah," Jake agreed. "I'll keep an eye on it, though."

Dr. Markham reached for a prescription pad. "I'll give you something in case he becomes agitated. It'll help him rest."

Beau came rushing in with Ben's clothes and Elise tried to put them on Ben, but he kept crying, "No me mom-E, 'ou me mom-E." Elise gave up and gathered two blankets around him and Beau drove them home.

Aunt Vin, Althea and Wags met them at the door.

''Thank God,'' Aunt Vin gushed. ''We heard on the news, but I just had to see for myself.''

Wags jumped up and down barking, trying to reach Ben.

Althea caressed Ben's hair. ''Ben's home.''

''Me 'ome,'' Ben repeated as they carried him to his room.

Elise sat with him in her lap, snuggled tight in the blanket, his face against her chest. Wags pushed his nose into Ben's lap. ''Look, Ben,'' she coaxed. ''Wags is glad to see you. He's missed you.''

Ben threw both arms around Wags and hugged him. ''Me 'ome,'' Ben said.

Wags barked happily and settled on the floor at their feet, now content. Taking a fortifying breath, Jake went to get Ben's pajamas and brought them to Elise.

''Let's put your pajamas on,'' she said to Ben. ''It'll be warmer.''

''No, no, no,'' Ben shouted, and clutched Elise tightly.

Jake knelt down in front of them again. ''Ben, look at Daddy.''

Ben turned his head and stared at Jake. ''Mommy and Daddy are here and we love you and we're not going to let anything happen to you. Do you understand?''

Ben kept staring and Jake showed him the red pajamas. ''Daddy has your Christmas pajamas. You remember Christmas? We had lots of fun and Ben got lots of gifts and Mommy bought you these warm pajamas. Let Daddy put them on you. Okay?''

Ben held out his foot. ''That's my boy.'' Jake felt a moment of relief and hurriedly slipped the pajamas on him.

Ben wiggled closer to Elise, muttering, ''No me mom-E. 'ou me mom-E.''

''Yes, I'm your mommy,'' Elise assured him.

Ben kept repeating the words, and as much as Jake didn't want to, he realized he would have to give Ben the medication Dr. Markham had prescribed.

''I'll take him to bed with me and maybe he'll quiet

down,'' Elise said. She went to their room, carrying Ben; Jake pulled the covers back and she crawled in with the child still clinging to her. ''Now you can go to sleep right here in Mommy's arms.''

'''Ou me mommy,'' Ben kept on.

Elise kissed his face with a lump in her throat. ''Yes, I'm your mommy and I'm right here.'' Elise thought if she said it often enough, Ben might finally relax.

Jake arranged the covers over them and Wags jumped on the bed, curling up next to Ben.

''Jake?'' Beau stood in the doorway and Jake walked up to him.

''Is Ben okay?'' he asked in a low voice.

Jake raked a hand through his hair. ''He keeps saying that Elise is his mommy. Sherry told him she was his mother, and he can't get it out of his head.''

''Once he goes to sleep, he probably won't remember much of what happened today.''

''Yeah, but getting him to sleep might be easier said than done.'' Jake fished the prescription out of his pocket. ''Would you please have this filled? I have a feeling we're going to need it.''

''Sure, right away.''

Jake returned to the bed. ''Is he asleep?'' he whispered.

''No.''

Jake sank down in total physical and mental exhaustion, but he knew this night was long from over. Leaning against the headboard, he rubbed Wags's back and watched Ben. As if sensing that someone was looking at him, Ben stirred and saw Jake, then crawled out of Elise's arms to his father.

Jake locked his arms around him, finally accepting that Ben was back. Ben was safe.

Soon Beau was back with the medication and Jake put it in some juice. At first Ben pushed it away, but eventually he drank it. Within a few minutes he was sound asleep in Elise's arms. Jake straightened the covers.

''Caleb's in the den,'' Beau said. ''Can you talk to him?''

He reached down and kissed Elise. ''I won't be long, honey.''

Her free arm crept around his neck and held his face against hers. They were safe.

''We're all home,'' he whispered, sensing her nervousness. ''Everything's okay.''

Was it? She wasn't sure. Fear still occupied every corner of her mind and she couldn't control it or ignore it, especially when she saw Ben's distress. Feeling Jake's breath on her skin eased the turmoil in her…for now.

He kissed her again. ''I'll be right back.''

Jake walked into the den and was surprised to see the room full of people.

''How is he?'' Althea asked.

''He's finally asleep and it would probably be best if everyone went home. It's been a long night.''

Peggy and Carl got to their feet. ''I'm so sorry,'' Carl said.

''It's not your fault,'' Jake assured them. He didn't blame them for Sherry's actions.

''I wish we didn't feel it was,'' Peggy said, patting Jake's shoulder as they left.

''I can stay,'' Althea offered.

''No, Mama, but thanks.'' Jake put his arms around her and hugged her for several seconds. It was so natural. ''Go home and get some rest. I'll call tomorrow. And Andrew, thanks.''

''No problem.''

Constance, Judith and Stan slipped on their coats. ''Is Elise okay?'' Constance asked.

''She's shaken up, but now that we have Ben back, she'll be fine.''

''Please call if you need us,'' Judith said.

''I will, and thanks.''

The room soon cleared except for Beau and Caleb. Jake glanced at Caleb. ''What happened in the trailer?''

''Evidently Sherry was afraid Fobbs would really kill Ben and she pushed him out the window.''

Jake squeezed his eyes briefly. ''She finally did something good in her life.''

''Yeah, when it came right down to it, that biological bond was there.''

''Where's Sherry?''

''When Fobbs realized what she'd done, he shot her. She's dead.''

Jake ran both hands over his face, wishing he could feel some sadness, but he was just numb. ''And Fobbs?''

''He shot himself before Coltrane could stop him.''

Jake swallowed the constriction in his throat. ''You could hear the respect Fobbs had for Elijah. For a second back there, I thought Elijah could talk him out of the trailer.''

''Yeah,'' Caleb murmured.

Jake took a deep breath. ''Elijah saved our lives and Ben's. Where is he? I'd like to thank him.''

''He's gone.''

''What do you mean gone?''

''He did his paperwork and left.''

''Where did he go?''

Caleb shrugged. ''Coltrane's not exactly the type of man to invite confidences and I wasn't about to ask.''

''He's our brother,'' Jake pointed out.

''That doesn't seem to mean a whole lot to him,'' Caleb said.

''Elijah's a Texas Ranger so he can't be too hard to find,'' Beau reasoned.

''Don't you two get it?'' Caleb asked. ''Coltrane doesn't *want* to be found by us and I can't exactly blame him.''

Silence tiptoed through the simmering emotions.

Jake released a heavy sigh and put an arm around Caleb. ''Elijah knows where we live and maybe someday he'll want to meet us, but we can't force it.'' He sighed again. ''I sure would like to thank him, though.''

''If I get an address on him, I'll let you know,'' Caleb conceded.

''Thanks, and now I have to get back to my wife and son.'' He moved toward the hall. ''Thanks for all you did today for me and Elise and Ben.''

''That's what brothers are for,'' Caleb responded lightly.

Jake nodded and walked to the bedroom. Elise was sleeping with Ben in her arms. He should wake her so she could put on her gown, but decided to let her sleep. She needed it.

He stood for a moment and watched them, and he said a profound prayer for everything he'd been given back. It was over. The nightmare was finally over.

CHAPTER EIGHTEEN

IT SOON BECAME CLEAR THAT the nightmare was far from over. Elise held Ben most of the next day. He screamed if she left his sight. He went from Elise to Jake, but he wouldn't respond to anyone else. He wouldn't sing the putt-putt song or the I-love-you song. He cried a lot and Jake's heart broke a little more every time he witnessed Ben's pain, and he was helpless to do anything to comfort him. He had to give Ben another dose of medicine to calm him down so he could sleep.

He phoned Dr. Markham and the doctor said it was natural for Ben to be feeling afraid and clinging, but he was young and in a few days his memory would fade and he should be better. If not, they'd have to take other measures.

On the third day Ben was better. He was out of Elise's arms playing with Wags and an enormous weight lifted off Jake, until a more urgent problem surfaced. Elise. He'd been so worried about Ben that he hadn't noticed the signs. She was afraid. Instead of letting Ben walk, she carried him and held him constantly. She refused to start Ben's therapy or exercises again, saying it was too soon because Ben's shoulder was bruised. Dr. Markham had come out to the house and said Ben was fine, so Jake knew it was a whole lot more. She was smothering Ben, trying to keep him in a world where nothing or no one could hurt him again. He tried talking to her, but he wasn't getting through. He even installed a security system in the house, hoping it would ease her mind. It didn't. He was at his wits end and he didn't know what else to do.

The nightmare went on and Jake cursed what Sherry had done to their lives. Peggy called and said Sherry's body had been brought back to Houston and they'd buried her next to Irene and her father. Peggy said that Irene would have wanted that and Jake had to agree. Sherry's parents had loved her, but she never got over her father's death. Drugs had been a way for her to forget. Sherry had caused Irene a lot of heartache, but in the end Sherry had saved her son's life. That's what Jake would remember about her.

Three weeks later, Jake was still struggling for answers. Ben slept with them at night and Elise wouldn't hear of his sleeping in his own bed. Every day Ben took another step backward, he was even falling again, and Jake knew this couldn't go on.

He sat in the den, wondering how much longer they could live like this, how much longer they could live in fear.

"Jake?" Beau called from the kitchen.

"I'm in the den."

Beau and Caleb strolled in.

"Aren't you two supposed to be working?"

"We could say the same about you," Beau replied. "I saw tractors in the fields. Isn't it time to get the land ready for planting? Why aren't you out there?"

"Mike's taken over the farm, and I haven't had time to do anything but worry."

Caleb frowned. "Elise isn't any better?"

Jake stood and ran a hand through his hair. "She's more paranoid every day and Ben feeds off her fear. She's hurting, and I don't know how to help her and that's killing me."

"Where's Elise now?" Beau asked.

"She's getting Ben up from his nap and probably sitting in the rocker holding him. If I didn't force her, she wouldn't come out of that room."

"This isn't good, Jake," Beau said quietly.

"Don't you think I'm aware of that?" Jake snapped. "I

just don't know what the hell to do. I—'' The doorbell rang, cutting him off. ''I'm not in a mood to talk to anyone.''

''I'll get rid of them,'' Caleb offered.

''No.'' Jake stopped him. ''We have to start living again and it starts now.'' He walked to the door and opened it. Judith and Duncan stood there.

''I'm sorry, Jake,'' Judith said. ''I should have called, but Duncan wanted to play with Ben for a while. Is that okay?''

Jake had made a decision a moment ago about living again and now he had to carry it out. He had to let the outside world into their lives once more and Duncan was the perfect person to begin with. ''Yes, it's fine,'' he replied. ''I'll get Ben.''

Elise was sitting in the rocker holding Ben, just like he knew she'd be. He prayed for the strength to do what he had to. ''Ben, you've got company.''

''Tell whoever it is to go away,'' Elise said coolly. ''Ben's not ready for company.''

Jake inhaled deeply and took Ben from her. ''Yes, he is.'' He moved toward the door.

Elise leaped to her feet. ''Jake, what are you doing? Ben's not ready!''

Jake closed his mind to the distress in her voice and carried the child to the den. ''Look.'' Jake pointed to Duncan. ''Look who's come to play with you. And there's Uncle Beau and Uncle Caleb.''

Beau stepped forward. ''How about it, champ? Want to go outside and play ball? It's a beautiful sunny day.''

''Ben can't go outside,'' Elise said from behind.

Jake turned to her, seeing the anguish, the pain in her eyes, and he almost weakened, but he had to do this for *them,* for all three of them. ''Yes, Ben can go outside.''

Ben glanced from his father to his mother, clearly confused. That expression drove Jake on. He handed Ben to Beau. ''It's okay, Ben. You can play with Duncan.''

Beau quickly ushered everyone out the French doors. Elise started after them, but Jake caught her. "No, Elise, let Ben go. He needs to start playing."

"He's not ready," she cried again. "Why can't you see that?"

"He is," Jake insisted. "Look."

They watched as Ben and Duncan ran after Wags, both of them laughing.

"You don't know what's out there," Elise muttered.

"It's our backyard. I know exactly what's out there."

She swung to him, her eyes cloudy. "Why are you doing this?"

"It's time, Elise," he answered. "We can't keep Ben locked in this house. It's time to start living."

"Living is when they take your child and rip your heart out, and then you have to watch that child suffer. No, I refuse to go through that again. I won't let *Ben* go through that again." She reached for the door and Jake pulled her back.

"No," he said sternly. "Look at Ben. He's having fun. For God's sakes, look at Ben. Let him have fun."

"How can you do this?" she wailed, and ran to the bedroom.

Jake let out an agonized breath.

"I'll speak to her," Judith said. Jake had forgotten she was even there.

He blinked back tears, feeling his world torn further and further apart, and he wasn't sure if he could ever put it back together.

ELISE DROPPED TO THE BED, trying to still the anxiety in her, but it didn't work. Nothing worked. She knew she was going overboard and she couldn't stop that, either.

Judith sat beside her. "Jake's right. You can't live like this."

"You've never had your child snatched from you," Elise said sharply. "You don't know that feeling."

"Excuse me?" Judith drew back. "My husband picked my son up from school one day and called and told me that he wasn't bringing him home and that he was filing for permanent custody."

"It's not the same," Elise said. "You knew where your son was and you knew he was safe."

"It may not be the same," Judith admitted. "But my son was gone and I know what that feels like."

Elise didn't respond and Judith added, "Stan and I are working out our problems. He and Duncan are moving back to the house."

A child's scream echoed outside and Elise jumped up and ran for the window. Beau was holding Ben in the air so Duncan and Wags couldn't reach him. Ben's screams of delight continued and Elise felt them echo through her heart.

"See," Judith said as she came to watch the scene. "Ben's happy."

"Beau shouldn't be holding Ben that way. His shoulder is still tender. Ben needs to come in the house." The sentences sounded like a chant.

Judith caught her by the shoulders and turned Elise to face her. "You're falling apart, Elise, and I think you know that. Ben needs a mother, not someone who's so afraid she can barely breathe. You've been through a traumatic ordeal, but it's over. You have a husband who loves you and a son who—"

"Shut up, shut up..." Elise shouted, running into the bathroom and slamming the door. She sank to the floor, pulled her knees to her chin and clamped her arms around them in a protective gesture. She was drowning. She could feel it. She wasn't in water, but she was drowning all the same. Her lungs were clogged with fear, and every second they grew tighter and tighter, burning. It was choking, smothering the life out of her. She was drowning and she couldn't save herself.

Happiness had been taken from her too many times and

now she couldn't stop the fear that was controlling her mind. She had to keep Ben safe. That was the only thing that got through to her. Ben had to be kept safe.

LATER THAT EVENING AFTER everyone had left, Jake knew he couldn't let up. He had to be strong, but every time he glimpsed Elise's tortured expression, his resolve faltered. Only for a second, though.

They gave Ben a bath and put on his pajamas. While Ben played with Wags, Jake took Elise to their room because he didn't want the boy to hear them. "Ben sleeps in his bed tonight."

"No, no, he'll be scared. No, Jake!" Her voice grew frantic.

"This isn't up for discussion. Ben sleeps in his bed tonight."

"No, I refuse to let him sleep in there alone. Anyone could..."

Her voice stopped as Jake met her eyes. "We've installed a security system. If a door or window is opened, it goes off. Not to mention that Wags will bark if anyone even steps foot in Ben's room. We're right across the hall. We're in our home, and we have to give Ben a sense of security. We *have* to do this, Elise. I know it's hard, but—"

"If you do this, I'll never forgive you." Her voice was cold.

Jake stepped back as if she'd hit him. "Don't come in unless you can encourage him," was all he could say, then he turned and went to Ben.

He was on the floor playing and Jake picked him up. "Time for bed, son, and tonight Ben sleeps in Ben's bed."

"Mom-E," Ben cried, and held out his arms for Elise, who was standing in the doorway.

Jake dredged up every ounce of courage he possessed and pulled the covers back and placed Ben in the bed. Wags jumped up beside him.

Jake knelt on the floor. "This is Ben's bed and Ben has to sleep in his bed because he's a big boy."

"Mom-E," Ben said, but this time it wasn't so strong.

"Mommy and Daddy will be across the hall, and Daddy will sit here until you go to sleep. And Wags will be right here, too."

Wags barked.

"'Ags." Ben patted the dog and Wags licked Ben's hand. "'Ac-tor, 'A-dy."

"Oh." Jake had to search for it because Ben hadn't held the tractor or his teddy lately. He'd only been holding on to his mother. They were at the foot of the bed.

Ben clutched them and rolled onto his side. Jake rubbed his back. "Putt-putt tractor, have you any wheels?" Jake sang.

"'Es-'ir, 'es-'ir," Ben responded, and Jake knew he was doing the right thing. But he felt like hell. He kept singing, though, until Ben's steady breathing told him he was asleep.

He walked into their bedroom, his whole body numb. Elise was in bed, curled in a fetal position, and the numbness saturated his heart. He was hurting her, but he didn't know what else to do. Eventually, he hoped she'd understand that he had to take drastic measures.

He took a shower, checked on Ben and got into bed. He never felt so far away from her; he wanted his wife back. He reached for her and instead of pushing him away, she jerked into his arms, crying silently, her face wet.

He swallowed painfully. "Elise, stop this, please."

"I can't," she sobbed on his chest. "I can't help it. I try, but I can't. I'm so afraid."

He rubbed her back much the same as he'd rubbed Ben's. "I know, honey, I know."

"Plea-ease," she hiccuped. "Plea-ease, please help me."

"Shh, shh," he said softly, continuing to stroke her shaking body. "Go to sleep and we'll talk tomorrow."

Somehow she fell asleep and Jake just held her. They

had to find a way to deal with what had happened to them, and they had to find it together. It was the first time she'd asked for his help and he knew that was a good sign. Tomorrow had to be better.

JAKE WOKE TO AN EMPTY BED. Elise wasn't there. A flicker of apprehension coursed through him, then he realized where'd she'd be…in Ben's room. He slowly crawled out of bed and walked across the hall. Ben was asleep, Wags beside him, but Elise wasn't there. Wags raised his head and Jake put a finger to his lips so Wags wouldn't bark.

A moment of alarm gripped him and he hurried to the kitchen. Aunt Vin was making coffee. "Is Elise here?"

"Elise?" Aunt Vin looked puzzled. "No, I just got up and I haven't seen her. Jake…?"

But Jake wasn't listening. He was running toward the hall. God, where was Elise?

The bathroom door was closed and Jake slowly eased it opened. A foul smell greeted him and he saw Elise sitting on the floor by the toilet, resting her forehead against the tank. He took the scene in at a glance and quickly flushed away the vomit. He grabbed a wet washcloth and a glass of water. Handing her the glass, he said, "Wash your mouth out. You'll feel better."

She rinsed her mouth and spit into the toilet. Jake flushed it again, then knelt beside her and wiped her face with the cloth. "You probably have the flu."

"No, I'm…I'm pregnant," she said.

Jake's whole body stilled, and before joy had a chance to take root, she added, "I don't *want* to be pregnant, Jake. I can't be. I don't want a baby. Ben needs me. He needs all my attention. I don't want to be pregnant."

Jake sank back on his heels. "You don't know what you're saying."

"Yes, I do," she said stubbornly. "I don't want another baby."

Jake's heart slammed into his ribs and he fought for a

way to help her. "We've both wanted a child for so long. Remember our plans? How can you say you don't want it?"

Elise felt the fear that controlled her and she couldn't get beyond it. The only thing between her and the pain was Jake's voice. All she had to do was reach out to him and...

"Jake, help me," she cried. "I want to feel the sunshine on my skin again. I want to look forward to tomorrow, but I can't. I'm so afraid. Jake..."

At the entreaty in her voice, his heart sank in the pit of his stomach, and he felt tangled in so much misery he was powerless to help her. But he would; he just had to find the right way. He smoothed the damp hair from her forehead.

"Mom-E. 'A-dy," Ben called.

"Oh, Jake, don't let him see me like this."

Jake struggled to his feet. "I'll be right back," he said, and met Ben and Wags in the bedroom. He swung Ben up in his arms, holding him tighter than necessary. "Ready for breakfast, son?"

"Mom-E," Ben said.

Jake kissed his cheek. "Mommy's in the bathroom. She'll be out in a minute." And he prayed she would.

"What would you like for breakfast?" Jake asked, trying to stay sane and reasonable.

"'Eam, 'A-dy, 'eam," Ben replied.

Jake was only half listening. He kept thinking that they were having a baby. They should be happy.

He put Ben in his high chair. "Aunt Vin, would you please give Ben some ice cream?"

"Ice cream?" Aunt Vin asked in a shocked voice.

Jake didn't hear a word. His mind was on his wife and her pain. *They were having a baby.* How did he make her understand, comprehend, accept that wonderful news? In a split second he knew and he went charging out the back door. He tripped the alarm system because he hadn't punched in the code. The alarm shrilled through the house and he quickly turned it off.

"Jake, what's wrong with you?" Aunt Vin asked worriedly.

"Just take care of Ben," he said, and ran to his workshop. He grabbed the cradle and headed back to the house.

"Where're you going with...?"

Aunt Vin's voice trailed away as he hurried down the hall. He set the cradle in the bedroom where Elise could see it from the bathroom. When he gave it a push, it started to play "Rock-a-Bye, Baby." He sat on the bed and waited, counting in his head. *One, two...*

Elise heard a sound and she raised her head from the tank.

"Rock-a-bye, baby."

Oh God, Oh God, the sound jolted through her, warming those places that were so cold, so locked with fear. *"Rock-a-bye, baby."* Slowly the fear around her heart began to ease, crack, then release until she could actually breathe without pain, without paranoia.

"Rock-a-bye, baby."

She crawled on her hands and knees until she could touch the cradle. It was so beautiful, so perfect, so everything that was good in this world. She had thought she could survive anything as long as she had Jake's love. Fear had made her forget that. She lifted her eyes to Jake's, eyes that weren't crying, eyes that were full of joy.

Fifteen, sixteen...

"We're having a baby," she said brightly.

Relief blew through him and it was the best feeling he'd ever had in his life. He dropped to the floor beside her. "Yes, we're having a baby."

She threw her arms around his neck. "Thank you, thank you," she breathed against his face. "I can *feel* again, Jake, and I can see tomorrow and I'm not afraid. Oh, God, I'm not afraid anymore."

He cupped her face in his hands. "I can't promise you

we'll never have sadness or heartache or pain in our lives. That's life and it doesn't come with any guarantees, but I can promise that I'll always be here for you and Ben and the new baby. No matter what we have to go through, I'll always be beside you, loving you.''

''I know,'' she whispered, knowing it so deeply that it had brought her back from that awful place. ''Jake, what happened to me?'' she asked in a pitiful voice.

He leaned against the bed and held her. ''Too many knocks in a lifetime, I think it's called, and this time you shut down, shut out everyone and everything, except your love for Ben.''

''And you,'' she said, her hand caressing his cheek. ''My love for you saved me.''

They enjoyed the moment, just holding each other.

''We're having a baby,'' she said excitedly. ''All the times we tried so hard, following my cycle and other ridiculous instructions and it never happened. Now without trying, I'm pregnant. I'm not sure how since I'm on the pill, oh…''

''What?'' he asked anxiously.

She grimaced. ''I was so busy with the holidays I forgot a couple of times. When we confessed our love on Christmas Eve, I didn't even think about it, and on Christmas day I was so tired it slipped my mind, too. After trying for months and nothing, I…I…I can't believe it happened so easily.''

''It happened because it's the right time and you didn't have to put your feet in the air or anything weird.''

She smiled. ''No, I just had to love you…completely.''

His lips moved toward her and she buried her face in his neck. ''No, don't kiss me. I've been vomiting.''

He kissed her hair, her ear, her neck. ''Doesn't matter to me,'' he muttered. ''I love you any way, anywhere, in any shape.''

''I love you, too,'' she murmured.

Jake stroked her hair, hating what he had to say, but they

had to get everything out into the open. "You might not be pregnant. It might just be the stress you've been through."

She lifted her head, still smiling. "If I am, that's okay. If I'm not, that's okay, too, so you don't have to worry. I just got derailed with all the senseless pain that I couldn't control." She paused. "I never knew I could love Ben so much."

"Yeah, and you're the woman who thought she didn't have motherly instincts," he teased, and it felt good to be able to do that again. "Let me tell you, lady, you have instincts in spades."

"Mom-E, Mom-E, Mom-E," Ben shouted a moment before he and Wags burst into the room. Ben had chocolate ice cream all over his face and Wags was licking it off.

"Wags, stop that," Jake scolded, and Wags dropped to the floor with a whine.

Ben wriggled himself between Elise and Jake.

Elise lifted an eyebrow at Jake. "Ice cream?"

"Well, yes," he admitted with a twinkle in his eyes. "I had to keep him busy for a while."

"'Hat at?" Ben asked pointing at the cradle.

Elise used the washcloth she'd dropped on the carpet and wiped Ben's face. "It's a cradle."

"'Or me?"

"No." Elise kissed his cheek and it was probably the first time she'd ever said no to him. "It's for a baby and Ben's not a baby. He's a big boy."

"Big." Ben raised his arms high above his head.

Jake and Elise glanced at each other and in silent agreement they decided to wait and tell Ben when they were sure.

"I love you," Jake whispered, losing himself in the glow of her eyes. It had been so long since he'd seen that look and it was taking him away to where he wanted to be—in love with her forever.

"'Ove 'ou, too," Ben said, and held up two fingers.

Jake and Elise laughed, a happy, resonant sound that echoed around the room. She had survived the most traumatic experience any mother could. Tomorrow was hers and now she would step into the future stronger, braver, with a man and a son she loved. She knew that life wouldn't always be easy, and when things got rough, she'd rock this cradle and remember the one thing that was unshakable. Love…Jake's love.

EPILOGUE

Two and a half years later

A FAMILY.

Jake drove the Suburban to the curb and stopped. He glanced at Elise and a silent message passed between them—no tears today. Getting out, he went around the vehicle and opened the passenger door, then the back door.

"Ready, son?"

"Yes," Ben replied, and undid his seat belt without a problem. Ben had improved so much that Jake could hardly believe this was the same little boy who'd needed help with everything. Ben was no longer in the lower five percent of his age group. He was now in the fifty-per-cent group and gaining. The coordination on his left side was still off, but not enough to keep him from starting school.

Today was the first day and Ben was enrolled in kindergarten. Ben was in real school.

He was so excited he could barely sit still. Jake and Elise were the only ones nervous. It would be his first step away from them and they were trying to be brave and not start crying.

Ben grabbed his backpack, then started to get out, but quickly turned to his baby sister, Althea Katherine Eve, who was sitting in her car seat. They had named the new baby after Jake's mother because he'd wanted Althea to know he loved her and had truly forgiven her. Katherine was the name Elise had always wanted for a girl, and Eve because they knew she'd been conceived on Christmas Eve—their baby by Christmas.

Ben gave her a quick kiss. "Bye. I gotta go to school, Katie." He said the words perfectly, no faltering, no missing syllables, no splitting his words. The messages were finally getting to his brain like they should. Some days he struggled, some days he didn't, and they knew this would be a pattern for him. Eventually, though, the doctors had assured them that Ben would function like a normal little boy. And he already was.

"Bye, Ben," Katie said just as perfectly. At almost two years of age, she was clearly very bright. She did everything ahead of schedule and Jake was grateful for the bond between brother and sister. Katie followed Ben everywhere and Jake knew this was going to be a difficult day for her.

Staring into his daughter's eyes, Jake's heart swelled with love. From the first moment he saw that beautiful face, he knew his life would never be the same again. It was richer, fuller, and at times he felt a pang of sadness that he'd missed those first years of Ben's life. He didn't dwell on it, though. He'd been given so much.

"Bye, Wags," Ben said, and hugged the dog who stuck his head between the seats. "Watch out for Katie, 'cause she's little." Wags whined and Ben kissed him, too.

A BMW drove up behind them and Duncan bounced from the back seat. Stan walked around to the passenger side and helped a very pregnant Judith get out.

"I'll walk Ben to his room," Duncan offered. "I know where it is."

"Okay?" Ben said brightly, looking at his parents.

Jake glanced at Elise, unsure if this was the right thing to do. He wanted to walk Ben to his room to reassure him that his parents were here. But in truth, and it was so hard to admit, Ben just needed them to let go. They had to let him be a little boy. Jake hadn't realized how difficult this would be.

He squatted down in front of Ben. "Daddy and Mommy will be here when school gets out."

"I know," Ben said.

Jake wanted to ask questions. Was he scared? Was he okay? Did he need anything? But he didn't say a word. He just hugged Ben, tightly.

Elise hugged him, too, fighting tears. "Remember this afternoon Granny Althea's making a cake to celebrate your first day of school."

Ben smiled. "Granny makes good cakes."

Elise bit her lip and didn't know if she could do this, but knew she had to. This was part of being a parent—letting your child grow up.

Ben sensed her sadness and put his arms around her again. "I'm okay, Mommy. I'm big." Ben slipped on his backpack and Jake and Elise had to stop themselves from helping him.

"Let's go, Ben," Duncan said. "The bell will ring soon."

Duncan took Ben's hand and they walked up the steps to the big doors. At the door, Ben turned and waved, then disappeared inside.

Jake expelled a long breath. "Do you think I should make sure he's okay?" he asked Elise.

Elise shook her head. "No, I think now we have to go home."

"It'll get easier," Judith said. "That first day is always difficult."

"How are you?" Elise asked, trying to think of something else.

"Terrible," Judith sighed. "Having a baby at forty isn't easy."

"But you're happy." Elise knew her sister was by her voice, her manner and the light in her eyes.

Judith placed a hand on her stomach. "Yes, ecstatic."

Stan rubbed her back affectionately. "Come on. Time to get you off your feet."

As they left, Elise said, "Be sure and call when the baby comes."

"Don't worry," Judith joked. "You'll hear me screaming."

Elise smiled, glad her sister had finally found happiness. There was a lot of that going around. Turning to Jake, she saw he was staring at the building with an anxious expression. She knew exactly how he felt and slipped an arm through his.

"We've talked to his teacher several times and she's well aware of Ben's history. She has my cell phone number and yours. If Ben becomes the least bit distressed, she'll call us."

He stared into her eyes. "You're very calm about this."

"I'm not," she assured him. "I'm a bundle of nerves, but I know how happy Ben is and I can't let myself be paranoid and ruin this day for him."

He admired how far she'd come since the trauma of Ben's kidnapping. He'd made the journey with her and every day he thanked God for Elise and her love. Their union was now stronger, fueled by heartache, pain and love. Love overshadowed the rest, and for better or worse they had made it through.

"Mommy," a little voice called from inside the vehicle.

"We'd better go," Elise said. "Katie's getting restless."

Jake kept staring at the building, unable to leave.

"Did you notice his face?"

Jake blinked. ''What?''

''Did you notice Ben's face when he waved at us?''

''Of course.''

''Well, then, you saw his look that said I'm big and going to school like everyone else.''

Jake relaxed. ''Yeah.''

She stroked his arm. ''It's what we've worked for and now we've achieved it. Ben's achieved it. And we have to go home.''

He knew that. He just needed her to remind him.

''Daddy,'' a little voice chirped.

''Yes, baby,'' Jake responded. ''I'm coming.''

They got in and Jake started the engine.

''She's going to miss Ben terribly,'' Elise commented. ''Wags will, too.''

''They'll be looking for him the rest of the day.''

''Mommy, Ben,'' Katie said, looking back at the building.

''Ben's in school, baby. We'll pick him up later,'' Elise replied looking at Katie, blond hair in a topknot and big brown eyes like Jake's. She loved her daughter with everything in her, but that didn't mean she loved Katie more because she'd given birth to her. Ben was her firstborn, and it didn't matter that she wasn't his biological mother. She was in every other way.

''I'm having second thoughts about returning to teaching,'' she said forlornly.

Jake raised an eyebrow. ''You've already told the dean you'd be back this semester and you're only teaching one class. You'll be home by noon.''

''Ben and Katie are only small once and I don't want to miss anything.''

''And how are you planning to explain this to my mother

and Constance, not to mention Aunt Vin? They have the baby-sitting schedule all worked out.''

Elise groaned and leaned her head back.

''You're looking forward to it, so don't feel guilty. The kids will be fine. I'm always around and you can be home at a moment's notice.''

''I guess,'' she admitted. They'd talked about this so much and decided that when Ben went to school, she'd start back at the university. It had sounded good at the time, but now all her instincts were chiming in and she was wondering if she'd made the right decision.

''You have,'' Jake said, reading her mind.

She reached out and caressed the hair at his nape and was so glad she had this wonderful man to keep her sane.

''I wonder if Caleb's on duty this morning?''

''Jake,'' she sighed annoyingly. ''Caleb will call you when he has any news.''

Jake and Caleb had grown very close. They had more than made up for the lost years, sharing hopes, dreams and plans. Caleb had confided his dream of becoming a Texas Ranger. He had already applied and was waiting for an answer. Jake was more anxious than Caleb.

''With Caleb's credentials, I don't understand what's taking so long.''

''A vacancy for one thing,'' she pointed out. ''Vacancies are rare.''

''Makes me wonder how Elijah Coltrane became a Texas Ranger.''

Elise knew that Jake needed to meet Elijah again, to know about his life, but Elijah didn't want anything to do with the McCains. ''It doesn't matter, Jake, he's made it very clear how he feels. He's returned all your letters and he won't answer your phone calls. I don't know what else you can do.''

"I'm not giving up," he said stubbornly. "Beau never gave up on me and I'll never give up on Elijah. He just doesn't realize he wants to be a part of our family, and once he gets to know Caleb, I believe all the pieces will fall into place."

"Honey." She stroked his neck. "Don't get your hopes up."

He kissed her arm. "I'll meet Elijah again someday."

"I love you," she whispered.

Before Jake could respond Katie shouted, "Two," and held up two fingers. Jake and Elise smiled. So much love, but Elise knew Jake wouldn't feel completely at peace until the last McCain was brought into the family.

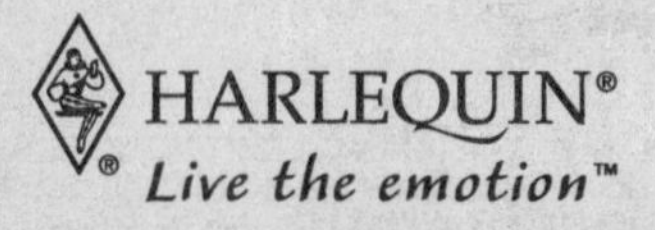

HARLEQUIN®
Live the emotion™

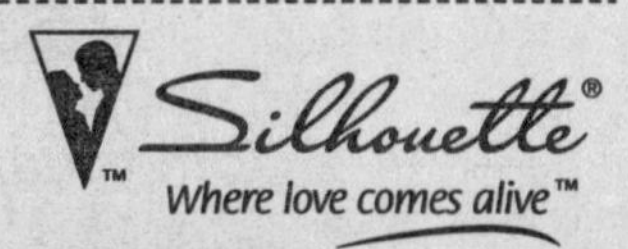

Silhouette®
Where love comes alive™

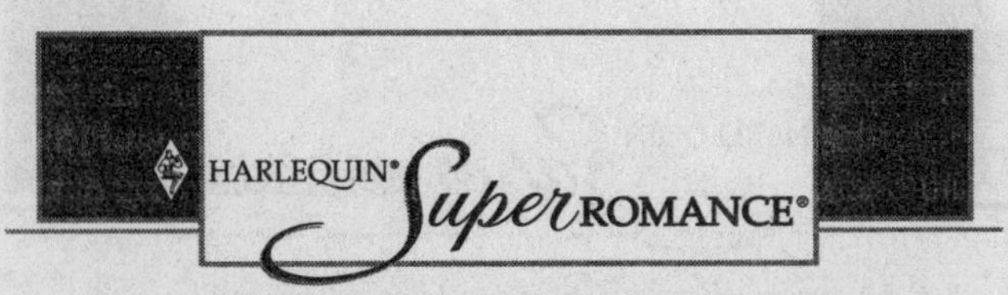

COMING NEXT MONTH

#1170 LEAVING ENCHANTMENT • C.J. Carmichael
The Birth Place
Nolan McKinnon is shocked when he's named his niece's guardian. He knows nothing about taking care of a little girl—especially an orphan—but he still would've bet he knew more than Kim Sherman. Kim's a newcomer to Enchantment—one who seems determined not to get involved with anyone. But Nolan can't refuse help, even if it comes from a woman with secrets in her past....

#1171 FOR THE CHILDREN • Tara Taylor Quinn
Twins
Valerie Simms is a juvenile court judge who spends her days helping troubled kids—including her own fatherless twin boys. Through her sons she meets Kirk Chandler, a man who's given up a successful corporate career and dedicated himself to helping the children in his Phoenix community. Valerie and Kirk not only share a commitment to protecting children, they share a deep attraction—and a personal connection that shocks them both.

#1172 MAN IN A MILLION • Muriel Jensen
Men of Maple Hill
Paris O'Hara is determined to avoid the efforts of the town's matchmakers. She's got more important things to worry about—like who her father really is. But paramedic Randy Sandford is determined to show her that the past is not nearly as important as the future.

#1173 THE ROAD TO ECHO POINT • Carrie Weaver
Vi Davis has places to go, people to meet and things to do—and the most important thing of all is getting a promotion. So she's not pleased when a little accident forces her to take time out of her schedule to care for an elderly stranger. She never would have guessed that staying with Daisy Smith and meeting her gorgeous son, Ian, is *exactly* the thing to do.

A great new story from a brand-new author!

#1174 A WOMAN LIKE ANNIE • Inglath Cooper
Hometown U.S.A.
Mayor Annie McCabe cherishes Macon's Point, the town that's become home to her and her son, and she's ready to fight to save it. And that means convincing Jack Corbin to keep Corbin Manufacturing, the town's main employer, in business. Will she be able to make Jack see the true value of his hometown...and its mayor?

#1175 THE FULL STORY • Dawn Stewardson
Risk Control International
Keep Your Client Alive is the mandate of Risk Control International. And RCI operative Dan O'Neill takes his job very seriously. Unfortunately, keeping his foolhardy client safe is a real challenge. And the last thing Dan needs is the distraction of a very attractive—and very nosy—reporter named Micky Westover.

HSRCNM1103